A Question of Time

A Question of Time

This is a work of historical fantasy. While some of the places and characters depicted herein are based on real locations and people, the specifics are the product of the authors imagination and should be treated as such.

Published by Piscataqua Press
32 Daniel St., Portsmouth, NH 03801
www.ppressbooks.com

Printed in the United States of America

A Question of Time

∞

A Novel

S.W. Jenness

Messages XI.15
Thalese to Tacitus

"You ask me, as his confidant, to tell you of him. Was he a god? The answer is no."

Thalese of Pompeii

For Mary Ann Engle Jenness

My Appia

New York Times
Science Times
Dinosaur Size Egg-shaped Object Found in Nevada Offers More Questions Than Answers.

By Mary Morgan JAN 12, 1980

On October 22 of last year, a large, egg-shaped object was discovered embedded in sandstone in Red Rock Canyon, Nevada by fossil hunters Rick Martin and Casandra Lin. "We saw what looked like a small, very shiny, flat rock exposed in the sandstone," said Ms. Lin. "It was the same color as the surrounding rock. Had it not been for sunlight reflecting off it we might have missed it."

What they found, following meticulous excavation, was much bigger than the proverbial bread box. The "Object of Interest," as it is known for lack of a better understanding, measures 20' x 10' and is hollow. There is an oval shaped entrance into its interior which houses a small bathroom, storage bins, and a single seat set before what appears to be some sort of control console. There are no controls or gauges. "In fact," Ms. Lin explained, "there's no wiring or any kind of mechanics that one would expect to find if this thing was some sort of device."

Mr. Martin pointed out that there are no windows either, and if that isn't enough, the exterior "shell," as he calls it, appears to be a "smooth, glossy, supple plastic that has somehow survived in pristine condition while being encased in ancient sandstone. It's not even scratched! However, there is plenty of dust on the interior, but that dust didn't come from outside the Object. Nothing of the surrounding soil that encased the Object seems to have fallen through the oval entrance into the interior."

When asked if they believed they had stumbled upon something of extraterrestrial origin, both Mr. Martin and Ms. Lin were quick to dispel that notion. Mr. Martin said they have been "pestered" by self-proclaimed "ufologists" ever since he inadvertently used the word "hull" to describe their discovery in a local publication. Ms. Lin called ufology a distraction. "We are professionals. We don't subscribe to pseudoscience. What organic material we've collected is both terrestrial and human. The bigger question is how did this obviously contemporary object come to be encased inside Jurassic era sandstone?"

PART I

"The trouble with fear of the unknown is that you never know what that fear will be like until it's too late to do anything about it."

Michael Palin
Pole to Pole

I

∞

"Can you hear me, Aaron?" It was Liam Cullen's voice coming in loud and clear over the headset. Dr. Liam Patrick Cullen was the project manager. He was an MIT grad, a talented aerospace engineer and problem solver, adept at converting concepts into functional equipment.

"Perfectly," I replied as I buckled myself into the ergonomic pilot's seat. The day of the launch had arrived. All the months of hard work and preparation had come down to just a few short minutes. My excitement was tempered with a healthy dose of nervousness. No matter how much I loved to travel, I was always a little apprehensive at departure, especially when traveling alone, and this was no ordinary trip.

"You're all clear to power up," Liam said.

"Copy that," I replied. I took a deep breath and then swept my hand across the surface of the control panel. The panel came to life. Buttons lit up. Holographic gauges appeared, floating before me while the whole upper half of my egg-shaped craft went from opaque to transparent. It was as if the top had been removed and yet it was a one-way transparency. I could see out, but nobody could see in. From the outside, the ship looked like a big, shiny, silvery egg with no windows or hatches or any markings or indentations of any kind. All portals were hand motion activated, but functioned only with individuals who were paired with the system.

If this sounds a bit futuristic, it is, in fact so much so that the original researchers assigned to study this puzzling find, which at the time was labeled only as an "Object of Interest," considered it nonfunctional. They left many questions unanswered, but since they could find no military or strategic value in continuing the study, the funding for further research was cut. In their final analysis they determined that the "Object of Interest" was "most likely" a failed cold war era military experiment that was deliberately buried, noting that such action was not unusual for the times.

"How are you holding up?" It was Dr. Christina Ruiz. She was the head of the project and owner of the device I was sitting in, but more importantly she had figured out key elements of its primary function and a way to operate it.

"Well enough," I replied. "This is by far the most insane thing I've ever done, and I've done some pretty crazy things."

"You don't have to do this," she said. "I'm insane for letting you talk me into it. I should be going."

I laughed. "You get airsick on a step ladder. Tell me again how high up I will be going?"

"Never mind," she said with a smile. It seemed strange the way I could see her so clearly and she couldn't see me at all. "Please, if you have any doubts..."

"I don't. I'm always nervous before a trip. At least the outbound leg will be quick."

"It should be almost instantaneous."

"One hundred and fifty million years in less than a second," I said. "I might see a dinosaur."

"But you can't stay there," she said. "You've got to get this thing heading back as quickly as you can. You're not prepped for that era."

"I know that."

"And I know you," she said. "Your spirit of adventure is stronger than your sensibility sometimes."

"We're almost done out here," Liam said. "You can go green. Good luck."

"Thanks." I looked at the gauges as they hung in space before me. I put my hand over the red button to initiate the starting sequence. That was followed by a series of bars as power was applied to the forward sender unit. Once all the bars were lit, the red button turned green. "I'm on green," I said.

"Everything looks good out here," Liam announced.

"Good," I said, "but you shouldn't be in here with this thing set to launch."

The ship was resting on four ski-like protrusions inside a specially constructed containment room. Shielding within the walls, ceiling and floor of the room was designed to dampen the effects of the tiny, artificial black hole that would be briefly generated when I initiated the launch sequence. The black hole would literally last for a millisecond. It wasn't the black hole that was important, but the eddies, or wormholes it created around the nose of the hull in the process. These eddies were the route to the past. The ship was essentially lassoed and swallowed up by one of them, sending it back to its Date of Origin. The fact that the Date of Origin was in the Jurassic era meant that the builders of the device were most likely not human or terrestrial.

"We're fine," Liam said. "It will be just a couple more minutes. I want to make sure all the sensors are reading you."

"I wish I could see you in there, Aaron," Christina said. "Are you sure you have everything? I know how anxious we all were this morning. Maybe we missed something."

I picked up the clipboard with my list of travel items. "I have three checkmarks in front of every item," I replied, "from you, Liam, and Aine. Toga, tunic, meds, utility vest, not to mention plenty of food. So, stop worrying."

Traveling into the past was a two-step process. Step one could not be controlled. It simply sent the ship back to the Date of Origin. Knowing the precise date was not necessary for this step. The only thing that mattered was that the ship's Date of Origin be a date that preceded the selected target date, which meant any date between 150 million years ago and the present could be chosen.

Step two was the controlled, or piloted leg of the trip. From the Jurassic, or Date of Origin, the ship will travel into the future towards home, stopping off at our selected target date along the way. January, 79 CE near Pompeii, Italy, was selected as the target date and location to satisfy the goal of the project, which was to determine if the past could be changed to affect the future. If we learned that history cannot be altered, then Christina would make her work public, but if we learned differently, knowledge of the ship would stay secret and eventually die with us.

This goal would be achieved by altering a well-documented artifact or work of art in the past. One set of printed images of all the potential Pompeiian options for alteration would be time-sheltered inside the ship with me. These materials included picture books along with personal photography I took specifically for the trip. Duplicates of the same materials would remain in the lab for post trip comparison. Any differences would mean the past could be altered. I also carried a flash drive with all my photography from ancient archaeological sites in Italy as a backup.

Pompeii was a good choice because there were countless numbers of available publications with detailed pictures of the ancient site and its artifacts to choose from. I had majored in Roman history and knew Pompeii well. I could read and write in Latin, which helped me learn to vocalize the language. There may have been no way to know the various dialects and subtleties regarding how the ancients spoke their language, but at least I understood basic grammar and knew enough vocabulary to communicate on some level if I absolutely had to. Lastly, 79 CE was the year Pompeii was destroyed by the last Plinian eruption of Mount Vesuvius. Should the unthinkable happen, and I inadvertently do something that puts history as we know it at risk, the eruption would act as a containment mechanism. Pyroclastic events have a way of doing that.

Thought was given to conducting this experiment closer to our time, perhaps going back to yesterday to rearrange the lab for comparison. That would seem to be a safer logical first step if it was possible, but it wasn't. It would create a paradox, or contradiction in space/time, meaning there would be two of me existing at the same point in time, the consequences of which were unknown but potentially disastrous.

"I wish I knew why the ship was abandoned in the Jurassic," Christina said. "Was it deliberate or did something break down? There's plenty of human DNA but no body. At least it proves we weren't the first humans to figure it out."

"I know we're not the first humans to use it," I said, "but are you sure they were from the future?"

"Absolutely," she replied, "and they were the last to use it. They found it and adapted its workings to human physique and physiology. The technology they used to accomplish that feat is certainly beyond ours, but enough like ours for Liam to configure a way to connect to it. The ship itself is a whole other animal. Whoever built it had to have a working understanding of quantum gravity. We don't even have a working theory yet."

The plastic-like material of the hull and related items were not plastic at all, but trillions of microscopic interlinking bits of artificially programmable intelligence. They were not to be confused with living matter. They did not think for themselves. They did not alter programming except where the programming allowed alterations within a set of specific guidelines, but they did replicate to repair damage, which is why the hull was always shiny and smooth. Individually they were weak, but in combination with others, their power and capabilities grew exponentially.

Christina believed the ship was meant for deep space travel more than time travel, perhaps even as a kind of shuttle from a much larger craft. She felt the capability to return to the ship's Date of Origin made it possible for space travelers to visit places lightyears away without finding their homeland decades or even centuries ahead in the future upon their return.

"I guess this is it," Christina said reluctantly. "You can still back out. There's nobody here who'd think any less of you."

"I'm not doing that," I said. "Next stop the Jurassic. Wow. I can't believe I just said that."

"But you can't stay there," she said, "and don't leave the ship for any reason. I don't want you breathing any unfiltered air from that era."

"I won't. And you're repeating yourself."

"But it's worth repeating. I know how much you'd love to see a dinosaur. Not this trip."

"I promise," I told her. "My biggest concern is syncing with the ship once I'm there. That's the first thing I'll do. If that fails, I may as well breathe the air because I won't be coming back."

"You'll be fine," she said. "You're only talking hand placement. You're already synced. It will respond to your commands."

I took a deep breath and tried to relax. I waved to Christina and then remembered she couldn't see me.

"Have a great trip," Liam said. "See you in a few hours."

"Last chance to change your mind," Christina said.

"Nope," I said. "I'm ready." I watched as they left the chamber and sealed the door behind them. I was already beginning to feel alone.

"I love you, Aaron," Christina said. "Never forget that."

"I won't," I replied, "and I love you too. We'll pick that date when I return." I placed my hand over the green button and waited. There was a low-level hum that moved around me from the back of the ship to the front followed by a sudden flash and then darkness. The ship tilted slightly and then righted itself as a powerful feeling of emptiness washed over me. For a moment it left me confused as my mind went blank. I looked at the green button, which flashed for a moment, and then shut off. My memory returned. I knew what that meant. I was in the Jurassic.

II

∞

Christina did indeed know me, and quite well. She was a high school friend of mine. She was my date for the senior prom, and while I was more athletic than classroom scholarly, she was truly brilliant, not to mention attractive. I went on to the University of New Hampshire for a degree in history while she chose MIT, receiving a doctorate in mechanical engineering.

She was very much into astronomy and space related sciences, and a gifted mathematician who saw engineering as her way into NASA. She was persistent, and after several tries, she finally landed a job at the Aerospace Center in Houston. That's where the "Object of Interest" first caught her eye.

She discovered the final government report on the "Object of Interest" while doing a key word search of the NASA research database during a lunch break. She had top-secret government clearance and was studying classified early space program experiments involving or relating to solar radiation and thermal energy. She nearly dismissed the report out of hand because it had been declassified and seemingly misfiled. However, there was one notation that caught her eye. The outer shell registered no thermal radiation. She looked for an explanation in the report but found nothing.

The more she read the more questions she had. Nobody knew who made it, what it was, or even what it was made of. The reports referred to the "shell" material as being a kind of plastic, but she found no records of any lab testing that verified it. Plastic will scratch, and the "Object of Interest" supposedly had no scratches despite being buried in very gritty soil. But her biggest question remained – what happened to the thermal radiation? Everything above absolute zero emits thermal radiation. Was it just a typo? She had to find out.

She began by driving to the Nevada warehouse where the Object had been placed in storage, but when she got there she found it had been moved to the Davis-Monthan Air Force boneyard near Tucson, Arizona where it rested outside amid a row of retired helicopters.

The first thing she did was touch it. It should have been prohibitively hot under the scorching sun, but it wasn't. It felt inexplicably cooler than the sunlit areas of the helicopters, but it wasn't void of thermal radiation. It did feel soft, almost soft enough to create indentations by pressing her palm or fingers into it, but no marks were left by her attempts.

There was an oval entrance. Christina looked for markings that would indicate the prior existence of hinges or a locking mechanism, but she found nothing. The oval opening was smooth all the way around. When she stepped inside, she found it comfortably cooler than the outside. It wasn't like it was air-conditioned, but there was a marked difference.

She set up an experiment inside the Object designed to detect the amount of background radiation penetrating the shell. After a one hour-long session the results showed zero. She ran the same experiment inside one of the helicopters and came up with a reading of 42 cpm. She reran the experiment inside the Object and got another zero reading despite the oval portal being wide open.

She couldn't understand how something so anomalous to anything she'd ever encountered before could be so readily dismissed. When she expressed her frustration to one of the security officers, he suggested that if it was that important to her, she should buy it. She didn't know she could do that, but he insisted she could. Nobody knew what to do with it. There was some titanium and aluminum in the seat and interior fixtures, but it was so minimal it was hardly worth stripping, and the shell wasn't made of a strategic material. The plan was to crush it and bury it.

She bought it for a dollar.

Christina and I had had an on again and off again romantic relationship that lasted for a couple years, until distance became a factor. She was the first to leave New Hampshire while I stayed.

On the surface Christina and I appeared to be very different people. She was organized and studious, and always making the honor roll. Logic was her salvation, and planning and organization helped her to make sense of the world. I was less organized and seldom on any list. I enjoyed competitive sports, competing in everything from judo to baseball. I especially enjoyed track, including cross-country running and javelin. Christina preferred the structure of noncompetitive group exercise classes. Where she was cautious, I was adventurous. She knew what she wanted and had plans to get there, and I just had plans to make plans later.

Eventually, she found a career at NASA while I became a traveler. I'd discovered a love of history, especially Greek and Roman. My hope was to supplement my European travels by being a guide to the very places that interested me the most, but it wasn't quite that easy. I had to begin more modestly. My first paying job was shuttling competitive shooting teams, both club and college, to various events. It was hardly what I would have chosen, but I had to start somewhere, and it paid well enough to cover expenses. I also learned how to shoot. I'm not a hunter, or have any interest in hunting, but competitive target shooting was fun, and I found I had a talent for it.

With time I was able to grow my little company into a profitable business, offering hiking and biking tours of the White Mountains in New Hampshire, and once that business was established, I found a way to partner with a Swiss airline in order to offer similar options for travelers to the Alps.

By that time, I had the contacts and experience to be able to shift my focus and offer guided tours of archeological sites in Greece and Italy, including Pompeii. I sold my half of the adventure travel business in order to hire professional archaeologists and historians as guides, adding Renaissance related options in the process. That's where Christina and I became reacquainted. She purchased one of my ten-day Florence packages.

When I saw her name on the list, I offered to reimburse my per-ticket portion of the earnings, but she wouldn't hear of it. Instead, she had an offer for me. I'd inherited an old farmhouse that belonged to my grandfather. It was a cozy place to live, but parts of it needed restoration. Christine needed a quiet, secure place to house and study her newly purchased "Object of Interest," and my idle barn would do nicely. Her offer included a complete barn renovation, as well as the addition of a small laboratory.

That trip reignited our romance, and four months later she took a leave of absence from NASA and moved into my farmhouse. Her equipment followed a day later, and her "Object of Interest" arrived on a flatbed truck a week after that. It didn't look like much to me, but within a few days she made her first big discovery. She discovered the shell material was made up of what amounted to microscopic computer chips or nanochips as she called them. By using a glove she found tucked up under the seat, she could activate the control panel, and with that she discovered she could sync herself with the Object. Once she was synced, she no longer needed the glove to activate the systems. That meant she could open and close the portal just by sweeping her bare hand over the location. There was no door in the normal sense. There were no handles or hinges. The door would simply fill in the open space to close, and spread out to open, but it only worked with people who were synced. I couldn't open the portal until I'd synced with the Object the same way she had.

More experiments led to more discoveries, including an almost microscopic microprocessor embedded into the control panel. It was clearly an advanced technology, but a different and more familiar type than the control panel. Christina needed help, so she invited Liam Cullen to study it, and they discovered it was a kind of link, or bridge, between two seemingly incompatible technologies. Once its function was determined, Liam constructed a wireless adaptor that offered a way to communicate with the "Object of Interest." That was the breakthrough that led to an understanding of many of the Object's functions via a series of digital notations that were actually in English, a modified version, but still English.

By being able to communicate with the "Object of Interest," Christina concluded that the Object was originally constructed by an ancient, most likely extraterrestrial, civilization that predated humanity by tens of millions of years, and at some point in the distant future it was discovered by future humans who adapted it and used it.

That didn't answer the questions of who built it, how it got to Earth, and why it was either stranded or deliberately left in the Jurassic. However, what Christina did know was how fantastic the discovery was, as well as how potentially dangerous. That meant specific questions had to be answered before she could ever consider going public with her find.

III

∞

Christina and Liam watched the launch from the safety of the lab by using a computer that was hooked to a webcam inside the containment room. They saw the ship appear to distort and flutter, followed by a brief flash and then the screen went blank.

"What do you think?" Liam asked.

"I think it worked," Christina replied. "I can feel it. He's gone. He's really gone." Aaron's departure left her with a sudden physical sense of loss, something beyond what would be considered normal.

"I feel it too," he said.

"This is a mistake. I never should have agreed to this."

"Hold on, Chris," Liam said as he took a first look at the reading from the launch. "These numbers look good. It all looks good." He turned to his wife. "What do you think, Aine?"

Dr. Aine Sayers Cullen was a medical researcher, and an old friend of Christina's. Christina assigned her the task of creating an immunization plan for Aaron for the year 79, including the protection of that era from anything he might carry in his system. The goal of rendering anyone completely immune to all the potential bacterial and viral risks of any age was unachievable, and they all knew that, but with knowledge of the past, greatly enhanced with modern DNA research, it was possible to minimize those risks with vaccines and a compact, battery powered air filtration mask should he inadvertently wander into a high-risk situation. There would be a quarantine chamber setup where Aaron would spend at least two weeks in quarantine following his return.

"What is there to think?" Aine replied. "No ship, no data. My readings are flatlined – dead."

"Not helpful, Aine," Liam said. His purpose in asking was to make Christina feel better.

"I'm fine," Christina said and she looked at her watch. "He should be initiating his return right now."

Liam smiled. "He initiated his return one hundred and fifty million years ago Christina. He's already been to Pompeii as well. He should be just a few hundred years from home by now, so we'd better get ready."

The trip to the Jurassic may have been almost instantaneous, but the return, not so much. A separate technology was required. This technology compressed space around the ship in a way that altered time. It caused the ship to rise off the surface of the planet while being pulled along by gravitational forces. The planet would appear to be spinning faster and faster beneath the ship as it rose. Each rotation represented a day by Earth time.

Christina had found data indicating the ship was capable of traveling at 850,000 rotations per minute. That translated into a minimum three hours of travel time from the Jurassic to the present, but that didn't take into account acceleration and deceleration times or the time spent at a location. Acceleration and deceleration could be relatively rapid because it wasn't about speed in the normal sense. The ship was essentially stationary, situated at various altitudes depending on its speed through time.

She estimated it would be at least five or more hours before the ship's return, at which time it would appear to be floating downward as a balloon might upon landing. The ship would be hard to see. In a technical sense it was visible as it traveled into the future, but virtually transparent depending on its onboard speed through time. The outer shell could mimic the colors of its environment much like a chameleon, but with greater detail. It also had no radar, heat, or tracking signatures. It was clearly designed to hide in plain sight.

The three of them ate and made small talk to pass the time. It was a warm, wonderfully sunny summer afternoon, perfect for sitting outside by the quarantine room, and that's where Christina sat through the afternoon and into the evening. She refused to let her fears get the best of her, but that got harder with every passing hour. Liam and Aine were getting concerned too. Landing at night wasn't ideal, but it wasn't likely either if the ship was functioning properly.

"I'm sleeping outside tonight," Christina said.

"With the coyotes?" Liam asked.

"I don't care," she replied.

"We'll join you."

That was all well and good until a series of powerful thunderstorms came through at around four in the morning. The three of them ran into the main house for cover. Storm driven gusts of wind pounded against the kitchen window as Christina tried to focus on the grounds outside. The ferocity of the storm had killed the electricity. With each flash of lightning came a glimpse of the grounds, and rather than moving away from the window, she remained with her face almost pressed to the glass. Like her fear of heights, she always feared lightning, but not on that night. Each flash bathed the grounds in an eerie blue light that spoke to her of things surreal. Great crackling sounds split the sky with brilliant flashes for a few brief seconds, before everything was plunged back into darkness.

Blasts of thunder nearly matched the frequency of the bright bursts of light. One bolt appeared to crash into the trees behind the barn just as a rippling sheet of rain pelted the glass near her face.

Another flash, and Christina's eyes were drawn to the soaking grounds and a hazy halo-shaped ring of light. St. Elmo's fire came to mind, but that wasn't quite right. It reflected in the nearby puddles below, while the house physically shook from the rumble.

She jumped back for an instant, but quickly returned. There was a flash and another rumble followed by another flash.

"My God!" she cried at the sight of a wobbling, radiant crescent of ghostly blue light that glowed electrically like neon for an instant, before fading into the blackness. She stepped back and rubbed her eyes fearing the storm was playing tricks, but then came the next flash, and with it, the solidified shape of something she knew.

"I don't believe it," she said. Her mind was moving faster than her eyes could react and she tripped and fell in the darkness. The occasional sporadic flashes from outside lit the room with broken shadows. "He's back!" she cried out while picking her way to the front door. She turned the handle and a sudden gust of wind ripped it from her hand, nearly blowing the door off its hinges as it slammed against side of the house.

"Are you crazy?" Liam yelled from the dark hallway behind her. "You can't go out there now!"

"He's back!" Christina said. "He's back!" And she disappeared into a sheet of driving rain.

Aine was groggy and stumbling into the kitchen. "What's going on?" she asked.

"I don't know," he replied. "I think she's finally cracked. See if you can figure out why the generator didn't start, and I'll chase her down."

"It's dangerous out there, Liam."

He looked at her, shrugged, and braced himself for the weather, but then the sky lit up and he saw the silhouetted figure of Christina set against the familiar shape of the ship.

“Holy shit!” he gasped, the words barely able to escape his tightening throat.

“What?” Aine asked.

“It really is the ship,” he replied as he stood frozen in the doorway with the rain driving against his face, and then he gathered his willpower and charged into it.

“Aaron!” Christina cried out repeatedly. “He doesn’t answer,” she told Liam when he joined her, “and I can’t find the door.”

“Aaron!” they called out together.

“He has to be here,” Christina said as she ran her hands along the hull. “The door should have opened.”

“It’s on top,” Liam said when a lightning flash lit the grounds, “and it looks open. We’ve got to get up there.”

The outside flood lights came on as the generator kicked in. Liam turned to see Aine in the doorway. “I need a flashlight,” he told her before running into the barn for a ladder.

Christina was near panic as she tried to push the ship upright, but the hull was terribly slippery and too difficult to budge without equipment. It seemed like an eternity by the time Liam returned with the flashlight and ladder. The open portal was facing practically straight up, making it very difficult for him to see inside, even from the ladder, but he managed. “He’s not here,” he said once he’d had a chance to circle the interior with the light.

“He has to be,” Christina said. “There’s no way he had time to climb out with the ship tilted like that.”

“He’s not,” Liam insisted as a gust of wind blew stuff around inside the cabin. Rain was pouring in as well.

“Can you see inside the bathroom?”

“The door’s open,” Liam replied. “I can see the whole cabin. He’s just not here.”

“No!” Christina cried out as she fell to her knees in a puddle, her clothing soaked and sopping wet hair clinging to the sides of her face. Her worst nightmare had just come to pass.

IV

∞

A great storm raged all around me and I had all I could do to keep from being tossed into the heavy seas. Lightning danced across the sky, crackling in bright, blinding flashes, while wind and rain lashed in oscillating sheets against my face. The roar of thunder and sea was deafening. I clung with white knuckles to the ropes that held my small wooden raft together as waves of increasing intensity tried to knock me off. There was a bright flash of white light and my raft shuddered from the hit.

"No!" I screamed in terror as the planking loosened and gave way. With nothing solid beneath me I fell between the separating timbers, hopelessly grabbing for anything solid as they spun away and vanished into the stormy darkness.

I was frantic, gasping for air. "Help," I cried out repeatedly, "help!"

I quickly became confused and was breathing in more water than air. With one great thrust I broke the surface for the final time, and exhausted, I slipped quietly under the waves. The violent world above was silent, and in its place was an oddly comforting feeling of resignation and peace. The panic was gone, and I became content to drift along in the darkened calm, watching with curiosity as my lifeless hands floated gently before my face.

It was a wonderful sensation, peaceful and completely relaxing, except for an odd, raspy, buzzing sound that didn't quite fit with the whole cloud-nine scenario. A cicada? It sounded like there were at least two sources of the buzzing somewhere nearby. There was also renewed sensation in my hands and soreness developing throughout my body. Suddenly I felt a sharp pain over my right eye, and with a toss, I woke up.

"Incredible," I muttered while remaining perfectly still to let the pain subside. I took a deep, calming breath, comforted by the knowledge I was still alive. My eyes were watering, but as my sight became clearer, I found a modicum of serenity by looking up at the imperfections in an otherwise smooth, white ceiling. I was content to study the many tiny cracks in the plaster until I realized the ceiling was not familiar.

"What the heck?" I tried to sit up. My neck and shoulders were so sore and stiff that I could only lift myself a few inches before falling back against the pillow. I was terribly weak and that one small movement left me shaking.

I took a few more calming breaths while looking more closely at my surroundings. The room was a small, windowless rectangle with an eight-foot high ceiling. The primary light source was an open doorway just a few feet from the foot of the bed that looked onto what appeared to be a well-groomed courtyard. The walls of the room were painted with a semi-gloss sheen and the colors were vibrant. A rich red, detailed with yellow pin striping dominated the room, while impressions of windows were painted in azure-blue squares on the walls paralleling the bed. Each square contained multi-colored architectural motifs that may have lacked a realistic sense of perspective but were graphically pleasing to the eye. The combination of the colors and design was comforting.

There was a wooden stool in the corner by the door and a small table next to the bed. The table had a square, gray, marble top, and once I'd finally summoned the energy to roll onto my side, I noticed it had meticulously sculptured wooden legs standing on carved cat's feet. Resting on the table was an earthenware pitcher flanked by a pair of thick, glass goblets that displayed a faint, greenish-purple luster on the surface. There was a light breeze entering the room through a narrowly cut vertical opening in the back wall behind my head. It was only about an arm's width wide and apparently designed for ventilation rather than viewing.

I eased back again and looked up at the ceiling. There was also an annoying throbbing just above my right temple. Even the slightest touch produced a penetrating sharp pain that shot down my neck to my shoulder.

"That's not good," I sighed as I continued to stare up at the ceiling. The right side of my face was swollen as well, affecting my jaw. My movements were slow and my joints stiff and sore, and when I tried to sit up a second time I fell right back again.

"*Noli temptare consurgere.*" It was a young woman's concerned voice coming from the doorway. She appeared only as a dark silhouette against the bright sunlight of the courtyard.

"Huh?" I mumbled. I hadn't caught a word she'd said, nor was she familiar once I could see her more clearly. She was about five feet tall and elegantly dressed in a flowing, pastel-green wrap belted at the midriff. She was also quite pretty. Her hair was thick and chestnut-colored, and pulled back into a single braid that hung almost to the middle of her back. Several long, artificially created curls framed both sides of her face.

"*Quaeso*," she pleaded as she stepped closer, "*noli temptare consurgere*." Her words were inconsistent with those that seemed natural to me, but I knew what the word *quaeso* meant, and then I realized she was telling me that I shouldn't try to sit up. She had a point.

"Hello," I said, "do I know you?" Instead of a reply she looked confused. "Who are you?" I asked in a stronger voice, but all I sensed was a developing dilemma.

She stared at me for a moment, which made me a little nervous, but then she took a breath and spoke much more slowly, "*Me paenitet. Non intellego quid dixeris*." It appeared that my predicament was more than just being in a strange room, but even so, once I adjusted to her pronunciation, I recognized the problem. She was speaking in a different language than the one that came most naturally to me, but it was not unfamiliar. I knew what she'd said. She was apologizing for not understanding me.

"No," I said in words to match hers. "I apologize to you. Do you understand me now?"

She gave me a questioning look, but then she smiled, "Yes."

"Good," I sighed, relieved that communication, although difficult, was at least possible. "Who are you?"

"I am a friend," she said simply and clearly.

"A friend? Does that mean I know you?"

"No," she replied as she stepped closer, "but I feel like I know you…ah…Gnaeus," and then she pointed at me.

It was my turn to stare questioningly. "Me?" I said with raised eyebrows. "Are you calling me A Gnaeus?"

"Not…A Gnaeus," she chuckled. "Your name is Gnaeus." I felt my blood pressure spike when I realized I didn't even know my own name. "What is it, Gnaeus?" she asked.

"My name is what?" My voice trembled noticeably.

"You don't know?" Her smile melted into a look of concern.

I shook my head. "No."

V

∞

She stepped to the side of the bed and placed her right hand flat against my forehead. "Perhaps it was the illness. You were quite hot for several days."

"I had a fever?"

There were aspects about the way she spoke that differed from what seemed correct to me, but even so, I was already starting to understand and speak more easily in words she understood. We continued to talk slowly, but my use of the word *febris* for fever confused her, so I rephrased the question and asked if my body was too hot.

"Yes," she said as her smile returned. "You also had terrible shakings, but we kept you well covered. The signs were bad, but somehow father knew you would survive. He will be most pleased."

The more she spoke the more I realized how clumsily I was speaking. My sentences were broken, and it seemed like I had to dig for every other word. I couldn't enunciate the same words in the same way she did either. Second language or not, it was like my brain had atrophied to the point of affecting my speech.

"How long have I been ill?" I asked nervously, suddenly realizing my sickness may well have caused brain damage.

"Ah," she said, "you were found sitting by the side of a road six days ago. You were very ill. You have been here ever since."

I was getting tired of lying down and decided to try to sit up again. Modesty kept me from pushing the covering aside when I realized I was naked underneath, so I held the bed sheet over my waist. My new friend took my arm to steady me, and once I was sitting up, she sat beside me. The stone flooring was invigoratingly cool against the bottoms of my feet, but the real shock was my physical weakness.

"Thank you," I said. I needed a moment to catch my breath from that one small movement. "You seem to..."

"Please," she said kindly, "relax. You've been terribly ill. There will be plenty of time to talk later."

It was clear I'd been ill, so I took her advice and rested before rephrasing the question. "You know who I am, but I don't know you."

"Ah," she said with a very warm smile. "My name is Maria Secunda, but my friends call me Appia."

"Appia?" The word produced a recollection. "Is that like the road?"

"No," she chuckled. "It's like my father. My father is called Appius Marius Caupo. My real name is Maria like my sister. But she is Maria Prima, of course."

"Of course," I said, even though I didn't have a clue.

"I am told that when I was a child, I followed father all around the villa. Apparently, I liked to mimic him. Father's friends gave me the nickname Little Appius. Instead of losing it when I grew up, I became Appia."

"Appia. You have a pretty name." Despite my physical discomforts I was still alert enough to notice her natural attractiveness. What makeup she wore she didn't need, but she wasn't quite as young as I first thought, perhaps mid or even late-twenties. There was gentleness in her smile that was disarming, and the warmth in her hazel eyes was unavoidable while her manner was comforting.

"I must look awful," I said.

"Not at all," she replied. "Today there is much more color in your face."

"Have I been shaved?" There was only light stubble on my chin.

She laughed. "Of course, and bathed as well."

I glanced at the pitcher on the table and asked, "Is that water?" I raised my arm to reach for it, but the motion made me lightheaded.

"Gnaeus?" she said with great concern. "Are you all right?"

I was about to reply when I felt myself slumping to the side. Oh, good, I thought as the world became hazy again. Perhaps it really was a dream, but I could still hear Appia's voice somewhere in the distance. She called for somebody named Thalese, and a moment later I was being lifted back onto the bed. The lightheadedness passed once I was lying down, but my weakness continued.

"I think he needs more rest," Appia said to a concerned man standing next to her. He was holding my wrist while she was straightening out the folds in her green wrap.

"I think you're right," he agreed. "He's been terribly sick."

"He doesn't seem to know who he is," Appia told him.

"Really?" He sounded more curious than surprised.

"We spoke of it specifically. He doesn't."

"Did he tell you where he's from?"

"No. How can he? He doesn't know his own name!"

"Hmm," the man muttered. "I'm pleased he has awakened, but I hope the illness hasn't left him feeble."

"He's not feeble," she said. "He's…well…I don't know. But not feeble. He's not from here. That's for sure."

The man elevated my head and shoulders by adding another pillow and Appia handed me a glass of water.

"Thank you," I said graciously and I took a sip. "Thank you both." The taste was pure ecstasy and my body absorbed it like a sponge. After the first glass I drank a second and then a third.

If Appia was five feet tall then Thalese was five and a half. He looked older, perhaps 50, but it was hard to tell. He was quite thin. He had a slender face with tiny wrinkles at the corners of his mouth and brown eyes, but his tightly cropped, dark-brown hair showed no signs of gray. His one-piece, tan tunic was simple and plain, and he had a very kindly manner about him.

"Do you know me?" I asked Thalese.

"You are Gnaeus," he replied.

"No," I said. "I want to know if we have ever met before now."

He glanced at Appia. "No."

"You both know my name, but neither of you know me." I wanted to ask if I was carrying any identification, but I didn't know the word.

"We know who we think you are," Thalese said. "The name Gnaeus Octavius Getha was sewn into your clothing."

Appia grinned. "Why did you do that? Did you expect to forget your name?"

"I don't think so," I replied with a smile. Her comment was strangely amusing. "But maybe if I could see my clothes I might remember."

"What do you remember before today?" Thalese asked.

I didn't have to think very hard to reply. "Nothing." It was a chilling realization.

Appia sat down at my side again. "Most of your clothes were so badly soiled that we had to take them to the laundry. But the material was so unusual, and, well, they just came apart. I'm sorry."

I asked her to repeat her words because she was speaking more quickly than I could process. It seemed like I had enough vocabulary to draw on, but trying to communicate was just not coming naturally.

Appia had a comical grin, apparently amused by something about me.

"I apologize for my speech," I said. "I must be hard to understand."

"It's not that," she said. "I was thinking that you might want to talk to your tailor. I've never seen formalwear cut so…oddly." She looked away as if trying not to laugh.

"I have no idea what you're talking about," I said in frustration.

"I'm sorry," she said, and she gently took my hand. "Don't worry; father will be able to help." They watched with concern as I drank another glass of water, and didn't leave until I assured them I wasn't about to pass out again.

A third visitor quietly stepped into the room. She was a mature woman with a wisp of gray in her hair. She had a tan tunic wrapped over her arm. Her clothes were very plain, like those of Thalese, but loosely wrapped the way Appia's had been. She seemed oblivious to me while carefully folding and setting the tunic on the stool by the door. I was not up to conversation, so I said nothing, and without so much as a glance she hustled off.

I was nearly asleep when an impeccably groomed man, sporting a pure white wrap, entered the room. The word *toga* came to mind when I studied him more closely. He was a little heavy set, and I would guess him to be at least fifty years old. He wasn't much taller than Thalese and his walk was well practiced, giving an air of importance to his appearance. His attire was in sharp contrast with everyone else's, clearly meant to impress.

"Greetings, Gnaeus!" he said in a loud voice. He was also displaying a wide smile. "I'm Appius Marius Caupo, but my friends call me Appius! So, you're finally awake."

"That's one possibility," I said soberly.

"I see," he said, but what he saw was a mystery to me. Then his voice dropped about five octaves as he dragged the stool over and sat on the tunic. "I've been told you have an odd inflection in your speech. So, speak to me," and he stared at me in a way that demanded a response.

"What would you have me say?" I replied.

"I don't know. Why don't you begin by telling me a little about yourself?"

"A little is all you will get because I don't know anything."

"I was told that too," he said.

"I know my clothing was cause for amusement, but none of the clothing anyone else is wearing is familiar to me either."

"What is familiar to you?" he asked.

"I don't know," I said. "It's just a feeling. I can't explain it. I can't explain anything." It seemed impossible to be any more confused than I was at that moment.

He looked concerned, but all he could say was, "Interesting." However, he was having no apparent trouble understanding me.

"You understand me better than the others," I noted.

"It's not so hard," he grinned. "In my travels I've had to deal with far more difficult dialects than yours. But yours is unique. Your speech is very pure in structure…surprisingly so."

"I should also tell you," I said, "that the name Gnaeus is not familiar. They said it was on my clothing, but I still don't know it. Maybe my clothes were borrowed."

He smiled, stood up and then stepped to the end of the bed. "That's possible, but there are aspects…facts if you will…that lend support to the name Gnaeus."

"Facts?"

"Facts!" he stated emphatically. His expressions changed quickly. He would be smiling one instant and serious the next. "Aside from the name in your clothing, and this is of equal importance, you were witnessed being born from a cloud. And secondly, the very morning of your arrival, the chickens…"

"What did you say?" It seemed like I was having more problems with the language. "It sounded like you said I was born from a cloud."

He stared at me as if I'd spoken out of turn. "That's correct," he replied, "and don't look at me like I'm the one who's been whacked on the head."

"Is that like a metaphor?" I asked in bewilderment.

"No," he replied as if such a bizarre notion made sense. "It's what was witnessed."

"Are you talking about a real cloud like in the sky? Because that makes no sense."

"That was my first thought as well, but it's a fact that can't be denied. And when nonsense makes sense we must look for a deeper meaning."

I sighed, "What does *that* mean?"

"I'm still working on that," he said thoughtfully, "but I'm certain of divine implications."

"Divine? That's not…I mean…well…what do you mean?"

"Relax, Gnaeus, and let me finish." There was little else I could do so I eased back into the pillow. "Now," he began, "when we found you, you were dressed in unusual clothes with pockets full of unusual items. You clearly have knowledge of things foreign to this region, or any I've visited. And I've visited them all!"

"What items?"

"Please let me finish," he replied with a wave of his hand. "You see, Gnaeus, you are an anomalous being. You appear to be a foreigner and yet you're not. Your accent is not of this land, but your diction is too pure to be from anywhere else, and your name is distinctly local, which may link you to a very important family. It's important to know what deity is involved and why that deity has chosen to link your family with mine."

"Or not," I said as I understood most of his words, but little else. "What are you talking about?"

He paused briefly, but ignored the question, and then proceeded with the story in an even more dramatic fashion. "Clouds have cast shadows over this villa in recent months. My client base is uncertain."

"Client base?"

"My supporters," he replied. "They do my bidding. They give respect. They can be escorts. Most importantly they offer political support including votes as needed. A strong client base is critical to the future of my family."

"They're like employees?"

"No," he said as he shook his head, "they're not like anything. They're clients. It's a mutually beneficial arrangement. I have the wealth and ranking, so I can offer legal counseling, meals occasionally, gratuities, goods, livestock, blah blah blah, other support. You name it."

"You said they're uncertain. What are they uncertain about?"

"Me," he replied. "I'm old. Supposedly eccentric," and he shrugged. "A political has-been. I know what people are saying. They think I'm weak. Unfortunately, most of my clients are unbound. They can leave for another patron, and a few have, which makes your arrival most fortuitous."

"Now you've lost me again," I said.

He was back to pacing. "It's quite simple Gnaeus. You're a gift from the Gods." I wanted to laugh, but I couldn't because he'd made the statement with such sincerity. "You look doubtful," he noted, "but you were witnessed being born from a cloud. I can have the witnesses tortured to see if that changes their testimony, but they all said the exact same thing, so I believe they're telling the truth."

I stared at him for a moment. "So how come I know nothing of this? Did I pop out of this cloud and bang my head or something?" I thought I was being sarcastic.

"Very possibly," he said with a straight face, "but I believe it's a little more complicated than that. You see, memory loss is also an effect of rebirth. You get a new slate and a fresh beginning."

"Rebirth? From a cloud?"

"Yes, Gnaeus! A mysterious cloud appeared low on the horizon above the vineyard. It drifted slowly like a seed in the breeze. From within the center a divine messenger emerged. His head and shoulders appeared first as he fell headlong to the ground. And then the cloud was gone!"

"And I'm supposed to be that messenger?"

"Yes," he replied with a straight face.

"Okay," I said with a chuckle, "but why would the gods choose to introduce their gift in such a traumatic and painful way?" I thought the question would stump him. "It's like giving someone a broken present. How does that make sense?"

"It makes perfect sense," he stated with a knowing smile. "Are your injuries not consistent with a headfirst tumble?"

"I suppose they are," I replied. My wrists and head were banged up.

"Birth is a traumatic experience by design," he explained. "It's the first real test of strength and character!" He seemed to have an answer for everything, and I was growing too tired to care. "You rest. I'll be back later."

I nodded and he left. Conversing was much easier with him than the other two, but I did struggle with some of the words. It sounded like he said something about torturing witnesses? I must have been mistaken.

I closed my eyes, and sleep came easily. Dreaming came easily, as well, and as I drifted off, I found myself walking amid a cluster of badly damaged buildings. None had roofs or second floors. Their crumbling brick walls lined the streets like rows of broken teeth, while colorfully dressed people were milling about the empty chambers.

From behind, an ominous shadow crept over the land, quickly plunging everything into darkness. I turned around to see the ghostly blue silhouette of a mountain swelling to mammoth proportions before my eyes. It was crackling and cracking as it expanded, and then it began to break up sending huge boulders rumbling down its slopes towards me.

"Whoa!" I gasped as I shot straight up in bed. Sweaty and shaken I glanced around the room. "Just a dream," I muttered as fear welled inside me, accompanied by a sickening bout of lightheadedness and disorientation. I gripped the bedding and concentrated on calming down. I finally fell back to sleep, mercifully too tired to dream.

VI

∞

When I awoke it was from pangs of hunger and a near desperate need for a bathroom. The creaking of the wooden bed frame acted as a signal to a woman outside the door. She was by my side before I was fully upright. It was the same woman who had left the tunic on the stool earlier.

"Can I help you?" she asked in a formal tone.

"I think so," I replied. "I need to go to the bathroom."

She appeared to be perplexed. "You want to bathe now?"

"No," I replied, "not bathe." The combination of the words bath and room weren't consistent with her vocabulary. "How about water closet?"

She glanced at my empty glass. "You want more water?"

"No." I couldn't help smiling. "How about this? Is there a room for, say, making earth?" Then I held my stomach and feigned a pained expression.

"Oh," she chuckled as her eyes lit up.

"I'm sorry I can't remember the proper word."

"Latrine," she explained. "There's a pot beneath the bed if that's easier."

I looked down and saw a terracotta handle sticking out by my left foot. "No," I told her, "I'd prefer to get up. I would like to try and walk to see if it helps."

She handed me the tunic from the foot of the bed. With her help we pulled it over my head, followed by my first attempt to stand. My legs were terribly wobbly, and the way the wooden bed frame creaked when I shifted weight was a little disconcerting, but I made it to my feet. My head throbbed but the pain quieted after a few seconds.

"What's your name?" I asked.

"Leita," she said and she took my arm.

The weather was wonderfully warm and very bright. The light was a little overwhelming, and I needed to shade my eyes and let them adjust. My room opened onto a neatly groomed, rectangular courtyard, which I realized was actually called a peristyle. A nicely crafted portico with yellow and white columns offered protection from the sun and a pair of marble benches were welcome resting spots along the way to the latrine.

There were sculptures meticulously positioned to give a flavor of elegance amid a setting of well-groomed trees and bushes. There were small palms and cypresses along with oleander, and wandering among them were peacocks and other delicate creatures. The air was abuzz with the sound of cicadas, and overhead were lots of birds fluttering in the breeze. At the center of the courtyard was a gray stone fountain ringed by matching stone benches, and nearby was a white marble bust set on a tall, fluted pedestal. "Who's that?" I asked.

"Emperor Vespasian," she replied. "He's a good friend of my master."

"Emperor Vespasian?" The name was familiar. The word Rome came to mind as well.

"Yes."

"I think I know him," I said. "I mean, I know of him. Actually, I don't know what I know of him, but at least his name is familiar…I think."

That brought a smile to her face. "I like you," she said. "You have a friendly manner." We walked the length of the portico until reaching a door in a corner. "Here," she said with pride, "the latrine. We have two. Both with running water!"

"Running water? Is that considered unusual?"

"Well, yes," she replied as if my question was a little odd, "but Master Appius has his ways. Are you all right to go in alone or would you like some help?"

"I'm fine," I told her, but my situation was getting critical.

"I'll be here if you need me."

My eyes had adjusted to daylight, so it was difficult to see inside the dimly lit room, but the smell confirmed the location. The air was muggy and unpleasantly still. The smooth stone flooring was damp and greasy against the bottoms of my feet and I could hear a steady gurgling of water.

There was a fixed wooden seat set against the back wall. The word outhouse came to mind. A small, continuous stream of water flowed beneath the seat exiting through a clay pipe on the right. A cloth-tipped stick was set vertically against the left wall. It looked like an unlit torch; however, I didn't have to think very hard to understand its true function.

My physical need quickly overcame my queasiness. Needless to say, I didn't dawdle. Leita was waiting outside and steadied me on the walk back to my room. After straightening the bed and refreshing my water glass she returned to the main building. Had she actually used the word *master?*

I didn't feel like going back to bed so I stepped outside and sat by the fountain. The soft sound of bubbling water was very soothing, but not quite enough to wash away my worries or the brief periods of light-headedness.

Of greater concern was the injury above my eye and the way certain movements continued to cause shooting pains down the right side of my face.

"Gnaeus!" It was the booming voice of Appius. "You are up and about! This is indeed good news!"

"Yes," I replied. "I'm feeling a little better."

"Amazing! Simply amazing!"

"Are we near Rome?" I asked.

"No," he replied. "Rome is some distance north. Several days travel depending on your rush."

"I think I've been there."

"You think?" he said thoughtfully. "So you're not sure?"

"I am sure because I remember things." Thinking about Rome was producing actual memories that came easily without concentration.

"What things?"

"Impressive buildings…a crowd of people in a square."

"What square?" he asked.

"I don't know," I replied, "but I think it's in the middle of the city. I see a hill to my left…not a big hill. But there's a magnificent temple on top. I remember the brilliant gold trim."

"Interesting," he said as he slowly paced back and forth. "What else?"

"Well, I remember standing on a set of stairs of a basilica. I think it's a basilica."

"Are you facing this basilica or…"

"It's behind me. I'm standing on the steps of the basilica facing the square."

His face lit up. "The Basilica Julia, perhaps?"

"Possibly," I replied. "That name sounds familiar."

"You're in the Forum."

"Yes," I smiled, "that's exactly it. It is the Roman Forum!"

"Very good, Gnaeus!"

I stood up and walked over to the bust of Emperor Vespasian. "I know I have a lot more to remember, but it's just not clear."

"Try, Gnaeus," he encouraged. "You're doing very well."

I looked around the courtyard attempting to pull as much as I could from my memory. "I think I saw an emperor in the square that day."

"An emperor? Not the emperor?"

"I don't know," I replied.

"Can you describe him?"

"Is it important?"

He shrugged. "Possibly. I don't know."

"He was old," I began, but a disquieting image flashed in my mind. "He seemed to be..."

"Seemed to be what?"

I sighed. "I think I saw him die. I mean, I really think I saw him die." Appius shrugged again and shook his head. "Could this be from a dream?" I wondered. "I've been having strange dreams."

"Perhaps," he replied. "What makes you think he died?"

"I'm not sure I actually saw him die," I said, "but I know he died. There were lots of soldiers and it was soldiers who killed him. I remember now! His own soldiers turned on him. He was helpless. It was chaos around me, and I was trying to get away from it. But I did see a man killed."

"The emperor?"

"No," I replied, "a different man. He wore a white toga. He was trying to run when he was attacked. They slaughtered him. It was hideous! No wonder I don't want to remember anything!"

Appius appeared to be in deep thought. "Does the name Vitellius or maybe Galba mean anything to you?"

"Yes," I said as the image suddenly gained clarity. "It was Galba! Yes! He was the emperor I saw. The crowd pushed his litter around and his own people dumped him onto the ground. It was a horrible sight!"

"I imagine it was," Appius said quietly. "It was a horrible time to be in Rome."

"Then it wasn't a dream. It was real."

"About as real as it gets."

I was anxious to move on to hopefully better memories, but it was like I hit a brick wall and I quickly became lightheaded again. "That's all I can do right now," I said as I sat to try and quell the dizziness. "I'm sorry, but all this memory work makes me sick. I don't understand it."

"Relax, Gnaeus. It will all become clear to you in time."

"I hope so. Maybe I'll remember more when I see more familiar things. Everything I just told you came to me when I saw that bust over there."

"Emperor Vespasian?"

"Yes," I replied. "Leita said he was your friend."

"Indeed," he smiled. "He's a very good friend, but what do you know of him?"

I shook my head. "Nothing really. His name is familiar. That's all. But that's when I thought of Rome."

"That's good, Gnaeus. Maybe one day you'll get to meet him. He visits from time to time. It gives him a brief respite from the trials and tribulations of his office."

"What office?"

He looked puzzled. "He's the emperor."

"The current emperor?"

"Yes," he replied.

"That doesn't make any sense…"

"It will in time," he said with a smile, "but right now I've got something to show you. I'll be right back." The peaceful beauty of the peristyle made it easy to follow his directions. When he returned, he laid a heavily laden gray vest at my feet. "What's all this?" he asked.

I looked at the vest lying in a heap on the ground. It had several fat outer pockets, including one with a handle sticking out and another with a wad of hose rolled tightly inside. The hose was connected to an odd-looking canister clipped to the outside pocket. I immediately knew it was a breathing device for filtering out biological threats.

"It's familiar." I said.

"We thought it wise not to touch anything until you've had a chance to explain it."

I lifted the vest from the ground and placed it in my lap. I felt a connection as soon as I touched it. The label on a bottle in one of the pockets read acetaminophen/codeine/50 tablets. He touched it gingerly as if it was something hot.

"Do these words have meaning to you?" he asked.

"Yes," I replied. "It's a pain medicine."

"Really?"

There were a host of other medicines, mostly in packets. One of the narrower pockets was zipped shut. Inside were two capped injectors for allergic reactions to bee stings. I knew what everything was, but they awakened no new memories the way the bust of Emperor Vespasian had.

"So," Appius asked, "does this stuff have meaning to you?"

"Yes," and I undid the snap holding the handled object. I immediately knew it was a gun, and with my fingers wrapped around the handle, I knew it was mine.

VII

∞

"Most curious," Appius commented. "None of us knew what to make of that. It's quite nicely finished, but offers no obvious function."

"You don't know what it is?"

"No," he replied with a shake of his head. "Is it like a club? But that would mean you're holding it by the wrong end. It's a mechanism. I'm sure of that."

"You really don't know? Everyone must know what a…" and I paused. I didn't know the word for gun in his language.

"Know what?" he inquired.

"It's hard to explain."

"Thalese believes it to be some sort of weapon."

"Thalese is correct," I said. "It is a weapon, and a most dangerous one if not handled properly."

"Interesting," he said thoughtfully. "But how can something that small be effective?"

"It's effective," I told him.

"How can such a small weapon do much of anything?" he quipped.

"It just can," I replied. I needed time to think and he wasn't giving it to me. It was hard enough fighting with the language, but I was also becoming more confused and irritated. My fingers tightened around the handle of the gun as I closed my eyes. Nothing was making sense.

"I don't understand," he said. "How can you make such a bold claim? Do you remember something?"

"Please," I pleaded, "just let me think."

"But how?" he repeated with greater insistence. "You must be able to tell me that much!"

"Maybe later," I replied in a feeble attempt to put him off.

"Why not now? Have you another agenda?"

"Another agenda? What other agenda could I possibly have?" My frustration level had reached its peak and I buried my head in my hands.

"I'm sure you must understand why I ask. I'm only trying to…"

"Do you really want to know?" I blurted out in frustration as a burst of adrenal energy brought new life to my weakened body. "Do you?" My hands were shaking as I pressed three rounds into the revolving barrel.

"Hmm," Appius muttered, "I guess so." I must have looked like a man possessed. My aggressive tone had given him second thoughts, but I wasn't about to let him off the hook.

"All right!" I said as I jumped to my feet while slamming the barrel shut. I spun it once and took dead aim at a second marble bust about ten feet away.

Boom! Boom! Boom! I fired off three rounds in rapid succession. The sound split the air, ricocheting off the walls and columns. The powerful force of the blunt nosed projectiles easily shattered the soft marble head. Stone dust flew in all directions. Shell fragments peppered the solid wall beneath the portico. Plaster cracked with brittle, angular bits raining to the ground.

"What is happening to me?" I cried out to the sky in English and I threw my arms in the air in frustration. My body went limp and I sunk to my knees. My head was pounding again.

Appius was seated on the ground after having tripped when he heard the shots. There was a look of awe on his face and for once he was left speechless. I tried to rationalize what had happened, while being appalled at how recklessly I'd handled the gun.

"You command thunder like a god," he said quietly as he dusted himself off. "Like the eagle! Like the great Hercules himself!"

"What?"

"Hercules," he said. "The trials of Hercules. You must know of them? But of greater importance is that I finally know which god has sent you. I should have seen it sooner."

"Please don't do that," I said shaking my head. "I'm confused enough as it is."

"Hercules is a prominent guardian among my Lares," he explained. Then he glanced at the damaged statue. "What did you say when you called out to him?"

"Called out?"

"To Hercules. You called out to him in some strange tongue. I heard you."

"I don't remember," I replied, not wanting to talk about it. "I wasn't thinking clearly."

"You spoke clearly enough, but I didn't recognize your words."

"I was simply mumbling in frustration." I realized I had inadvertently spoken in my more comfortable language.

"You need not explain," he commented as he stepped towards the shattered target, "but I'm sure you can understand my curiosity."

"Sorry about the damage."

"It's all right. I asked for it." He took a moment to study the ruined statue and then he looked at me. He sighed and looked back at the statue again. All that was left of the head were several large chunks of broken stone lying on the ground around the pedestal. "I can only imagine what that would do to a real head."

"Sorry," I said sheepishly.

"One thing for sure, you're a very powerful person."

"I don't know what I am," I said as I watched him examining one of the marble fragments. And as I said it, I was afraid.

VIII

∞

"I think we should wait until the storm passes," Aine said when Christina and Liam came in from outside. "Maybe wait until it's lighter out. Get a little rest first," she added as they rushed by her on their way to the equipment shed. "Just a thought." She had a good point. It was a time machine. Whatever had happened to Aaron had happened ages ago, so time was not of the essence, but for Christina, sleep was out of the question and fear of the elements was negated by her fear of personal loss.

The first thing Christina and Liam did was to get the ship righted. The four stabilizing skids formed once it was upright which made it easier for Liam to push it into the quarantine room with the tractor. Why it hadn't righted itself on its own was one of a growing list of questions on everybody's mind. However, only one question was at the forefront – what had happened to Aaron?

The fact that the hatch was open was concerning, but not because he might have fallen out while in transit. The hatch closes automatically upon panel activation. The seemingly obvious conclusion was that he was not in the ship when it took off. That would explain why the hatch was open, but the panel could not be activated unless he was in front of it. To activate it from outside was a logistical impossibility.

Rain had gotten inside the ship, but not nearly as much as they'd expected. There were papers strewn everywhere, but most disturbingly they also found blood on a wad of cotton gauze and on the control panel. Luckily, they found Aaron's camera. The first thing Liam did was download the images into his computer. The first photo he pulled up was a colorful shot of a series of wharves framed by a marble arched bridge.

"Wow," Aine said. "Is that really from the past?"

Christina was shaking. "It has to be. Look at the shoreline. That's not modern."

"These next two are street scenes," Liam noted, "and look at the wharves in this next one. Look at those boats. That's definitely ancient. And look at the bridge photo again. That looks like a river, not a bay."

"Check out this beautiful building here," Aine said. It was a shot of a golden trimmed temple on a hill above other buildings.

Christina carefully studied each image. “Have a look at this one,” she said. It depicted a regally dressed person being carried through a crowd in a sedan chair. “Tell me what’s wrong with this picture.”

“It means he made it,” Aine said in quiet awe. “He really made it. I guess sometimes things don’t sink in until you see something tangible.”

“But where did he make it to?” Christina asked. “I don’t think that’s Pompeii!”

“Are you sure?” Aine said while pointing to the photos of street scenes.

“You’re right, Chris,” Liam said. “Where’s Vesuvius? He was fixated on that mountain.”

“Exactly,” Christina agreed. “This is not Pompeii.”

“Then where is it?” Aine asked.

“Rome?” Liam said with a glance at Christina.

“That would be my guess,” she replied as she enlarged the photo of the man being carried in the sedan chair. “This man may be an emperor.”

“Right again,” Liam said. “He has a standard and bearers. He looks old.”

“He’s too old,” Christina said.

“What do you mean too old?” Aine asked.

“This is a very old man,” she explained. “Titus was emperor in 79 CE, and he was much younger than the man in this photo.”

“Are you sure?” Aine asked.

“Pretty sure,” Christina replied. “If that’s the case it means we missed the target in more ways than one.”

“You’re saying this is not 79 CE?” Aine asked. Liam had already made that deduction and returned to the ship to sort through the paperwork. He found Aaron’s log. He opened it to page one and laid it out on the table.

Departure: Amazing!! Almost instantaneous! It happened so quickly it defies logic.

Landing: No sense of motion. Dark outside. My first thought was somebody shut the lights off in the chamber.

Travel Time: 0.89 seconds! Wow!

Date of Landing: Time log at 0.

Lat/Long Coordinates: No data.

Time: No idea. It’s obviously night.

Temperature: 88 degrees F.

Outside air quality: High CO2. Still in breathable range. I have no plans to breathe it.

Landing site: Class unknown. 360° view. Feel too exposed. I have to remember nothing can see in. 3/4 moon on horizon to my right. Orange! Looks big. Swollen! Weird. Not an illusion. Calm ocean or large lake to horizon. Must be on a beach. A tree line to my left. Tall trees. Too dark to see much else.

Physical/Emotional state: Feel gutted by a growing and unnatural feeling of intense loneliness. This is scary. 150,000,000 years in the past? No time or desire to confirm. I just want to get out of here.

"That's good," Christina said. "Log at zero. He made it to the Date of Origin safely."

"Looks like a good departure too," Liam added.

Departure: Perfect lift off. 30,000 feet! I can feel the pull of the Earth which is spinning so fast it looks like a big white cue ball beneath me. Not feeling well. Disoriented. It doesn't help that the stars are moving as well.

Landing: Easy. Very controllable.

Travel Time: 37 hours, 11 minutes, 52 seconds.

IMPORTANT! *Time travel causes illness that includes dizziness, nausea, disorientation and brief but worrisome lapses of memory. Meds offer NO relief. Speed through time may be the culprit. Speed reduction during landing was the cure.*

"I don't like the look of that," Aine said. "I thought the hull was supposed to protect the pilot from the effects of time travel."

"I did too," Christina said with concern, "but he used the word cure, so he was fine when he landed."

Liam flipped the page.

Date of Landing: Unknown! Data just numbers: 1746276.80944. What is that? Gauge error?

Lat/Long Coordinates: 96698-09-87y897. No DMS! No elevation! Another gauge error? No mountains or bay either. NO Vesuvius. This IS NOT Pompeii! Coastal approach consistent with Italy. Ground indicators consistent with target date. Will assume 79 CE. Landed near a river that runs from the coast to a city. Definitely a city. Rome? Wishful thinking? At 0800 I plan to walk in the direction of the city to confirm time and place. Perhaps still possible to satisfy project goal.

Time: Visual best guess 0700? Set watch to 0700.

Weather: Clear. Temperature: 49 degrees F. Warm for target month but still within range. Vegetation consistent with target season. Will assume January as planned.

Air quality: Excellent overall. Some wood based and industrial pollutants but markedly different from home. Possible first confirmation of era.

Landing site: Class 2. Dense forest. Low risk. No need for camouflage. Last landing site option. No suitable cover from here to horizon. Trees probably harvested.

Physical/Emotional state: Tired but ok. No reason to panic. Every reason to proceed. Nervous but excited. Still a dream come true!

Liam turned to page three, but it was blank.

"That's all?" Christina said as she flipped through the rest of the small book.

"He made it safely," Liam noted.

"To where?" Christina said in frustration. "Rome? What is 96698-09-87y897?"

"I don't know," Liam said. "That meter was reading in degrees when he left."

"What about the date data?" Aina asked.

"I don't know that either," Liam replied in frustration. "Everything was supposed to read in our Gregorian, year, month, day, time right down to fractions of a second. It was reading properly when he left."

Christina sighed. "Then let's look at what we *do* know. The pictures look like Rome, but it's not confirmed. Why not Naples? It's closer to Pompeii. Most big cities were probably built on rivers. Emperors visited other cites too."

Liam shook his head. "No. Naples is on a bay, not a river. He thought the city was Rome and he would know better than any of us."

"You're right," she agreed. "He would also know that meant there was a problem, so why did he leave the ship? He should have come straight home!"

"Why would he?" Liam replied. "He was already there. Putting off his departure wouldn't make a difference with regard to ship operations. He knows a lot about ancient Rome too. He felt like he might still satisfy the project goal."

Aine was studying the bloody gauze they'd found in the ship. She thought he may have simply had a nosebleed, but after looking over the mess in the cabin she reconsidered. The first aid kit was open with its contents strewn about the floor along with other items that should have been in bins. Aaron was a more organized person than that, unless he'd had a serious problem.

"What about the materials he carried?" Liam asked. "The books and photos. Maybe we should be looking for differences between the sets."

"Hold on," Aine said. "I think we need to step back and discuss our options first. Do we have any options? Even if we figure out what happened to him, can we do anything about it?"

"Our option is to go and get him," Christina replied without a hint of doubt in her voice.

IX

∞

The morning sky was a brilliant blue overhead and the peristyle was filled with busy birds. It was warm, as well, which was nice to wake up to. My body was stiff, and all those various aches and pains were waking up with me. Leita seemed to have come from nowhere to help me sit up.

If I had to guess her age, I would guess mid-40s, but it was hard to be sure. In some ways she looked younger, yet older in others. Her hair was dark brown, thick, lightened with a few wisps of grey, and naturally curly as it hung to her shoulders. Her eyes were hazel, much like Appia's, and she had a youthful smile that belied the tiny wrinkles at the corners of her eyes. She stood a foot shorter than me, at about five feet, but she was strong, and her grip on my arm was firm.

"Thank you again," I said, and I gently held her hand for a moment before letting go. She replied with a warm smile and accompanied me to the bench by the fountain.

Thalese called from the main house. "Please come," he said in a gentle voice. Appius greeted me at the villa entrance with overdone enthusiasm. His double handshake was firm, but clumsy since it appeared I wasn't familiar with that style of greeting. He was completely unfazed, and after passing through a short corridor, he ushered me into a very large room with a high ceiling. The ceiling had a square opening to the sky at its midpoint, while directly below was a similarly shaped basin built right into the floor.

"Impluvium and compluvium," I said.

"Very good, Gnaeus," Appius said in a comical way for my having verbalized the obvious. We continued on to a much smaller adjoining room. There was a wooden table in the middle, which was surrounded on three sides by interlocking couches.

"Curious," I said as the arrangement struck me as odd, and yet familiar.

"Here we are," he said, and he directed me to the couch on the right. My instinct was to sit upright, while he preferred to recline at an angle. The way the couch was designed was more consistent with his posture, so I decided to mimic it. "Figs," he said as he pushed a bowl towards me.

"Thanks," I replied. It was a familiar food, but its heavy, sweet taste settled poorly in my stomach so I put it down.

"Don't like figs?" He seemed disappointed so I picked it up again, but I just couldn't eat it.

"I think I'm too hungry for such a sweet food."

He called for Thalese who was dutifully waiting by the doorway. Leita entered the room carrying a large ceramic pitcher and began pouring water into our goblets. She was followed by another woman carrying something that smelled like cooked chicken. I knew that smell very well, and I watched with growing delight as she placed it before me on the table.

When she straightened up, I caught her glance and warm smile. Her look was one of familiarity, and I smiled back. She was a naturally beautiful woman with a dark olive complexion. There was something exotic about her, perhaps in her eyes, or her long, straight, black hair, which fell in partial disarray about her shoulders.

"Who's that?" I whispered to Appius after she left the room.

"Ah!" he responded with a knowing smile. "Do you like her?" He tore off a chicken leg and handed it to me.

"Do I know her?"

"Do you?" he replied as if it was a riddle.

"When she looked at me, I thought I saw something familiar."

"Indeed," he said as he took some chicken for himself. "Her name is Nubia. She watched over you during your illness. It was she who bathed and shaved you."

"I should thank her."

He chuckled oddly. "Yes, you can do that. So, how do you like her?"

It seemed an odd question given it was such a brief encounter. "I don't know. I'm sure she's very nice."

"But are you attracted to her?" he asked. "I saw a twinkle in your eyes."

"She has a nice smile." I couldn't hide my amusement. My eyes were sore and probably bloodshot, and unlikely to register on a twinkle meter.

"She likes you," he said confidently.

"She doesn't know me."

"But she does like you."

"That's nice," I said.

"You don't believe it? Because it's true."

"If you say so."

"I do," he stated. "That's my point."

"I'm afraid I don't understand your point. I seem to be misunderstanding a lot of points, so it's probably just me. It may be a vocabulary issue."

"You may be a little dusty," he said, "but I think you're doing quite well. Your diction is nearly perfect. You can take pride in that. You would put many good citizens to shame."

"But I'm still different. My manner of speaking is not like yours, and not like anybody here."

"That's because you're not like anybody here," he said. "Look at you. Your features are different, and you're big too, athletically conditioned, not unlike a gladiator."

I knew that word. "Do you think I'm a gladiator?"

"Not really," he replied. "I see no evidence."

"But you're not certain."

"I'm certain enough," he replied. "Your athletic look lacks practical toughness. Your hands and feet are soft and I see no evidence of gladiatorial training. You can trust me on this. My ability to appraise the practical worth of combatants is well known as are my successes."

I studied my hands for a moment with no idea of what he was talking about. "So I'm big and athletic, but soft, without toughness," I chuckled. "That doesn't sound good."

"It's merely a base to build on," he said, "and not a judgment of character. It's all about your nature. Who you are inside."

"Nature?"

"Yes," he replied. "What you say and how you act tells me all I need to know about you regardless of your past."

"I doubt you've learned much so far," I said.

"On the contrary," he told me. "I've learned a lot."

"Really? Like what?"

He looked pleased by the question. "It's your nature to speak your mind. Therefore, you're not a servant or combatant, and you're powerful. You clearly have knowledge of things unknown anywhere I've ever been, and I've been everywhere. The point of my questioning is to reveal your instincts. Instinct reflects nature, and by revealing your instincts we will learn who or what you are."

"What I am?"

He chuckled. "I didn't mean that as an affront. I only meant that you may be special in ways yet undetermined, and you're free to develop your instincts within this household. Live by your instincts. That's how you will learn who you really are."

When Nubia returned to clear the table, I paid little attention to her so as not to add more fuel to Appius' imagination. Thalese entered with some sort of ledger, which Appius took time to read thoroughly while I relaxed.

"Is Nubia a family member?" I asked after she left.

Appius smiled. "Indeed she is. She's a most dedicated servant and one of my best purchases."

"There we go again," I said as I nearly dropped my glass. "That's exactly what I'm talking about. To my ear it sounded like you said she was a purchase, as if you bought her like a commodity. Part of my problem may simply be vocabulary."

"You heard me correctly," he said without looking up from his ledger.

His answer left me dumbfounded. "I want to be absolutely certain I understand. You bought her with money?"

He finally looked up. "No."

"That's a relief," I sighed.

"I paid with garum. It's often favorable to deal in commodities rather than money."

"That sounds like slavery! I thought slavery was abolished ages ago."

"Abolished?" he chuckled. "Wherever did you get such a notion?"

I thought about it for a moment, but I had no reply. I seemed to have a lot of ideas and feelings I couldn't support. The concept of slavery was so abhorrent to me it didn't seem like I would need to have to explain my reaction. "I wish I could answer that, but I can't. All I know is the idea of slavery bothers me."

"It's not just an idea," he said, "it's a fact of life. They know it, I know it, and everybody knows it."

"That makes no sense to me. Do your slaves wish to be slaves?"

"I don't understand."

"Is being a slave a choice? Did Nubia choose to be a slave?"

"What kind of a question is that?" he said, sounding offended. "People are what they are. That's life. Society and culture depend on it."

"I don't understand," I said. "I can't imagine a society based on a class of captive, downtrodden people."

He shook his head and shrugged. "Who said anything about downtrodden? I'll tell you what. Feel free to discuss it with any members of this household. They'll tell you they're better off here than where they were before. I guarantee they're not downtrodden. Start with Thalese. He was stolen from his home on Samos and impressed into maritime service. How such a gentle man survived a year of hardship on a Greek galley I'll never know. It was because of slavery I was able to extricate him from such a hopeless beginning. He's had the best education, been given an income, and been elevated to the level of steward and tutor to my daughters. Two years ago, he purchased his freedom. His loyalty remains steadfast to this day! He's indispensable as my confidant and business director. Had he chosen to have children, they would have been born into this world as citizens with the birthrights afforded all freeborns."

"Aren't all people considered to be created equal?"

He gave me another one of his confused expressions. "Equal? How?"

"Life, freedom," I couldn't think of an equivalent word for liberty. "And the pursuit of happiness. All people having the same chances in life from birth."

He took a sip of wine and picked up a piece of bread. "People are born, they live, and they die. Everyone comes into this life differently. Society has strata. It could not exist if everybody was the same. The pursuit of happiness? What's that? Life is about the pursuit of honor. Honor is everything. Without honor we are nothing!"

"You own slaves," I said. "How is that honorable?"

He slapped his hand on the table. "Never question my honor in this house! Never! I may not have lived a perfect life, but I have my honor!"

"Fine," I said as I quickly backed down. "I'm sorry. I'm simply trying to understand why my senses and feelings seem so utterly foreign to what I see and hear around me. When I hear the word slavery I think of abuse – of people being treated as something less than human."

"You've spoken with Leita?"

"Yes," I said.

"Does she seem abused in any way?"

"No," I replied, "not that I can tell, but I haven't been here very long either."

"Does she look beaten? Does she appear stressed in my presence?"

"Not that I can see."

"I bought her when she was fourteen years old. I considered her situation abusive. My action probably saved her life. I admit I didn't purchase her solely for that reason. I did need a trained cook, but her plight determined my choice."

"She was a trained cook at fourteen?"

"She showed promise," he smiled. "She knew enough. And what of Nubia you ask?"

"I didn't ask." I chuckled.

"She was bound for an Egyptian brothel had I not purchased her," he said. "Now she helps Leita care for my home and on occasion has the honor of sharing my bed. Please, talk to her, or anyone in this household. Ask anything you wish."

"She has the honor of sharing your bed?" I said with a note of sarcasm.

"I force nothing upon my servants," he replied. "That would be an affront to my honor." It was clear the question irritated him. "I promise you, any children born under this roof will be registered freeborn. I take my obligations seriously!"

"I'm sure you do," I said, tiring of the conversation.

He leaned back and stared at me for a moment. Thalese stepped into the room but Appius waved him away. "There is a lot left for me to teach you," he said. "But you look tired."

"I am," I replied. "It seems I get tired quickly. I'm fine one moment and about to collapse the next."

"It will take a few more days before you are fully fit," he said. "How are you feeling, otherwise?"

"A little headache," I told him, "but not serious."

"Please don't hesitate to let somebody know if it gets worse."

"I will."

X

∞

"Let me play devil's advocate for a moment," Aine said. "Suppose we find anomalies between those identical sets of books. That means history can be changed. Maybe we got lucky this time. Should we tempt fate again? That's what a rescue attempt would be."

"Are you suggesting we bury the ship in the backyard and wash our hands of it?" Christina asked, sounding quite upset.

"Please," Aine said, "don't take it the wrong way. I want him back as much as you do, but we still have an obligation to ask the tough questions."

Liam had been sitting, quietly listening. He understood both points of view but saw no resolution. "I believe the prudent thing is to research all the data before making any decisions. Only the data can tell us whether to go after him or not."

"I can't believe what I'm hearing!" Christina said.

"I'm sorry," Liam said. "Of course our goal is to bring Aaron home. Just the same, only the data can tell us what happened and where he is. But you know as well as I do that won't be easy. The only data we can decode is what's stored in the human based technology. All the critical navigational data is undecipherable to us."

"At least we can see it," Aine said.

"We can see something," he said, "but it's gibberish to me. Code breaking is not my field. Quite frankly I don't know anybody who would know where to begin with this."

"Chris does," Aine said with a smile.

"Oh no," Christina replied, "not Kamden. There has to be somebody else."

Aine shook her head. "Do you know any other code breakers you can trust? I hear he's become one of the best government cyber intelligence specialists there is. He hacks the hackers."

"But he's still unmarried," Christina said.

"Keeping tabs on him, are you?" Aine chuckled. "It seems to me nothing should stand in the way of getting Aaron back."

"You're right," Christina sighed, "but let's see what we can figure out first."

The next step was to organize and analyze all the papers and other items they found in the ship. Most of the clothes Aaron wore at the launching were there, but for his toga and vest. Having found his camera and the pictures he'd taken was proof that he'd left the ship and returned. The bloody gauze meant he'd been hurt, but it didn't indicate how badly; although, it meant he was conscious enough to treat himself. The lack of any notes following his last log entry was as worrisome as it was frustrating.

"We can't rule out head injury," Christina said. "There has to be a reason why he didn't complete his notes. If he had time to bandage himself, he had time to write unless he was in and out of consciousness. I know he'd have written if he was able."

Liam and Aine simply nodded in agreement even though they saw little evidence to make any judgements. They chose to start comparing the photos between the two sets of books. After several hours of page by page analysis they found no anomalies.

Meanwhile, Christina focused on extracting any useable data from the control panel related to Aaron's location when the ship left ancient Italy for home. She came up empty.

"We've been through the rest of his things," Aine said as they gathered to discuss their findings. "It appears he left with a full vest if it makes you feel any better. That means he has meds and a breathing apparatus."

"His weapon?" Christina asked.

"We can assume that," Liam replied. "Perhaps that's a good thing."

"That gun was never meant for protection," Aine said. "It was only to be used to satisfy our project goal. I agreed with the idea, but I was never truly onboard with that method."

"I don't recall you offering any alternatives," Christina noted. "We needed a way to scar an ancient item for analysis. It had to be something that could be done quickly and from a safe distance. A gun was ideal. One bang and he's done. Nobody nearby would have a clue. Even if they repaired the item, or replaced it, it would be different."

"That's why the large caliber," Liam added. "It was about punching a chunk out of a marble bust or something similar, not defense. There are better choices for that."

"I know the logic," she said, "and I did agree. I've just never been comfortable with it."

"I have no issues with it," Liam said. "Aaron is well trained and principled. He was the one who drew up the *Time Traveler Principles of Conduct*. Of course, it's all common-sense stuff, but he felt it was important enough to document. Don't shoot somebody is a major biggie. And we all know he will strictly adhere to the dictates of that text. That's just who he is. In fact, I see even less reason to question this decision now that we've found no evidence his visit caused any alterations to the past. Remember, whatever he did is done. We can conclude the gun was not a factor."

"We can't conclude anything," Christina said. "All we've done so far is a quick comparison of the photography between the two sets of books. We will need to conduct a much more thorough examination, including all the text, before we can make any claims. That will take time."

"What about the data?" Aine asked. She was looking straight at Christina. "Can you extract any more that we can actually read?"

"No," she replied, "not at this moment."

"So, what's the best we can hope for?"

Christina shrugged, but she was obviously getting anxious. "I don't know. You're asking me questions I can't answer yet."

"I do know," Aine said. "We need help."

"Do you think your friend Kamden is capable of figuring out extraterrestrial data?" Liam asked Christina.

"I don't know," she replied. "Ask your wife. She recommended him."

"Yes," Aine said. "If anybody can, he can. And we can trust him. What do you say?"

Christina thought for a moment and said, "Nobody has yet deciphered Linear A. Many brilliant minds, including code breakers, have tried. And that's a human script...Minoan. Egyptian hieroglyphics were not deciphered until the discovery of the Rosetta Stone. We have no intergalactic Rosetta Stone for extraterrestrial data, so is it realistic to think anybody of this Earth has a chance?"

"Come on Chris," Aine said, "you know I'm right."

Christina shook her head and looked away. "Shit," she muttered. "Yes. Okay. I'll call him."

XI

∞

The next thing I remembered was waking up in the cool darkness of night. For the briefest of instances, I thought I'd awakened in a different and more familiar place. I don't know what triggered that response. The only sound was the buzz of a lone cicada that didn't seem to care whether it was day or night.

I got up to go to the latrine. I was relieved to find nobody posted by the doorway. There was a distinct chill in the air outside my room and the stone tiling was cool on my feet. I was wide awake by the time I was back in my room and there was little else to do but lay there and think. My general knowledge was so limited I grew tired of rehashing the same thoughts, but with nothing to distract me I couldn't shut it off. When Appius came to wake me, I was already dressed and anxious to do anything.

"How are you on this fine morning?" he asked.

"I'm fine but restless," I replied.

"Headache?"

"No." I smiled. "I actually feel pretty good." I passed my hand over the right side of my face. "The pain is not as sharp, and the swelling seems to be down."

He took a closer look and nodded. "Hungry?"

"Starving."

"Starving?" he said with a look of concern. "You ate more than expected yesterday so I hardly…"

"I didn't mean I'm dying of starvation," I chuckled. "I only meant I'm very hungry." We entered the triclinium where my attention was drawn to what looked like hardboiled eggs. "These look familiar," I said as I picked one up, but then I dropped it because it was hot. "How were they made?"

"You'd have to ask the chicken," Appia said as she entered the room right behind us.

"We have a comedian in our midst today," I chuckled. "But these were boiled in water, right?"

"Yes," Appius replied. "Have you had them before?"

"I think so," I said as I started to peel one. "This is very familiar. Especially the smell."

"That's good," he said, and then he turned to Appia and asked her to fetch Thalese. "What do you require with regard to the deities?" he asked as he turned his attention back to me. "We have a lararium as you may have observed. We gather for family rituals every morning and before sunset, or individually whenever any of us wishes. We have our ancestral deities and household spirits, and a special place for Hercules, but I realize you may require something even more specialized."

I shook my head. "I don't know about any of that."

"I understand," he said. "You will know when the time comes. In the meantime, keep asking questions. I will try to answer what I can."

The eggs and honey rolls were good and I probably ate more than I should have. Appius was watching me as usual and he seemed pleased. He was always watching me. He seemed to be continually assessing my words and mannerisms, and it was starting to get annoying because I was never quite sure why, or what he was really thinking. I was glad when Thalese finally appeared.

"The bath is ready," he announced.

"Fine," Appius said. "I think we're done here," and he motioned for me to stand. I thought we were heading back to the courtyard, but instead we made a sharp left into a narrow corridor beneath the second-floor stairwell. It was musty smelling and dark enough to require an oil lamp to see the fabric-covered doorway ahead.

"What's this place?" I asked.

"The bath," Appius replied. "Watch your head," and I had to duck to pass beneath an unusually low door jam.

In the first room was a marble bench. There were several niches built into the wall above it. The air was warm and moist. There was another fabric-covered entrance to the left of the main entrance, and when I peeked inside I was met by markedly more humid air.

"Frigidarium?" I asked.

Appius displayed a wide grin. "Yes," he said.

"And then the tepidarium, and beyond that a caldarium. Am I right?"

He clapped his hands together. "Exactly right! My bath may be small, but it has all the amenities."

It was wonderful to have another bit of memory return. From those recollections, I figured I must have been in similar places before and I wasn't bothered when Appius motioned Thalese to remove my tunic. After that, I was handed a pair of wooden sandals, which I knew were to protect my feet from the hot floor of the warmer rooms to come.

We left the changing room and passed through the cold room, up a pair of steps beneath a fabric covered doorway, and to the next much warmer room. I immediately I broke into a sweat. Thalese began applying oils to his former master's skin. I wasn't comfortable with the idea of such assistance. Appius found it funny when I applied my own oils, but he didn't fight me on that one issue at least.

Thalese handed me a set of oddly shaped metal utensils. I watched to see how he used them on Appius before trying them on myself. He was mostly scraping off the sweat and oil from his skin. When he finished, Appius thanked him and sent him away. I mimicked Appius as he continued to use the tools on himself. The setup of the bath may have been familiar, but such an odd method of cleansing brought back no recollections.

"Have you soap?" I asked as the word came to mind.

"Actually," he replied with surprise, "I do have a chunk somewhere around here, but it's a terribly expensive novelty. I'm amazed you've heard of it."

We passed from the warm room through another fabric covered doorway to a narrower and much hotter room. Inside on the left was a round marble basin and straight ahead a rectangular brick bath filled with steaming hot water.

"Wow! This is hot," I said as the drape was closed behind me. Appius smiled and motioned me towards the bath. I could a feel my blood pressure rising as I slowly settled into the steaming pool.

"Not many private hot rooms have a hot water bath," he noted with pride.

"It's certainly invigorating," I said, but the heat took some getting used to.

"Good," he said. "How are you feeling overall?"

"Much better," I replied. "Definitely stronger. I couldn't have taken this heat yesterday."

"That's excellent," he said thoughtfully. "I have business in Rome. Your speedy recovery means I can probably take that trip sooner rather than later."

"Will I be going with you? Perhaps it will help my memory."

"No," he replied, and then he paused to wipe the sweat from his brow. "I think your time is better served right here for now. You'll have Leita and Nubia here to advise you, and spend time with Appia. She's a lot like you.

She questions everything. She can be exasperating sometimes, but I do love her so." He smiled and I found myself smiling as well.

"I was just thinking," I said, "the word Rome also speaks to me of political intrigue and poison being a common method of political upward mobility. I know that sounds silly, but that's what came to mind."

"If you've been to the theater lately," he replied, "or read anything contemporary, everyone who's anyone gets poisoned at one time or another. If poison was as popular in real life as it is in literature, it would have to be listed as a natural cause of death."

"That's funny," I said, but he wasn't smiling. His mind had moved on to something else.

"I've been giving thought to your words," he said in rather dramatic, yet hushed voice. "I don't want this repeated beyond these walls, but you spoke of people being created equal."

"That's right." I was surprised he remembered.

"Such a concept seemed utterly absurd at first," he said, "but it did give me pause, and frankly, I can't give you a just reason as to why we get labeled at birth. I can recite the rules. I know what qualifies one person a slave and another freeborn, but if you put ten newly born infants in a room together, there's no way to assign social status simply by looking at them. In certain instances, I can make that call under this roof, but there's nothing divine about that. That's just a rule. I understand that societies need rules to avoid chaos, and I'm not questioning that, but rules are not divine. Rules can be unjust. Rules can be changed!"

"Wow," I said, "but why the secrecy?"

"Resistance to change," he replied. "Change can be frightening, and when honor is involved, potentially dangerous. I've had my ups and downs. Maybe that's given me insights others of my rank don't have. I don't know. I've tried to enact better protections for those in our service, but I'm always met with resistance. Even my son-in-law, Caestus, is diametrically opposed to everything I believe in. And he stands to inherit my estate!"

"Appia's married?"

"What?" he replied as he was still in thought.

"I didn't know Appia was married."

"She's not," he said with a chuckle. "I have two daughters. Perhaps you'll have a chance to meet Maria before I leave."

"That's right," I said. "You have another daughter, also named Maria. Which begs the question, why did you name both your daughters Maria?"

He shook his head. "Unbelievable what the gods have left for me to teach you. I'm Appius *Marius* Caupo. My first born is Maria Prima. My second is Maria Secunda. It's not so difficult."

I closed my eyes and dunked my head. I came up smiling. "You said you bought Leita when she was 14."

"She was a concubine at 12," he noted.

"Is that like being married?" I asked.

"Sort of," he replied. "It's common when marriage is prohibited by law. Her spouse abused her. By buying her I probably saved her life."

"Is it common to be a concubine or married so young?"

"Not common," he replied, "but legal. Most girls wed around 15 or so. Boys are older, usually in their 20's."

"Interesting," I said. "So how did Appia escape marriage? She's clearly well past 15." He looked uncomfortable by my question. "You don't have to answer," I said. "I was just curious."

"Appia has never been wed," he replied. "She's perhaps too old by most standards, and perhaps a little too headstrong. Sometimes I think she's too much like me, and that's not necessarily good."

"Really?" I said. "I would think a man would be glad to find a woman who thinks for herself."

"Curious comment," he chuckled. "A smart woman has little advantage over others, unless of course she has property."

"Appia's very attractive as well," I added. "You can't tell me that's not a criterion."

He studied me intensely for a moment. "It is," he said in a solemn voice, "but circumstances have made Appia a special case."

"What does that mean?"

"Let's leave it at that for now," he replied. "I love Appia more than my own life. It wasn't always that way, but her perseverance melted through my selfish ignorance and I saw myself for what I was. I owe her everything I am today. I'd gladly give it all back to secure her future and future happiness."

"Sounds like you're a very lucky man."

"I am," he replied, "but it took a lot of adversity to see it."

We left the hot room for the cold room. The cold room was hardly what I'd call cold due to its proximity to the hot room, but it felt refreshingly cooler after the heat of the bath. Thalese was waiting for us in the changing room where my tunic had been replaced with a beige toga cut similarly to the white one Appius wore.

"That's yours," Appius stated with a smile. "Now you'll look more like the freeborn the gods intended. The next step will be to get you on the census. An interesting challenge for me."

"Census?"

"Every citizen must be listed on a census somewhere," he explained, "along with his property, which we'll need to arrange for you as well."

I turned to Thalese. "What's he talking about?"

"When the time comes for you to step outside this villa, you must have the documentation that confirms your rank," Thalese said.

"A difficult task," Appius added, "but it's another reason why you've been left in my care, and I feel energized by the challenge of this divine calling."

"He has a clean slate," Thalese said to Appius. "That will make it easier."

"What's that mean?" I asked.

"You come to us with no history," he explained, "no records, no rank, no property, nothing. Like raw clay ready to be shaped. That's better than having to replace an old past with a new one."

"I'm sure I have a past," I said, "and a name, but it's making me insane that I can't recall anything! Am I married? Do I have children? What pain or hardship has my absence caused those I left behind? You seem to be going to an awful lot of effort for something I'm not entirely clear on. I could regain my lost memory at any time, and then I might be obligated to leave."

Appius smiled. "Should that be the case, then I will welcome your discovery and assist you in any way I can to reunite you with your clan. I recognize how very difficult this situation is for you, and yet I must caution you not to dwell on it too much. The answers you seek may not be forthcoming."

"Fine," I said, "as long as you understand my position."

"I do, but regardless, if I'm correct, as I believe I am, I must act now. It's no risk to you."

"Really?" I said. "What you're talking about can't be legal."

"Don't worry about legality," Appius said. "Yours is an entirely unique and extraordinary situation. It transcends the normal bounds of the law. Such situations require extraordinary solutions."

Thalese turned his attention to me in order to straighten out the mess I'd made of my new toga. I could see by their smiles my inexperience was entertainment for them; although, I was beginning to feel a little self-conscious.

"I don't understand," I said.

"I know," Appius said. "None of it is your concern. Just leave it all to me."

From the bath we reentered the atrium where he explained that the room was originally the atrium of one villa while the peristyle was the garden of another.

He led me upstairs to a walkway that was open on one side, offering a fine view of the atrium from above. There were three bedrooms on the other side. The entrance to the second was open, beckoning us with a comforting breeze from a large open window. "Oh my," I gasped at the view that lay beyond the trees and terracotta rooftops.

Appius found my reaction curious. "What is it?"

"That mountain," I replied.

"What of it?" he said.

My eyes remained transfixed. There was an eerie familiarity about that mountain, perhaps in the way it dominated the countryside, because its shape wasn't familiar. It wasn't conical on top but had a basin-like form that was open to the sea about two thirds of the way up. Its highest point was on the opposite side of the basin.

"I think I may have climbed it," I said. "Or maybe it just resembles the mountain in my dream. This may sound silly, but I had a dream where a mountain suddenly swelled in size and violently blew apart."

"That's some imagination you have," he said, "but as you can see this mountain is at peace with our little village here."

"It is beautiful," I said, and it was. The colors all seemed to go together, from the earthen reds and whites of the structures to the silvery green of the mountain, which was streaked by thin, wispy clouds at its peak.

We returned to the ground floor and proceeded across the peristyle to my room. My strength was generally better, but I still suffered with occasional bouts of dizziness and disorientation. Leita met us en route to offer her assistance, but I just thanked her for her gracious offer and Appius sent her away.

"Have you a preference?" he asked once she was beyond ear shot.

"A preference for what?"

"Your personal servant," he replied. "You need one. It will have to be either Leita or Nubia. That's not ideal, but they're the only ones able and available."

"I don't need a personal servant," I said with a halfhearted chuckle. The notion struck me as absurd.

"I'm thinking you do," he said. "You need to learn the particulars of your social rank. That's why I believe you've been left in my care. So, who will it be?"

"Let me sleep on it."

"Leita has the most experience," he added, "but Nubia's quick to learn. I'd purchase you a new slave, but there's no time, and anyway, it's for educational purposes only so male or female doesn't matter. The only thing that matters is that you learn how to be a citizen of rank. Either one can teach that."

"I'm sure we can figure this out later," I said in an attempt to put it off.

"I'd rather we do it now," he stated. "Your choice will affect the daily routine, so I'd like everyone settled before I leave for Rome."

"I don't want anyone changing their routine for me. Perhaps a better time would be after you return from Rome. Such a rushed decision might impact the daily routines more than you realize."

"How do you mean?"

"Well," I replied, "suppose my decision affected the quality of meals?" The food was excellent, so I reasoned he might want to rethink rushing my decision since it appeared everyone had a role in meal preparation.

"Then Nubia it is!" he announced to my great surprise.

"Huh?"

"You're absolutely right," he said. "Leita's the best cook I've ever had. Being in your service might affect her routine. Good thinking, Gnaeus! Very good!" All I could do was sigh. "I'll take care of the details. I know Nubia will be pleased as well."

The moment I sat down I felt vibrations through the bedposts as dust fell from the ceiling. "What's that?" I asked when the goblet on the table began to chatter.

He looked concerned for a moment, but his smile returned quickly once the tremor passed. "It's nothing." His words were meant for me, but he was studying the cracks in the plaster.

"Does that happen often?"

"It happens so often you won't even notice," he replied, and he left with a smile, talking to himself all the way across the peristyle.

Every muscle in my body thanked me as I stretched out across the bed. I had no idea how fatigued I'd become, and I dropped off to sleep the moment my head came to rest on the pillow.

XII

∞

It took Christina longer to find Kamden than it did to convince him to join the project. She began her search based on an assumption he was still working for the government, when in fact he was much closer, teaching at MIT. She swore him to secrecy and then told him about the ship. She explained why his special skills were needed without mentioning the part about having lost the pilot.

He was excited by the prospect of being the first human to decipher extraterrestrial data, and perhaps equally excited that Christina had come to him. It didn't matter that she could only afford to cover his food and travel expenses. The lab was just an hour's drive from his home, and since he taught only three days a week, he had time to assist on a part-time basis.

His enthusiasm on his first day on the project was in stark contrast to the melancholy disposition of his fellow teammates. Liam and Aine didn't understand why Christina kept him in the dark about Aaron. They reluctantly played along, but they knew once Kamden had full access to the data, he'd know she'd withheld information.

The one pleasant surprise for Christina was that Kamden had matured. He came across as a calmer, more self-confident version of the smothering, insecure man she dated in grad school. He did ask her out. He wanted to treat her to dinner and dancing, to which she told him she was in a serious relationship.

"I'd like to meet your boyfriend," he said. "Is he a part of this project too?" The distressed way Christina looked at him made him think he'd spoken out of turn. "I'm sorry…"

"No," she said, and she reached for his hand. "I'm sorry. I lost track for a moment. Yes, Aaron's a key part of the project, but unfortunately, he's away. He has a travel business and he's often gone for weeks at a time."

"Well," he said, "I'm profoundly flattered that you could look past my faults and include me on your team. I wish I could express how truly excited I am to be here."

"I'm glad you're here too," she said with a warm smile. "Maybe dinner isn't such a bad idea. As friends."

Kamden's eyes lit up. "Fine, yes. As friends."

"We'll go Dutch, okay?"

"Absolutely," he replied. "Now, how about showing me that extraterrestrial data? Are you sure it's extraterrestrial?"

"It has to be," she replied. "The ship was built millions of years before there were humans."

"Maybe they aren't human," he said, "but still a terrestrial intelligence. Perhaps they left the planet in ships like what you discovered or became extinct long before we evolved."

"I don't think so," she said.

"If we're talking late Jurassic," he said, "that was a time of high greenhouse gases and acidic oceans with CO2 numbers ten times today's high levels. Could that be a sign of industrial pollution?"

Christina couldn't hide her smile. "No. Absolutely not. There's no fossil record. There are no structures or the remains of any advanced ancient civilization to support that. This is a unique technology. It has survived over tens of millions of years. You'd think we'd have found more examples if it was terrestrial, but so far this is a one of a kind. I could go on."

"No need," he said.

The first thing Kamden did, once he logged onto a computer, was look at the alien data, marveling at the technology used to create it, and it didn't take him long to find a course of action. He was so transfixed by what he saw, several hours passed before he realized he hadn't eaten or taken any breaks.

"How's it going?" Christina asked later that day. "You know you can take breaks. I encourage it."

"This is my break," he replied as he stood up and stretched. "This is fantastic. Are you absolutely sure these ancient extraterrestrials aren't actually human? Perhaps from a more distant future than the future humans you've already identified?"

"I'm sure," she said. "The laws of physics won't allow it."

"Maybe the laws are wrong," he said. "Let me rephrase that before you take my head off. We've come a long way in understanding the universe. We have two theories of relativity and quantum mechanics and so forth, but more is needed. All the really big questions are still out there with discoveries to come that may well change all the rules."

"I know that," she said, "but I can't just make things up. I have to go with what I know until something new comes along that disputes it. Why do you ask?"

"Because this alien data isn't so different," he replied. "Granted, this technology is beyond fantastic, and Liam showed me how future humans created a technological bridge that made it possible to process it into a more familiar form, but the data itself is not incompatible at all. It's more like an advancement, or next step from what you've already learned."

"You can interpret it already?" she asked with surprise.

"Hold on," he said as he raised his hands. "I'm not that good. But I think with the right tools, I can create a kind of filter that will make it possible to convert much of it into something we can read and understand."

"What kind of tools do you need?"

"The kind I'll have to make myself," he replied. "Liam can help me with the hardware. He did a remarkable job building a connection between our technology and that of the future humans. I think he will be able to build a similar tool to access the alien data directly once I know what I need."

"That would great," Christina said.

"But it's going to take time," he said, "a lot of trial and error. But at least I know where to begin."

She nodded but she wasn't smiling. "Thank you. Tell me what you need, and I'll see you get it."

Kamden took his hands off the keyboard and sat back in his chair. He looked into her eyes. She wasn't beaming with excitement the way he'd hoped. In fact, she looked more like she was about to cry. "Okay, Christina," he said, "what's going on? You should be invigorated, excited by what you have here. Think of the potential. This is a remarkable discovery. Beyond remarkable! You should be dancing, and yet it's been like a morgue around here all day."

"I'm sorry," she said. "I'll get perkier later."

"I don't want perkier," he said. "If you're concerned about me being here, I'm not that dopey, insecure kid you knew in college. I've grown up. You told me to do that and I did. There's another man in your life. I respect that. You can trust me."

"I do trust you, Kam," she said somberly. "What you've told me just now is much more than what I expected. You've given me real hope. But I have to be careful not to expect too much."

"Chris," he said as he scratched his head, "you can expect what you want. If you're worried that I'm being overly optimistic, don't be. If I wasn't sure I could do it I would have said so. But how have I given you real hope?

Hope for what? You haven't once told me your ultimate goal. What are you planning to do with this thing?"

She took a deep, reflective breath and sighed. "You'll figure it out anyway."

"Figure out what?"

"We've already tested the ship," she said pensively.

"I know," he said. "Liam explained the static testing. You figured out how to make it run. You should be congratulated."

"I should be shot," she stated bluntly. "We lost somebody."

"What do you mean you lost somebody?"

"Exactly that," she said. Kamden's smile melted away. "It was a piloted test. The ship returned but the pilot didn't," and she looked away as tears welled in her eyes.

"Holy shit," Kamden uttered in disbelief. "I take it the ship went back in time."

"Yes," she said with a subtle nod. She was shaking and obviously having trouble holding back her emotions. "I asked Liam and Aine to stay silent because I wasn't ready to tell you everything. I'm sorry, Kam."

It didn't take much effort for him to put the pieces together. "Where's your boyfriend?" he asked. She wanted to reply but the words caught in her throat. "I'm sorry," he said. "You can count on me, Christina."

"He's actually my fiancé," she said as she wiped the tears from her eyes. "And now he's dead."

"Don't say that," he said.

"But it's true. The photos we recovered show he made it to ancient Italy. That means he died two thousand years ago. I hate to think how."

"And you plan to go back in time to rescue him."

"That's the plan."

"Then that's my plan as well." He wanted to ask why they attempted a piloted trip without having unlocked more of the data. That seemed out of character for the Christina he used to know, but despite that, he realized it was not the time to bring it up.

"And that's why we're not dancing in the streets," she said.

"He's not dead until I say so," Kamden stated, "and that will only happen if I can't hold up my end of the bargain, and that, my good friend, will never ever happen."

"Thank you, Kam. Your work is most critical. I'm hoping that somehow the alien data will tell us what went wrong and give us a time and place for extraction. We expected the ship would return one way or another, but we never anticipated it would take off without him."

Kamden thought about it for a moment. "Can it do that?" he asked.

"We didn't think so. But if that's true, where is he? If you have another thought please share."

"Is there a reason why he might have chosen to stay?" he asked.

She shook her head. "Not to my knowledge. He sounded fine in his log. He said time travel caused disorientation and possibly memory loss, but he was fine when he landed. He did leave the ship, but there are no log updates after that. The date might still be 79 CE, possibly Rome."

"You don't know?"

"The data is unclear," she replied. "His photos support that era and location. They also prove he returned to the ship after his walk. He was injured at some point, but you'd think he'd have left us a note if he'd chosen to stay."

"The first thing we need to do is establish the exact date and place of his arrival," he said. "Was 79 CE Rome the target? Why do I know that date?"

"Rome was not the target location," she replied. "Pompeii on the Bay of Naples was."

"Of course," Kamden said. "Mt Vesuvius."

"We selected 79 CE because that's the year Mount Vesuvius erupted and buried the town of Pompeii. Aaron knows Latin and Pompeii. Should his visit put future history at risk; the mountain would be there to correct it."

"The eruption was your backup in case of a screw up," he said.

"That's correct."

Kamden listened but he saw flaws in the logic. "Just landing in another time might be considered invasive to history. The bigger question is if history is changeable or not."

"Which was the whole point of the mission," she said. "Now you know what we know. I know what you're thinking and you're right. A piloted test never should have happened. We thought we had extracted the data we needed. We were wrong. I know that. It's my fault and mine alone. But beating myself up won't fix anything. That will have to wait until we've brought him safely home."

XIII

∞

After several hours of uneventful sleep, I was revisited by images of the mountain. Rather than a repeat, the mountain had changed from a simple blue silhouette to a vision with a shape similar to the one I'd seen from the upstairs window. As I watched, it swelled grotesquely and blew apart like it had in the other dream.

I awoke breathless, sweating and gripping hard at the bed as if still trying to evade the falling rocks and debris. The dreamscape seemed so frighteningly real that I remained shaken for several moments afterwards, making further sleep out of the question.

The courtyard was bathed in the cool light of a nearly full moon. My room was in shadow, but there was enough reflected light to see someone had left food for me on the nightstand. I took a moment to savor a few bites along with a full cup of water. The dream had left me thirsty.

There was little point in staying in bed as I was fully awake and the courtyard beckoned. The air was cool and the ground damp as I made my way to one of the benches by the fountain. There was a wonderful feeling of tranquility in the air, and I loved the soft bubbling sound of the fountain. I could just make out the small birds moving about in the bushes, giving life to everything.

Despite all the peace and tranquility, my mind returned to the mountain. There was something strange about the way I continued to dwell on it, especially in my sleep, and soon I felt a need to confront the problem directly. With the countryside bathed in moonlight, it seemed I might be able to observe it from that second story window where I'd seen it before, so I quietly made my way upstairs. The room was completely dark when I entered and, unfortunately, there wasn't much to see outside either. Rooftops glistened with dew, but the mountain was, at best, an unclear mat of black serving only to block out stars. When I turned to leave, I saw the flickering of lamp light in the corridor, and then the burly figure of a man entered the room.

"Sir?" he said.

"Who are you?" I asked as I didn't recognize him.

"I am Caelus," he replied in husky voice.

"Are you a servant as well?"

"Yes," he replied.

"Oh," I said, suddenly feeling uncomfortable.

"Master Appius has talked to you then," he said. He was standing directly between me and the door.

"We've talked many times."

"She's over here," he said, and he stepped past me to shine the light of the lamp over a bed in the corner. I hadn't remembered there being a bed in the room, but regardless, there it was, complete with a woman Caelus seemed intent on waking.

"What are you doing?" I whispered. "Don't do that," but her eyes were already open. It was the servant girl Nubia.

"Did you not come for her?" he asked.

"Come for her?" I replied as he motioned me closer. By then she was sitting up and yawning, barely clad in a loosely fitting night wrap that she proceeded to take off.

"I'll just go back downstairs," I said as politely as I could. "I didn't mean to disturb anyone."

"Of course," Caelus said as he took hold of my wrist before I could make good my retreat. He had a strong grip. "It's okay. Just come."

"Yes," Nubia said as she got up and took my hand. "Master Appius has explained everything."

"Explained what?" I asked in bewilderment. "I came up here to look at the mountain. I didn't realize there was anyone here."

Caelus looked into the blackness outside and chuckled. "I'll see you're awakened for morning meal." He left and pulled the drapes shut across the doorway.

"I shouldn't be here like this," I said as I looked at Nubia.

"Why not?" she asked. I didn't have a good answer as a whole host of feelings skewed my thoughts. "Don't you like me?" She began smoothing her hands over my chest.

"It's not that," I said as I tensed. "Of course I like you, but…"

"I'm for you," she said. Her warmth and openness quickly soothed my anxiety, and I readily gave in. There seemed no reason not to. During those marvelous moments of bliss, my mind was finally void of confusion.

Afterwards we remained together, entwined in each other's arms as the coming of dawn slowly brought with it a sobering thought – Nubia was a slave.

"Nubia," I asked, "did you want to make love with me?"

She gave me a puzzled look. "Did I do something wrong?"

"No," I replied, "of course not. I was wondering if you wished it or was it a duty?"

"A duty?" she repeated, sounding confused. "If you are asking if I'm allowed to make those choices, I am." I nodded but I wasn't certain she understood the question. "Master Appius explained everything to me," she added, "and I'm very pleased that you selected me."

I realized she was talking about the personal servant duty. "He told me how you took special care of me during my illness," I said. "It must have been quite a chore."

"It wasn't a chore at all," she said. "I wanted to."

"That's nice of you to say."

"I mean it," she said. "You're special. I know it."

"Special? How?"

"Something I can't put into words," she said. "Something everyone has felt from the first day you arrived. Even mistress Appia mentioned it, but Master Appius has better defined it."

I sighed and eased my head back into the pillow. "You have an active imagination."

"Master Appius explained my role as your personal servant."

"Your role?" I asked.

She was smiling and seemed honestly happy. "It's something I want to be a part of more than anything."

"Being my personal servant is that important to you?"

"Of course, it is," she replied, "and all that goes with it."

"What goes with it?" I asked.

She smiled and looked up at the ceiling and said, "Everything I never dared wish for."

"Like being freed?" I asked.

She looked at me as if it was a joke question. "There are many freeborn women who would gladly trade places with me. I'm lucky to be in this household, and in time you'll see what I mean."

There was more I wanted to ask, but the booming sound of Appius' voice in the corridor brought a quick end to our personal moment. We didn't even have enough time to cover up before the drape was flipped open and he was in the room. There was a wide smile on his face when he glanced at us, but rather than leave, he stepped to the window.

"So, he's indeed a whole man," he said with a glance at Nubia.

She hesitated, but then uttered meekly, "Yes."

"Good," he said, and he looked at me. "She's yours you know. Of course, you can imagine my surprise when Caelus told me where you were this morning."

"I couldn't sleep," I said sheepishly. "I came up here to study the mountain. That's the truth."

He smiled. "When Caelus told me that I laughed. But on second thought, I realized that's exactly what you did. I'll bet you didn't even know she was here."

"I didn't," I replied.

Nubia had been quietly lying at my side, but I could feel her becoming increasingly anxious. "I have chores," she whispered. "I should be helping Leita."

"That's right," Appius said, and he looked at me. "She still has a few household duties to manage, but outside of that, she's yours."

Nubia dressed quickly and left. I got up and started to get dressed, but then I got angry. I didn't like what had just happened or the way Nubia reacted to it. "Is it common practice for people to walk into occupied bed chambers?" I asked as I finished dressing.

"Does it bother you?"

"Yes," I replied frankly with growing indignation.

"Well," he said with a nervous chuckle, "it isn't exactly the same as…"

"The same as what?" I shot back. "With a non-slave? Is it acceptable behavior because she's considered property?" He glared at me, clearly surprised by my aggressive behavior towards him. "Perhaps my senses are confused," I said in a calmer tone, "but I feel there are some aspects of life that demand a degree of privacy."

"It was unthinking of me," he said, "and for that I apologize. All I was going to say was," and he sighed. "Never mind. You'll yell at me again. It was only meant as a joke."

"A joke?"

"And not too funny now that I think of it," he said. "I was uncomfortable and embarrassed, and I handled it badly. I knew I'd find you here, but normally Nubia's up well before this time of the day. As you'll soon learn, sexual pleasure is an area where self-control is an indication of a man's character. One must have control over one's passions. That means, you go to your partner, do your business, and leave. And, by all character standards, it is considered a daytime activity."

"What?" I chuckled. "That's ridiculous. I may not know much, but I do know love and passion are important aspects of any extra-personal relationship."

"No, Gnaeus," he said. "Passion has its place, but it's also a weakness that needs to be controlled. It's part and parcel of the testing that confronts all of us each and every day. It's important as a citizen that you understand this or you risk being labeled as effeminate."

"Effeminate?"

He shook his head in frustration as he turned away. "Have all the sex you want!" he blurted out. "Nights! Days! Nubia, Leita, whomever! I don't care! But the appearance of control must be maintained at all times. Is that better?"

"This is a dumb conversation," I said. "You don't really expect me to answer that?"

"What I expect is for you to listen," he said. "This is important. If self-control is the first word of personal conduct..."

"Isn't that two words?"

He glared at me. "Then the second is discretion, especially if you're having trouble satisfying the first. A Roman citizen is always discreet."

"Quick and discreet," I said.

"Exactly," he said with a smile, thinking I was beginning to see it his way. I looked out the window to escape the conversation, but the image of the mountain was just as disquieting, so I sat on the bed. "You must be hungry."

I was hungry, so we headed downstairs. I went straight to the bath to dunk myself in the tepid pool water of the unheated hot room before rejoining Appius for the morning meal. The bath was obviously an integral part of life, but apparently not before breakfast.

Nubia looked radiant as she set food out on the table in front of us. Leita had prepared the eggs, and the aroma brought back a good feeling that touched on some distant past. Caelus entered the room, and Appius officially introduced us.

"I'm sending Caelus to Stabia today for supplies for my trip to Rome," Appius said as he cracked the shell of a hardboiled egg.

"When do you leave?"

"Tomorrow," he replied, "before dawn. Caelus will accompany me."

"That soon?"

"Yes," he said. "I'm an old man so there's no time to waste. And I have a big favor to ask."

"Of course," I said, "anything."

"I'd like you to be in charge of the household while I'm away."

"What?" I said as I wasn't sure I heard him correctly.

"I want you to be acting master of my home. I think you're ready."

"Ready?" I said with surprise. "How can I…What about Thalese or Appia?"

"I'm sending Thalese to Asia on an important errand," he replied. "Appia will take care of things outside the villa. Use her for advice, or Leita, or even Nubia. What I mostly want from you is to keep my daughter safe."

"Do you fear for her safety?" I asked.

"Not really," he replied while reaching for a second egg. "I just worry when I'm away, but having you here helps, and if there are decisions that need making, you must make them."

"And you trust me to do that?"

He looked at me and pushed his bowl aside. "I believe trust is not just a one-way street. I've asked you to trust me, and therefore I must put equal trust in you."

"Aren't you forgetting our conversations?" I said. "We obviously reason differently."

"Perhaps," he replied, "but it's because of those conversations that I know it's the right choice. You're a caring and thoughtful person, and you question things. I can't see you making any decisions without discussing them with the rest of the household first. Am I right?"

"You are," I agreed.

"Gnaeus," he said, "you are the only male resident under this roof of citizen rank besides me. That's important."

"Okay, I guess. Fine."

"Then what's the problem? Will you honor my request?"

"Yes," I said, "of course. How long will you be gone?"

"Twenty days to a month," he replied, and he called for Leita to fetch his purse. When she returned, he instructed her to hand it to me. It was heavy and full of coins. "There's a ship leaving for Ostia at first light, so I probably won't see you before I go. Spend that as you see fit."

"I'll try not to use it all," I said. "Only in an emergency."

"No! It's your money to use in any way you wish. Be smart, be frivolous, be whatever. I don't care. I've got to go."

His plan was to sleep onboard the galley that night so he wouldn't have to get up early or risk missing his departure. I didn't understand that since he owned the shipping business and the ship. Technically, he could leave whenever he wanted, but he explained how important shipping schedules were. That was the last time I saw him before his departure.

My first few days as acting head of the family went quite smoothly, perhaps too much so. Nubia and I were rapidly transitioning into a deepening relationship that had no clear outcome. With no memory of home, family, and friends to keep me connected, it was easy to assimilate into a new situation.

Despite being surrounded by kindly people, I knew I wasn't of their kin. I also knew I came from somewhere very distant, which perhaps explained my inner loneliness and rapidly developing relationship with Nubia. However, our relationship wasn't born from what I considered a natural evolution. I'd been a strong verbal critic of slavery, and yet our relationship began the night I inadvertently took advantage of one of the very perks freeborn slave owners have over their slaves. It's true it wasn't by design, and it's true that she was welcoming, but it's equally true it wasn't innately consensual. Nubia's understanding of love and lovemaking were from the perspective of a slave. Her personal needs and desires were secondary to those of her master, conceivably to the point where she no longer knew the difference.

Perhaps, the ethical response should have been to end it when I first came to that realization, but I didn't because I recognized there was something more happening between us – something we both needed.

About a week following Appius' departure, Leita made a surprise visit to my room. It was shortly after sunrise and Nubia had just left.

"Good morning, Gnaeus," she said with a nervous look. "I hope you slept well."

"I did," I replied. "What can I do for you?"

"I'm sorry," she said, "but I feel compelled to speak."

"Please," I said. I motioned for her to take a seat, but she chose to stand.

"Master Appius had hoped that by putting you and Nubia together she would awaken the hidden master in you."

I looked at her and sighed, "Maybe there's no master in me to be awakened."

"Let's hope there is," she said. "You like Nubia."

"Very much."

"She likes you too," she said, "very much, but that's not good."

"You can't mean that."

"You and Nubia are engaged in a romantic relationship," she said. "It pleases me that she's experiencing a kind of happiness she might otherwise never know, but it's also not working."

"What?" I said. "Why not?"

"You need to put more effort into becoming a master," she said. I could see she was shaking. "She knows what you need to do, and you need to listen and not distract her. You should work with all of us, and perhaps spend less time alone on that hill of yours. I know you like to go there." She was right. There was knoll in back of the villa that offered wonderful views of the whole area right down to the bay and distant horizon. "I say this only because I want the best for you."

"Sometimes I feel like I've awakened into a world turned upside down," I told her. "Appius said that I'm free to partner with Nubia and even you. Apparently, that's okay as long as it's quick and discreet. But don't fall in love. Don't have a relationship! Oh no, don't do that! Do you see a problem with that thinking?"

She shook her head. "I don't know what to tell you. I can only advise."

"Tell me this," I said. "What would you do if I ordered you into bed right now so I can partner with you?"

"I would do as you ordered," she said without hesitation.

I sighed. "I guess you would."

"Is that what you'd like?"

"No," I said. I should have realized the folly of the question. "I was hoping you'd say no because of Appius. Because you love him. And you do love him. I may be blind to many things, but not everything."

She looked puzzled. "Whomever I may love has nothing to do with what you require of me. Duty comes first and it's the same for you. Nubia and I are here to make sure you understand what is expected of you as a male citizen of honorable birth."

"And that saddens me," I said. "I put relationships well before anything else."

"That's why this is so hard," she said, "but Nubia understands. Listen to her. Learn from her. The enjoyment doesn't have to end, but the romance must. Your actions must reflect your social status, not hers." I saw an honest look of concern on her face. "The perceptions of your peers are absolutely everything. They will be your judges. They will determine your political strength. What happens here may be practice, but it needs to be practiced to a point where it's second nature."

The pitcher next to the bed had a little water left in it, and after filling two goblets, I offered one to her.

"Thank you," she said, and she took my offering. "That's the sort of thing I'm talking about. I should have done that for you. You should have instructed me. It's really quite simple."

"Thank you for coming to me," I said. "I'll try. That's all I can promise."

"Please don't judge me too harshly for speaking out. I thought if you understood it would help."

After our talk I accompanied Leita to the kitchen. There was a large bowl on the counter from which she pulled out several pieces of cut chicken. She placed them on a cutting board and began removing the bones.

"Chicken again tonight," I chuckled. "I can eat chicken every night."

She smiled. "Not tonight. This is for a friend. I take a little something to him every once and a while. He hasn't got much."

"He must be a special friend then."

"He is," she replied with a detectable note of sadness in her voice. "He's my son. I've had four children. Two survive. He's a fine young man. He has a wife. She's pregnant with their first child. They share a flat in the bay area projects with two other families, but there's so little income. I do what I can."

I asked her not to go anywhere and I hurried off to my room for the purse Appius had given me. "I don't know how much money this represents," I said upon my return, "but maybe it will help," and I poured some of the coins onto the counter.

"What's this?" she asked.

"Have you spoken to Appius about your son's situation?"

"He's inquired about Paris," she said, "but he didn't father him. Of course, he still owned him at birth, but circumstances were not favorable. My master placed him in another home."

"I don't want to pry," I said, "or maybe I do. I'm confused. Where was his actual father?"

She smiled but she wasn't really smiling. "That was a very difficult time for my master," she replied. "For everyone in his domain." It was clear she didn't want to elaborate.

"What happened to Appius that was so bad?" I asked. "I've heard things, but I've gotten no explanations."

"Politics, I suppose," she said. "Backing the wrong side. My master has always been eccentric. He was also foreign to the region. No Oscan heritage. His so-called friends deserted him and then feasted on his misfortune like vultures on a carcass. We had to leave our home in the middle of the night. We barely escaped with our lives."

"I'm sorry," I said. "Who is we? Where did you go?"

She sighed and began chopping up what looked like asparagus. "It was my master, his wife Lucretia, Thalese, Appia and me. My master knew Rome wouldn't be safe either, but he had friends in Gaul."

"Appius was married?"

"Yes," she replied. "She was a niece of the emperor. Of course, he wasn't the emperor then, and since the emperor came from humble beginnings like my master, the marriage was more about emotions than politics. He was devastated by her passing. We all were."

"I'm sorry," I said. "How long ago was that?"

"Thirteen or fourteen years ago now I think," she replied. "She became ill shortly after we'd settled in Gaul. It was a particularly harsh winter."

"You didn't mention Caelus."

She shook her head, "He and Nubia joined our family after our return here."

"Why did you have to leave so abruptly?" I asked.

"Proscriptions," she replied, "or the threat of proscriptions. I'm not sure they actually happened. Word was out about a list. My master didn't believe it. He refused to leave even when his client base dwindled down to almost none. Perception is everything. He was perceived as being weak and therefore he was, but he continued to dig his heels in even when it was clear to everyone else all was lost."

"Could he have done something to avert this obvious calamity?"

"He could have compromised his sense of honor, I suppose," she replied, "but that is not in his blood. By the time we left it was much too late for that."

"What finally made him leave?" I asked.

"When he learned Appia had been assaulted," she said.

"What?"

"Appia was lured into an abandoned shop by a supposed family friend," she replied, "a man who'd visited and dined with my master many times."

"Assaulted, how?" I asked.

"Raped," she replied. "I'm probably speaking out of turn so please keep it to yourself."

"Of course," I said. "That's most disturbing."

"Luckily, Appia's had time to heal and get past it."

"Nobody ever truly gets past it."

"But they do," she said. "Life isn't without its horrors. We all learn to cope."

"I must be misunderstanding something. I would think such an act would create anger and bring people together to join Appius and hunt this man down."

She gave me one of her knowing smiles that meant I still had much to learn. "She was assaulted by three men, all of whom were prominent citizens of rank. It was planned and Appia was stalked. It happened at midday, near the Forum."

"But why?" I asked.

"They did it to send a personal message to my master," she replied. "It was meant to show they could do anything to him without fear of reprisal. That's how weak he'd become."

"If he was that hated and weak why didn't they just kill him?"

"That would come next had we not left," she replied.

"How old was Appia?" I asked.

"Almost fifteen if memory serves me."

I was angry at that point. "Where are these criminals now? Do you recall their names?"

I saw her studying me as she added the chopped chicken to the pot of stew she was making. "There's nothing to be done," she said. "My master has had his satisfaction."

"What about Appia's satisfaction?" She was getting upset and didn't answer, so I changed the subject. "Do you know what your son makes in wages?" I asked.

"What you just handed me is about a months' worth," she replied.

"Has he any experience in carpentry or masonry?"

"He's had to be about everything in his young lifetime. His former master is a nice man, but comparatively poor. He freed Paris because he couldn't afford him. Paris has had to fend for himself most of his life."

I knew I needed to dispel any doubts about my assertiveness and there appeared to be an opportunity here. "I'd like to hire him," I said. "The ground tremors are continually cracking the walls and ceilings. I think we need a maintenance person to keep up with repairs."

"Master Gnaeus, what are you saying?"

"Appius told me I have the right to make decisions, so I propose to offer Paris a job. I'll cover room and board for him and his wife in exchange for maintenance work on the villa. You can give him that money as a bonus."

"You mean it?" she asked as she appeared to be ready to jump for joy. When I smiled, I received a big kiss on the cheek.

"You can tell him I can't promise anything right now, but I will speak to Appius about offering him a regular wage. At the moment I have no resources for that or I'd offer that as well."

"I feared I might be too far away when the baby comes. This is so perfect. I'm a midwife you know."

"I take it you've done it before," I said with a smile.

"Twelve times in sixteen years," she replied, "and I haven't lost a single one. Not one!"

"Congratulations," I said with a clap. "What's his wife's name?"

"Therasia."

"They're lucky to have you."

I was feeling good when I returned to my room. Perhaps elated was a better word. Not only was there the good feeling of being able to help, but I had just added a sense of purpose to my life.

The next day I was awakened at first light by another one of those ground tremors. It was the worst so far. I jumped out of bed. Appius and the others may have written them off as inconsequential, but I wasn't so sure. I was in Nubia's room at the time, and from her window I had a good look at the mountain. I felt a connection. Somehow, I knew the tremors were a portent of disaster, and the mountain was a clue, so I decided to climb it. I had no idea of what to look for, but I felt I'd know it when I saw it.

Appia was in and out most of the day, but I didn't talk with her until the evening meal. During the conversation I discussed the mountain and we decided to climb it together the next morning. I told her it would take a lot of time to complete the trip, so we should leave early and take advantage of the cool morning air for as long as possible. She said she knew that, and that she wasn't born yesterday. In fact, she told me not to worry about anything, because, as she pointed out with a chuckle, I was the one born yesterday.

Nubia stayed in my room that night, and I slept so soundly I never heard her leave, or Appia enter to wake me. In fact, hearing Appia's voice in the dark did more to confuse me than anything else, and I muttered something in my delirium about going back to sleep.

"There you go speaking in that strange tongue again," she said.

"What?"

She laughed. "I'm sorry, I thought you were awake. I just passed Nubia so I figured she'd awakened you."

"Oh yes," I said while I attempted to sit up. "I must have dozed off again. Hey, it's still dark out."

"Of course it is," she said, "and kind of cold. But remember, you were the one who said we needed an early start, so don't even think about going back to sleep on me."

She laughed and left me muttering to myself, but awake. I had no idea what time it was, but it had to be very early because only the palest of pink highlights showed on the upper branches of the higher trees. In fact, I never ever knew the exact time, and nobody other than me seemed to care. There was a stone sundial in the peristyle that was reasonably accurate for telling midday. I had a watch in my vest, but I couldn't figure out how to keep it set. There were twelve hours in a day, counted from sunrise to sunset, but that meant summer hours were longer than winter, and my watch made no provision for that.

Appia came to breakfast dressed in a modified boy's tunic. She altered it in way to increase her range of motion. I was impressed by her ingenuity. She brought along a pair of straw hats with wide brims for protection against the sun, and then announced that our ride was ready when we were.

"Our ride?" I asked.

"You didn't think we were going to walk all the way to the mountain when we've got horses?" she replied.

Her excitement was infectious, and we ate quickly. Nubia helped us fill two ceramic containers with water, and handed Appia a cloth satchel filled with honey rolls and date bread. Leita was at the front door with the horse.

"Can he take two people?" I asked, noting the thinness of a saddle that had no stirrups.

"Of course," she replied. "This is my strong one. His name is Democritus."

"I know that name," I said. "Wasn't he a Greek philosopher?"

"No," she said, "he's always been a horse…teehee." Appia was in complete control of Democritus as we clopped along at a healthy pace, making our way over dirt roads that meandered through the mildly hilly terrain and sleepy little villages. We passed one town she called Boscoreale. I knew that name. We crossed open areas and through hollows where low patches of fog added an eerie, almost mystical feeling to the small parcels of woodland that rose with the slope. The day continued to brighten as we made our way north, but the sun didn't crack the horizon until we'd almost reached our climbing point.

The peak was horseshoe shaped with an elevated central basin that opened towards the bay. I thought we should begin on the sea side of the mountain and climb to the central basin first. From there we could climb the milder southern slope to reach the lower side of the peak and then walk around to the higher northern side to get a good perspective of the entire structure.

When the grade became difficult for Democritus we dismounted and Appia led him to a spot beneath the shade of an umbrella pine. She tied him with enough rope so he could reach a fresh patch of greenery, and then emptied one of the water containers into a bowl that we left for him.

I tried to figure out the best way to carry the other water jug. It had a long neck with a single handle and a wooden stopper. The problem was awkwardness; however, by wrapping my belt once around my waist, and then a second time through the handle of the jug, I was able to carry it on my hip with relative comfort. Appia carried the food simply by using a cross body strap.

"Have you ever climbed this before?" I asked as I studied the slope ahead. The opening to the basin was at least two thirds of way up the mountain, probably three and a half to four thousand feet above sea level.

"No," she said. "I've explored lower areas and the vineyards, but never gone higher than this."

We kept a steady pace as we made our way through a patch of tall fir trees. There were no vineyards on this western slope, but there was a weathered foot path that made walking easier. The vegetation thinned out once we reached the basin. It was a good time to rest, so we found a comfortable spot where we could sit and look out across the beautiful bay. The brilliant sea sparkled. I pointed to what I believed was Surrentum about three quarters of the way out on the stretch of mountainous land to the left. The island of Capri was visible just beyond. Stabiae and its port were closer on the inner shore to the left, and Neapolis was visible to the right.

The basin had enough vegetation to make it impossible to study from where we sat, so I suggested we continue up to the southern peak where we could look into the basin from above. The inner walls of the basin were steep, so we opted for the less demanding ridge, but even so, it was much more difficult to climb than what we'd experienced up to that point. The trees were smaller at the higher elevation, looking like brambly caricatures of themselves, and the soil was looser and grittier, causing us to slip occasionally.

When the sun appeared from behind the mountain it caused a sudden rise in temperature. My suggestion of a water break was met with welcomed acceptance. I was thirsty too, but my need for relief from carrying the water jug was even greater as it seemed to be carving a niche in my hip.

I kicked into the soil around my feet. It had a dry and sandy consistency below a thin crusty cover. The unusual reddish color set it apart from any of the soils around the villa.

"What is it?" Appia asked as we shared the water.

"Curious stuff," I replied as I studied a handful of subsoil.

"How so?" she asked.

"This is volcanic soil," I replied as the word suddenly came to mind. I stood up to get a better look at the basin below. It was clearly a volcanic caldera. There was a small forest at the open end, while near the center was a semi-circular pond abutting a large mound of uplifted earth. The mound stood out for its lack of vegetation and a multitude of cracks covering its crusty surface. It had to be a good twenty-five feet high and at least triple that across from the caldera wall to the pond. "Have you ever heard of this mountain erupting?"

"Erupting?" she uttered. "What are you talking about?"

"This mountain is a volcano," I said.

She shook her head. "I don't know that word."

I had to think. "There are mountains that actually explode. That's called an eruption. They're not like regular mountains."

"Like Etna?" she asked. "It burns sometimes and spews rivers of fiery lava."

"Yes," I said. "I know of Etna. It is a volcano."

"Oh," she said thoughtfully. "Are you saying our mountain is like Etna?"

"Yes, and no," I replied. "Mostly yes. But I fear this one may be different."

"Why? Do you see something?"

"Look at that weird mound down there," I said. "Unless I'm wrong, that's what's called a lava dome, or volcanic dome."

"What's that?"

"It's a weak place in the land," I said, "where pressure from below has forced subterranean material upward."

"Okay," she uttered sounding totally confused.

"See how it stands out," I replied. "It's relatively new compared to the land around it. The way it's cracked..."

"Water causes cracks too," she said. "I've seen them along riverbanks where the mud has dried out and shrunk. Maybe those were caused by a heavy rain."

"That's a possibility," I said even though I didn't really think so, but I had to applaud her logic. She was indeed a refreshing change from her father's way of thinking. "But there's something else. Look very closely. Does that look like steam rising?" She studied the mound but couldn't see what I was talking about. When I looked I couldn't find it again.

"There," she said excitedly. "Look at the water." I looked but I didn't see anything odd. "It's gone. It looked like smoke or steam but I don't know where it went."

"You're absolutely sure you've never heard of this mountain erupting or seen smoke near the peak after a tremor?"

"Nope," she replied.

I decided our best option was to climb down into the caldera for a closer look. Appia agreed and so we retraced our steps down the ridge to the basin and then through the small forest to the mound and adjacent pond. It all looked a lot bigger below than it did from above, and there were wisps of steam rising from many of the cracks in the mound, much of it collecting above the pond as thin, almost transparent vapors. Appia did a quick taste test of the water before I could stop her.

"Don't drink that!" I said.

"Yuck," she said, and she spit it right out. "This water tastes bitter and it smells of rotten eggs." I handed her the water container so she could rinse her mouth thoroughly. "That was stupid."

"Are you okay?" I asked.

"Fine now."

"Good," I said. "This thing is most definitely a volcano, and I fear it's waking up. This mound is indeed new. It's created by something called magma. Magma is rock that's so hot from subterranean pressure it turns to a liquid that sometimes gets pushed upwards. It's not far below our feet. I think magma is pushing up under this mound, but it hasn't broken to the surface yet."

"I have no idea what you just said, but is it dangerous?"

"Normally I might not be as concerned," I replied, "but given all the earth tremors we're having, yes, I believe we have a very serious problem. It appears this mountain hasn't erupted for quite some time. The most dangerous, explosive eruptions come from volcanoes that have long quiet times between eruptions."

"How do you know all this?" she asked.

"I don't know," I said in frustration. "I just do," and I sat with my head in my hands. "I just do. I look at things, and the answers pop into my head. This thing is scary."

"Vesaevus has always been our great fortune," she said. "The soil is incredibly fruitful. It's not at all scary, Gnaeus."

"Do you mean Vesuvius?"

She shrugged. "Vesaevus, Vesuvius, sure."

"This mountain is really Vesuvius?" I wanted to be certain.

"Yes," she replied. "That's always been its name. Is that a problem?"

"Yes," I replied firmly.

"What?"

"This is a very, very dangerous mountain," I said. I studied the steaming mound again. "The tremors are a warning that magma is moving upward. That mound may be a release point."

"Suppose the cracks do get bigger?" she asked. "How bad could it be? Wouldn't these walls block that liquid rock you said was a problem?"

I looked at her and said, "I'm not sure I know how to explain this."

"I know you fear it," she replied.

"We spoke of Etna," I said. "You know about lava."

"Yes."

"Lava is also magma," I said, "but hotter and runnier so whatever gas is in that magma escapes before it explodes. Unfortunately, I believe this mountain is the kind that explodes. Its magma is not quite as hot, trapping the gasses which detonate as gasified rock. Instead of a fiery river of lava, it blows upward as a massive cloud that rains volcanic rock and ash over the land."

"Like snow?" she asked. "I remember snowstorms in Gaul that buried the land up to my waist."

"It might fall like snow," I said, "but this kind of snow is gritty and abrasive to breathe. There would be larger stones mixed in with it. Enough of it will cause roofs to collapse."

"Do you think it could reach our villa?" she asked with great concern.

"Not just our villa," I said, "but the entire region, and that's not even the worst of it. At some point the energy that holds that massive cloud up will weaken, and when it does it will fall and spread out over the land. This material is so hot and so toxic that nothing living can survive it. Any people it strikes will die before they have time to fall down, and no shelter is safe. Hiding in a cellar will not save lives. A mountain like this has the potential to bury whole towns so completely you won't be able to find them afterwards."

She sat quietly for a moment and looked at the mound and the pond. She picked up some of the dirt around her feet and rubbed it between her fingers. "This is different than most soil," she said. "It's gritty and abrasive."

"I know I've given you a lot of information to consider," I said. "Feel free to doubt me. I can't tell you how I know these things, but I can tell you I'm not making it up."

"I know you're not making it up," she said. "Nobody could make that up. Sometimes I think Father may be right. You know of things that only the gods know."

"No," I said. "I learned this somewhere. I was taught."

"Yes, the gods taught you."

I shook my head. "No. My senses completely reject that idea."

"Mine do too," she said, "but I can't think of a better explanation."

"That's still not a good reason buy into it," I said.

We made our way back down the slope, stopping once to give our weary quads a rest. If they were tired going up, they were doubly so on the way down from doing all the braking. We shared the bread and finished the water. A warm, welcoming breeze filtered through the trees.

"I have a question," I said. "Do you know how much decision-making power I actually have while your father's away?"

"Father made you head of the household," she replied. "I would assume you can decide anything."

"That's good to hear," I said, "because I recently made a big decision regarding Leita."

"I know. You gave her money to give to her son."

"Yes," I said, "I did do that, but I did more. I offered her son steady work at the villa in exchange for room and board for him and his wife." I thought Appia's chin was going to hit the floor. "He's hard working," I explained, "and I thought we could use somebody to repair all the damage these earth tremors are doing to the villa."

She grinned and took my hand. "You certainly don't need my approval, but it sounds like you're doing just fine. It will be interesting when Father gets home."

"There's also a child on the way."

Appia chuckled. "Make that very interesting."

It didn't take us long from there to reach Democritus. The moment he saw Appia he started swinging his head side to side and stomping the ground like an excited child.

"Democritus, my good boy," Appia said as she rubbed his fuzzy nose. Once he'd calmed down, we hopped on and began our ride back to the villa.

It was late afternoon by the time we finally arrived home. Nubia was waiting for me by the fountain. She looked stunning in a pinkish-orange pastel wrap.

"You are so pretty," Appia said, and then she looked at me, and then back at her. "Uh oh…"

"What?" I said.

"Father isn't going to like this."

"What?"

"You're supposed to be her master," she said, "only."

"Appia," I said, "I can't own people. I can't boss people around to prove my authority. I can't treat intimacy as a self-centered, unemotional act of dominance. I can't, and I won't be something I'm not."

"I know," she said with a sigh, and then she reached up and kissed me on the cheek. "You are something different alright, and I don't want you to change either."

XIV

∞

Creating a kind of digital decoder reminiscent of the Rosetta Stone was Kamden's first objective. He began with three language groups, contemporary English, future English and Alien codex. Contemporary and future English were very similar in narrative or common form, but technical writing differed considerably.

After six months, he'd become obsessed. He quit his job at MIT and moved into the farmhouse. His workdays became longer and longer, the last being twenty straight hours. It was three in the morning when he knocked on Christina's bedroom door to apprise her of his latest breakthrough. It was late, but it couldn't wait, so she tossed on her robe and followed him to the lab.

He took a seat before his computer. "You know, the ship remains capable of traveling into the past only because it's never been turned off since its creation?"

"Yes," she replied.

"I suspect that live outer shell has something to do with that."

"I don't know that it can be turned off," she said. "Is that what you woke me up for?"

"No," he said with a smile, and then he pulled up the first screen. It was a graph he'd created from the readable navigation data recovered from the ship. "Here it is. The ship's actual Date of Origin, or when the ship went live so to speak." Numbers flashed on the screen and stopped at October 12, 172,492,152 BCE. "That date coincides with the Gregorian calendar as we know it."

"The aliens used the Gregorian calendar?" Christina asked.

"No," he replied with a chuckle. "However, the future humans created a precise numerical dating system where zero is the build date. The numbers can be used to calculate dates in old Julian, revised Julian, our Gregorian, or any other system you choose to employ."

"That's brilliant, Kam. It's the first actual evidence that Aaron arrived in the Jurassic."

"That he did," he said, "but there's more, a lot more," and he pulled up a chart full of lines and text that looked like a horizontal family tree of sorts. "I made this from the navigational data recorded during the return. Each point along the central zigzagging line is a course adjustment. The blue lines point to the corresponding data. We now know what the ship did even if we may not know why."

Liam and Aine entered the lab having been drawn by the commotion. Christina's excitement was contagious as they all pulled up seats around Kamden. "What does it show?" Christina asked.

"It shows," he said as he traced the center line with his first finger all the way across the screen practically to the end, "that the ship was precisely on course to this point." He enlarged the image until the last two and a half thousand years filled the screen. "The only time the ship fully landed prior to its arrival here was January 15, 69 CE by the Roman calendar." He pointed to a big black dot on the screen. "But this is data you've had in front of you all along."

"What do you mean?" Christine said with surprise.

"It's in his log," he replied. He picked up a printout of the log. "Date of landing, 1746276.80944. That's January 15, 69 CE at 7:25 and 36 seconds AM by the Julian calendar. How did you miss that?"

Liam looked shocked. "I'm sorry. That's on me."

"Me too," Christina said.

"That's not just the wrong year," Aine noted, "but the wrong day. We targeted January 17th because that's Aaron's birthday."

"The day is correct Aine," Liam said. "The 15th is also the 17th. We're talking different calendars. The Romans used the old Julian version, but Aaron wanted his arrival to coincide with our Gregorian calendar. In fact, I applied the Gregorian calendar mode as our base for the trip, but I must have made a mistake since the data reads as Julian."

"Not necessarily," Kamden said. "I see all your dates are Gregorian conversions. That's good. I'm surprised you got that far without breaking the alien codex."

Liam was still shaking his head. "I don't understand why the date displayed that way."

Kamden pulled up a data readout on his monitor. "Probably because the program hadn't finished, which may explain the odd landing coordinates as well."

"That data makes no sense," Liam said.

"But it does," Kamden said as he pointed to the graph again and enlarged the image so only the years between 50 CE to 100 CE were visible. "It's simply untranslated data. There was nothing wrong with the programming. This is definitely pilot error. He took control of the ship at five thousand feet altitude, and manually landed it from there."

"In 69 CE?" Liam asked.

"Yes," Kamden replied, and he pointed to a midpoint on a curved line.

"Aaron was supposed to take manual control at five thousand feet," Liam explained. "That way he'd have a clear view of the coastline as he descended."

"If there was nothing wrong with the programming," Christina asked, "then why was the ship descending ten years too soon when it should have been at 30,000 feet?"

Kamden pointed to a series of numbers and text at the bottom of a printed data sheet. "It's called Routine Terrestrial Verification. The ship is programmed to descend below five thousand feet prior to its intended target date in order to verify location and fine-tune its approach for a more precise landing. It was still on its way to 79 CE when Aaron took control ten years too early."

"Ten years to the day," Aine said.

"The programmed verification began at precisely ten years out," he said. "The month and day remain the same, which I might add, means this ship must have been programmed for use on this planet. Maybe it wasn't built by an ancient alien intelligence after all."

"No," Christina said. "The future humans most likely modified the alien programming."

"The question now becomes intent," Kamden stated. "What was Aaron trying to do when he left 69 CE? Was he trying to come straight home, or was he attempting to satisfy the original goal?"

"Come straight home," Christina said. "Except, we haven't established that he was actually in the ship when it took off from Rome, only that he'd returned after his walk."

"Well," Kamden replied, "if he intended to come straight home, he made one critical mistake. He never reset the navigation timer to zero."

"I don't understand," she said.

Kamden closed his eyes and sighed. "This is why I woke you up so early. That's the most important step. He may have landed in 69 CE, but the original program was still running. The ship was still heading to 79 CE Pompeii!"

"I didn't know it did that," Liam said somberly.

"Neither did I," Christina uttered.

"Okay," Aine said, "so what if it did continue on to 79 CE? The ship still came home. It did what it was supposed to do, except without Aaron."

"Did it land in Pompeii too?" Christina asked.

Kamden enlarged the image on his monitor further to get a better reading. "It's so close it's hard to tell. It slowed almost to a dead stop, for maybe, say, two or three seconds. It couldn't have been more than five or six feet off the ground."

Christina stood up. She was frustrated. Kamden had done what he'd promised, but his answers had only produced new questions along with a navigational function they'd missed altogether. She knew Kamden needed sleep, but she needed more answers. She made coffee.

"What's with all the curlicues?" Aine asked, and she pointed to a faint, squiggly line that traced the ships line of descent to 79 CE, followed by its subsequent ascent towards home."

Kamden studied the lines more closely and looked at the corresponding text. "Pitch and roll," he said as he rubbed his eyes. "Good catch. I hadn't noticed that before. Except it doesn't make sense."

"Why not?" Christina asked.

"Pitch, roll, and yaw are automatically controlled by the nav system," he replied, "but this indicates Aaron manually overrode that control feature."

"To what end?" Christina asked.

"I don't know," he replied with a shake of his head. "But the ship was perfectly stable until just before its target date. Mere moments. And then it started to roll."

"You're thinking Aaron did that?" Christina said.

"Yes," he replied. "That's what it looks like."

Liam recalled the disposition of the ship when it landed. The hull was 90 degrees out of alignment with the door open to the sky. "If the hull was rolling," he said, "the door would have been open to the ground too. I know he's not supposed to be able to fall out, but maybe…"

"Maybe not fall out," Kamden said.

Christina poured coffee for everyone while she listened.

"We still don't know for sure if he was actually in the ship," Aine reminded them.

"He had to be." Kamden spoke slowly and thoughtfully. "And since he didn't know what the ship was really doing…" He pointed to the descent into Pompeii. "Look. The ship never got up to speed between 69 and 79. Instead of 30,000 feet, it barely reached two miles. It took over thirty-five hours to cover those ten years. I hate to think about what he was going through."

"He must have been frantic," Christina said. "Probably attempting to gain speed."

"That can't happen without adjusting the programing to add that variation," Kamden stated.

"He knew not to touch anything program related," Liam said.

"He never touched the programming," Kamden said.

"If we factor the ship's reduced rate of speed between 69 and 79 CE," Christina said, when she realized what Kam was thinking, "how long would it take the ship to cover the distance between 79 CE and now?"

Kamden did the math. "Two hundred and ninety-six days."

"When did the ship begin to roll?" she asked.

Kamden enlarged the image as much as possible. "At about five-hundred feet altitude during the descent."

"A 360-degree roll?"

"No," he said. "It started as a slow rocking, 45, 55, 80 degrees, back and forth."

"Controlled?" she asked.

"I would say, yes." He looked more closely at the screen. "As the ship accelerated away from 79 CE, the rocking became a slow 360-degree roll all the way home. That appears to be uncontrolled."

"What are you thinking, Chris?" Aine asked.

"Let me ask you this?" she replied. "What would you do if you faced two hundred and ninety-six days in a tiny ship with food and supplies for only a month at most?"

"Bail out," Liam said. "He knows we can't save him if he dies in the ship."

"Then why didn't he leave us a note?" Christina lamented.

"Because it was last minute," Liam said calmly. "He was hurt, probably frantic. The ship was inexplicably slowing to land. He probably recognized the bay, Capri, Vesuvius. He was back on manual control then, right?" and he looked at Kamden."

"Yes," he replied. "He could land anytime. He just couldn't accelerate, or change course without zeroing out the timer."

"I think," Liam said, "time was against him. He saw where he was, assessed the situation as best he could, and he made the hard choice to bail out and send the ship home."

"Logistically difficult," Kamden said, "but possible."

"How?" Aine asked. "He'd have just two seconds to get out through the hatch once the return was activated. We know that. He knew that."

"Yes, he did," he replied. "Two seconds isn't enough time from an upright position, but by rolling the ship to 80 or 90 degrees, two seconds is enough to fall, or dive out. That explains why the hatch didn't close automatically. He wasn't inside and linked to the control panel."

"I see," Aine said, "but this is just so much speculation."

Kamden sighed. "The sad part is the trip back from 79 took fewer than three hundred hours. He had enough food and water for that."

"Let's not go there," Christina said. "We know where he is, so let's concentrate on that."

"No, we don't," Aine corrected.

"I think he made it to Pompeii," Liam said.

Kamden looked up from his screen. "I'm leaning that way too."

"Actually," Christina said, "Aine has a point. We are speculating. Corroborating evidence is what we need. We need to go over all the data – everything again." That drew a collective sigh from the others. "Look," she added, "I know it's a lot of work, but we may only have one shot to get it right. That's a time machine in the barn. The one thing we have is time. Time to be certain."

"What if we come up empty?" Liam asked.

Christina shrugged. "We'll deal with that then," and she turned to Kamden. "Thank you, Kam. Now get some sleep."

"Aye aye Captain," he said.

XV

∞

It was another beautiful morning. Warm rays of sunshine poured in through the narrow opening behind my head, gently nudging me awake. I had no idea what day of the week it was. It didn't really matter. One day followed another with a comforting similarity. I was feeling good about myself. Paris and his wife Therasia had accepted my offer and Leita couldn't have been happier.

It sounded like there was a cicada actually in my room, but it was probably just outside on a column. The birds seemed to be louder too, as was another sound I hadn't heard in weeks.

"Appius?" I said. I climbed out of bed too quickly and nearly fell on my face. I tossed on my tunic and staggered into the courtyard.

"Gnaeus!" Appius called out the moment he saw me.

"You're home," I said as I made my way to the main house. "Did you have a nice trip?"

"We need to talk," was his reply and he disappeared inside. The atrium was a hub of activity with Appius choreographing the action. Even Appia was put to work, rushing about with arms full of tablets.

"Did you have a nice trip?" I repeated.

"I did," he replied, "but it's always nicer to be home." He offered me a strong handshake adding, "Come, Caelus has heated the bath."

"A bath before we eat?"

"After three days at sea, I think it's time." Nubia and Leita glanced in my direction as they carried supplies towards the kitchen. Both sporting wide grins as if they knew something I didn't. Appius wasn't smiling which made me uncomfortable. "What have you done to my home?" he asked upon entering the bath.

"What do mean?" Rather than answer he went straight to the hot room. Caelus joined us with his arms full of fresh clothing.

"I left you in charge of a household of four, but I've come home to six."

"Seven," I said, "if you count the unborn child."

"That's right," he sighed, "which is fine if you have the means to provide for them. My question to you, Gnaeus, is what do you propose to do with them?"

"I believe that depends on you," I replied. "You left me in charge. You told me to make decisions so I made one. Is that correct or were we just playing a game?"

"It was not a game," he replied. Caelus left momentarily and came right back, but Appius waved him away. "I trust you also know I can cast them out."

"But you won't," I said.

"How do you know that?"

"Honor," I replied. "You gave me the authority to act in your name. It's your honor as much as mine."

He smiled. "Good answer. You assessed the situation, and you took swift action. You didn't use the household money I gave you for personal indulgences. Your instincts are indeed those of a master. Therefore, Paris and his family will remain, and you, Gnaeus, have done well. Perhaps I haven't as much to teach you after all."

"I hoped you would pay Paris a wage as well," I said.

"Me?" he chuckled. "My honor was satisfied by honoring your decision, but that doesn't make me responsible for them. All decisions regarding their future disposition remain yours." I was speechless. "You look a little pale, Gnaeus."

"You know I'm in no position to do anything for them," I said. He just sat there grinning. "Now I get it. You must want something from me." I had to give him credit. He was always a step ahead of me with his understanding.

"Here's what I propose," he said. "You're entitled to monetary benefits as my understudy. You can offer Paris a modest wage from that if you choose. He and his family are your property now. I need to see how well you manage people dependent on you for their survival."

"I don't own them," I said. "They're not slaves."

"Semantics," he said with a shrug. "The point is you changed their living conditions and you're responsible for them moving forward. You could squander this opportunity, or this could be the beginning of your own support group."

I sank deeper into the hot bath. "Their future is up to them. All I wanted to do was make Leita's life easier."

"I know exactly why you did it," he said. "That's why Leita will be your new personal servant. Naturally, Nubia will be returned to my service as soon as possible. I have much for her to do."

It took me a moment to process his words. "Nubia and I are doing so well together."

"I agree," he said, "and your progress will continue with Leita." I must have looked like I'd just been kicked in the head. "Don't be sad. It's not like she's going anywhere."

"I'm just surprised," I replied.

"Leita is a pleasure to have around. Her experience will be a big part of your next level of training. I was going to make this change anyway, but your development has allowed me to up the schedule."

"What about meals?" I asked. "I thought Leita was your best cook?"

He chuckled. "She isn't going anywhere either. There's no reason to pull her off kitchen duties. And by the way, Gnaeus," he added, "the college of priests in Rome has evaluated the circumstances of your rebirth. Their assessments were consistent with mine." My mind was on Nubia so I wasn't very interested. "This is important, Gnaeus. It's tangible proof of your divine heritage."

"Are you actually telling people I was born from a cloud?" I asked.

"Of course not," he replied. "Those priestly findings are not to be made public." He was smiling and obviously quite pleased with himself. "I envision great things for you, Gnaeus. You may feel like nobody listens to you, but I assure you they do, and now I know the source of your thoughts." My mind had wandered back to Nubia. "Did you hear what I just said?" he asked.

"I'm sorry," I replied as I tried to refocus. "I'm still waking up."

"I want you to know I've given great thought to your ideas. There will be changes."

"That's good, I guess," I said as I sat up. "What are you talking about?"

"I've walked many of the same Roman streets a hundred times, but never before did I look into the faces of the landless poor. I had to ask, what makes me better? Wealth and property? That just makes me luckier."

"First slavery and now landless poor," I said. I was genuinely surprised by his words. "You've made some great strides in understanding. But I guess such insights will be a hard sell to others of your rank."

"It's your rank too," he reminded me.

Appius was finally ready to eat so we left the bath and joined everyone else in the summer triclinium that looked out onto the courtyard. Appius, Appia, and I took our places, while Caelus, Nubia and Leita served the meal.

Appius talked of his trip to Rome. The emperor provided Appius with personal servants and a room on Palatine Hill at the former palace of Emperor Tiberius. Caelus stayed at Appius' second home, what he called the Villa North, near the warehouse district in Rome. He ran errands for Appius in Thalese's place. It was interesting to note that the family wealth had nearly doubled in six months as a result of a growing need for river craft and an imperial agreement that Appius had just renewed.

Appius spoke of great meals and thrilling races at the Circus Maximus. He was impressed by a new amphitheater under construction at the site of Nero's palace. He believed it would be the grandest, most colossal structure in the civilized world.

Thalese arrived shortly after breakfast. Appius left to speak with him in private before the rest of us had a chance to welcome him home. He sent him away again before rejoining us.

"Where's Thalese?" Appia asked.

"He'll be back," Appius replied. "He went into town on a special errand. He has important information regarding Gnaeus that must be entered into the registry as soon as possible."

"What information?" I asked.

Appius smiled. "This information will secure your freeborn status so you can officially take your rightful place in society."

"You discovered who I am?" I asked excitedly.

"Your name is Lucius Valerius Getha," he stated. "I sent Thalese to Asia, to Ephesus where he pieced together your name and family pedigree."

"My real name?" I said with surprise. "He found my family?"

"Not exactly," he replied. "He recovered evidence."

"What evidence?" I asked.

"I'll explain it all later," he said, brushing me off.

"So, I have a life before coming here after all," I said sounding more confused than excited. I already knew Ephesus was a big city, but hearing the name produced no new memories the way the word Rome or the name Vespasian had.

"I didn't say that," he said.

"I should probably be heading there as soon as possible. Do I have a wife...kids? I have no memory. Are you sure that's my name?"

"Yes," he replied.

"Yes, what?" I said. "I have a wife...kids?"

"No," he said, "I mean I don't know. All I know is Lucius Valerius Getha is your name. Unfortunately, there's no family there for you to return to."

"But didn't you just say I have a family?"

"No," he replied somberly. "I said family pedigree. It's proof of your free born status and your legitimacy as such."

"It seems like Ephesus would be a logical place to start looking for my past," I said. "Maybe once I'm there I'll see things that will spark my memory."

Appius was shaking his head. "Trust me, my friend," he said as he put his hand on my shoulder, "you'd be wasting your time. What you seek is here. Not there. Of that I am most certain."

"That means you're not Gnaeus anymore," Appia said to me. "You're Lucius, or we can call you Getha like you thought."

"Getha feels more correct," I said. "I like it better too."

"Then Getha it is!" Appius announced.

"But that's not the name you said was sewn into my clothing. I believe that was Gnaeus Octavius…"

"The clothes you arrived in were too badly soiled to be sure of anything," Appius stated. "That toga could have been a rental or borrowed. It doesn't matter. Lucius Valerius Getha is who you are."

"How did Thalese figure this out?" I asked. "How did he even know to go to Ephesus?"

"He's a very clever and resourceful man," Appius replied.

"Apparently," I said while scratching my head.

Appius stood up, but when I started to stand, he told me to stay seated, and then he removed the gold medallion from around his neck and handed it to me. A signet bearing the name of the Flavian family was embossed into the gold face.

"As Emperor Vespasian once gave this medallion to me for my protection," he said, "I now present it to you, Lucius Valerius Getha." I was stunned. I didn't know what to say. I didn't even know the point, but by the solemn faces all around I knew it meant something important. "You have proven your value to me and my family," he stated. "I have no son to follow in my footsteps. This family has no future without a freeborn male heir. This dilemma has caused many sleepless nights, but tonight I will sleep soundly."

"What are you talking about?" I asked.

"It came to me in a dream," he said. "It was corroborated by priests this very morning."

Appia looked as surprised as I was.

"Your arrival couldn't have been more opportune," Appius added. "You belong here. Your presence ensures this family has a future. Not even Caestus can now lay claim to Appia's inheritance through his marriage to Maria Prima."

"Caestus," I said, "your son-in-law? You've spoken of him before I believe."

"The law allows for a son-in-law to lay claim to a father-in-law's property when there are no male heirs, but not if I have a son."

"You don't like him very much."

"What's there to like? He's a fence sitter and I don't trust him," he replied.

"But father," Appia said, "you've never given him a chance."

"And I never will," he stated firmly. "He talks behind my back. He says things in public he shouldn't. Why can't he be more like Getha and direct his criticisms to me? To my face?"

"Maybe if you were nicer to him, he would feel more comfortable speaking with you."

"It doesn't matter," Appius said, and he took the medallion from me and handed it to Appia. "I'd like you to put it on him." She closed her hand on it, but she wasn't smiling.

"Maybe this isn't such a good idea," I said noting her discomfort.

Appius leaned over and kissed Appia on the cheek. He whispered something in her ear, to which she nodded and smiled. "I'm glad you are a member of our family," she said to me, and she carefully placed the medallion around my neck.

"Are you sure?"

"I am," she replied.

"What about my age?" I asked Appius. "I would think you'd want somebody younger. I've got to be 40."

"I'm thinking more like 35," he replied.

"For some unknown reason 38 feels right."

"No matter," he chuckled. "You're healthy, strong, and well over a decade younger than I am, and you're mature. You can't teach maturity to a youth and I don't have time for nature to finish polishing a roughhewn stone."

"I guess I have a lot to think about."

"The thinking's been done," Appius said. "In a few weeks we'll make the adoption official. We'll offer testimony before my colleagues at the Curia, and then, as my son, we'll proceed to the Temple of Jupiter to make our public proclamation." I looked at the writing on the medallion. "It can protect you," he said, "should you ever need imperial favor," and then he held out his cup of wine. "This cup represents the solidarity of the household. To drink from it is to be one with this family."

He took a sip and passed it to Appia. "For you, Getha," she said, and she took a sip and passed it to me.

"What if we find my family in Ephesus?" I asked.

Appius sighed. "You are now effectively linked to the emperor through me. You aren't just doing me a great service as my son, but such a link benefits all those in your personal sphere, whether known or as yet still unknown, whether family or not."

My hands trembled as I looked at the cup. For an instant it felt wrong, but as that feeling passed, I could think of no rational objections. I quickly composed myself and took a sip before passing it to Leita. Everyone was smiling.

"Getha," Appius said with a kindly smile, "whatever may befall me in the future, I just want to know my daughter will be alright," and he looked at Appia. "I want to know she'll be safe and happy. That's what I seek."

It had been an eventful day, and I was in need of a quiet place to think. No matter what each new day brought with it, late afternoon would find me sitting on the knoll behind the villa letting gentle breezes soothe both body and soul. It was nearing sunset and the warm glow of the late afternoon sky was beginning to blanket the landscape with vibrant yellows, oranges and reds. The sea sparkled as seabirds enlivened the air with their sounds. Overhead, a smattering of puffy cumulous clouds were quietly rolling in from the bay to add dynamic contrasts to the already colorful scene.

Appia came out to join me, but I was so engrossed in my daydreaming that I hadn't noticed her.

"May I sit?" she asked in a quiet voice to politely alert me to her presence.

"Of course," I said with a smile. "It's been quite a day."

"Indeed," she agreed as she took a seat beside me on the smooth stone outcrop that made for a natural bench. "In all the years I've lived here I've never sat in this spot,"

"I find it soothing" I said.

"It's wonderful," she replied. "I can see why you spend so much time here." I pointed to a flock of gulls that had found something of interest near the city walls. Appia laughed at the sudden flutter of wings mixed with squawks and general clamor. One of the birds suddenly rose sharply away from the rest with a beak full of something, leaving the others to follow in hot pursuit. Appia took that moment to move closer. "This is nice," she said.

"And nicer to be sharing it with a friend."

She smiled. "Even nicer to be sharing it with my brother."

The next several weeks were spent preparing me to meet the public. Caelus became my fitness trainer, seeing to my physical conditioning while teaching me sports and games. Appius took on the task of explaining the local political system, including in-depth descriptions of the various personalities I'd be meeting. Thalese was directed to refine my language skills and educate me on the finer points of upper-class etiquette. He was to educate me on the local festivals while tutoring me on how to dress properly. Appius was concerned my inexperience would be exposed if my toga fell into disarray. Properly wrapped togas were difficult to put on correctly. They were woolen and heavy, very restrictive, and I had a habit of wiggling my left arm free, fatally altering its shape.

Appius was often away after evening meal. He had become the consummate politician, despite not officially running for office, going from villa to villa, tossing around ideas with anyone who'd listen. This method of politicking relied less on clients and more on personal interaction, a style considered radical by many, and one he'd developed from remarks I'd made.

The more I learned about society, the more I became concerned about Appius. Thalese had taught me how important protocol was in public, and Appius was modifying centuries-old traditions. The fact that he had accepted my earlier ideas regarding slavery and a slaveless society added to my concerns. It wasn't that I'd changed my mind, but I was beginning to understand that radical ideas posed risks if they threatened to upset the status quo by stirring emotions in the lower classes. I suggested he slow down and limit his politicking to the voting public first, but he would not hear of it. He believed Hercules had spoken to him through me, making it an honor bound duty to put the word to the street regardless of who it upsets.

When I asked him how he knew which of my comments were from Hercules and which ones weren't, he said the ancestors made it clear through his offerings. I shouldn't have been surprised. He was on a roll with a newly found sense of purpose that his ego demanded. People were starting to listen too, and while his peers were discounting his rhetoric as nonsense from a senile old man, his words were finding resonance among the lower classes. Thalese understood my concern while assuring me the worst that could happen was he'd lose a few clients.

A couple nights later Appius held a formal gathering of associates and clients to explain his still evolving ideas after learning there was a lot of misinformation being shared among them. He was still undecided as to when to introduce me to the public, so I stayed out of sight.

With little to do I wandered upstairs to sit in the small front room balcony that hung out above the street. I liked to go there on occasion to look at the city walls and to the distant sea. I wasn't there very long when I heard voices below.

"The old man's lost it," the first voice said.

"It makes you wonder if he ever had it," another said with a chuckle. It sounded like there were at least two others chuckling along with him.

"Do you think he'll be a problem?" a third said.

"No," the second replied. "He's a nuisance but not a problem. Even his clients don't know what to make of him. His own son-in-law thinks he's mad."

"What about the emperor?" the first asked.

"Hail Appius!" the second said with a laugh. "Do you honestly think the emperor really takes his ramblings seriously?"

"No," was the general reply.

"What's his point?" the first asked. "It isn't like he's seeking public office."

"I beg to differ," the second said. "He's thinking Duoviri, or perhaps even Duoviri Quinquenalles. What do you think this little gathering is really all about?"

"I'm not so sure," the third man replied.

"So where's he getting these crazy ideas anyway?" the first asked. "He's always been eccentric, but now he's ridiculous. Could they be coming from Appia? She doesn't always know her place."

"Appia," the second said with a long moan. "I've been trying to get under that wrap for years." I peeked down at the street and saw the speaker making a lewd jester with the front of his toga. "She's a bastard child you know."

"Really?" the third said with surprise.

"Bore by one of his slaves," he replied. "Probably a slave father as well.

Details seem to be deliberately clouded."

"That's ridiculous," the third replied. "She's freeborn."

"Are you sure? There may be evidence to the contrary."

"What evidence?" the third said. "If any real evidence existed the situation would have been dealt with. You know the penalty for misrepresenting class. It wouldn't have been tolerated."

"The facts may be hazy," the second replied, "but where there's rumor you eventually find truth."

"Not true," the third said. "This is not a joking issue. If you have proof, make your claim in public…otherwise shut up."

"Whatever," the second said in a lighter tone, "but if I ever catch her alone without that goon Caelus tagging along, I'll make her another way."

"You and about twenty others," the first man said with a chuckle.

"I may have fanaticized about her too," the third said, "but I like Appia. I wouldn't want to see any harm come to her."

"But you know what she did to me in public," the second said bitterly. "What gives a bitch with her questionable heritage the right to embarrass me the way she did?"

"You're married, Sextus," the third reminded him. "She's not like one of your slaves and she's not looking for your kind of attention."

"If it turns out she's not freeborn," Sextus said angrily, "I'll have her as I like! It sounds like you actually like the wench."

"I do," the third replied. "And as I understand it, she had good reason to slap you."

"In public?" he said. "She slapped me in public! If her father screws up, as I expect he will, I'll see she ends up in a brothel where everyone has the chance to *like* her," and he chuckled.

"You were invited here as a friend of Appius," the third man reminded him. "We all were."

"That's just how deluded Appius has become," Sextus replied. "How many real friends are here besides you? Nobody listens to him. They humor him. He's rich. The emperor's his friend. I'm here for the food. His cook is just about the best around. I will give him that."

"I say we drop this," the first chimed in, "and rejoin the others."

The conversation had made me angry; although, some of my anger was diffused by the third man. I wondered who he was. He was clearly a friend, so I hustled downstairs to get a better look at him, but instead I accidently met Appius at the foot of stairs conversing with a guest.

"Sorry," I said as I came to a sudden stop.

"Getha," Appius said in a surprisingly friendly voice, "come here."

"I didn't mean to disturb you," I said as I cautiously joined him.

"Getha, this is my good friend Marcus Piso."

"So, you're Lucius Valerius Getha," Marcus said. "Appius was just telling me of you. Welcome to Pompeii."

"Thank you," I replied tentatively.

"Do you like the games?" he asked, but before I could answer he added, "Of course you do. You'll have to join me, or better yet, we'll do midday meal sometime."

"Fine," I said. Appius gave me an approving nod along with a look that told me it was time to leave. I left with so much nervous energy I nearly collided with Nubia in the courtyard. After sharing our surprise and a few chuckles I asked her about Sextus.

"He's a friend of my master," she said.

"He's no friend," I stated flatly, and I told Nubia about the conversation I'd overheard. I also wanted a better look at him, so she led me to a place where I could discretely look in on the meeting.

"He's the one to the right of Marcus Piso," she said. He was younger than I thought and I committed his image to memory.

I wanted to spend some time with Nubia because we had barely spoken since Appius made the switch, but she had duties to perform. I was tired, and even though the meeting was still going on, I went to bed and fell fast asleep.

It was somewhere in the early morning hours that I awoke to a bright flash of lightning followed by a clap of thunder so loud that it seemed to shake the bed posts. More lightning and more thunder had me sitting straight up in bed.

The air felt damp and charged as the first drops of rain struck the roof over my head. One drop followed another until the sky let loose with a torrent that quickly flooded the gutters, sending sheets of water cascading off the overhangs to stand in puddles on the soft ground below. Amid a broken burst of energized light, I caught a glimpse of someone crossing the courtyard in my direction.

"Appia?" I said when the female form appeared only as a silhouette against the bluish white flashes.

"It's Nubia," she replied. "I'm scared."

"Please come in," I said. She was soaked and shaking so I offered her my blanket and she got into bed with me.

"Do you still like me?"

"Of course," I replied as I dried the dampness from her forehead.

"Even if I was once prostituted?" she asked.

Her question caught me by surprise, but then nothing completely surprised me anymore. "I suspected as much," I said, "but that hasn't happened since you've come here, right?"

"My master has treated me well. I still don't know why he selected me. There were many other women better suited to his servant needs. He knew I wasn't a virgin, but he still paid a top price for that."

"Appius is different," I reminded her.

"But do you still like me?"

"Of course," I said with a hug, "and I'm here for you. I'll always be here for you." A second thunderstorm moved in from the bay to brighten the night sky with continued displays of energized blue light. She started crying. All I could think to do was hold her. "We've become so close so quickly," I added, "but regardless of what Appius has in mind for us, you'll always be a part of me."

"You are most definitely a part of me," she said with an unusually strong hug. The tears that had been straddling the rims of my eyes suddenly found their freedom, and I returned her embrace with one of my own. As the storm intensified, the rain began to beat hard on the tiles above our heads again.

"Tonight is for our pleasure," she said with a kiss.

"You said our? Not your, but our. Now that's music to my ears."

The night was electric as was our passion. Two more storms followed, and through the violence of the night, we stole from the storm's energy to remain together until the first light of dawn. Peace returned to the land and with it came a gentle, soothing breeze that further comforted us as we lay exhausted in each other's arms.

"I must go before Master Appius calls," she whispered with a kiss to my cheek. "You will always be with me. Always."

"That sounds so final," I said. "I'm not so far away."

"I know," she said, "but your life will soon change in ways you can't imagine."

"Nothing has to change. This shouldn't be an ending but a beginning."

I heard sadness in her voice as she ventured a reply. "My master has a plan for you, and that plan doesn't include me."

"No," I said for lack of a better reply.

"I wish the world was a different place," she added, "but it's not, and no matter what happens, or how distant I may seem, remember this night. This night is the truth that's inside me always." She gave me a gentle kiss and then placed a finger on my lips to keep me from speaking. I sighed and she left.

XVI

∞

It seemed like my eyes had barely closed when I was awakened by the booming voice of Appius. "It's getting late," he called out. "There's work to do!" He tossed my tunic to me and I dressed and followed him into the courtyard.

"Hope you're well rested," he stated, "because it's another day with Caelus. He's worked you pretty hard, and it shows!"

"Great," I muttered as I staggered to the fountain in order to splash my face.

The workouts with Caelus had begun almost from the moment Appius returned from Rome. He had instructed him to teach me the physical demands my new social life would require. Appius wanted a strong, able bodied son who could hold his own in public. He felt the friendly competitions that took place in the exercise area at the main city bath would be a good place for me to begin making a name for myself. Such lighthearted combats were not life and death struggles; however, they offered bragging rights to the victorious relatives who often made wagers, and Appius loved to wager. I was taller than most men. He felt that my physical advantage gave me the potential to enhance our social positions within our class and the community.

Caelus was intense and sparring with him often made me nervous, and I think that was his way of making me work harder. My longer reach meant I could punch harder, but that was about it. The rest of the time I was on the defensive.

The only time I beat him convincingly at any contact sport was the one time he came at me hard while wrestling. In the heat, or fear of the moment, I reacted instinctively to his thrust by using a leverage move that sent him sprawling over my hip and onto his back. He was stunned. He had retired undefeated as a gladiator, and never once had an opponent put him so completely on the defensive. The word Judo came to mind but he'd never heard of it. Just the same, I had something I could teach him.

Caelus was mostly impressed by my ability to throw a javelin. My first attempts weren't very good, but once I discovered a motion that seemed familiar, I found I had a power that left him momentarily speechless. He said he'd never seen anyone throw a javelin that hard with accuracy. I won all those competitions. I found it great fun.

"What are we doing today?" I asked Caelus when I saw him wander into the courtyard. I'd hoped it would be a quiet day. He shrugged as if he didn't know and he looked at Appius. Appius motioned for him, Thalese, and me to follow him inside where morning meal was all set up. From all the smiles I figured something was up.

"Then are we all agreed?" Appius asked while looking at Thalese and Caelus. They both nodded and turned to me.

"We've decided to visit a city bath tomorrow," Appius announced. "It's time to take that first step into society. The eagle must be set free."

"Tomorrow?" I said. They all laughed. "How's my accent?" I asked Thalese. "It was only yesterday you told me I still had a lazy tongue."

"That happens only when you get tired," he replied. "You've come a very long way quickly. You'll be fine."

"And you feel I'm ready?" I looked at Caelus.

"You have the gift of size and ability," he said. "You would make a fine gladiator with the right training."

"But Caelus," Appius said sternly, "I didn't ask for a gladiator, just an education in the less aggressive sports."

"He's no gladiator," Caelus replied. "He has not hardened his heart. Getha has a soft heart. He sees the games as sport and not survival."

"As well it should be," Appius said happily.

Caelus chuckled and leaned back against the wall. "A pity though," he added, "with what I've taught him he could break any of your friends in half."

To my great relief, Appius told Caelus to go easy on me. He let out a great belly laugh adding, "By the looks of it he's already had a days' worth of specialized training."

Caelus followed his master's orders to the letter and I returned to the villa only mildly fatigued. Leita was there to greet me with a pleasant smile and to escort me to the bath.

The next morning, Leita woke me with a happy smile and a new set of clothes.

"This is the big day," she announced. "I'll wager I'm more nervous about it than you."

"What big day?" I asked as my first attempt to sit up failed.

"Master Appius is taking you to town," she said happily. "You must remember that."

I did indeed, and once I was standing, Leita led the way to the bath. Thalese met us there where I was shaved, bathed, and dressed. The toga Thalese selected was made of a fine white material and was truly elegant even if somewhat restricting. Appius patiently waited for us in the courtyard. Nubia stood next to him, and I'd never seen her so radiant.

"Will you be coming too?" I asked her.

She looked at Appius and back to me. "No," she replied.

Leita squeezed my hand for luck when we passed through the house. I stopped and grabbed a honey roll and quickly washed it down with a swig of water. I wasn't about to go hungry. Thalese joined us and the three of us were on our way. As we entered the city all the townsfolk stopped what they were doing to watch us pass.

"This is weird," I said. "Are you sure this is such a good idea?"

"It is," Appius assured me. "I've set the groundwork, and everybody who's anybody has heard of you. I'm sure they're all dying of curiosity."

"Which reminds me," I said, "where did my name really come from? You promised me an answer." He nearly gagged and Thalese pulled the two of us off into a deserted side street.

"All right," Appius replied in a hushed voice. "It's better you know now before you bring it up in the wrong company." He looked around and told Thalese to keep people away.

"I purchased you a name," he said.

"You can do that?"

"Obviously I can," he replied, "but you are never to speak of it. It's not a great name, but it's freeborn and you're in the census with a traceable heritage."

"I knew it!" I said. "I knew it was all wrong."

"Wrong?" he said. "I hardly think so. Nothing could be more perfect. There's even a service record, although nothing distinguished. We'll only use it for the adoption. After that your name and heritage will be mine."

"This can't be legal," I said. "Who is the real Lucius Getha?"

"He's about 35, give or take," he replied. "He's landless and losing his faculties to a degenerative mental condition."

"We should get going," Thalese said.

"It's a good situation for all concerned," Appius said. "Now he'll have the means for the care he needs. Both families are well served."

"If I have his name, whose name does he use?"

"Will you quit worrying," he said. "Thalese has it all worked out."

"Even the documentation?"

"Let's just go," he said as he shook his head. "We'll discuss it later."

"It's a perfect setup," Thalese said as we reentered the main street. "Ephesus is great because it's far away, big, chaotic, and a wonderful place to make special business arrangements if you know where to look."

It seemed to take us an eternity to reach the baths, and then another smaller eternity to get through all the people at the entrance looking to greet us.

My nervousness made everything a blur. Thalese led us into the changing room where he handed me my sports clothes, which amounted to little more than a belted waist wrap and athletic sandals. Appius and I had gotten separated in the crowd, but over other voices I heard him call out the name Sextus. I couldn't believe it. Sextus Secundus was the vulgar guest at the party and the first of his supposedly better friends that he insisted I meet. I remained polite when introduced, but the sight of him turned my stomach. He seemed a little smug to me, but I decided it best to play along for the moment. I was then introduced to Quintillius Nextus and Darius Polonia, each putting on an air of charm while finding discrete ways to study me.

In the palaestra, people were jogging while others were wrestling or jousting with wooden sticks, and still others played a kind of ball game; however, most were just standing around chatting.

"Let's get you involved in something," Appius said, "perhaps the bowling. Caelus says you're good at skill sports."

"What about a friendly contest with Sextus?" I said when I saw him enter the exercise area.

"Why him?" Appius asked.

"Why not?" I replied. "He's almost my height. He's obviously athletic. It seems only fair."

"He doesn't bowl," Appius said, "and I doubt he will wrestle with you. He only competes when he thinks he will win, and he doesn't know you yet."

"I think he'll wrestle me," I said confidently.

Appius studied me. "Really?" he said. "He'd never voluntarily take on someone who's clearly of equal strength or stronger. Especially a stranger.

He will simply pass the task onto one of his slaves."

"Would you care to bet on it?" I said with a grin.

Appius's eyes lit up. "A wager?" he said. "An interesting concept coming from a man with few means."

"There must be something you want from me."

"What about you?" he asked. "You must want something from me to make such a suggestion."

"You first."

He thought for a moment a said, "If I win, you let me choose a wife for you."

"You're kidding?"

"So, you're not so sure of yourself after all," he chuckled.

"Alright," I said, "but if I win you must register Nubia's enfranchisement at the first possible chance. There will be no cost to her or other obligations whatsoever to you. If she chooses to stay, you will pay her a proper wage that will better her condition."

"Is that all?"

I looked around and said, "Yes, I think that will do it. So, who's uncertain now?"

He gave me one of his stern looks and said, "But we need to agree to one rule first."

"What rule?"

"Sextus must initiate the contest," he said. "Any fool can go up and whack somebody to start a fight."

"Of course," I said. "I wouldn't have it any other way."

He stared at me. I could sense the cogs were grinding in his head. "Alright," he said, "I'll take that wager. I don't know what you have planned, but you're thinking something." I smiled and started towards Sextus, who was standing on the other side of the palaestra. "One thing about successful gambling," he said. "Never agree to a bet until you're certain you've got all the angles covered."

"I do," I said.

"That makes two of us."

Sextus saw me coming so I approached him in a friendly manner. "Sextus my friend, how are you?"

"Hello," he said.

"Would you walk with me?" I asked and I put my hand on his shoulder. "We need to talk."

"Okay," he said while looking a bit perplexed.

I led him to the center of the grounds and stopped. "A little bird told me you have a problem with Appia," I said. "You need to know that if you have a problem with her, then you have a bigger problem with me."

"What?" he said as he stepped back from me. "Is this a joke or some half-baked threat?"

"Oh no," I replied, "it's fully baked. A word to the wise. Next time you make threatening remarks towards anyone close to me, make sure I'm not within earshot."

"Just who do you think you are?" he said in a loud voice for all to hear.

"Help me here, Sextus," I said cordially as if we were old pals. "I'd like very much to be your new friend, but there's this issue of a public apology to Appia. I think that would be a nice gesture. What do you think, big guy?"

I could see the rage in his eyes as he tried to assess my prowess. "I suggest you choose your tone with me a little more carefully," he stated firmly as more people became aware of our standoff, "but because you're new, I'll let it pass this time."

"Sounds like the words of a coward," I said loud enough for all ears. "You're a big talker when it comes to abusing women, but man to man you're just what I figured, a gutless wonder," and then I laughed and spit on the ground near his feet. "I can't wait to tell Appia and her friends this one," and I turned away to give the appearance of leaving in disgust. "You make me sick!"

Sextus was caught flat footed by my unexpected attack on his honor. The anger seethed within him as I'd left him with but one option to save face. I heard him muttering something under his breath, followed by the awkward thump of sandal clad feet as he dove at me. I simply pivoted to the left, causing him to crash wildly into my shoulder, and then I dropped him over my knee to the ground with a move Caelus had taught me. It was almost too easy to be satisfying as I pinned him while twisting his right arm up against his back.

"Do you give up?" I said. He grunted, so I added more torque to the twist.

"All right!" he cried out. "I give! I give!"

"Just kidding," I said. I let go and jumped back to my feet.

"That hurt," he said angrily.

"That's nothing," I said for his ears only. "Call it a friendly warning." He gave me a truly hateful look while dusting himself off, but he made no more threatening lunges.

"What was that all about?" his friends asked when he rejoined them.

"Nothing," he replied, "just have to teach these newcomers a lesson every once and a while."

They were laughing as I made my way towards Appius who didn't seem very pleased.

"Explain," he said sternly.

"Just establishing a presence," I replied.

"I can see that," he said, "but this isn't the arena. These grounds are for friendly games. That wasn't friendly, Getha."

"It wasn't meant to be," I said. "I don't like him."

"That much is clear," he said, "but how can you possibly know enough about anybody to have any opinions?"

"I just do."

"Sextus is too important to toy with like that," he said, "and I hope he doesn't take permanent offence."

"I had my reasons," I said as I began to mellow, "but I suppose that may not have been appropriate for the long term."

He tried to remain stern, but then he smiled. "I despise that man," he admitted. "I have no idea how you could have picked up on that so quickly."

"Then there's the matter of the wager. I believe there's a debt to be paid."

"There is indeed," he said sounding unconcerned.

We passed a bakery and a pottery shop on our way out. The crowd was gone. Thalese walked so quietly behind us that I found myself forgetting he was even there. Appius led us to a side street and into a quiet little tavern near the city gate. He told Thalese to go home and get everything ready for the special family feast he had planned.

"How long have you been with us?" Appius asked as he purchased two goblets of wine. He handed one to me.

"I'm not sure," I replied as we took seats in a room in the back. "Maybe five months." We were the only patrons.

He seemed to agree. "In that time, I've had the good fortune of watching you develop at an astounding rate. I hope you understand why I cut your conversations short today. I didn't want you having to scramble for answers to any leading questions. I have no doubt that in another month you'll be able to hold your own without my help."

"That's the goal, I believe." I said while sipping my wine, which didn't taste good that early in the day.

"What I'd like to know is," he said, "will you remain a member of my household once you've reached a safe level of independence? You'll have my name and your freedom. It will be your decision as promised. And with that said, I'd like to add that your presence at my side as my son is even more important than ever. I believe that together we can make a difference."

"I have no plans to go anyplace else, unless of course I regain my lost memory, but even then..."

"Let me finish," he said somberly. "There remain a few things you need to know before you make a final decision."

"The decision's made," I replied.

"Even if Nubia becomes my concubine?" he said.

"What?"

"I know the two of you are especially close," he said. "I realize that goes against every principal regarding the master/slave relationship, but I celebrate it."

"You do?"

"I could never say that in public, nor should you, but your loneliness was hers as well, and it bears fruit."

I took a healthier swig of wine. "What's fruit got to do with anything?"

"Nothing in a literal sense," he said with a hearty chuckle. "But Nubia is with child."

I almost dropped my cup. Appius called for refills. The bartender responded and I took another healthy swig. "I don't know what to say."

"There's nothing to say," he said. "I thought you should know. I apologize for neglecting to take your emotional needs into account, which must have been considerable given the obvious confusion of rebirth."

"Then I should marry her," I said.

"You can't marry her any more than I can," he said with a smile.

"Well, at least not while she's still a slave."

"I have a confession to make. I planned to enfranchise Nubia as soon as this week, and as my concubine her status improves. The child will be freeborn with my name."

"Let me get this straight," I said. "Is it that you can't marry her or won't marry her?"

"I can't marry her," he replied. "We are a Roman region and thus we must subscribe to Roman law which forbids marriage between freeborns and any class other than freeborn. Freed is not freeborn. Concubinage may not be ideal, but it's the best solution for her and the child."

"She agreed to this?"

"Of course," he said with a smile. "She knows the rules. She knows this is for the best, and I assure you, what we do now is for the best. Think about what you want to do. Everyone considers you a part of the family. We all want you to stay."

We finished our drinks and headed out into the sunlight. We weren't far away from the city gate, and once outside the city we were in sight of the villa. "I'm not going anywhere, Appius," I said, "especially now."

"Nubia's not going anywhere either."

"How long has she known?" I asked. "Why didn't she tell me?"

"Getha," he said, "the child is mine."

I didn't know what to say. It didn't seem likely either. "Are you sure?"

"Yes," he chuckled as if I'd asked a silly question. "Absolutely. That much is certain."

I had to admit it wasn't entirely out of the realm of possibility, and he had that familiar look of confidence in his eyes. I had no doubt his words were sincere, so I dropped the subject.

I put on a smile when we reached the villa, but beneath my facade I felt a cool, emotional numbness. The whole family was there to greet us, including Appia. Leita took my arm and led me to the courtyard where the makings of a great midday feast were all laid out. I overheard Appius explaining to Caelus how I put Sextus in his place, and while he'd suggested to me that my conduct was improper, he was speaking of those same actions with a degree of pride.

Nubia was there as well, but I found it hard to look at her. Her role in the household was already in transition. The clothes she wore were more like that of a wife, and there was a more confident tone in the way she addressed Appius. No doubt he could do more for her than I could.

The feast turned into a pleasant family event, and I snapped out of my depression. When I saw Nubia entering the main house, I followed her on the pretense of needing to fill a wine pitcher.

"Congratulations," I said when I caught up with her on the stairs. "I just found out."

"Everything?" she asked with a quiver in her voice.

"I think so," I replied. "I can't imagine what else there might be." My presence was making her uncomfortable, so I turned to leave.

"Wait," she said, but then she didn't speak.

"You don't have to say anything," I said. "I understand, and I'm happy for you." Her eyes welled with tears and she hustled upstairs. I was tempted to follow but decided against it.

Appius had gone to great lengths to make it a special day, and as the afternoon turned to night, townspeople began dropping by. Marcus Piso, who apologized for missing my bout with Sextus, showed up with his wife. What had begun as a small family gathering slowly grew into a gala event.

I was under the impression that social gatherings were limited affairs due to imperial paranoia regarding plots against the leadership. I don't know where I got that idea from, but it certainly wasn't the case here. There were lots of people showing up and lots of food and drink. Appius had been planning this supposedly impromptu festival for over a month. He got the idea when he was in Rome and the planning began then. People came from all around the region. There were city officials from Oplontis and Stabiae, as well as a pair of businessmen from Neapolis. There was a curious fellow by the name Gaius Plinius. He was accompanied by his nephew and a friend by the name of Pomponianus. I had no recollections of Pomponianus, but the name Plinius was very familiar. Appia explained that Plinius was a famous admiral and a surprise guest at the party. Somehow I knew that, but his face was completely unfamiliar.

The feast didn't end until around midnight. Leita had joined me and remained by my side until after the last guest had departed. I bid her a good night at the stairway, and then I went straight to bed.

I was finally alone. Sleep was impossible as my mind worked overtime; although, little of it was productive. I rolled around and around, and when my frustration reached its peak, I got up and walked out into the darkness of the courtyard.

"Whoops," I said with surprise when I nearly bumped into someone coming towards me. "Nubia?" She didn't answer at first, but when the moon broke through the clouds, I could see her face.

"Yes," she said. She was trembling. "I couldn't sleep."

"Neither can I," I said, "but you could get hurt out here in the darkness."

"I hope you don't hate me."

"I could never hate you," I said, "but it might be smarter if we talk in my room." She agreed, and soon we were sitting together on the bed, but it was hardly like old times.

"Appius said you're going to have his child," I said. "I suppose I should say congratulations."

"Lay with me," she said, "I'm cold." It wasn't all that cold outside, but I laid down with her and spread the blanket over us. She was still shaking.

"I am to have his child," she said, "but it will forever be yours to me."

That seemed like a strange thing to say. "I have to admit I was surprised to find out he fathered your child. It didn't seem like there'd been enough time…"

"Getha," she said with surprise, "you fathered this child. I haven't been with anybody else and he hasn't touched me in a very long time."

"So he lied to me! I can't believe it. He said the child is his."

"He didn't lie," she said with a smile. "He's not claiming to have fathered the child. He's claiming his legal rights as would any master. Whether I'm his slave or concubine, any children I bear are his no matter who fathered them. It's something he wanted very much and I'm happy for it too."

"He wanted you pregnant?" I asked.

"Yes," she replied, "by you."

"What?"

"You're the son of a god," she explained, "and any children you father will share that heritage."

"I hate to disappoint you, but I'm no son of any god and you of all people should know that. Does this mean that all we shared together was false?" Rather than answer she turned away. It was as if the life had been sapped from her. "Every day comes with new surprises. This one beats them all."

"I was surprised the night when you first came to me," she said, her voice trembling. "It was sooner than expected. But I knew what my master wanted and I accepted his proposal. I assumed you would be like other men. I expected you'd have your pleasure and go when you were done."

"I wish you'd told me that then," I said.

"But that night was different," she said. "You're different. Maybe it was improper without your consent, but I'm glad it happened. There is nothing about me or my feelings that are false."

"Neither are mine," I said.

We shared the rest of the night together, awake, hoping it would never end; however, dawn arrived regardless of our wishes. Appius did as he promised and registered Nubia's enfranchisement. He even spoke of it to very select audiences, but only as an example of his reformed character.

I tried hard not to dwell on Nubia, but it was difficult. We'd glance at each other during meals and we spoke on occasion, but the intimacy we once shared was over. Her life had been an education in adaptability, and she was far better at it than I was. The issue of the child had become my greatest dilemma, but it represented such deep, personal pleasure for her that I decided not to discuss it further. My feelings were muddled and confused at best. The situation just felt wrong to me. However, it was clear that I was the only one plagued by such concerns. From Appius' perspective, everything was morally acceptable and perfectly on schedule.

Paris had completed all the restoration work on the main house prior to the Ides, and had moved on to plastering the bath. Sporadic ground tremors continually threatened his finish work, but he had developed a method of plaster reinforcement that seemed to retard the spreading of new cracks.

He was also a man of ideas, and he would share them with us at evening meals. Life in the household had elevated his self-esteem, and while he was a little naive, no one could deny his honest desire to help. He was still young, and from listening to the conversations between Thalese and Appius, he spent much of his time studying business and politics.

Appius grew fond of Paris, and with the villa nearly repaired, he offered to buy out my work contract with him. I found it curious at first, but Appius explained how his enterprises in Rome had grown to the point where he felt he needed a junior assistant to oversee the operation. He said he made two to four trips to Rome per year, spending close to four months total at the Villa North, not including travel time. As it turned out, he was indeed thinking of running for political office, and should he succeed, his trips to Rome would have to be cut back or put on hold altogether. Paris had proved he had a knack for commerce, and with a capable aide to travel between the two households, Appius would have the time he needed to pursue his political aims at Pompeii.

On the eve of my adoption, I couldn't imagine a happier household than the one I lived in at that moment. The atmosphere was infectious, with everyone working together and fully enjoying each other's company, including Caelus. Our daily workouts had evolved into carefree games of skill, and since the need to impress people with my physical abilities had been satisfied, I truly enjoyed the exercise. Caelus could always move quickly and run in sudden bursts, but I introduced him to jogging at which he proved to be naturally gifted. Every other day was set aside for distance runs done at a sustainable pace which often lasted as long as an hour. His stamina in all things was phenomenal.

That afternoon we put on a lighthearted display of wrestling in the courtyard for the family and a few impromptu guests, and afterwards I joined Appius at the bath.

"You've come a long way very quickly," he said as he eased himself into the heated bathwater.

"I'm trying," I told him. "I've still got a great many things to work on, but all in all, I feel pretty good. And you've come a long way yourself." He leaned back and closed his eyes to enjoy the moment. "What about Appia?" I asked.

"What about her?" he said.

"Is she actually freeborn?" I asked.

"What?

"Never mind," I said. "I'm speaking way out of turn. Sorry."

"Does this have anything to do with that spat you had with Sextus?" he asked.

"It did," I replied. "At your party I overheard him questioning Appia's legitimacy."

"He had no right to do that!" he said angrily. "Appia is freeborn. She's in the census as such."

"So am I," I said, "and we both know that's not legitimate."

"We know nothing of the sort!" he stated emphatically. "You're in the census therefore you're legitimate. End of story."

"Fine," I said, wishing I hadn't brought up the subject.

Appius relaxed and let the soothing warmth of the bath work its wonders. "Appia was my second child," he said calmly. "Leita was supposedly barren. I originally refused to acknowledge my role in Appia's conception and I handled it badly." He paused and studied me for moment. "Please keep this conversion just between us."

"Of course," I said. "So, Leita is Appia's natural mother."

"My wife Lucrecia was unable to have another child," he explained. "She nearly died giving birth to Maria Prima. I wanted a male heir, but it wasn't happening. Leita's pregnancy came as a complete surprise. She was supposedly infertile. But she gave me a girl when I needed a boy. I had no interest so I did nothing."

"What was there to do?"

"I should have proclaimed her my daughter immediately," he said. "I should have drawn up a birth certificate at her birth. Instead, I vacillated, bemoaning the lack of a male heir. I was stupid!"

"She doesn't have a birth certificate?"

"First off," he explained, "birth certificates are not required, but they can be of great benefit should freeborn legitimacy ever come into question. Appia has one. Postdated. Listing Lucretia as her birth mother."

"Does Appia know any of this?" I asked.

"Part of it," he replied. "She knows her birth certificate was postdated, but she doesn't know Leita is her birth mother. You once asked why she remains unwed. Once again, that's on me. Her prime years were lost due to circumstances...my folly."

"I know you were driven from here," I said. "To Gaul I believe."

"Do you know why?" he asked.

"I know Appia was assaulted."

He nodded. "Did she tell you?"

"No," I replied, "nor have I mentioned it to her."

"Unfortunately," he said, "such events do more than personal harm. They can also rob a young woman's marital value when virginity is a key factor," and he chuckled sarcastically. "I have had offers to buy her. Some quite lucrative."

"You thought about selling Appia?"

"Absolutely not!" he replied. "All they wanted was her body to sell by the hour. It's illegal for married men of our rank to have extramarital relations with freeborn women. That's why fallen freeborn women command such high prices in that somewhat less than legal market. I'd sooner die than subject her to that. I love her too much."

"But no offers of marriage?"

"There have been inquiries," he said. "Mostly much older men. All came after I'd reestablished my honor and returned to Pompeii. That was eight years ago."

"You apparently turned them down," I said.

"No," he replied with a smile, "Appia did. Those decisions are hers alone. None of my peers understand that. But she is her own person and I love her for it."

"Ya, well," I said, "I understand it and I applaud you for it. Interestingly, it didn't sound like Sextus and his friends know about Appia's assault. I might be wrong."

"You're probably right," he said. "That was thirteen years ago and we left for Gaul right after. Given all the political upheavals and purges during our years away, a lot of things were forgotten. Some conveniently so. Anyone who sided against Vespasian, or any Flavians or friends of the Flavians, wants those days dead and incinerated. I have a long memory. I know who turned against me and they know I know. Trust me. They aren't about to say a damn thing."

"You know your daughter's an incredible person," I said. "To have suffered abuse and gotten beyond it to become such a strong and self-confident person is remarkable. I'm sure you had a lot to do with that."

"Leita was the one," he said. "She's no stranger to abuse, and her experience and her love brought Appia back to us."

"But you've never told Appia about Leita," I said. "Why not?"

He shrugged. "Appia was the light of Lucretia's life and Appia loved her mom. I believe the attack on my daughter caused the illness that killed my wife. The gods should have punished me and not her."

He may have been right, but not for the right reasons. Grief and depression can make people more susceptible to disease, not to mention the added effects of sudden homelessness and a harrowing trip north to Gaul. It's a wonder any of them made it. "Will you ever tell her?"

"I was planning to," he said. "I was waiting for the right time."

"She is in her twenties," I reminded him.

"I know." He smiled and he looked at me. "Your arrival has brought me great comfort. I know she'll be alright after my passing. That she'll be safe and happy."

"You look pretty healthy to me," I said, "so I expect you've got a lot more life to live before you have to worry about that."

Appius felt a good night's sleep would be more beneficial than any adoption eve celebration we might be thinking about. He understood our desire to celebrate, but promised a big surprise after the adoption, followed by, "the greatest celebration to hit these parts in a long time." I could see by Thalese's smile that he knew what Appius meant, but he wasn't about to tell.

XVII

∞

I went to bed relaxed and at peace that night. I was feeling good. I was feeling strong. The injuries and illness that hampered me upon my arrival at the villa were healed, but for one. Dizziness coupled with disorientation remained an issue whenever I tried to access my lost memories. Like vertigo, each bout came on suddenly, but unlike vertigo, I could quell the effect by relaxing my mind, which is exactly what I did. I didn't want anything to spoil the moment.

As I happily drifted into deeper phases of sleep, it soon became apparent that my subconscious mind wasn't on the same comfy, serene page with its conscious counterpart. Images began to appear that I hadn't encountered before. There were tall maple trees with fiery colored leaves, their trunks surrounded by perfectly manicured grasses. I saw a wooden barn and a rusty white pickup truck. "What?" I was suddenly awake and sitting up. "What the hell was that?" I said as I tried to catch my breath. "A truck?" I was shaking and sweaty as I forced myself to focus on the imagery of that dreamscape, but then a heavy rush of dizziness and disorientation shut everything right down. I felt nauseous and I had to lay back and let it pass. "This is freaking ridiculous!"

"Getha?"

"Leita?" I replied as I recognized her voice.

"Are you all right?" she asked. "I heard you yelling."

"Sorry," I said. "It was a nightmare and nothing more."

"Are you sure? I could stay with you if that would help?"

"I'm fine," I said, "but it would be nice to get through one night without this mental silliness."

"Alright," she said. "You know where to find me if you change your mind."

"I do," I told her, "and thanks."

My nightmares had been getting progressively more elaborate and absurdly contradictory. I knew what a truck was, but I also knew nobody else would. I had to wonder if Appius was right about me.

I finally managed to fall asleep and the next thing I remember was Appius waking me at first light. The dizziness was gone. It was a new day. A beautiful day. A day to put aside all doubts and disquieting dreams. A day to simply enjoy and share in the company of those I'd come to love. I felt like a great weight had been lifted and I didn't want anything to disturb that.

The whole household was going to the Forum for the event. That meant the villa would be empty. Pompeii was not without its share of burglars and burglaries. That's why all first-floor windows were either very small or had bars. I couldn't risk losing my vest, so for peace of mind I wore it under my toga.

I joined Appius who was waiting patiently for me in the atrium, and with Thalese as our escort, we set out for town. Our first stop was the familiar public baths south of the Forum where I'd had my run-in with Sextus. Appius seemed to love the attention from friends and well-wishers, and we spent some time socializing. From there we began again for the Curia, but with many of those we met tagging along beside us.

We entered the Forum at the southern end and found Appia waiting. By design, Appia was there to join us for the walk across the Forum to the Temple of Jupiter. It was the way Appius wanted it. His new son, and the daughter he loved dearly, were to make the symbolic trek with him.

The rest of the plan called for Nubia and Appia's sister, Maria Prima, to join us when we emerged from the Temple of Jupiter, and from there the five of us would return home as one family. Caestus, Maria Prima's husband, was conveniently out of town. His absence greatly pleased Appius.

Thalese and Leita were to return to the villa once the Curia had ratified the adoption to begin final preparations for the post-adoption feast. Paris and Therasia were not present as Appius had sent them to Oplontis on a business matter, and Caelus's job was to escort Nubia to the Temple of Jupiter. Appius had the whole day planned and orchestrated for maximum effect, and the results of his efforts were already evident by the way the Forum was filling with people.

"Come," Appius said with a smile, and I followed him inside the Curia which was at the opposite end of the Forum from the Temple of Jupiter.

It was difficult to see once inside because our eyes were still adjusted to the bright daylight, although I could feel the many eyes scrutinizing me.

Appius spoke first, and as my eyes adjusted, I began to recognize many of the men in the room. Most sat with stern expressions while others had genuine smiles. He spoke of family and honor. A few of his clients offered positive words of support, and then Appius asked for Curia ratification of the adoption. Supposedly, the ceremony was unnecessary. The adoption was a done deal, but unanimous approval by the town fathers was an added layer of security, making it next to impossible for anyone to question the legitimacy of my name.

When I heard Appius ask for their approval there was a momentary silence, but then he was rewarded with a healthy chorus of yeas. I was then proclaimed Appius Marius Valerianus Getha of Pompeii, giving me a new name and official home. After accepting congratulations and hearty handshakes from everyone in the room, we finally left the building.

"What would you have done if someone had disapproved?" I asked Appius once we were outside in the bright light.

"No one would," he replied confidently, "as I already explained to you, I only gamble when I know I can't lose." We chuckled and stepped out to where Appia was waiting to join us. Appius raised my arm in the air in a triumphant manner that brought cheers from the many well-wishers who had crowded around us at the south end of the Forum.

"I told you I had friends," he said as we began our slow journey across the square to the meet the priests inside the Temple. He would use them to provide the final act of social legitimization.

People continued to gather, creating an almost carnival like atmosphere. Appius was the center of attention, and I'd never seen him so pleased. He appeared to know everybody and called each one he greeted by name. Unlike those I'd seen at the villa and in the Curia, it was a group primarily made up of working-class freeborns, many in the textile and shipping businesses.

What had begun as a medium size group burgeoned into a large procession that was barely making its way across the Forum. That gave me time to study the many faces that gleefully moved with us. It struck me, however, that they were mostly men, and virtually all unfamiliar to me, and then I noticed my toga and how it had already started to loosen around my shoulders. It seemed I just couldn't wear one properly for any length of time. I had a habit of pushing against the tight areas until the clasp either bent or the material gave a little.

"Oh well," I said as the feeling of liberation was welcome, and then I looked up at the sky to note that even the gods had seen fit to provide a perfect day. Clear skies were pretty much the rule, and the temperature was more comfortably cool than I expected when I got up.

My eyes were drawn to a two-storied portico leading to a building that looked to have something to do with textiles. Above the first-floor columns were carved the words CONCORDIA AUGUSTA, among others. I stopped as a chill ran through my body.

I looked around at other buildings, and then to the mountain, and back to the words CONCORDIA AUGUSTA. It wasn't the meaning that had my attention, but the carved letters themselves. I'd seen them before. I'd stood in the exact spot and seen those exact letters, but the building I pictured in my mind was different. It was in ruins.

"Italy?" I uttered. "My god!" And I scanned the scene again as a wave of dizziness nearly upset my balance, but this time it was followed by a flood of conflicting, yet familiar information. It was jumbled, and none of it made sense, but for the first time it felt like I had a tangible hold on something of my true past. "What am I doing here?" I said under my breath.

"Congratulations!" a cheery voice said as I felt my arm being taken in a friendly Roman style greeting. I returned the gesture, but was too excited to fully focus on what was happening around me. "Thank you," I replied to another well-wisher as I looked at the mountain. There were more greetings but I wasn't focused on them. I'd been suddenly thrown into a mental state of confusion with too much information coming at me at one time. "Thank you," I repeated, but the sensation of disorientation was growing progressively worse, and I found myself in desperate need of a quiet place to think. That's when I heard a piercing scream followed by an audible groan that rose from the crowd.

I looked for Appius, but he'd gotten several feet ahead of me and I couldn't locate him. "Appius!" I yelled as I quickly regained my focus. I began pushing my way through the crowd. I hoped that he'd just stumbled, but I feared something worse, and then I was bumped from behind. In the same instant a sharp, searing pain shot deep into my left shoulder. There was the turn of a blade and I heard my vest tearing beneath its wool covering.

"Damn!" I screamed in agony, and as I spun away, I caught sight of a bloodied knife blade rising to make a second strike. I immediately dropped to the ground as all remaining mental confusion vanished. I have no recollection of drawing the gun from beneath the tatters of my torn clothing, just the loud bang when I locked both arms straight out and squeezed the trigger. An adrenaline enhanced fear drove me, and I rolled away from the falling body before it smacked the ground. People began to scurry in all directions. I jumped to my feet, hastily ripping away fabric until I finally had complete range of motion.

I could see where Appius was down, and through the crowd I saw a man above him tucking a blood-stained knife beneath his toga. I raised my weapon to intercede, but to my left I saw a man grab Appia roughly by the throat.

Bang! I dropped her assailant with a single shot to the face a split second before he could slit her throat with the hooked knife in his hand. Blood and tissue sprayed in all directions as his body crumpled to the ground. What followed was like some sort of dream sequence to me. I felt no pain or emotion. There was no thinking or confusion, just a cold singularly focused resolve. I turned to the right and fired two shots in rapid succession at Appius' fleeing attacker, both ripping violently through his back, sending him sprawling, arms out, and face first into the white limestone flooring.

The frightened crowd scurried for cover while I continued to pivot menacingly in all directions until the Forum was cleared. Three assassins lay dead on the ground, but the damage I feared most was done. Appius had been struck with multiple knife wounds, and his motionless body rested unceremoniously in a pool of blood. Appia knelt whaling at his side, clutching at his lifeless form.

I wanted to cry as my emotions returned, but I had to stay in control and think of a way out. Appia was blood stained and visibly upset, but otherwise appeared physically unhurt. I reached down to check Appius' pulse, but quickly stood again as the clatter of cleat treaded boots drew my eyes to the south end of the Forum where a small band of plainly dressed soldiers entered with swords drawn and javelins at the ready. They were taking aim at us.

"Stay back!" I yelled and I fired a warning shot into the air. "What do you think you are doing?"

The crack of the exploding shell stopped the group briefly, but after a few seconds they cautiously inched forward again. At first there were six, but then from the basilica entrance came two more holding tall bows, and then I heard the sound of heavy sandals coming from the north, and I spun around to see a pair of archers entering from the right of the Temple of Jupiter.

"Don't!" I yelled in panic while pivoting back and forth in short rapid motions to try and cover both groups. "Don't, or you die!" I pulled the trigger again to fire a second warning shot, but heard only the click of an empty chamber. The gun was short one round.

"Shit!" I muttered under my breath, but I kept calm enough to flip open the barrel and dump the five empty shell casings onto the ground.

"It will go easier on the girl if you surrender now," a gruff, commanding voice called out. I fumbled through the lower right pocket of my vest for the hand full of extra shells I knew I had somewhere on me. "She has a certain value if you know what I mean," he added. I could hear chuckling from behind buildings and columns.

"It will go easier on you if you leave us alone," I replied. My fingers felt like sausage links as I reloaded the gun, which I kept aimed at the soldiers so at least I'd look dangerous. Those few seconds seemed like an eternity, and the instant I snapped barrel in place, a loud command rang out and the soldiers moved to let loose with their weapons. The die was cast.

My whole body was a mass of compressed nerves set to react in an instant, and the two archers by the temple were down before drawing their bows. A javelin whisked by my shoulder from behind as I turned and dropped onto the hard flooring, and then I heard the subtle rush of an arrow passing by my left ear.

Two more shots from ground level felled the other archers, while a pair of poorly thrown javelins from retreating soldiers clinked across the stone surface behind us. Appia hugged her father, making her a low target. I could finally check Appius for a pulse. Even though I was certain of the result, I would never have forgiven myself if I hadn't checked.

"They want to kill us," I said in nervous disbelief as I released his arm and began to confront the situation. "Why?" An eerie silence followed, broken only by a light breeze and Appia's quieted sobs. She seemed oblivious to our plight. I had to think.

We were surrounded, but our attackers were clearly confused by my weapon and had no idea how vulnerable we were. I wondered where Caelus was. We could certainly have used his help, but it wasn't hard to realize he'd been attacked as well. Heads were peeking out from behind columns. It was clear some soldiers were using the buildings as cover in order to inch their way closer.

"We've got to go," I said and I reached for Appia's arm.

"No!" she cried out while tightening her grip on her father.

"We've got to go now!" I repeated, and I grabbed her wrist. "Please!"

I was hurt and bleeding. The pain in my shoulder might have disabled me had it not been for the fear that kept me focused.

People were starting to edge back into the open areas, so I spun around with the pistol pointed, and they scurried for cover again. My heart was in my throat. Our escape was taking far too long, but just as I reached for Appia again, a familiar figure, braced by a pair of archers, approached from the north.

"Marcus Piso," I yelled in relief at seeing a friendly face.

He stopped and stared. His expression was that of disbelief. "Why is this barbarian still standing?" he hollered. "Kill him! Kill him and his bastard sister!"

The archers aimed, but I fired. The first fell before he could get set, and the second dropped his bow and ran the instant I took aim at him. That left Marcus alone, and no more than 50 feet away. I looked at Appius on the ground, and then back at Marcus. There was one more live round in the barrel.

"You killed my friend," I said angrily as I placed my finger on the trigger. "My father."

"No!" he replied. "You killed him!" He was spitting mad. "You and your subversive…treasonous ideas!"

"What?"

"We controlled Appius until you came along to infect him," he said in a nasty tone. "Who are you anyway? You don't talk like us. You don't act like us. A god perhaps?" He stepped back. "I doubt it. Look!" he yelled for all to hear. "The mighty god bleeds!" and he turned and ran for the nearest archway.

I was ready to shoot, but I hesitated, and then a sudden crackling sound broke at our feet sending sharp splinters in all directions.

"Ohh!" Appia cried out in pain. An arrow fired from a hidden position had caught the edge of a limestone paving block and shattered. Appia stood up with a piece of the shaft lodged in her arm.

I returned fire in the general direction of the Curia, and then drew Appia close to protect her. Her wound looked ugly, but the large, wooden splinter was at an angle and not deep, so I yanked it from her arm.

Time was up and I knew it. No doubt the initial shock of my surprising power had been diminished by the fact I was visibly wounded. Soon arrows from hidden positions would fill the air, and I could hear movement closing in on both sides from behind the columns and building facades.

When I wrapped my good arm around Appia's waist to usher her out, I caught a glimpse of my own blood that had painted the ground with a smattering of small drips. This can't be happening, I thought as bits and pieces of lost memory produced an image of Christina, followed by a rush of images, my entire life – my life as Aaron – flashing before my eyes. "Help," I cried out as I looked to the sky, and with no live rounds left in the barrel to further frighten our pursuers, about all I could do was aim the gun menacingly and back away. The chase was on.

I could hear the distant sound of armor clattering behind us as we passed to the left of the Temple of Jupiter. Despite my mental disorientation, fear kept my mind sharp. I knew soldiers would attempt to close in on us quickly, so I deliberately took a right at the Forum baths to make it seem like we were heading west and towards home. That maneuver blocked their view long enough for us to take an immediate left in an attempt to sneak out via the coastal route unobserved. We would exit through what I knew as the Herculaneum Gate in my time. It was the only trick I could think of, and not all that tricky, but I was hopeful it would buy us enough time get beyond the city walls. As we half ran and half stumbled in our cumbersome clothes, I felt around in my pockets for any more live shells that remained.

The ploy had apparently worked, but I knew it would gain us only a moment or two at most, and then we heard something neither of us had ever heard before in Pompeii, the sound of military trumpets coming from inside the city walls. I knew it had to be some sort of alarm, which meant the trap went beyond the area of the Forum.

"Can we hide in a building?" Appia asked as we passed by one under repair.

"No," I replied. "If we don't get outside the city now, we never will."

She was struggling, so I dropped our pace to a fast walk as we turned onto the main road that led to the city gate. The soldiers may not have witnessed our maneuver, but plenty of townspeople had, so it was even more imperative that we got out as quickly as possible.

The gate looked quiet as we approached, but then Appia pointed out a pair of soldiers on alert manning the gate's upper level.

"Shit!" I said as we slowed our pace to avoid arousing suspicion, a silly notion considering our bloodied and disheveled condition. Rather than interfere, people simply fled. Thankfully, it cleared the street of uninvolved bystanders but unfortunately it left us alone in the open.

"I've never noticed soldiers on the walls before," I whispered to Appia, and as we neared the archway, I reloaded the gun with just three rounds. That was all I had left with me.

"They're not like any soldiers I know," she replied. "Certainly not imperial troops."

"Mercenaries?" I asked.

"Halt!" boomed a voice from high in the ramparts.

"Damn!" I cried out in English. "More fucking archers!" It was a race to the draw. I lifted the gun the instant they raised their weapons and fired twice. I missed with the first shot but hit the second archer squarely in the face.

"Aww," Appia groaned, and she turned away from the gruesome sight. I grabbed her arm to pull her under the archway, and out of the line of fire.

"The others must have heard that," I said between breaths.

"But why are they doing this?" Appia asked.

I didn't know any more than she did, and with her hand in mine we ran the rest of the way through the gate and outside the city. The other archer was waiting for us, but that's what I expected, so I turned and fired my last round before he could release his arrow. I missed. The bullet ricocheted off the tufa wall by his head. The crack and spray of stone fragments startled him, buying us time. I hurriedly pulled Appia with me to the side of the road to put a cypress tree between us and him.

One arrow whooshed by my head, and then another slammed into the stone pavement. There were lots of people around, but that didn't prevent our attacker from continuing to take pot shots at us from an ever-increasing range. We passed tombs on both sides before passing a series of shops on the right. I saw a narrow footpath between a pair of tombs, and steered Appia onto it. We were hidden briefly before the terrain opened up making us visible again. The situation was intolerable, and I frantically scanned the landscape for better cover.

Fortunately, the turmoil I'd caused seemed to have retarded the chase effort, and we safely reached a patch of woods just northeast of the city. It wasn't a lush hardwood forest, but at least the gangly trees provided some cover and a chance to slow down, and as we did, additional memories returned along with a chilling sense that more was wrong than just the attack. I should not have been there, much less a center of attention. It was all wrong.

"I'm sorry," I said as I stopped to give Appia a supportive hug. She was trembling, and her eyes appeared abnormally dilated. I checked the wound on her arm and found it closed, yet very red and sore looking. It was clear we couldn't keep up our frantic pace indefinitely. "How do you feel?" I asked.

"Sick," she replied in frustration.

The torn clothing around my wound was a problem, so I attempted to tear away more of it, but the vest material was too tough to remove completely. "I'm sorry, but we must keep going," I said. "They can't be very far behind." I was lucky in one sense. I must have moved just before being struck, because the knife entered at such an extreme angle as to have glanced off my shoulder blade. Of course that didn't make it hurt any less.

"I know," she replied somberly. "What do you think has happened to Thalese and Leita?"

"That's why we're going back to the villa."

She looked surprised. "Father told me long ago, that if an attack on him should ever succeed, the family should head to Rome."

"He must have known he had potential enemies."

"Certainly not Marcus Piso," she replied, "but ever since Gaul he's talked of situations where honor might dictate violence against him. But he never expected this."

"This attack was much more involved than just a couple disgruntled compatriots acting on honor. There's an army out there, and that took time and effort to plan."

"Unbelievable," she said, "a whole army. That means all the roads will be blocked."

"I'm not going to worry about that just yet," I said. "I've got to get to the villa first. I don't want to leave without the others."

"*We've* got to get to the villa," she corrected. "I'm not leaving your side," and she followed me to the southern end of the thicket where we could see our home in the distance. "Piso's smart. He must figure that's the first place we'd try to reach."

"On the other hand," I said, "he may think we'd be too smart to do something that predictable."

"Do you really think so?" she asked.

"Not really. For all we know he's got the manpower to cover the villa and the roads."

"Maybe," Appia said, "but maybe not. The soldiers in the city may be all he has if he was confident of trapping us there. The only reason we escaped is because of that noise maker you have, something he couldn't have known about."

The villa may not have been far away, but because of all the open land it took a couple hours to carefully circle around to reach a hidden position on the bushy knoll overlooking the back of the building by my room. After several moments of lying on the ground, studying the quiet scene through the brambles, it appeared safe so Appia started to get up.

"Wait," I said, and I grabbed her by the arm, "look."

From our elevated position we could see over the roof above my room, across the courtyard, and into the second story windows on the back side of the main house. The middle room was dark, but I was sure I saw something moving.

"That was close," I said.

"Will that help?" Appia pointed to my gun.

"No," I replied. "Its power is used up unless I can get to my room for more of these," and I opened the barrel and dumped out the spent shells. "This isn't good. I'll be too exposed if I try to go down there now."

"Maybe we can get closer after dark?"

"That's what I was thinking," I replied, "but for now we need to stay put."

"Do you really think we can get inside?"

"I don't know," I replied, "but if I can get to that narrow window at the back of my room, I might be able to reach the pouch I tucked in behind the closest bed post. Then I can use my weapon again."

We finally had a chance to relax, if one could call it that. We were both in pain, but I had the added discomfort of having discovered who I really was, and while all the pieces hadn't come together yet, I knew I'd come from a very different place.

"Getha?" Appia asked. "How did you know those streets well enough to find a way out of the city?"

I knew those streets from my era, but I couldn't tell her that. "You must have taken me there before."

"No," she said. "I don't believe any of us ever took you through that part of town."

She studied my expression, but before she could press her inquiry further, the thunder of soldiers on horseback drew our attention back to the villa. They quickly dismounted and took positions outside the walls in a way that implied a defensive posture. It was becoming clear there was more going on than just the search for us, and any idea of sneaking onto the grounds was out of the question.

I shook my head in frustration. "What else can go wrong?" and then I caught sight of the mountain. The fragmented pieces of my past life were quickly coalescing into cohesive memories.

"What is it?" Appia asked, picking up on my elevating tension.

"This is only June?" I said. "Is that right?"

"Why?"

"How about the year?" but as soon as I spoke, I realized she wouldn't be able to tell me in a way I'd understand. It didn't matter. The ship's target month was January which coincided with the month Appius found me. It was a good bet the year was 79.

"What is it, Getha?" Appia said. "You're scaring me."

I looked at the mountain again. Its shape was different from what I recalled from my era, but there was no mistaking it. It was Vesuvius, and no doubt preparing to play its most famous role in history. It was finally sinking in just how alien I was to her era. I remembered the *Principles of Conduct*. "I'm sorry," I said with watering eyes. "I really am very sorry."

"For what?" she asked as she took my hand. I couldn't tell her, so I tried to turn my attention to the soldiers positioning themselves around the villa, but my mind was elsewhere. There was no historical record of any such violence in the region of Pompeii prior to the eruption. The horrors we'd just experienced were not supposed to have happened. I felt sick. Piso was right.

"I'm so very sorry," I said. I looked again at the hazy blue/green slopes of Vesuvius. If there was any consolation, it lay with the mountain itself. The massive eruption that I knew was to come had the potential to minimize any historical damage I'd inadvertently caused.

Appia was puzzled by my comment, but not up to dealing with it. For several moments we observed the grounds below in silence as the soldiers continually repositioned themselves at greater distances from the villa walls, which meant they were getting closer to us.

"It looks like they're setting up a defensive perimeter," I said. "That will mean controlling the high ground. That means this knoll. We need to go."

"Where to?" she asked.

"I don't know," I replied. "Perhaps back to the trees."

More soldiers rode in. I studied their manner and confused variety of dress. Most of them wore what looked like a mixture of pieces and parts from several varieties of uniform. None wore the polished helmets and armor characteristically associated with Roman fighting men.

"Look," Appia said, "that fat one acts like some sort of commander."

"Nobody's taking him very seriously. Where do you think a motley group like this came from?"

"Hard to tell," she replied. "Marcus Piso has many outside connections," and she sighed, "I can't believe he hated father that much."

"Then you were aware of my confrontation with him in the Forum?"

"I was aware of everything," she replied, "but mostly I was aware of one brave man standing alone against an entire army."

"It's not bravery, Appia," I said, "it's called survival." The sky was darkening as an ominous, slowly rotating cloud moving in from the bay blotted out the sun.

She paused for a second to wipe a tear from her cheek. "If that was all," she said, "you'd have left me there."

A thunder clap drew my attention to the threatening clouds nearly overhead. I remembered how violent the storms could be when they came in off the water. Bright flashes of lightning were followed by rolling thunder as the storm seemed to have its sights on us.

"We need to find cover," Appia noted.

"I think our cover is finding us," I said as darkness spread over the land.

Lightning began hitting the ground close by, followed by a saturating, wind driven rain. The thunder was jarring, but we ran. We ran with the storm, hand in hand, away from the villa. We didn't look back until we reached the edge of a stand of tall fir trees. Nobody was following us, at least as far as we could see. The rain was heavy and cleansing, and despite the danger from above and beyond we stopped and drank from it.

When the veil of rain passed, we stepped into the trees for cover. Unfortunately, it wasn't dense enough to properly hide us, but Appia knew of a place closer to the mountain that would better suit our needs. It was a little bit of a hike through prickly brambles and brush to reach it, but it was well worth the effort. It was a small opening within a stand of mountain pines. The ground was soft with grasses and moss and near the center was the crumbling remains of an old building foundation. Appia explained that pirates once used the location to bury pilfered loot. The pirates chose well. There were no occupied structures nearby, and we were hidden from view in all directions.

"We can't get to Rome, can we?" Appia said as we sat with our backs against an exposed section of the old foundation.

"I doubt it," I replied. "Even if the roads aren't blocked, we're in no condition to make that kind of journey." I lifted her arm to look at how the rain had cleansed her wound.

"We need rest," she said and I agreed. She studied my wound while I reached into my vest and took out a pair of shiny packets.

"This might hurt a little," I told her while ripping open a packet and applying the greasy antiseptic gel to her arm, "but it will help your injury heal faster."

"It feels cool," she observed. "Will it help your shoulder too?"

"It should," I replied as she carefully spread the contents of the second packet over my wound as I had done for her. The feeling sent raw chills of pain to my teeth.

"Are you sure this stuff helps?" she asked after noticing my pained expression. There wasn't time to explain about germs, so I simply groaned an affirmative. "I think this is going to be sore for a long time," she added, and then she looked at the unusual markings on the packet. "What sort of writing is this?"

"I'm not sure," I replied as I took the empty packet from her. I wanted to give her a better answer, but I knew I shouldn't until I'd resolved the issue of how to handle my presence in her world. Ironically, the labeling contained Latin medical terms, which no one in her era would understand even if I tried to explain it.

"I think you know," she said.

"Not precisely. I got these from a doctor friend. I know what they're for and how to use them."

"A doctor friend? You're remembering things, aren't you?"

"Yes," I said with a sigh.

"You've been here before too," she said. "I mean, before we found you."

"Yes."

"I thought it was strange the way you knew those streets," she said. "Does that mean you remember who you are?"

I nodded. "I remember who I was, but I don't know who I am now." My cryptic reply confused her, but to my great relief she wasn't ready to dig any deeper.

Appia had courageously held her emotions in check long enough to lead us to a safe haven, but once we were in the woods she broke down. She clutched at my clothes and wept into my chest in convulsive, wailing spasms. The intensity of her grief worried me. All I could do was hold her and try to stay in control of my own emotions.

"Grieve for your loss," I whispered, "but don't compound it with guilt.

There was nothing you could have done. Hold on to the truth, the truth that he loved you more than anything else in this world, the truth that you brought him happiness each and every day. I know because he told me." When she stopped crying she sat and stared off into the distance as if in a hypnotic trance.

It was quiet in our hideaway lair. Only the sound of a light breeze filtering through the nearby trees broke the silence. I worried about those left back at the villa, lamenting my inability to save them. I was beginning to come to grips with the fact that my presence had changed the dynamic of the region.

The image of Christina flashed in my mind as it had earlier, followed by the images of Liam and Aine. I thought of the lab and I could almost smell the fresh coffee brewing as I remembered it on those cold winter mornings, and then I remembered the ship. It had to be around someplace.

I had recovered much of my lost memory, but gaps remained. I remembered my target was Pompeii prior the eruption of Vesuvius, but instead I landed near Rome. I remembered landing, and even where I landed. I recalled walking along the Tiber River to Rome and the docks and sneaking through a warehouse to avoid detection from ruffians bullying dockworkers. I saw barrels of corn being guarded by soldiers, and in my excitement, I was nearly run over by an ox cart. I saw great buildings and smelled some very pungent aromas, some pleasant, but others not. I remembered sitting on the steps of the circular temple at the Forum Boarium. The air was filled with the smell of fish, but that was also where I experienced my first bout of disorientation and momentary memory loss.

I recalled thinking I could still satisfy the project goals in Rome almost as easily as Pompeii, but that first bout of disorientation scared me enough to change my mind. Returning to the ship became my priority but I didn't go straight back. The Roman Forum was very close by so I decided to loop around Palatine Hill and pick up the river trail on the other side of the Circus Maximus. Of course, I wasn't expecting to walk in on an assassination. I remembered the chaos of the moment as I hustled out of the Forum. I remembered trying to ask directions and getting insulting replies. I remembered passing through narrow, garbage fouled streets lined with tightly packed, multistorey tenements, but that's where my memory stopped. I couldn't remember how I managed to get back to the ship, or how I ended up in Pompeii.

I removed what was left of my toga and vest. I spread the toga out on the ground for Appia to lie on. She curled up into a ball and went to sleep. Darkness was upon us by then, but I was still too stressed to sleep. I paced back and forth in an effort to remember what happened to the ship. I had no idea.

I finally grew weary and lay down next to Appia. The events relating to our escape were beginning to haunt me and my hands started trembling as if registering some latent sense of shock. The horrible images of what the bullets did to those struck returned in a clear and vivid fashion. I wanted more than anything to believe it was all some horrible dream, but I knew there could be no such easy way out. Aaron couldn't have done such things, I thought, but Getha had.

Hours later I awoke to the pleasant sound of birds and the pale blue of early morning light. I was groggy in a way that kept my mind void of thought. I was hungry too, so I started to get up.

"Whoa," I moaned when I moved. Pain and stiffness sabotaged that first halfhearted effort and I remained on the ground. My feet and arms were covered with small cuts and scratches as was the right side of my face. My left shoulder was nearly paralyzed by stiffness around the wound.

I turned to see Appia awake and sitting up, staring off into the trees. "There's an owl in that tree," she whispered. I saw the subtle outline of a large bird nestled in the branches. "Do you believe its hoot to be a bad sign?" she asked. "Or even a good one? I've been watching him for some time, and he doesn't seem to have much interest in our fate. He seems more interested in what moves on the ground."

I smiled. "To hear an owl hoot only means you've heard an owl."

"Some might consider that statement an affront to the gods."

"Perhaps," I said, "but an owl is still just an owl. It flies, it hunts, and it makes baby owls. If the true purpose of its existence was to provide us with insights into the future, then where was it yesterday morning?"

"You have a unique understanding of things. Your words have so often clarified much about life that I've questioned."

"And why not?" I said following a pain shortened stretch. "After all, you are my sister."

"That's true," she said with a smile. "You know your name has changed again?"

"Yes," I replied, "but I'm still Getha."

"Appius Marius Valerianus Getha," she said. "That's who you are now, and I know it made father proud." She studied me as I seemed to be staring off into the distance. "What are you thinking?"

"I'm going back to the villa," I said as I started to get up. "I've got to get inside somehow."

"Give me a moment to adjust my clothes," she replied.

I took a closer look at our wooded sanctuary. No place could be perfectly safe, but this was a good choice. The clearing was slightly elevated and surrounded by a small forest cluttered with untrodden brambles and brush. It was about as safe as we could hope for. "I'd feel better if you stayed here," I said.

"I want to be with you," she said.

"I know. I don't like the idea of going alone either, but it's suicide for us to try and enter the villa together. I'd rather know you were safe here."

"I can't do anything from here if you're caught."

"I don't want you to do anything," I replied. "If that happens you must go straight to Rome."

"I'd rather we're captured together," she said. "If you don't return, I don't want to be left wondering."

"No," I said. "You must remain safe, if not for yourself, for the others. There's nobody left in our family with more influence with the emperor than you."

She grew silent as she fought the urge to cry. "Then hurry back," she said, and she drew me into a hug. "I don't know how long I can handle being alone."

"I'll be as quick as I can," I told her. "I promise."

I left our hideout, confused and very out of sorts. I didn't know if it was the shock of the past two days or maybe there was just too much happening all at once, but I couldn't even begin to fully organize my thoughts and emotions. The newest emotion was guilt. My sense of responsibility was becoming as overwhelming as the situation itself, and not long after leaving the hideout, I broke down in tears.

I thought of Appius lying dead in the Forum and I realized I had no idea how much damage I'd caused to history. I wondered if there was any possible way to fix it. Obviously, I couldn't bring Appius back, but if I could find ways to correct at least some of the effects of the disaster, I might minimize its impact on the future.

Moving alone made the trip a little quicker as I jogged in spots; however, I wasn't prepared for what I saw when I finally reached the villa. The whole area had been turned into a military camp with a pair of large tents on the plain above the knoll that overlooked the back of the villa, and what seemed like hundreds of soldiers crawling about the place.

I flirted with idea of sneaking up on one of the bigger soldiers in order to knock him out and steal his clothes. Dressed like the soldiery I might sneak inside unnoticed, but such plans are better suited to movie scripts than reality. I couldn't get within fifty yards of the villa, much less an unsuspecting soldier, with so many troops clearly on alert.

I had no choice but to return to the hideout. It was dark, but there was enough moonlight to find my way back where I found Appia pacing in front of the old foundation.

"I was so scared," she said when she saw me.

"I'm sorry. I won't go off like that again."

"You must be hungry," she said. "I picked berries while you were gone. I found wild carrots too."

My mind wasn't on food. "The place is a fortress," I said sadly. "I couldn't get close."

"I'm just glad you're back."

The night was comfortably warm, and with our minds worn out and energies drained, we quickly dropped off to sleep. It wasn't until the morning sun rose above the surrounding trees that I finally came to. I'd been restless for quite a while, but I didn't have the willpower to fully awaken until it became a matter of comfort. Appia was already up and about and sat patiently waiting.

"We slept a long time," she said. "It must be midday. That's good."

We inspected each other's wounds. Hers were healing nicely while mine was uncertain. It didn't look infected, but it wasn't healing as quickly as I hoped. Appia helped me spread more antiseptic on it, but it bore watching.

"Feels like I've been hit by a wagon," I said.

"By the size of the bruise across your back," she said, "it looks like the wagon won."

As safe as our little sanctuary might have been, it offered little in the way of sustenance. The berries and carrots helped, but we needed more. Appia suggested sneaking into a nearby village, but if we were going to take that much of a risk, it seemed like we may as well go back to the villa. With time to think about what we were up against, I had ideas about how I might be able to steal what we needed and perhaps even retrieve my ammo. This time we went together.

It was foggy when we left our hideaway. The roadways were surprisingly devoid of people. It didn't take us long to reach the military encampment setup at the back of the villa.

"See the tents?" I said.

"Yes," she replied, "but where are the soldiers?"

"They're there," I assured her.

"It looks awfully quiet to me," she said. We watched for several minutes, but there was absolutely no movement on the grounds anywhere.

"You stay here," I told her. "I'm going to see if I can get a little closer."

"Getha," she said. "I'm not going to stay here alone."

"I know," I replied. "I'm going in for a closer look. If it looks safe, I'll motion for you to join me. I'm not leaving you here. I promise."

"All right."

I squeezed her hand warmly, and then pulled the gun out from its front vest pocket. The barrel was empty, but it still looked menacing, and perhaps it would work as a bluff. I gave Appia a quick kiss on the forehead and stepped into the open. I kept the gun low, and held it nervously with both hands while approaching the back of the first tent. The closer I got, the eerier the situation became. The area was dead silent. There wasn't so much as a bird singing, and although I was tense, my level of confidence rose. Either everyone was still asleep, which didn't make sense, or the tent was empty. I reached down along the lower edge and peaked in under the flap. The tent was empty, so I motioned for Appia to join me. She kept a low profile and we entered the tent together.

"Where do you think they went?" she asked.

"I haven't a clue," I replied, "and there's nothing useful here either." The contents consisted mostly of crude bedding and empty crockery. There were no weapons at all so we moved to the next tent. That tent was empty too.

"Do you think they're gone?" she asked.

"I don't know," I replied. "This is pretty strange. There are no weapons or much in the way of clothing, but there are personal items." I picked up a small chest. There were a few coins inside and a hairbrush. "This stuff wouldn't be here if they'd left for good." I gave the place one more look to make certain there was nothing usable, and then we crawled to a spot on the crest of the knoll overlooking the villa. A few of the bushes had been beaten down by the storm, but they still offered some cover.

The villa looked quiet. There were no guards posted or any movement in the windows above the peristyle, but Appia did notice wisps of smoke rising from the vent over the kitchen.

"This is too weird," I said. "Obviously there's somebody inside. But I think I can reach what I need, so please, stay here for now."

"What if I see someone coming?" she asked.

"I don't know," I replied, "but just don't yell. Stay put."

"That's not a very good plan Appius Getha," she said. "I can't simply lay here and watch you get caught."

"If it comes to that," I told her, "you'll have to. After all, you have the future of the family resting on your shoulders. If you can warn me without drawing attention to yourself, fine, but otherwise forget it." She wasn't happy with my comments, but offered no further objections.

I made one last scan of the area and then I crawled on my stomach down the slope to a point where the back wall blocked the view from the second story window. It all seemed too easy and I feared a trap. Once I'd reached the back wall of the villa, I looked back at Appia. I could see her in the bushes, and if I could see her, so could anyone else. There was no time to waste.

Once I'd reached the wall I stood up and stepped closer to the narrow window at the back of my room, and then I peaked in. "Damn," I said when I saw the room was so packed with furniture there was no view into the courtyard. They were using it for storage.

The opening was so narrow I could barely get an arm through, but by pressing my good shoulder into the slot I found I could touch the floor. I'd kept the extra rounds in a small leather sack right under the left-hand corner of the bed. They were just behind the front bed post and theoretically reachable. When I found the bed post and no sack, I thought someone had taken the shells, but it was just a matter of reach. With my arm tingling, and elbow joint overextended to the point of pain, I found the very edge of the leather. My strength was gone from the loss of circulation, but after a brief respite I reached in again and dragged the sack closer with my fingernails. The feeling of relief when I finally held it in my hand was short lived. Appia, for some inexplicable reason, had crawled out from under the bushes.

"Go back," I said in an excited but muted voice as I signaled for her to stay down.

"Getha!" she called out in a loud voice for the entire world to hear. She was pointing to the corner of the building by the latrine.

"Shit!" was all I could utter, and then I flipped open the gun barrel, managing to load only three shells into chambers as the rest spilled on the ground.

"Getha, no!" she cried out as I slammed the barrel shut. I stepped away from the wall with both arms out, the gun cocked menacingly forward.

"Get down!" I hollered to Appia.

Soldiers suddenly appeared from the left. They froze when they saw me. Their weapons weren't drawn so I held my fire. More soldiers entered from the right causing me to start inching back towards the knoll in order to cover both flanks. It seemed like the Forum all over again.

"Appius Getha! No!" Appia called out as she stepped behind me. "Brother. It's all right. These soldiers are friends! They're friends!"

"What?" I said while maintaining a defensive posture.

"These soldiers are the emperor's elite guard."

"Are you certain?" I asked, while noting their more professional appearance.

"Yes, I am," she said, and then she placed her hand over the top of the gun. "We can relax," she said as her voice trembled. "It's over."

"Really?" I was suddenly aware of how stunned each of the soldiers looked.

"Yes," she replied, "it's over. It's all over."

XVIII

∞

There was a collective sigh of relief when I lowered my arms and placed the gun back in its pocket.

"Appia," one of the soldiers said with a nervous chuckle, "I like your new hairdo."

"How are you, Cornelius?" she replied. "It's called, on the run."

"It's nice to see you again," another said.

"Hello, Darius," she replied as she wrapped her arm around mine. "Is this your command?"

"It is," he said proudly, and he stepped to the front.

"They truly are friends," I said while trying to stop shaking.

"That they are," she replied, "very welcome friends. I've traveled in their company with father before," and then she announced to the group, "This is my brother, Appius Getha."

"We figured that out all ready," Darius said.

"Is he as powerful as they say?" Cornelius asked.

She chuckled. "Let's just say it's a good thing no one flinched."

Darius approached us and saluted. "There are people inside who'll be relieved to know you're safe."

"Is Caelus here?" I asked as we stepped forward, but then I remembered the bullets I'd dropped on the ground. I was quick to pocket them in my vest.

"Caelus?" he said as his voice perked up. "Oh yes, he's here, and so is Mistress Nubia."

"How about Leita?" I was anxious to know.

"There may be a Leita," he replied, "but I don't know everyone inside. There's a servant by the name of Thalese, and of course the emperor."

"The emperor?" I said. "You mean the actual emperor is here?"

"I bet that was father's surprise," Appia said. "If the emperor was anywhere in the area he would certainly have come for the adoption."

The sight of all those soldiers still made me a little uncomfortable, and the fact they were apparently friends did not completely erase my paranoia. Marcus Piso was supposedly a friend too.

"You're still tense," Appia said to me. "I feel it."

"I know," I told her as I reached inside one of the vest pockets for the gold medallion Appius had given me. "Do you think this would be appropriate?"

"Very much so," she said with a smile, "and you can take your hand off that weapon now. If we can't put our trust in the emperor, then our situation's hopeless anyway." She took the medallion from me and placed it around my neck.

There were guards posted on both sides of the big doors and several impressive wagons and carriages parked just off the road next to the city wall, and then, just as we made the turn to enter, Thalese came bursting out with the biggest smile I'd ever seen him display. "Thank the gods that you're both all right," he said as he attempted to give us hugs; although, I had to politely back away due to my wound. "I knew they couldn't kill you."

"What of Leita?" I asked.

"She's inside," he replied. "She had a tough go of it. She'll be fine, but for now she's resting upstairs in Nubia's care."

"What happened?"

"We'll talk of it later," he said. "She needs rest right now. She's alive and we're all thankful for that."

"Where's Piso? What about his army?"

"Dead," he replied. "Most of his soldiers too."

"Come on," Appia said, "try to relax. The fighting is over."

Thalese told us we wouldn't recognize the villa because it had been trashed so badly, and he was right. The floor was mostly tracked dirt with places where the once beautifully inlaid mosaic tiling was broken up. There were several military style cots along the walls, and strewn about were broken bits and pieces of the furniture that once adorned the various rooms. All the statues were either smashed or disfigured.

He went on to explain the disposition Appius' body. As a final act of devotion, he used the confusion in the aftermath of the attack to organize an immediate cremation and interment to avoid the public abuse of Appius' body by his killers. Minimalist versions of the essential rituals were performed to ensure his spirit was at peace before his urn was placed inside the family tomb. A feast could not be arranged at that time, but thanks to the emperor, that rite would soon be rectified.

We passed through the atrium and into the courtyard where we were greeted by a pair of well-polished guards who immediately stepped aside.

Behind them stood a rather unassuming man dressed in a plane white toga. Although he was ruggedly built, there was a gentle, almost fatherly look about him. Appia started to cry, and then she rushed forward to greet him with a hug.

"Your father's passing was a great shock to me," he said solemnly as he took her into his arms.

"The emperor?" I whispered to Thalese.

"Yes," he replied.

The emperor said something privately to her that caused her to smile, and then he kissed her cheek before letting go. "This must be the man of whom all the talk is about," he said, and he began walking towards me. He saw the medallion around my neck and smiled.

"That was presented to me by my father," I said nervously.

"Indeed," he said with a nod of approval.

"You look tired," Appia said as she studied the obvious wrinkles under the emperor's eyes.

"Perhaps fatigue's all it is," he replied. "I've certainly felt better than I do today, but I'm sure it'll pass. Anyway, I've got excellent food coming, and spirited libations. The months to come will be trying as you make your way through the grieving and loss, but tonight I'd like to offer up a very special feast. We'll try to dry the tears for a few moments and celebrate the life of your father, and one of my dearest friends. I think that's something he would have liked."

"Thank you," Appia said graciously and she gave the emperor another hug.

I started to back away but Thalese stopped me. "Appius Marius Valerianus Getha," the emperor said, "your influence was strong with your father, and I'd like a chance to understand those things that made such an impression on him. But since I must leave tomorrow, would you consider a visit to Rome sometime in the future? Hopefully in the near future?"

"I would," I replied as it hit me that I was speaking to a real Roman emperor.

"Good," he said with a smile, "I'll be looking forward to it."

I didn't know how to properly take my leave, so I simply nodded and stepped back inside the main building. I met Caelus coming in the front entrance. I'd never seen him so intense and full of purpose. He was dressed in a gladiator style waist wrap and a leather strap that crossed laterally up over his chest and shoulder and down his back. There was a large and very lethal looking sword at his side. He greeted me with a hearty Roman handshake and said, "We're all proud of you master, really proud!" He started to give me a slap on the back, but stopped when he saw the wound. "This is one tough freeborn," he announced to the soldiers in his company. "Trained him myself."

"It's good to see you Caelus," I said. "I knew they'd never catch you."

"They paid the price," he said in a strong voice, but then he mellowed. "Somehow it doesn't seem like enough."

"Try to relax," I told him. I could tell he hadn't completely let go of his anger. "I understand you're responsible for saving Nubia and bringing her back unharmed."

"Nubia is unhurt," he replied, "and still happily with child. I understand you returned Mistress Appia to us unharmed as well."

"She caught part of an arrow in her arm," I said, "but it's healing well, and otherwise she seems to be physically all right."

"You survived the attack in the Forum," he announced to all with delight. "There were more than a hundred mercenaries, and that was just in the Forum alone! And you beat the bastards! You beat them all!"

"I didn't see any hundred," I told him, "but I'd say we definitely lucked out."

"Right," he chuckled. "I saw the bodies of those you struck down. That was not luck that did that, but the hand of a greater power!"

"Caelus," I said, "I don't want to hear it. There was no greater anything there, just one mixed up human powered by instinct."

"I live on instinct," he said proudly and he slapped me on my good side. "Instinct is the gods work within us. It's when they take control of our actions." There was no sense in arguing, so I left him and went upstairs to look in on Leita. Nubia was there and we hugged. Leita was asleep. The room was kept deliberately dark with the shutters closed. I didn't want to wake her, but I took the chance to leave a kiss on her cheek before going.

"We'll talk later," I promised Nubia as I passed her on my way out.

The courtyard was a mess with all the greenery chopped and trampled and the statues destroyed. Even the fountain was knocked over; although, water still ran from broken pipes making the ground soft and muddy. All the back rooms off the palestra were stuffed with furniture and items that were considered in the way by the plotters.

I took enough time to empty my room and return the unbroken furniture to its rightful location. I was happy to see my bed still intact.

From there I watched the imperial servants work to prepare the courtyard for the promised feast. The broken pipes were pinched to give the ground a chance to dry out, and a tarp was brought in to cover soggy spots. There was a table and several seats added. Appia appeared with a fresh tunic for me. She'd found it stuffed in an upstairs room with other items of clothing and bedding.

"The bath is ready when you are," she announced. "At least they didn't ruin that."

"Thanks," I replied.

"How are you doing?" she asked.

"Not well."

"Me either," she said. "I can't stop shaking."

"Look at this," I said and I held out my right hand for her to see. It was visibly shaking. She held out her left hand which was trembling in the same manner.

"He's gone," she said.

"I know," was about all the prose I could manage in reply.

"I feel empty inside," she said, "like a big piece of my life has been stolen from me. I hope this is the end of the terror." As if on cue a tremor shook the room causing loose items to rattle and a cup to fall on the floor, but I remained quiet, knowing full well that another issue lay just ahead.

She walked with me to the bath where Thalese met us at the entrance. "Will you and mistress Appia be sharing the bath?"

We looked at each other and laughed. "Why not?" Appia said. "We've got no secrets left to hide." Meanwhile, Thalese spoke very highly of Caestus, Appia's brother-in-law, but not quite to the point of completely dismissing Appius' concerns. He believed Caestus to have been a fence sitter right up to the time when the attack forced him into choosing a side. Thalese believed the event made him finally take a stand and discover he had some backbone after all.

The emperor threw an impressive feast, and spoke eloquently of his friend Appius. He spoke of Appius's honor and bravery, touching on a time when enemy stones had cracked his kneecap and Appius rushed into a hail of arrows to help him to safety. When he finished speaking of Appius, he called his commanders together to issue an official proclamation. He stated that our villa and its inhabitants were to come under the protective jurisdiction of the Imperial Realm, and thus to attack it, or any of its people, would be considered an assault on the person of the emperor himself.

The feast continued well into the night even though the emperor retired early. The wine was sweet, and I allowed myself a little overindulgence because it temporarily freed me from my growing depression. Having my memory back had some benefits. I knew exactly who Commander Pliny was, and I made it a point to reintroduce myself to him and to his nephew when they arrived to offer their condolences.

I finally crawled into bed sometime after midnight. The bedding, that would be considered crude by the standards of my era, produced a feeling of pure ecstasy after the experience of sleeping on the ground.

XIX

∞

A long and frustrating year of digging through volumes of digital and printed material without so much as a scrap of corroborating evidence to prove Aaron's location had worn on everyone. On top of that, they were encountering issues with the science of time travel that limited their rescue options.

It had become clear that the ship's designed purpose was not voyages of discovery into the historical past, but rather a means of returning to the Date of Origin following a trip involving interstellar travel. That didn't mean such devices couldn't be used for voyages of historical discovery, only that this ship wasn't specifically designed for that purpose.

Kamden had done his part months earlier by breaking the alien codex with regard to technical data, but it was his discoveries of additional future human narrative records, including an operation manual and pilot's log that were most helpful. The log included entries from two piloted trips to the ship's Date of Origin in the Jurassic. In both instances the journeys were roundtrips without any stops during the return leg. In both instances the ship landed at precisely the same location in the Jurassic without issue; however, on the return the pilot was careful to land well beyond his/her starting point in the future.

That's when Kamden found the heading *Time Displaced Proximity* and a description of what happens when a time traveler or other complex living entity meets itself in the past. The good news was that such an event would not cause a violent reaction of galactic proportion, but the effect on a time traveler would be fatal due to a radical, uncontrolled cellular apoptosis, death on a cellular level. The future humans labeled the result *Inert Matter*. It also meant the planning for a rescue mission had become far more complicated.

"There's no third trip in this data," Christina said after having read Kamden's notes. "The ship was found in Jurassic stone. That means there was a third trip." The four of them were sitting around in the living room on a Sunday morning having coffee and discussing their findings from the previous month.

"I would agree," Kamden said, "but that's all the log data there is." He was referring the printouts Christina held in her hand.

"Interesting," she said. "No log data may mean no pilot and no pilot may mean they were trying to permanently lose the thing in the past. Get rid of it like we might be obligated to do at some point."

"I doubt that," Liam said with a chuckle. "You wouldn't send a time ship into the past to lose it. Somebody might find it. Like us! If I wanted to get rid of it, I'd blow it up! Boom, gone!"

"Good point," Christina agreed.

"But not my point," Kamden said. "We need to discuss *Time Displaced Proximity* because it will affect any rescue plan that involves sending the ship to a date and place in time where it's already been."

"We know enough not to land at the same spot," Christina said. "That's common sense."

"That may be so," he said, "but there's a lot more to it than that."

"Of course, there is," she uttered under her breath. "Let's hear it."

"From these log entries," Kamden began, "the only location where the ship can repeatedly return to in time and space without proximity issues is its Date of Origin. In our case, that Date of Origin is the Jurassic."

"Interesting," Christina said. "It seems like that would be an issue too."

"History," Liam quipped. "The Date of Origin is the first instant the ship was powered up after its construction. It has no history so it probably becomes one with itself or something like that."

"Time is not a constant throughout the universe," Aine said. "That has to figure into this somehow."

"No," Kamden chuckled, "forget that…"

"That must mean," Christina said, "that a time ship meeting itself anywhere other than its Date of Origin will have experienced different histories. It would be impossible for the two selves to rectifying such anomalies, which, for lack of a better description, would cause them to cancel each other out."

"Please," Kamden said sounding like he was getting frustrated. "Would you please just listen." They all stopped talking. "I'm sorry," he said, "but sometimes we lose focus when you all go off on tangents."

"Sorry" Christina said.

Kamden smiled. "Let's look at the 'whys' later and focus on just the facts themselves that pertain to our planning."

"You must have new research data," Christina said.

"From the Operation Manual," he replied.

"You finished deciphering it?" Aine asked.

"Yes," he replied. Now everyone was smiling. "Firstly, the Date of Origin is fixed. On this planet it's 172 million years ago. That's when the ship was first turned on, or made alive as the future humans call it...or will call it."

"That part we know," Christina said.

"Secondly," he said, "all other stopping and starting points are labeled as either *Journey Starts, Journey Stops* or *Journey Ends*. Our Journey Start was when Aaron begin the trip to the Date of Origin. Our Journey Stop is when he landed in 69 CE Rome, and the Journey End is when the ship returned here at the end of its programming."

"Common sense I suppose," Christina said.

"But not quite what the alien builders had in mind," he said. "Their Journey Start was also the Date of Origin. The ship we have was built, activated and stored somewhere on a home planet while separate interstellar spacecrafts took those alien travelers to star systems lightyears away. Of course, that meant that their home planet will have aged perhaps hundreds of years into the future upon their return."

"I see," Christina said with a smile. "So, when they got home, all they had to do was pop into one of these smaller ships and be back to the Date of Origin in less than a second. I didn't think it made sense that such a small ship would be suitable for interstellar trips. That's good information."

"I'm bringing up the alien piece," he said, "because you need to know where the future humans got their data. They made just two trips, without any Journey Stops along the way. Their operation manual covers Journey Stops, but that material is solely based on what future humans were able to translate from alien data. I might add that the data from the two trips they made confirmed what the aliens had written regarding the other two phases."

"That's good," Christina said.

"Okay," Kamden sighed, "now let's get into the not so good news. There are serious proximity complications with regard to a time ship returning to a Journey Stop where it's already been. That will most likely limit us to just one shot at a rescue because we can't return to a previously visited location in time and space."

"I'm not ready to think about second attempts until we have a plan for the first," Christina chuckled. "What would be helpful to know is how close we can get to Aaron's first Journey Stop in 69 CE Rome. If we arrive ahead of him, we can potentially send him home and avoid this mess altogether."

"Two of us could make the trip," Liam added. "One flies the ship home while the other waits for Aaron. Proximity issues averted. Disaster averted."

Everybody turned to look at Kamden.

Kamden took a sip of coffee before looking up from his printouts. "What?" he said.

"Where's the problem with that idea?" Christina asked.

"Who said there's a problem?" he asked sheepishly.

"I can see it in your eyes," she replied.

"I'm sorry," Kamden said. "You must think I'm looking for problems. Well, actually I am. That's my job. Unfortunately, that plan is probably unworkable. It would require the person meeting up with Aaron to stay longer than is practical."

"I don't think a few hours will be a problem," Liam said. "I'll stay. I'll take a lawn chair and a book."

"It's not that simple," Kamden said.

"Of course, it isn't," Christina uttered.

Kamden ignored her cynical glance. "The ship creates a protective barrier when it's in motion. This barrier protects the pilot from the ravages of time and elevated levels of radiation. That's because the ship is subject to millions of years of solar and space radiation all condensed into the few hours when it's in transit."

"We know that, Kam," Christina said.

"But did you know that time travel creates a kind of temporal backwash?" he asked.

"Like a wake?" Liam said.

"Yes," he replied. "That's what the ship's sensors read in order to avoid proximity issues. The ship knows when it's getting too close to a previous Journey Stop or Journey Start when it's not its Date of Origin."

"Fine," Christina said. "What would be a safe buffer that will allow us to meet up with Aaron in 69 CE? Hours? Days?"

"More likely months to a year," he replied. "Call it a year to be safe. A temporal backwash remains a constant at the time and location of the landing. It affects both the past and future, but the good news is it dissipates in both directions of time and space as you move away from its focal point."

"But that contradicts what happened to us," Liam said. "When the ship returned, it was just a couple days after the launch. Not months. Days! And it landed only a few feet away from its departure point. I mean, Journey

Start."

Kamden shook his head in a very negative way. "The ship arrived here on a flatbed truck. It had never landed here under power until it returned from our trip. The trip to its Date of Origin in the Jurassic did not create temporal backwash. That phenomenon is a product of the return only. No landings, no backwash. Does that make sense?"

"Okay," Christina said, "but since then, the ship has returned. That's a Journey End. So, there must be backwash."

"No," Kamden replied.

"No?" the others said in unison.

Kamden sighed as if tiring of the conversation. "No. There was backwash, but it's been a year since the ship returned. I'm confident it's dissipated, but if it hasn't, I'm sure it will have by the time we're ready to affect a rescue."

Christina was most appreciative of Kamden's hard work, but saw how frustrated he was. "Thank you, Kam," she said warmly. "Take a break."

He nodded, but his mind was still working. "There is one other option. Distance. A time ship can occupy the same point in time with itself with enough physical distance between the two selves."

"Any idea of what that distance might be?" Christina asked.

"A couple thousand miles," Kamden replied with a shrug. "Probably useless for our purposes."

Another thought came to Christina. "Since the ship never came to a full stop at Pompeii," she asked, "was any backwash created?"

"Yes," Kamden replied. "The data didn't record a stop, but all it really shows is he never landed. The ship had to have stopped for at least a millisecond when it switched from landing mode to takeoff activation."

"Assuming for a moment that Aaron was onboard the ship when it reached Pompeii," She said, "is a millisecond enough time to bail out?"

"Yes," Kamden replied. "He still had a window of a second on either side of that millisecond. But I hate to think of how unimaginably desperate he must have been to make that choice. And if he missed, the radiation from being caught out-of-era might have..."

"Well," Christina said to cut him off, "I doubt he was aware of any of that," and she paused, "which brings up the next obvious question, did he miss that window?"

"No," Kamden stated with certainty. "Rest assured, I'd have seen it in the data. However, having no data for that brief instant when the ship switched between decent and ascent does not confirm the assumption that he bailed out."

"Thank you again," she said. "You've given us a lot to think about."

"One more thing," he said. They all looked like didn't want to hear it. "The last thing, I promise."

"Go ahead," Christina said.

"The future humans were studying something they call *Time Displacement Disorder*," he said. "One of the symptoms they considered important was what they called *Temporal Amnesia*. I thought you should know."

"Amnesia?" Aine uttered.

"Aaron wrote of memory loss in his log," Kamden reminded them.

"Could amnesia be related to speed through time?" Christina asked. "Aaron said he felt better when he slowed down."

"Maybe in part," Kamden replied, "but it's an impairment related to being displaced in time, or living in an era other than your own. It may be a temporary condition, but that's all I know so far."

"We need to find him," Liam said. "We need to go through all those books again, including the text. We need to look for anything, even the smallest anomaly might help."

"I'm going to go on the assumption that he survived," Christina said, "and that any amnesia was temporary, so let's put ourselves in his shoes. He's either stuck in ancient Rome, or more likely Pompeii. His memory is back, so he wants to come home. What might you do to get our attention?" She picked up one of the books Aaron had carried with him in the ship.

Liam smiled. "I'd make a sign," he said. "I'd do something to some thing for us to find."

"But we found nothing so far," Aine said. "That means either history can't be changed, or he died too soon, or he didn't think of it. Or maybe the amnesia was permanent."

"I think we need to expand our search to include more books," he said. "How would you feel about a trip to the Boston Public Library?" He was looking at Aine.

"I'll go," she chuckled. "I don't know why, but yes, I'll go."

"Christina gave him a Roman name," he said. "You can read Latin. He might be mentioned in the ancient graffiti, especially if the amnesia is permanent. Amnesia doesn't necessarily bury all knowledge, which could have given him an advantage. Who knows, maybe he became a politician or some other big shot? Check out anything that looks odd to you."

"I can do some of this online," she said.

"True," Christina agreed, "but there's a lot of imagery in books that have never made it to the Internet."

Aine was shaking her head. "I have to be frank. This feels like a wild goose chase to me. My time might be better served figuring out the amnesia piece."

"If this works you won't have to," Liam said. "We'll just go get him."

Aine had no idea where to begin once she entered the Boston Public Library. The task was overwhelming with, "exercise in futility," written all over it. However, once in a great while, something pertinent falls into your lap, and in this case, it literally fell into hers. She was sitting on the floor of the library, surrounded by books, when somebody reaching over her shoulder to return a book to the rack accidently dropped it into her lap instead. She wasn't hurt, and it was apologies all around until her attention was drawn to the cover. The book was entitled *Oopart: Mysteries of the Ancient World.* Oopart stands for out-of-place artifact. The book was about ancient artifacts and discoveries that were inconsistent with the eras they appeared to have come from. It included the two-thousand-year-old Baghdad Battery and the Antikythera Mechanism, but there was one item that immediately caught her eye. It was from Pompeii, entitled, "Your guess is as good as ours." The photograph depicted a clump of time-melded ancient coins, but circled in red within the hardened clump were two rounded yet smaller coins. They were different from the rest, being made of oxidized brass with a hole made of some other metal in the center. The entire clump had been lightly scrubbed to make any inscriptions at least partially readable, and while most of the coins displayed the figure of a ruler, the smaller two didn't. All they displayed were the digits 44 REM. They were empty shell casings.

XX

∞

Quiet returned to the villa following the emperor's morning departure. He was still feeling poorly and left a little ahead of schedule in order to save a day's travel. That left everyone in the household free to deal with their grief on a more private level.

I looked up from where I sat under the portico by my room and saw Appia walking towards me from the main house. She looked terribly sad. Had it not been for my influence, her smile would be brightening an otherwise gloomy and rainy morning because her father would still be alive.

"You're getting wet," I said as she stepped around the puddles. "Why not use the portico?"

"It fits my mood," she replied. "How are you, Getha?"

"Fine," I told her.

"You're not fine," she said. "That much I know, but at least we all have each other. Am I right?"

I saw tears welling in her eyes, so I took her hand and motioned for her to sit next to me. "I'm aware of the pain everyone feels right now," I said solemnly, "but the healing process may take longer for some of us."

"I believe it's best to share our pain as we shared our happier times," she said. "We need to stay together more than ever. And Getha, you're not just part of the family; you're the head of it. Everyone looks to you for leadership."

I rubbed my hand across the stubble on my chin and then wiped away the random wet hairs from my forehead. It was hard to think about the immediate future with the problems of the recent past festering in my mind. Circumstances seemed to dictate a withdrawal of my influence, but that would make it impossible to rectify the damage I'd already caused.

"That's what Appius intended," I replied, "but you're just as capable of filling that roll. Power and influence are not strictly a man's province. The family assets are still intact. You have a solid base to start with."

"It's not a role I can fill," she said, "and it would be good for you."

"Think about what you're saying," I said. "Are you willing to allow ultimate family power to rest in the hands of some stranger who basically showed up on your doorstep?"

"Yes."

"You know nothing about me at all."

"How can you say that after what we've just been through?" she said. "I have all the information I need."

"I'm not sure I can be what you hope for," I said as I stood up. "I'm terribly confused right now." I didn't feel like talking.

"You're trying to put distance between us, Getha," Appia said sounding upset. "Why are you doing that?"

I turned and saw her wiping away tears. "I'm sorry," I replied.

"I'd understand if you have to go, but at least talk to me about it."

"I've never said anything about going anywhere," I said. "I've had to do a lot of thinking lately."

"About your past?"

"Yes," I said. "There are aspects of it that have complicated things for me."

"And you can't share them with me?" she asked. "Thalese taught me a long time ago that it's just as important to talk about our problems as it is to share our good times."

"Thalese is a wise man," I told her, "but I'm not sure this is a problem I can talk about."

"The day you became my brother was the day you began a new life. Whatever failings or mistakes you believe you made in the past have no relevance here."

"It's not like that," I said. "My past is full of good times and wonderful people. The issue is how I got here and the fact I should not have come in the first place."

"I'm not good with riddles," she said, "but to me that sounds like you're at least considering leaving us."

"I didn't say that."

"I'm not stupid, Getha," she said. "It makes sense you would wish to go back to where you came from. You must have family and friends. If it were me, that's what I'd do."

"Let me say this," I said. "This is my home now. However, in the unlikelihood it becomes possible for me to return to my world, I will be obligated to do so. I will have no choice."

"Your world?" she said with surprise. "You come from another world? I thought there was just one."

"You can't imagine," I replied.

"Where is this world?" she asked. "I've traveled this one extensively with father and I've never heard anybody speak of a second world."

I saw Nubia across the way. She looked out over the courtyard briefly, and then returned inside. "You've been a very good friend, Appia, and I know I owe you an explanation."

"Yes, you do."

Telling her anything of my past would be considered a conscious breech of *The Principles of Conduct*, but after all she'd suffered because of me, she deserved to understand why. "Can I count on your discretion?"

"Of course, but why?"

"Because I'm part of a special project," I said. "I swore to obey a code of ethics we called *The Principles of Conduct*. My visit was supposed to be basically noninvasive. I was supposed to be here and gone in a few hours, and nobody would know the difference."

She saw the stress on my face. "What are you talking about?"

"Okay," I said, and then muttered to myself. "How do I explain this?"

"Just try."

"Okay," I said. "Here goes. It's not where I came from that's important, but when. When I came from." She looked completely befuddled. "I came from the future, Appia."

"Future what?" she asked.

I paced for a moment. Now that I'd decided to say something, I didn't know how to say it. "This is going to sound like I'm crazy, but technically I haven't been born yet. In fact, I won't be born for about another two thousand years."

"Oh," she chuckled and she rolled her eyes, "is that all?" She stood and placed her hand on my forehead. "You don't feel feverish. You must be having nightmares again."

"I wish that were true," I said as I brushed her hand away. "Dreams may occasionally hold hidden truths, but they don't replace reality, and I'm fully aware of the difference."

She took a moment to ponder my words, and then she gently ran her hand down the side of my face. "I trust everything you tell me," she said, "but I'm not sure I understand. I think of the future as what will happen next, like tonight or tomorrow or next year."

"That's right," I said. "I traveled through time from a distant tomorrow to find myself here with you today."

"How is that possible? I can't imagine such a god-like power in a human. I thought we agreed you have no divine connections? We did agree on that, didn't we?"

"Yes, we did," I chuckled. "I traveled here in a mechanism. It's a ship of sorts, but where your father's ships link Pompeii to places like Rome, Ephesus and Alexandria, my ship linked my era to yours. Unfortunately, there are still parts of my memory that remain hidden. I don't know where my ship is and it's unlikely I'll find it anytime soon if ever."

"But if you find it," she said, "you feel obligated to leave us. That you would have no choice. Is that what you're telling me?"

"Yes," I replied somberly.

She shook her head. "No. I understand why you would choose to go home, but don't try to justify it as an obligation. You do have a choice."

"You don't understand," I said. "I never should have come. I shouldn't be here."

"Okay, maybe I don't understand. But if you want to go home, nobody will hold that against you, least of all me."

"It's not a case of what I want," I stated in frustration. "I came here as an observer only. I was a student of this time in history. Tantalizing bits and pieces of your world survived to mine. I've read the words of Pliny the Younger, Tacitus, Strabo, and others, and I developed a passion to see your world firsthand, and with my special ship that dream became reality." I began pacing again, using my hands to help me articulate. "I studied your history. I can tell you who all the emperors will be after Vespasian. I learned your language as best I could. Latin dialects didn't survive to my era, only the words survived. That's why I had so much trouble in the beginning. I thought I was going crazy."

"It's okay," Appia said, and she stepped in front of me and took hold of my hands as I was wringing them.

"No, it's not," I said. "I wasn't supposed to interact with anybody here. The concern was that any changes I make in this world might lead to serious consequences in mine. We thought we had all the angles covered. We were wrong."

"Wrong?" she said.

"Very wrong," I said sadly. "The fact is I've broken practically every one of those *Principles* I mentioned earlier and history has changed. It's all my fault, Appia, and mine alone!" I couldn't look at her so I stepped out from beneath the portico and into the rain. I felt sick and I started shaking. I dropped to my knees. I wanted to die.

Appia remained in the shadows for a moment, but then stepped into the rain and knelt beside me. "What did you do that was so bad?"

"I came here, Appia," I said. "I introduced devices and ideas prematurely. I empowered your father with ideas from my era. He thought I was sent by the gods. I would have thought the same thing in his place!"

"You can't know that," she said. "Father was always considered eccentric."

"But not dangerous," I said. "From what I know of history there was no violence here. There was no battle like what we just experienced. I can only hope I haven't destroyed the future too," and I glanced around the courtyard while gruesome images of that horrific day played in my head. "I suppose it's possible the past can't be changed. There are great minds, academics, theoreticians, who believe it can't. I'd love for a few of them to be here right now to tell me it'll all be okay."

"I don't what an acad..tician is," she said. "All I know is that this is not the past. It's the present. It's the here and now."

I sighed and looked her in the eye. "But the violence did happen," I said, "and your father is gone. You have every right to hate me. You should hate me, Appia! What I've done is unforgivable!"

"Appius Marius Getha," she said sternly. "Never EVER speak those words to me again! NEVER! I'm amazed that you of all people could feel that way."

"Appia, you don't understand."

"No!" she shot back. "You're the one who doesn't understand! Just what are these heinous crimes of yours anyway? Suggesting ways to make life better for more people? Saving me from certain death?" I looked at her but said nothing. The rain was getting heavy again. "What of your so-called code of ethics?" she said. "How ethical is it to have the ability to better people's lives and not use it? I don't know about the people in your world, but we're people too."

"Yes, you are," I said. "Nobody knows that better than me. And I believed I was doing the right things, but I couldn't have been more wrong. I haven't just done harm to your world, I've potentially harmed mine, as well."

"Or bettered it."

"Do you call this better?" I said as I pointed at the mess made of the courtyard.

Appia sighed and looked to the sky as the rain splashed against her face. "Sometimes I love the rain," she said calmly. "It has a cleansing feeling that washes away the stress. I'm sick about father's death, but I could never blame you. He was an aging and forgotten man before you came. That's worse than death to a citizen of pride and honor. You didn't kill father. Words don't kill, but people do."

"Words alone can't," I said, "but they can inspire actions that do. Your father believed my words came from the gods. He believed the gods would protect him as well. I can't change what happened, but perhaps I can fix some of this mess before it cascades into something bigger."

"Then do it now," she said sternly, "because you've got a family to run," and she turned and left before I had a chance to respond.

Realizing I'd said too much, I retreated to my room, but she'd made a good point, I did have a family to run. I had no choice. Appius's death wasn't supposed to happen, but it did, and the security of his family, and all he owned, was now in jeopardy because of me. My status as the only documented freeborn male in the immediate family meant that security rested with me.

Ideally, I needed to oversee the family and its businesses as he would have, but I wasn't him. I didn't think like him, and I couldn't in good conscience be a slave owner. It seemed like an impossible dilemma, but after giving it some thought, I realized I had options. Pompeii was chosen to satisfy our project goal for good reason. Mount Vesuvius was due to erupt at some point between mid-August and November. It would destroy the entire region, and possibly my mistakes along with it. I realized it wouldn't be wrong to let Thalese manage the businesses in my stead, as he often did for Appius, while I created a freer environment within the villa walls that would not harm the future.

The first order of business was to stabilize the situation by reaffirming that the family had firm leadership. I knew that would help to lessen the uncertainly and fears of those whose fate is tied to the family. For that purpose, I called a meeting. Before entering the atrium, where everyone was patiently awaiting my arrival, I put on the gold medallion Appius had given me.

Everyone stopped talking the instant I walked in. I saw a look of expectancy on each and every face and I found myself trying to fight a sudden case of nervousness. "Has everybody got a cup of wine?" I asked while looking around the room. There was some bustling about as the various empty cups were filled. I lifted my cup as I would have in my era. "This is to the memory of Appius Marius Caupo," I said, "a man of courage and vision. May he continue to live through our good deeds." I paused and looked at Appia and then added, "A man I'm proud to call father. To Appius!"

"To Appius," they repeated in unison.

"Appius, yes!" Caelus said enthusiastically. "Now to Master Getha. I drink to Master Appius Marius Valerianus Getha!"

"And I drink to you," I said before he could finish, "all of you. You've all been put under a terrible strain by recent events and have performed marvelously. I'm proud to call you my family." I noticed Leita was there, so I lifted my cup to her while continuing to address the group. She had suffered terribly during the occupation of the villa. The fact she was able to join us was a tribute to her inner strength and courage. "I'm not going to pretend I can fill the gap left by Appius," I said, "however, as head of the household I'd like to make my first decree. You are all freed, or you will be freed as soon as I can make it official. There will be no cost involved. You're just freed." I expected some sort of reaction, but the look of horror I saw on their faces wasn't it. "I have that right, don't I?" I looked at Thalese.

"Yes," he said as he seemed otherwise speechless.

"You need to understand I find the words slave and family to be incompatible. There are no slaves in my family."

"What exactly does that mean?" Thalese asked.

"It means you're all free to live your life on your own terms," I replied.

"I'm no longer a slave?" Caelus asked.

"That's right," I said. "None of you are."

"What if we don't want to be enfranchised?" Caelus asked. I saw concern on everyone's faces.

"This is how it will work," I said. "If you wish to live here and do the same jobs, which I hope you will, nothing's going to change except you'll receive better pay on top of food and board. The difference will be that nobody owns you. Should something happen to me and Appia you can't be claimed as property by anybody." I could see Thalese shaking his head. "What is it?"

"That's not quite true," he said. "When an estate is dissolved, claims can be made on all personnel that have no means."

"Okay," I said. "You're in charge of finances. You figure it out so that can't happen." He nodded. "What I want to try is something called profit sharing. In other words, the profit made by the businesses will be divided up among the family members once all operational costs have been met."

"You mean we will be given more money?" Paris asked.

"No," I replied. "You will have earned more money. Bear in mind that this profit-based income exists only as long as there is a profit to be shared. Profit isn't always monetary either, so some of it may exist only in the ledger. We will need to make decisions about how to handle all of those sorts of things, but we can do this, and be better off for it."

"Interesting," Thalese said. "Does that mean everyone shares equally?"

"Good question. That's the type of thing we need to discuss as a family. I believe we all should have an equal voice in the decision making process. I'm taking an active lead now because we need a coordinator to get things started. As time goes on, and you people begin to have a better understanding of what it's all about, my role will become less important."

"And what about those outside the family?" Thalese asked. "We have many slaves and freed men working the shipyards here, in Ostia and Rome, and the Villa North has a full complement of domestic slaves you've yet to meet."

"I'm not sure how we'll handle that yet," I told him thoughtfully, "but any slave owned presently by the family will be freed once we've reviewed the situation and can make a smooth transition."

"How will you keep them?" Nubia asked. "They could just leave."

"That's always the risk," I replied.

"I like what I hear," Thalese said, "but I have a concern. If we divide up all the profit where will the reserves come from in case of a bad season? The reserve has saved us in the past."

"That's a great question," I replied, "and a perfect subject for our first family business meeting."

"I don't know much about what you're saying," Caelus admitted. "I could just walk out that door and no one would hunt me down?"

"That's right," I said. "Are you thinking of leaving?"

"No! I like it here."

"Is anyone thinking of leaving?" I asked. "You all have that right."

"No one wants to leave," Thalese said. "I think the only concern is with change. All of us like what you say, but we've been through so much change already. I think we'd all just like to get back into our normal routines for a while."

"I understand," I said, "but look around the villa. Does anything about our home look normal? I think this is the perfect time for change. It's not traumatic. The duties won't change. The sun will still rise in the east and set in the west. The change is huge on an operational level, but not on the surface if you don't wish it.

"We worry because we don't see things the way you do," Thalese said. "The only slaveless households I know are very poor ones. What makes you so certain these nice ideas can work?"

"That's another good question that deserves a direct answer," I replied. "The fact is I come from a slaveless society. A wealthy society where there are no slaves."

"Oh oh," I heard Appia utter.

"None?" Thalese said.

"It's illegal to own slaves where I come from. The creed we go by is, all people are created equal."

"Does that mean you have your lost memory back?" Caelus asked looking quite bewildered.

"That's correct," I replied. "I have recently regained much of my lost memory. I'm sure most of you remember how different I was when you found me."

"Yes," Caelus said. "You were reborn that day. Master Appius explained all that."

"Well," I chucked, "that's not exactly right."

"Or perhaps completely wrong," Thalese added with a peculiarly knowing expression, and then I looked around at the others. Their eyes were intensely trained on me.

"Yes," I replied, "but I can understand why he thought that. Let me explain."

"That's not necessary," Nubia said.

"Let him speak," Thalese said.

"I thought you came from Ephesus?" Paris asked.

I had to smile because I had an answer for that. "Appius never claimed that I came from Ephesus, only that there was evidence of me having been there. Now that I have my memory back, or most of it, I know that in fact I have been there. So, he was correct." In that one sense I wasn't lying. I had been to Ephesus several times, but in my era. Of course, since my actual visits hadn't happened yet, one could also conclude I was lying. In any event, I didn't care. I needed a quick answer, and that one worked. I could tell by Thalese's nod that he liked my reply.

"You were saying," Thalese said.

"Oh, yes," I said. "It's unfair that I know so much about you, and you know nothing about me." I found myself staring at the floor momentarily. "Perhaps the most extraordinary thing about me is that I come from a land so distant that nobody here has any knowledge of it. That's where all the confusion began. I came from a different culture with different ways and ideas. That's why my peculiarities could only be explained as the work of the gods."

"Where is this place?" Caelus asked.

I had to think of what would make sense. "To the west. Well out to sea beyond Gaul. That would be the shortest route, but it would take months to get there by sail."

"There's nothing except cold and rough seas, not to mention horrific storms," Thalese said. "Ships that venture out too far seldom return."

"I'm not surprised, but regardless, there is a great land beyond."

"This isn't another one of those vivid dreams you have?" Nubia asked.

Appia chuckled, and then leaned over and whispered to her, "I already asked him that."

"This is no dream," I replied, "but what it means is I'm completely human just like each of you. I have no special links to any gods, and no superhuman powers."

"But the Forum," Caelus said.

"I understand why that looked like something divine," I said, "but my power came from the use of a manmade device common in my land, perhaps too common."

"Then you must come from a very powerful place," he said.

"I suppose that's true."

"To have come all this way you must have had a very powerful ship as well," Thalese noted.

"I did," I said, thinking his wording was curious. The sailing characteristics of Roman era ships would more likely be described as big, strong or especially seaworthy, but not powerful. Powerful usually refers to fuel-driven mechanical engines. "I believe I'm the first person from my land to have successfully made this trip."

"Where is this ship?" Paris asked as he moved to the edge of his seat.

"I don't know," I said honestly. "I still can't remember everything. Unfortunately, that's one of those things."

"Sunk?" Caelus asked.

"Possibly," I replied. "Anyway, that's basically what I wanted to say. We're all in this together as humans and equals under this roof. My voice is no more divine than anyone else's in this room." I sat down expecting a flood of questions, but was greeted by silence as people looked at each other. Everyone seemed a little uncomfortable except Appia and Thalese.

"I know what happened, Master Getha," Caelus said. "Don't you see? You're being tested by the gods. It's just as Master Appius had foreseen."

It was my turn to look befuddled. "What makes you say that?"

"It makes sense," he replied. "The gods work is beyond any of us to understand. The whole situation is too fantastic to be anything else."

Others agreed, so I decided it might not be such a bad idea to let them think what they wanted. The explanation I offered was only a half-truth and nearly as unbelievable as the truth would have been.

The meeting was more relaxed after that, so I took my leave and left with a better feeling about how it went. Thalese followed me to the courtyard and spoke quietly once we were away from everybody else.

"What is it, Thalese?" I asked.

"Can you tell me who the next emperor will be?"

"How would I know that?" I replied with surprise.

"I had to move to a room near yours since my old one was ruined," he said. "I overheard your conversation with Appia. I apologize. I should have made my presence known."

"How much did you hear?" I asked.

"Enough," he replied. "If my conclusions are correct you tried to tell Appia you traveled here from a distance far greater than she could readily comprehend."

I wasn't sure what to say, but it was clear he hadn't bought the version I'd just tried to sell to everybody else. "I don't think she wanted to comprehend," I told him.

"And you truly believe what you told her?"

"Which was?" I asked, to see if he really knew before I said too much.

"You told her you came here from the future," he replied. "I believe you said you won't be born for another two thousand years."

I nodded and then smiled. "That's just about right. I suppose now you must think I'm crazy."

"It is a little difficult to imagine," he said.

"And being born from a cloud makes sense?"

"Well," he chuckled, "I was the one who interviewed the witnesses. They saw something unusual, mysterious. Of that I'm certain. But you actually believe you traveled in time?"

"I do because I did," I said. "If you choose not to believe it, that's fine. I don't want it public knowledge anyway. Your discretion on this matter would be most helpful."

"I understand," he said. "I've been a student and teacher of historical writing and the past lives for me, but I've never dreamed it possible to visit bygone times. This is fantastic."

"But it can come with a high price," I said. "I wouldn't have done it if I knew what I know now."

"Your claim to know the successors to the imperial throne is more than a prediction."

"It is," I said.

"It's hard to believe such a thing is possible," he said. "I'm not implying any fabrication on your part, but the gods do work in curious ways."

"I could offer more proof," I said, "but I should warn you, there's a price that comes with this kind of information, so you'd better be very sure of yourself."

"I'm quite sure of myself," he said seriously, and I could see it in his eyes.

"This must stay between us," I added. "I'm holding you to your honor."

"I understand," he replied. "I will never speak of it to anyone."

I took a moment to sip some water from the cup on the nightstand. "I may be off by a day or so, but somewhere on or about the ninth day before the Calends of July, Titus will become emperor."

"That's not far off," Thalese said. "What happens to Emperor Vespasian?"

"He will pass away from illness," I replied. "You may recall he left here feeling poorly." He nodded. "And now I have a question for you. I know who I am, and I'm not from Ephesus. I'm not the person Appius listed on official city documents prior to my adoption. Does that render the adoption null and void?"

He chuckled. "You never were that person, but don't ever tell anyone that."

"But it's hardly legal."

"On the contrary," he said, "it's perfectly legal. That document makes it so. And your adoption wasn't just publicly endorsed by the Curia here and the College of Pontiffs in Rome, but by the emperor himself. That's as legal as it gets!"

"Alright," I said. "Any more questions?"

"Actually, yes," he replied, causing me to sigh. "You told Appia you are sworn to uphold a code of ethics. Isn't giving freed status to all your slaves inconsistent with what you told her? Forgive me for my confusion."

I couldn't help cracking a smile. I also couldn't tell him it didn't matter because the mountain was going to blow up. "You're not confused. Would you rather I change my mind?"

"No," he replied. "I applaud you."

"Well, don't. I've made a lot of mistakes." I looked out onto the courtyard and saw Appia walking arm in arm with Leita. "Let's just say my decision in this one matter is consistent with the direction Appius was heading in before he was killed."

"You told Appia you blame yourself for my master's death," he said.

"I do," I sighed.

"But your intensions were honorable."

"Then call it manslaughter instead of murder" I said.

He cocked his head back. "I don't know that term. I'm not sure I want to, nor can I truly speak to your unique dilemma. But the fact is we need you, and if you're guilt requires some form of chastisement from Appia and me, you will be disappointed."

The next few days went by with relative calm considering all the changes taking place. Leita's condition was improving despite having suffered both physical and emotional abuse. I set aside a part of each day to spend with her. Sometimes we'd walk together, other times we'd sit and talk. She still hurt, but her rate of recovery was astonishing considering the degree of violation she'd suffered. Perhaps I shouldn't have been so surprised. Violation and abuse were a part of her childhood, and to survive, she and countless others like her must have learned to accept their misfortunes as a natural part of life and developed strategies to stifle the pain and stay functional.

On the sixth day before the Calends of July, Thalese came to me with the news of Emperor Vespasian's death. "You were correct," he said gravely as he approached from the main house. "The emperor died three days ago at his retreat near Reate."

"That saddens me," I said, "I'm sorry, Thalese."

"But you already knew."

"I did," I said. "That doesn't make me any less sad." The news actually confirmed something I had assumed until that moment. The year was indeed

79 CE.

"He died of an illness just as you said he would. They claim he aggravated a fever by swimming in cold water.

I stepped over to the recently repaired bust of Emperor Vespasian. "Let's move this to a place of honor next to the one of Appius," I said. He agreed, but I couldn't avoid his stare. "What is it, Thalese?"

"Do you know what fate awaits us?" he asked.

"No," I said.

"I suppose you wouldn't tell me anyway."

"Not necessarily," I said, "but the written information that survived to my era is not that detailed."

"Can you tell me who will follow Titus?"

"Who do you think?"

"I don't know," he said hesitantly. "Titus doesn't have a son, but if his reign is short, I would suppose it would be his brother."

"You answered your own question," I said with a smile. "After Domitian there will be Nerva, but he'll be quite old by then. He'll have the foresight to adopt a son by the name of Trajan, then his adopted son, Hadrian. Do you want to hear more?"

Thalese chuckled. "That's not necessary. I just wanted to know something about the future."

He was satisfied and returned to the main house. I was glad to have him as friend and confidant; although, I wondered how that would affect my future decisions regarding the eruption. My feeble, virtually nonexistent attempt to distance myself from family members was a complete failure. It can't be overstated how previously clear-cut obligations become muddled when the people in history books become real lives.

XXI

∞

Two weeks after the attack, Therasia gave birth to a healthy 6 lb. baby boy. For the first time since the assassination the entire household felt like celebrating. The timing couldn't have been better for Leita. There's nothing more fulfilling for the suffering spirit of a midwife than successfully bringing a new life into the world.

Thalese reminded me that attention was needed with regard to the operation in Rome. He complemented the staff at the Villa North for holding the businesses together through the recent crisis, but stressed that one of us should be there to ensure continued stability in the aftermath of Appius' loss. He said recent messages from Rome had expressed a variety of concerns that only personal contact could address. I didn't see any reason not to send Paris if he still wanted the job. Appius had trained him for that precise reason. Thalese would prepare a tablet of introduction embossed with the family seal, and Paris and his family were to move to Rome as soon as it was safe for the baby to travel.

My personal plan was to simply let nature happen. I did my best to ignore the calendar, which wasn't difficult because Romans used a different convention to track days. I knew the date of the eruption to be nine days before the Calends, so I never bothered to pay attention to the date until after the Ides. That's when I'd become more sensitive to tremors and other indications signaling the eruption was imminent.

There was a decidedly more violent tremor, on the 19th of the month by my calculation. There was damage to the town, which included city water pipes. More telling was a thin halo of haze surrounding the mountain's summit. The mountain was venting.

Family members came to me looking for answers, but for once I remained true to the *Principles* and offered nothing, pretending to be as baffled as they were. I was hoping they'd decide to leave the area without my influence. Unfortunately, that hope was not realized.

Paris and his family departed on what I calculated to be the 21st day of the month. Thalese had arranged passage on a family-owned merchant ship heading for Rome at dawn on the 22nd. Sea travel was generally a safer mode of transport compared to traveling with a family overland. There was also what locals called the twenty, seven, one rule. A distance that required twenty days by foot could be covered in seven days by horse or one day by ship. It was quicker too.

The month of the upcoming eruption was of no concern to me, only the day. I'd seen enough to believe that the time was at hand. Between the gas emissions and the increasing number of daily quakes, it didn't seem possible the building force behind the eruption could be held back another month.

I decided I needed to make one last effort to find my ship. My plan was to climb the mountain on the day before the eruption and look for potential hiding places in the plain below; after which, if I found nothing as expected, I'd spend the remainder of the day at peace with my family. I couldn't predict how I'd feel once the eruption began, but all the decisions from that point on would be theirs. I would simply assume their fate.

Not so much as a cicada kept me up on the night before my climb and I quickly fell asleep. I was awakened around three in the morning by a series of mild tremors that roused a few birds. I couldn't go back to sleep, but since it was a such beautiful moonlit night, I began my hike before dawn. The calm air was filled with many wonderful herbal fragrances, and when the sun finally emerged from behind the distant hills, its warmth produced a misty, wonderfully mystical scene. It was going to be another beautiful day.

My search for the ship would begin from the mountain so I took the most direct northerly route. I decided to climb the southern slope and focus on areas between the mountain and Pompeii. My expectations were so low as to be comical. I'd already searched the most likely places multiple times with no success.

My family may have been asleep, but much of the local population wasn't. There were people hustling to and fro along roadways and paths, between buildings and groves, mostly preparing for the day's labors. Animals were being fed and let out of their pens, while empty wagons were positioned for loading goods.

I approached Vesuvius with some trepidation. It was a little unsettling to be climbing a volcano so close to its awakening, but its peacefulness and botanical beauty masked its true nature. A wispy, white cloud continued to ring the summit, but at that moment the mountain showed no other outward signs of the trouble brewing below.

Vesuvius wouldn't begin its eruption cycle until well after dark or more likely the next morning. Gas explosions would signal the start, followed by a quieter time, and then the major eruption sequence would begin around midday.

It's difficult to describe my feelings at that moment. In one sense I had given up hope of ever getting home, which should have left me depressed, but the fact that I was resigned to sharing my fate with the others had a calming influence on me. The inner turmoil of the past weeks was gone and I was living for the moment, and at that moment I was hiking the most famous volcano in history just one day before it created that fame. I was finally free to be the kind of explorer I wanted to be, so I decided to risk a trip to the summit to observe any changes in the caldera. The venting had to have come from there, perhaps from the lava dome itself.

It was 0602 by my watch when I reached the slope. That was a guesstimate, but probably close. I wanted to be back home by early-afternoon. I took a more direct route to the top than Appia and I had. This time I hiked straight up the southern slope. The walking was easy through the lower farmlands, but more difficult through the higher forest with all its tangled ground cover. There were gullies and fallen timber which gave way to brush and ground hugging plants above the tree line and nothing on top but gritty sand and porous, rusty rocks. It took about two hours to reach the summit.

The haze wasn't as noticeable at the top, but there was a steamy fog rising in stringy whiffs from the caldera. I could smell sulfur in the air. I was exhausted from my walk, but not too exhausted to cross the narrow peak and look down into the caldera. The first thing I noticed was an off-colored mist rising from the pond that was covered in a heavy, brownish film. There were multiple vents of steam jetting upwards from between widening cracks in the lava dome, and the small forest at the open end of caldera was bathed in a yellowish fog. If I had any thoughts about going down there, they were quickly dashed by the sight. Most likely the air was toxic.

"Wow," was about all I could say. Vesuvius was clearly active and nobody below had a clue. There were no farms or homes in the caldera because it was high above the plain and the soil and pond water were tainted. It was the perfect cover for an awakening volcano. No wonder the eruption seemed to come on so suddenly. Any visual precursors would have been out of sight and any associated steam mistaken for clouds.

I took a moment to study the dome and how steam was venting quite forcefully out from its cracked surface. It was bigger too, perhaps a quarter to a third larger than before. That meant magmatic pressure was forcing magma up through the blockage in the vent. That confirmed it for me. The thing was about to blow. It was hard to believe it wasn't about to blow right then; however, I was confident in the date. I had a good twenty hours or more before I needed to worry, but just the same, it seemed prudent to start back sooner rather than later.

It had been a brisk, six-mile walk from the villa to where I stood peering down into the caldera. I needed to sit and rest my weary legs before starting back. I found a nice spot facing the southern plain. It was a beautiful view on a perfectly clear day, not counting the thin whiffs of volcanic haze that drifted by. I could see Pompeii in the distance. It was characterized by the same oval shape that helped me find it from the top of Mount Vesuvius in my own age.

I had water left so I quenched my thirst. I was supposed to be searching for my ship, but one look over the terrain from that height underlined the ridiculousness of an idea I knew wouldn't work from the start. I suppose I didn't want to give up hope, except that hope is all that's left when there is no hope, so I officially ended my search there.

A whiff of sulfur was enough to remind me of the cauldron brewing behind my back, and yet it was quiet up there, perhaps a little too quiet. Where were the birds? Appia and I saw lots of birds on our previous climb. I'd read somewhere a rather unscientific account of how the birds had all fled the region just before the eruption. That was not a comforting thought, but perhaps it made sense given the nature of the volcanic haze and toxins rising behind me. Birds wouldn't hang around in that, nor should I for much longer.

I was about to get up when I became entertained by the way tiny grains of sand were dancing around the bigger stones as if catching mini-updrafts of wind. I found it an interesting sight until I realized there was no wind. A cold chill ran down my spine and I looked at my watch. It read 0834.

Instinctively, I pressed both palms to the ground, and through my body I felt a clear and distinct ground resonance. I wanted to pass it off as just another tremor, but this was different. It was closer.

"Oh no!" I gasped and I leaped to my feet. For one bone chilling moment I remained frozen in place trying to gather my thoughts. The ground resonance was quickly followed by a deep rumbling from below as the soil began vibrating and shifting, and then, as if coming from all directions at once, there was a loud, sonic boom, followed by a blast of steaming hot air to my back. I immediately fell to my knees as the earth shook, and then I looked up and saw a plume of grey dirt being hurled at high speed over my head.

Chunks of rock were blown into the air as if being expelled from some giant popcorn maker. Whatever goes up has to come back down.

There was no time to think. Just run. But before I had a chance to take my first step the tremors intensified with such ferocity the ground turned to mush under my feet and in the next instant I was tumbling backwards down the slope. Gas primed explosions continued to throw debris into air as I rolled and righted myself. Quickly up, I found I was running like a scared cat with his ears pinned back and all muscles in motion. I slipped again and slid about 50 feet into a small ravine just as a downpour of superheated bits of steam and volcanic matter rained from the sky.

I gasped from the stings as some of the more solid bits found exposed skin. Panic driven, I tried to brush them off as I scurried to my feet, but rather than fall away, they seemed to stick, searing my skin. The next wave of tremors sent me tumbling farther. It became impossible to move without falling, but at least I was headed in the right direction – down.

Quakes loosened stones that rumbled down the slope in avalanche fashion. There was nowhere to hide as even trees were being shredded by jagged rock fragments that began to smack the ground with increasing frequency. I was struck twice in the back by fist size chunks of rock before being overtaken by a tumbling avalanche of stone. Tree trunks absorbed the brunt of that assault, sparing me from certain death, but I didn't escape unscathed as a pair of large, bouncing stones collided behind me, striking me waist high with glancing blows that rendered me senseless for an instant.

I rose to my feet again only to fall as my hips gave out. I knew something was very wrong as there was no feeling down my entire left side, but I couldn't stop. An adrenaline powered fear kicked in as I hugged the ground in an effort to continue my slide down the slope, while much of the remaining rock debris bounced over me. Suddenly, whack! I saw stars and everything seemed to spin, and then blackness.

"Unfuckin believable," was all could I mutter to a throbbing wound on the back of my head as I slowly regained consciousness. It took me a moment to remember where I was, and then another to begin extricating myself from the loose debris.

Slowly and very deliberately I crawled free. My whole body felt outwardly pulverized and yet I had mobility, except for my hip, which was numb. I didn't try to stand at first, but instead continued crawling. The ground was vibrating as if there was a diesel engine buried below me, and when I finally did stand, I teetered on my bad hip and accidentally slid sideways into another ravine. That fall hurt, and was punctuated by a sudden sharp snapping in my lower spine when my upper torso twisted backwards against the forward thrust of my body weight. More than just my hip went numb.

I laid there frightened and out of breath. I felt a tingling in the area near where my back had snapped, and then feeling returned to my lower body. It took a great deal of effort, but I managed to get to my knees. I rested in that position for several moments until I was sure I had my balance, and then I eased myself to my feet. The worst hits had been to my left shoulder and lower back, but I couldn't ignore the pain from a small lump on the back of my head. That blow seemed less important because I was thinking clearly again.

This can't be happening I kept telling myself as I hobbled through a dangerous section of woods. Pliny the Younger had written in his letters to Tacitus that the date of the eruption was 9 days before the Calends, not 10! While it's true that only copies of his letters survived to my era, the day he ascribed to the event was a constant in most versions. I'd been caught completely by surprise. I looked at my watch. I'd been unconscious for nearly three hours.

The mountain rumbled like a furnace behind me, but it wasn't throwing out solid material the way it had at the start. A gaseous grey cloud hung over the summit producing a light rain of cooled bits of something unpleasant. It felt more acidic than rain because it stung against abrasions and any contact with my eyes. I knew about how gas explosions often preceded explosive volcanic eruptions, but I didn't realize how violent they were, and that was just a taste of what was to come.

The tremors that accompanied the first gas explosions continued, and I tumbled a few more times before reaching the farmlands on the lower slope. I met other fear driven people in flight, mostly farmstead workers. Many appeared to have suffered painful falls as well. I noticed few wore sandals, and that was when I realized I'd lost mine too, but in the heat of the moment it didn't matter.

The ground tremors all but stopped at one point, making the escape over the flatter countryside easier. My range of motion improved, and my hobble smoothed into a racewalk that took some of the sting out of my headache.

"This way," a concerned stranger called out as he passed by me on a westerly trail, "to the sea!" I thanked him, but continued on my southerly heading to the villa.

That's when it happened. A bellowing roar from within Vesuvius culminated in a titanic detonation that blew open the ancient caldera. The concussion from the blast was sonic and deafening. The ground lifted as a blast of compressed air, a shock wave, shoved me forward as if a rug had been pulled out from under my feet. My right arm stung as it absorbed the shock of the fall and I rolled onto my sore back. A continuing roar filled the air, while lesser explosions punctuated the heavily laden grey clouds that boiled and frothed angrily skyward from the freshly opened caldera.

"My god," I said in quiet awe, momentarily stunned by the sight, "this can't be happening."

XXII

∞

No matter how badly I wanted to reach the villa, I couldn't maintain a steady pace. My body hurt, my legs were fatigued, and the gravelly ground wore on the toughened soles of my feet. I walked quickly, and then jogged in short bursts, and then walked again. I wasn't limping anymore, and I had Caelus to thank for my level of fitness. Without his training I wouldn't have had the strength to cover the distance as quickly as I had.

It seemed like an eternity, but I finally saw the villa in the distance. I tried another short cut over a rise, but fell again as the ground gave way beneath my feet. My tumble followed the slope as if it were deliberate, and after rolling to my feet, I continued the pace until I reached the back of the villa.

I studied the sky. The rising volcanic plume had quickly spread southward overhead, blotting out the sun as gritty flakes of falling ash began to blanket the terrain. It wasn't as heavy as I expected, but I knew that wouldn't last. A good fifteen feet of volcanic ejecta would eventually accumulate right where I was standing.

"Caelus!" I called out as I turned the corner to see his familiar form moving towards the city gate. "Where are you going?"

"To look for you!" he yelled over the roar of the mountain.

I was nearly breathless as I rushed to meet him halfway. "Where is everybody?" I asked.

"In the courtyard," he replied. "Some of the walls and ceilings have cracked."

"How strong do you feel today?" I asked.

"I don't know if strength will help," he replied sounding uncharacteristically frustrated. "I can fight armies, but this? This is something very different."

I put my hand on his shoulder and looked him in the eye. "Can you control the mules in this?"

"The old one," he replied, "Warrior. He's a very good animal."

"Then hook a wagon to him," I said, "and bring it to the front door."

"Understood," he stated with renewed strength in his voice.

I nodded and back pedaled towards the house. "After that, grab any valuables you want, because we won't be coming back."

"Never?" he asked, catching the finality in my tone.

"Never!" I replied, and then I glanced at the ground before entering the villa. The ash was falling more heavily now, but it was nothing like the six inches an hour to come. A wagon might still work, at least for a while.

I passed quickly through the darkened home towards the courtyard. There I found the rest of the family huddled together beneath the security of a large door frame.

"Getha!" Appia cried as she got up to greet me with a hug. "I was so worried!"

"What's happening?" Thalese asked nervously.

"The mountain has blown up," I replied excitedly. "We've got to leave now."

"For where?" Nubia asked. "Wouldn't it be safer just to stay right here?"

"No," I replied trying to think of a way to emphasis my point. "We're standing in the path of the destruction."

"What happened to you?" Appia said with concern after noticing my limp. My hips had stiffened again.

"Minor problem," I told her hurriedly. "I'm fine."

"It's that severe out there?" Thalese asked, calmly taking note of the blood on the back of my head. "Are you sure you're alright?"

"I am," I replied, "and yes, it is that severe. Caelus is hooking up a wagon right now. Appia, if you would, help Leita fill a couple coverable containers with water."

"The water stopped running," she said.

"I know," I replied. "Use the stuff in the bath. We may need it for more than just drinking. Thalese, we'll need oil lamps and fuel…" and then I realized that wasn't the best use of his time. "I'll do that. You collect business records, coinage. We may not be able to save much, but it won't hurt to try."

"Sounds like were never coming back," he said.

"That's right," I replied sadly. "In a few hours there won't be anything left to come back to." They were stunned by the permanent nature of my words, but there was no time to explain. "I'm sorry, but we've got to go now. We'll also need protection for our heads and strips of cloth to breathe through."

"I can help with that," Nubia said.

"Okay," I said, "but be very careful. This trip will be a strain on all of us, but especially on you. I want all of you to understand, this is a matter of life and death. You need to trust me on this. I know exactly what I'm talking about."

"We do trust you, Getha," Nubia said warmly. "We waited for you. We knew you'd know what to do. I can wrap some food as well."

"Good," I replied as I stepped away from the group. "Let's get started. No telling how much longer we have." Caelus had brought the small, twin axle wagon around to the front of the villa as I'd asked. Warrior remained controllable at the front, but Democritus was jumpy after Caelus tied his reins to the back of the wagon. I loaded my lamps and helped Leita lift the water jug onto the transom, and then I saw Appia going back into the villa for more things.

"Hurry!" I yelled as she disappeared. Thalese emerged with the smaller of the household strongboxes.

"There are a couple things I want to get if we're not coming back," Nubia said as she scurried back inside.

"How about you?" I asked Leita.

"I'm fine," she replied, and she took my arm. "All I want is right here." I gave her a hug.

"What's the date?" I asked Thalese.

"The ninth day before the Calends," he replied with a curious look.

"The ninth?" I said with surprise. "I thought tomorrow was the ninth?"

"No, Getha," he said, and he suddenly stopped what he was doing.

"I'm confused," I said. "I've kept count. I haven't missed a day."

Thalese looked bewildered. "I don't understand. This is the ninth day. Of that I'm certain."

"Which makes today the…" and then I realized my error. Roman counting was inclusive. Pliny wasn't wrong. I was. It *was* the day of the eruption. It was also one mistake I didn't need to beat myself up over. The mountain had already done that.

"This is going to get much worse before it gets better," I said once everyone was ready. "It's going to get hot. There will be burning ash and difficult breathing. There will be chunks of falling rock, but we have time to make it to safety as long as we stick together and keep moving."

"What about father's horse?" Appia asked Caelus. "Where's Aristarchus?"

"I couldn't hold him," Caelus replied sadly. "I'm sorry." Appia was upset, so Caelus grabbed her by the arm when it looked like she was about to go after him.

"No, Appia," I said. "We can't get separated. Not now." She gave me a cross look but heeded my words. The gritty lapilli was building up under foot, so I hastened Caelus to turn the wagon south. "Are you sure you can control the animals?" I asked.

"They'll be better once we're moving," he replied. I pushed some of the supplies to the front of the wagon to make a place for Nubia to sit. Nubia wanted to walk with the rest of us, but I insisted she ride. I knew she'd have to walk if the ash got too deep for the wagon and I wanted her to conserve her strength for as long as possible. Once she was settled, I told Caelus to start the wagon forward.

Thalese and Leita stayed at the back to help Nubia should either animal spook. Caelus remained up front leading Warrior while Appia walked beside her horse.

When we reached the crossroads at the city gate, Caelus turned the wagon west.

"Whoa!" I yelled. "Not that way. Go east!"

"Are you sure?" he asked.

"I am," I replied.

"But everyone's heading for the port. We can escape by ship."

"No, we can't. Nobody can."

Thalese stepped forward. "You can trust him on this, Caelus. He knows what he's talking about."

"The sky looks worse over there," he said while pointing to the east.

"Getha knows," Thalese said. "Trust me my friend, he knows."

"All right," he said and he turned the wagon east.

"If we went to the sea," I explained, "we'd find the shoreline choked with debris and the sea too rough to launch boats. The coastal roads north are tempting, but possibly jammed, and we'd have much less time to reach safety. East won't be easy, but it's the quickest way I can think of to escape the greatest danger."

I left Caelus firmly on course and stepped back to where Thalese brought up the rear. "Thanks," I said.

"Caelus relies on his instincts," he said, "but you're practically a god to him. He'll always listen to you."

"I understand his concern. I just hope I'm right."

Thalese broke into an uncharacteristic grin. "You knew this was coming all along," he said with a chuckle, "and don't try to tell me differently. The problem was you couldn't read the calendar."

"Please," I replied with disgust, "don't remind me."

"What I mean to say is, thanks."

"For what?"

"For coming back," he said. "For recognizing that our lives count too."

I couldn't look at him. His comment was too unsettling. "Don't thank me now," I said as I stepped away. "We're not out of this thing yet."

I pulled out the compass to check the direction. The direction that made sense was almost due east. The road by the cistern gate branched off southeast across the river where it connected with the road to Nucerea. That would be the shortest distance out of the danger zone. It was a relatively smooth and direct route. The progressively heavier ash fall would make the road more difficult to follow, but once we were across the river it would be just a matter of heading east, and having a compass meant we had a decided edge once we lost our visual markers.

"Where are we going?" Appia asked as she came running in a panic towards me. "What about Maria?"

"Oplontis is in the wrong direction," I said. I hadn't considered anyone outside the villa. I was breaking enough *Principles* as it was.

"I can't go without her," she said with tears welling in her eyes. "You go on, I'll catch up later."

"No," I said. "It's too dangerous."

"But I have to," she stated emphatically, and then she turned and headed back towards the villa. "I can't leave without my sister!"

I told Caelus to stop the wagon and I brought Appia back before she'd gotten very far. If anybody was going, it had to be me. The risks involved with turning back for Oplontis were incalculable even with what I knew, but impossible for her given her minimal knowledge of the situation. I walked back to Caelus. "I've got to go back," I told him. "I hate to do this to you, but you're going to have to lead everyone out."

"Why?" he asked.

"I have to go to Oplontis," I replied. "See about Maria Prima and her family."

"I'll go for them," he said.

"No, my friend," I said. "You're the toughest person I know, and you're going to need all of that toughness to keep everyone moving when it seems like the whole world is burning around you. That's what I need from you. Keep moving, and don't stop for anything." I fidgeted through my pockets for the compass. "It's going to get harder," I said and I handed it to him, "harder to walk, harder to breath, and harder to see. Take this. This will help you stay on course."

"Won't you need it?"

"I know better than anyone how events will unfold," I explained. "That's my advantage, and this little device will be yours." Thalese appeared to find out why we were stopped. "This is a compass," I said, adding him to the conversation. I moved it around to demonstrate how the indicator remained true to one direction. "The arrow always points to the north. When the road becomes too difficult to follow, use it."

"I see," Thalese said with fascination. When I explained how following the arrow would lead them towards the volcano, he understood exactly how it worked.

I wasn't sure how the eruption might affect the magnetic field, but the compass seemed to be working fine. I knew from my time in Pompeii there were a few places where compasses didn't work well, so I cautioned him against total dependence on the device.

"Once you've crossed the river you need to head in a direction that favors east," I said.

"Inland," Caelus said firmly.

"Right!" I yelled over the mountains roar. "Most importantly don't stop. Not until you're well east and clear of this mess."

"How will we know where that is?" Thalese asked.

"Try to reach Nucerea," I replied. "That's what I'd planned to do."

"Nucerea?" Caelus asked with surprise.

"Or do the best you can," and then I removed my watch and handed it to Thalese. "Nucerea is in the direction you need to head, and it's the safest place I can think of offhand."

"What's this for?" Thalese asked while studying the watch.

"I know you can't read the writing," I said.

"It moves," he chuckled when the numbers changed from 04:08 to 04:09 PM.

"Those numerals are written in my native language," I said, "but that's not important," and I pointed to the 4. "That digit is the only part you need to worry about. What's important is the number of times that digit changes. Forget about the digits to the right of the dots." Thalese nodded while Caelus just looked puzzled. "Each change represents one hour. You need to be well clear of this general area by the seventh change. When that happens, that digit will have changed to two vertical lines. Do you understand?"

"I think so," Thalese said. "When it reads two."

I was about to say no, but then realized he was right. My eleven looks the same as his two. "Yes. When that reads II. Exactly."

"That's when we're to be in Nucerea?"

"Yes," I said, "and try to find shelter. That's when the mountain will begin its deadliest phase."

"So where will we meet you?" Thalese asked.

"Don't wait for me," I told him. "Rest if you need to in Nucerea. Then head straight to Rome. Go north by road if you feel it's safe, or go south to Salernum and seek passage by ship. That might be the better option. There will be ash and damage there too, but not like here. I imagine the place will be overrun with refugees, so expect chaos, but the harbor should be functioning. I wish I had a better plan, but the most important part is to get as far away from the mountain as possible. Do you understand?"

"Yes," Thalese said. Caelus nodded.

"Good luck, my friends," I said.

"You're not coming back this way?" Caelus asked.

"I don't know," I replied. I actually did know. I was planning to return and take the same route, but I didn't want them waiting. "Just get going. I want you safe as soon as possible. I'll see you in Rome."

"But?" Thalese said.

"No more buts. No good-byes," I said. "Just go! Hurry! We've wasted way too much time already!"

"You're not coming with us?" Leita asked with surprise.

"No," I replied and I gave her a hug. "I've got to get Maria Prima. Caelus and Thalese will see you through."

"But Getha," Nubia said sadly, "I will see you again? Won't I?" She hopped off the wagon to give me a hug.

"In Rome," I replied, and I helped her back up. "And keep that cloth over your mouth."

"Promise you'll be there?" she said.

"I promise," I replied.

XXIII

∞

Appia insisted on joining me on my trek to Oplontis to rescue her sister. I'd been there once, so I thought I knew where I was going. I tried to dissuade her, but she wouldn't hear of it, and with time becoming a factor, I relented.

We followed the city walls until we reached the road to Oplontis. The steadily increasing depth of the falling ash was becoming more of a factor, and once we reached the road, we found it difficult to follow. The other problem was the growing intensity of the mountain. The noise and vibration were unnerving and the continual ground resonance made each step uncertain.

"My mouth is dry," Appia said.

"So's mine," I replied, "but I'm sure Maria will still have water. Even if it's in the bath."

"Will we come back this way?"

"I'm counting on it," I replied.

The volcanically charged and sulfurous atmosphere was continuing to grow worse by the moment. There was a nasty, dry breeze from time to time, and the sound of thunder in areas away from the mountain. The seemingly harmless ash was becoming more of an irritant as fine glassy grains found their way under our clothes and into our eyes. Its grey particulate consistency was different from ordinary sand because of its harshness. It stung sensitive areas, while being a slow, but steady acting abrasive against our feet and legs as we waded through it. To make matters worse there were dangerously large chunks of rock starting to mix with the rest of the ejecta.

There were lots of other people out with us, and strangely enough, I saw little panic. Most seemed in flight, but oddly, a few appeared to be trying to conduct business like it was a normal day. We simply continued on course while maneuvering around the ghostly human forms as they passed in and out of the grey haze.

We trudged on for maybe an hour and a half before Appia recognized a building that confirmed our course. From there the trail became more difficult because we had to pick our way north along the less defined streets on the outskirts of Oplontis. That's when I realized I never would have found the villa alone. Everything looked the same in the haze, but fortunately, because of Appia, we could continue on.

It was phenomenal how quickly the ash was building up beneath our feet. The mountain was making up for its slow start which gave me doubts about getting out in time.

"Here," Appia said and she pointed to a pair of ash laden cypress trees. "No, here," and she led me up a narrow street and through a grove of trees to a building on the other side.

"We found it," she said triumphantly as we bolted up the steps and began banging on the front door. There was no reply. "Maria!" she called out. I tried to open the door, but it wouldn't budge.

"It's locked," I said noting the metal plate and square keyhole. "I don't think anyone's here."

"Somebody must be," Appia said. "They never leave the house empty." We yelled together, but no sounds other than the roar of the mountain were heard. I used my good shoulder to slam my body into the door with as much force as I could muster. There was a loud crack, but it remained shut. I slammed against it again but to no avail. "Can you break it?" she asked.

"I don't know," I replied, "but maybe. Stand back." I pulled the gun from its pocket and fired twice into the lock area. The first did nothing but split the keyhole; however, the second blasted out a chunk of wood between the locking plate and the jam. There was the clink of something metal hitting the floor, and with my shoulder lowered I gave the door one more shove and it popped open.

Appia rushed by me and immediately began calling for her sister. I recognized the place once inside. "There's nobody here," I said when we met in the courtyard.

"Where could they be?"

"I have no idea," I replied. "All I know is they're not here, and we shouldn't be either."

My statement was followed by a pair of nasty tremors that loosened plaster from the ceiling and sent us scurrying for cover beneath a marble table. A blast of wind caused falling lapilli to pelt the outside walls like hail.

"Are you sure we're not safer here?" Appia asked.

"I'm sure," I replied. We crawled out from under the table as the wind eased and the ground returned to milder harmonics.

"She could be in Herculaneum," Appia said. "They have friends there."

"Herculaneum?"

"Yes," she replied.

Just the thought of setting out for Herculaneum conjured images of the skeletons found at that excavation. I lost my nerve for a moment, but quickly got it back. "We can go in that direction if you wish," I said somberly. "But if we go that way, I doubt we'll make it out."

"She may not even be in Herculaneum," she said sadly. "I've endangered both of us with this wasted search. Let's rejoin the others." I didn't argue.

Appia led me to the bath where we found a foot or so of relatively clean standing water in the bottom of a square ceramic tub. I skimmed off the plaster dust from the top and we drank our fill before washing our faces and rinsing out the cloth masks. It wasn't very good, but it would have to do since there was no time to search for portable containers.

"What about pillows for our heads?" I asked.

Instead of pillows, Appia found two woolen, hooded cloaks. Yes, they would be warm, but they provided decent head and upper body protection from most of what was falling from the sky. The rain of lapilli was more annoying than deadly, and what *was* deadly would kill us no matter what we used for cover.

She spotted an enclosed, bronze oil lamp on the way out. I remembered the small lighter I had in my vest pocket and lit it for her. "I forgot I had this," I chuckled after seeing how startled she was by the gadget.

There was already over a foot and a half of ejecta on the ground in many places, but at least it was walkable. We couldn't locate the road we'd come in on, so we took the better marked coastal route south knowing it would turn inland towards Pompeii before we reached the salt marshes. That plan worked well enough at first, but turning back towards Pompeii was another matter. The coastal route quickly became less discernable, and visibility so poor that without the compass we were at risk of becoming hopelessly lost.

"This is impossible!" I cried out in frustration.

"I can't see anything either," Appia said over the continual drone of the mountain that offered surprisingly little help determining direction. "Nothing's familiar."

"This is not good," I said and I took her hand. "Let's not get crazy just yet. What we need mostly are markers."

"How about the coastline?" she said. "We can follow it north or south."

"Not north," I said thinking about the fate of Herculaneum, "and we've already lost the coastal road south."

"Not the road, Getha," she said, "the coast. We can hear the waves and use that for picking our direction." It was an impractical idea at best, born of desperation, but we were desperate. We'd need to be close enough to the shore to hear the waves over everything else. That meant lots negotiating around lots of structures and other obstructions, and the potential of a wrong turn putting us too close to the shore where erratic wave action might drag us into the bay. However, if it worked, it would be possible to reach the Sarnus River and the road to Nucerea by passing between the bay and Pompeii."

"I think that's our only choice," I said, and we were on our way again.

"How do you think the others are doing?" Appia asked as we continued southward.

"I'm hoping they're out of the death zone or close to it by now," I replied. "Although, it probably seems like the end of the world to them."

"Death zone?"

"That's when the deadly pyroclastic events will devastate everything west and south of the mountain."

"Are we in that death zone?" she asked.

"We are," I replied. "The others may be getting pelted right now, but the distance out of that zone is shorter."

"They can't have reached Nucerea yet," she said.

"True," I said, "but Nucerea is at least a couple miles beyond the death zone, so even if they don't quite make it there, they'll still be safe, relatively speaking. Of course, that is if my understanding of events is correct."

"What about us? Can we get far enough away in time?"

"That's the plan," I said, trying to sound upbeat. "We have to. I just hope I've made the right decision."

"I trust you."

We were trudging through a blizzard of ash, with visibility down to mere feet in places. There were times when we thought we could hear the ocean, but not clearly enough to confirm our direction. The rumble of the mountain had also proved too unreliable to trust. Sound bounces off of large solid objects, like buildings and walls, which creates confusion when those objects are hidden by darkness and ashfall.

Occasionally, other sounds, like the sharp crackling of breaking wood, trees falling, and the thud of roofs collapsing spooked us because we couldn't see anything. There were areas with lots of buildings and obstacles that often forced us to readjust our course. Just the same, it seemed like we were making headway in the right direction, and that was cause for optimism. "I think we may just make it," I said as more time passed without complications.

"When will we be on the road to Nucerea?" Appia asked.

"We'll make the turn for Nucerea once we've crossed the river," I replied.

We continued on, but as more time passed, I started to feel like something wasn't right. We had to be beyond Pompeii at that point. I tried to picture where the river was in relationship to the city. It didn't seem like it should be taking us nearly as long as it was to reach it. Each step was becoming heavier too. At first I blamed it on fatigue, but then I realized we were on an incline.

"What's that?" Appia asked as we came upon a massive tufa stone wall blocking our path. We couldn't see the top, or where it ended in either direction, but by the size of the stones it was a major structure.

"I don't know," I replied, but even as the words passed through my lips I was realizing the truth. "You've got to be kidding me!" I cried out in disbelief. "It's Pompeii. It has to be. There are no other walls like this in the area."

"It can't be," Appia said excitedly, feeding off my distress.

"Oh, but it can," I replied in frustration as I smacked the wall with my open palm. "All I've done is to lead us in circles. We've lost so much time – I'm so exhausted…"

Appia moved closer and put her arm around me. "I'm exhausted too Getha," she said calmly, "but it's all right."

"No, it isn't."

"Yes," she said, "it is," and she took my hand. "Would it be so terrible if we just go home?"

I set the lamp on the ground. "To die?"

"I love you," she said and she lowered her cloth mask, "with all my heart." When she looked up, I saw tears welling in her eyes.

Appia had become my closest and dearest companion, but until that moment I hadn't realized how much I cared for her, how much I loved her, how much I was in love with her. "I love you too," I said as the words came easily and freely without a hint of uncertainty. "With all my heart, I do love you."

I wiped away the loose particles of ash from her face and kissed her. "We're not going to the villa," I said as I gathered my thoughts. "We've still got time, a lifetime together if we can make this work."

"It can't end now," she said with renewed life in her voice, "not now." We gave each other big hugs. I picked up the lamp and we started again.

We hadn't noticed any tombs near the wall, which with other indicators, offered a decent guestimate as to our location and bearing. It also meant we'd passed Pompeii and gotten turned around. I looked at the wall and then at our footsteps. I made a best guess and we were off.

"How are you holding up?" I asked after about a half hour of trudging.

"Not the best," she replied, "but I'm okay."

I started to get concerned when we began climbing another incline. I couldn't remember any hills between the river and the city, and it seemed like we should have reached the river by then. I was just about to ask Appia for her thoughts when there was a boom from behind, punctuated by crackling sounds like distant firecrackers. I grabbed Appia and dropped to the ground. There were more booms. We looked behind us and saw the western slope of Vesuvius lit by the lightning and fire of a boiling, ground hugging volcanic cloud that literally thundered down the mountain to the sea.

"Damn," I said in awe.

"What's that?" Appia asked as she held me close.

"Remember when I explained pyroclastic events?" I replied.

"Yes."

"That's the first one," I said. The rumbling continued until the turbulent cloud reached the sea and dissipated into the darkness. "Herculaneum is dead."

"Everybody?" she asked.

"Everybody," I replied. "That includes Oplontis. Had we stayed at your sister's we'd be dead too." Appia was clearly shaken. The super-hot gasses had left a trail of fires in its wake. It made the familiar outline of its lower slope recognizable and the event painfully real.

"Is that to be our fate?" she asked.

"Not if I can help it," I replied. "The fact those fires are visible means the ash fall has eased. We'd better make time while we can."

"You tried to tell me about the mountain," she said as we trudged along, "but I didn't really understand. It's been at peace as long as anyone can remember."

We were starting to make better time as the buildup of lapilli felt a little firmer underfoot and we were encountering fewer obstacles, but we still hadn't reached the river. That was a concern.

"At last," I said when we came to a spot where the land dropped off abruptly. I put down the lamp and peered into the darkness below as faintly visible chunks of debris floated slowly by.

"It doesn't even look like water," Appia said.

"But I think we can follow it to a bridge," I said. "Any bridge will do. I hate to say this, but we'd better keep moving." I knew Appia was weakening and exhausted, but we were still well inside the death zone and time was running out.

The sound of another pyroclastic event rumbled in the distance. We dropped to the ground when the remanence of this one blew by as a dense cloud of ash, but nothing deadly of itself.

We began following the riverbank. Both sides of the bank had foot paths, but they were buried. There were trees and obstacles to step around as well. After an hour of walking, we needed water. The river was right there, but actually getting down the treacherous, ash laden embankment was a risky proposition in the dark. I left the lamp with Appia and gave it try. Once I was safely down, she joined me. It was a wasted trip. The water was full of grit and pollutants and just too rancid to swallow.

"We're not far enough away yet, are we?" Appia asked.

"No," I replied just as our lamp flickered out. I searched my pockets for the lighter, but I'd lost it. The appearance of hot embers overhead made a bridge faintly visible. "Let's cross while we can, and work our way south-east."

"Do you think we can still find the road to Nucerea?" Appia said.

"Not in this mess," I replied. "All we can do now is put as much distance between us and the mountain as we can, and hope it's enough."

I took her hand and we started across the bridge. The buildup of ash was higher than the railing, making crawling less hazardous than walking. A stream of fiery cinders blew past; the sparks swirling around our heads. They were a nuisance, but a better alternative to the absence of light, offering a chance to cross the bridge more quickly before being plunged into utter darkness again.

At some point after seemingly endless trudging, we hit a wall, a different wall – that of total fatigue. Sharp pains radiated around both of my knees, my injured hip had tightened, causing severe stress to my lower back, and there was no drive left in my legs. My quadriceps could do little more than quiver under the load. My personal discomfort and weakness only added to my appreciation of Appia's stamina. She was at least a full foot shorter than me, and yet she'd kept pace from the start, but there came a point that no amount of effort could overcome. With an audible sigh, her knees buckled, and she collapsed. I thought she'd tripped, but when she didn't get up, I knew our trek was at an end.

"I can't move my legs!" she cried out in panic as her fingers dug into my arm in a vain attempt to stand again.

"It's all right," I said, and I fell to the ground beside her.

"No," she said. "You go."

"I don't think so," I said as I took her in my arms. "Would you leave me if the situation was reversed?" She didn't answer, but tightened her grip on me. "That's what I thought," and then I dug some ash away to make the spot more comfortable.

"Are we far enough away?" she asked as her head came to rest against my chest.

"Possibly," I replied trying to sound optimistic, but Appia wasn't convinced.

"Honestly, Getha," she said, "tell me the truth. I need to know."

I looked into the darkness before attempting an answer. "Honestly, I don't know."

"Then we have to try again," she said while attempting to reposition her legs, but there was just nothing left in them.

"No," I said calmly. "We've done all we can. I've lost my sense of direction anyway. For all I know we may be heading right back towards the mountain. The rumble seems to come from all directions at once."

"I can't tell either," she said sadly, and with a sigh added, "We gave it a good try, didn't we?"

"We did. We surely did." I checked to make sure I hadn't lost the respirator. There was some comfort in knowing I still had it, but it would not protect us in an atmosphere where oxygen wasn't present.

"When it comes," she asked, "will it be quick?"

"I doubt we'll even know what hit us," I replied solemnly. I took a moment to fight back a sudden rush of sadness. "I'm sorry." She wanted to speak, but the words caught in her throat. I just stared off into the distance thinking that history may be self-correcting after all.

We remained in each other's arms until a sudden heavy rain of fresh material forced us to make adjustments. I attempted to dig a crude fox hole, but I was even too exhausted for that, so I removed my vest and rolled it into a pillow for a buffer between us and the ground. There was nothing else to do, but lay flat and use our cloaks as covers. For the first time in my life, I was completely out of ideas.

"Have you got the medallion father gave you?" Appia asked.

"I do," I replied. "It's right here," and I lifted it off my chest for her to hold.

"Good," she said groggily. "It will help father find us."

I couldn't keep my eyes open. Neither of us could as we fell into a kind of semiconscious stupor born from total exhaustion.

Our sleep was punctuated by fits of restlessness caused by gusts of turbulent air and the ever-rising level of ash. But it was the hard thud of something big hitting the ground that woke me up. I wasn't sure if I'd actually heard it at first, but the familiar rumble of the volcano told me it wasn't a dream.

"What was that awful crash?" Appia asked, while I brushed away the ash that accumulated during our rest.

"I don't know," I replied. Sore was the word for the day as every muscle and joint responded with various levels of discomfort. "I still can't see," I said once I was finally somewhat alert. "Are you all right?"

"We're still here," she said positively. "That's more than I expected."

"How are your legs?"

"Not good," she replied, "but I can move."

My eyes were usually good at adjusting to darkness, but there was no amount of adjustment that could compensate for such a heavy veil of particulate matter; however, every once and a while I could just make out Appia's movements from a faint orange background radiance caused by cinders passing overhead.

"Where is this place?" Appia asked.

"I don't know," I replied.

Our restlessness had kept us from being buried as we dozed; although, the vest was covered by a couple inches of ash. It was a mess, and I really didn't want to put it on, but I had to in order to keep from losing it in the darkness. The next thing I did was dust off the respirator and give our lungs a break with some filtered air.

"What do we do now?" Appia asked. "I don't like it here."

"Nor do I," I replied. "Perhaps we should just keep moving. Can you walk?"

"I think so," she said, and after two tries she got to her feet while I tried and failed. My hip was numb and my left leg immobile. For the moment I was grounded.

"Oh, Getha," she cried, "you really are hurt! I knew it back at the villa."

"It's all right," I said calmly. "I just got knocked down by a few rocks on the mountain. That's all." I knew I'd hurt myself, but I never expected to awaken quite so disabled.

"The mountain?" she said with astonishment. "You were on the mountain when this started?"

"Yes."

"Why?" she asked.

"No good reason," I replied, but my mind was on our current predicament. "It would help if we found shelter."

"There was another one of those ash storms," she said. "I woke up in the middle of it."

"Just one?" I asked.

"That's all I remember," she replied.

"How long ago?"

"Not long at all," she said. "The wind sounded worse than the other ones, but it wasn't. Is that possible?"

"I don't know," I replied. "What made it seem worse?"

"I heard a lot of wood breaking," she said.

"Could you tell which direction it was coming from?"

"Not really," she replied. "It was sort of swirling."

"Interesting," I said, and I turned around and began crawling across the ground, which rose abruptly.

"Where are we going?" Appia asked.

"Bear with me," I replied. "I've got a hunch," and then I came face to face with a wall. "It's a building," I said. "It must have shielded us."

"I thought nothing could protect us from one of those pyro things."

"Not if we're too close to the source," I said as I began feeling along the wall for an opening, "but they do cool and weaken, and just maybe…"

"Are we far enough away?"

"I don't know," I said, "but our chances improve if we can find a way inside." The ashfall had suddenly lightened, offering marginally better visibility.

"Do you think it's safe?"

"It's safer than out here," I said. The windrow of ash piled against the wall indicated a pitched roof. "This is promising, but we need a way in." Crawling through the ash along the wall was a slow and painful process so

I tried to stand again. With the wall for support, and Appia's help, I made it. We followed the wall around a corner to find the sills of several tall windows just above our heads.

"No doors?" Appia lamented. "Who builds buildings without doors?" She wasn't pleased when I started chuckling. "So, what's the joke?"

"This is the second floor," I replied. "The first floor is mostly buried."

"Oh," she uttered, "okay," and then she drew my attention to a depression in the windrow along the wall. "Could ash be falling into first floor windows?"

I looked. "I think you're right. Good catch."

The moment we began digging we found the top of a window. The wooden shutters were closed but there were gaps, and some of the slats were broken allowing ash to seep in. We dug a little deeper. There was no glass. "Hello," I yelled, but my voice was weak and raspy from the bad air and lack of water. There was no answer, so I tried again. Still no answer.

"This must be a villa," Appia said, and we continued digging, but our progress was frustratingly slow without tools. The ash was gritty and light and kept sliding back into our hole like digging in dry sand.

"A villa would be nice," I replied and then I stopped digging. "Do you recall any other big ash storms while we slept?"

"No," she replied, "but I dozed off a few times too. I did hear more booms like what we heard when Herculaneum was destroyed. It was right before you woke up."

I looked around. The sky was brightening over our heads. It had to be dawn. "I don't think Vesuvius is done with us yet," I said solemnly. "If there is another pyroclastic event left, it will be soon and it will be really big. We'd better dig faster."

"Shouldn't we try to get farther away?" she asked.

"No time," I replied, trying not let my anxiety show. "Dig, Appia dig…"

There was a distant crackling and a boom followed by another boom and more crackling.

My fear quickly turned to panic, and all my pains suddenly went away. A wave of bitterly sulfurous air mixed with a fresh cloud of ash blasted us as I turned my body to kick in the top of the locked shutters with my right heel. My first kick splintered the center slats, and the second was on its way when the ground beneath us sank as the shutter frames came apart. I immediately tumbled inside, riding a current of ash, smashing what was left of the slats along the way. I quickly righted myself in time to grab Appia who was swept in behind me atop an avalanche of ash. She was in turn followed by a great blast of hot air, sending us scurrying to the nearest corner. The heat quickly rose to intolerable levels as we huddled against the wall, overtaken by a fiery wind of swirling embers.

XXIV

∞

"My god," I gasped as I could feel what was left of our breathable air being literally ripped from my lungs. I pulled Appia hard to me. The walls reacted with frightfully sharp snaps, as the softer cement between the bricks crumbled from the abnormal stress load.

My head ached from the heat and pressure as the muscles contracted in my back, putting stress on my spine. The muscles in both legs cramped. There was a smell like burning hair. It felt like we were being broiled inside our cloaks. I could feel exposed areas of my body baking – the backs of my arms, my legs – and my strength was being drained by the second and I was helpless to stop it. When the ground vibrations forced us to the floor, I believed we were done.

"Hold on, my love," I said with my last breath. We rocked together in the turbulent winds, but as quickly as the temperatures rose, they moderated, and then it was over. The last frightful sound we heard was the ripping of tiles from the roof, followed by silence. We shared the respirator, but even that was difficult because the filter clogged so quickly; however, there was air, harsh air, and we could breathe again.

Pyroclastic material separates into two basic densities of lighter and heavier matter, the surge and flow. We survived because that sixth, most powerful of all the surges, had weakened enough to spare us, but there was still the issue of the denser flow. Being denser meant it retained its blistering temperature longer. It had the potential to entomb us forever, or at least until our remains were discovered and put on display in the Naples Archaeological Museum.

Seconds passed, and then minutes, and then we could start to relax when better air, relatively speaking, began filtering into the room. Greater density also meant the heavier pyroclastic flows didn't travel as far as the lighter surges, and we were the beneficiary of that rule. An ash storm accompanied by high winds, thunder and lightning blew by, but nothing we couldn't survive.

"Are you okay?" I asked as we remained huddled together. Our muscles relaxed.

"I'm alive," she replied. "I feel good about that, but is it over?"

"I hope so," I said. "I think so. That last one was the most powerful so far. We wouldn't have survived outside."

"But you don't know for sure?"

"No," I said with a shrug. My body had returned to crippled mode, so it took me a moment to get to my feet. I helped Appia up. It was nice to be standing on a hard surface again even though my legs were ready to give out.

"Should we try to find a better place to hide?" she asked.

I looked around the room. "No. The final surge is the biggest, so if there's one more left, it won't matter where we are. But it would be nice to sit down."

That last surge had left a dim orange glow outside which helped us find a bench on the opposite side of the room. There were traces of wood smoke mixed in with the ever-present volcanic pollutants. "Do you think this building's on fire?" Appia asked with remarkable calm.

"Maybe," I replied as I eased myself onto the bench, "but I think we're okay for now."

"Good," she sighed, and she gave me a big hug. "I love you, Appius Getha."

"I love you too," I said with a kiss. We sat together, quietly resting, awaiting whatever might befall us next. After several minutes had passed, I felt better about our chances. "If another was coming, it should have happened by now."

"Finally," Appia sighed.

"But of course, we still need water and food. There may be other people…" and she poked me in the side.

"Relax," she said. "Let's just savor the moment." The opportunity to rest was welcome, but it also gave our battered bodies time to protest all the abuse heaped on them. Stiffness was quickly settling into joints and muscles, but the specter of worsening pain couldn't dim the inner elation of simply being alive.

"We were unbelievably lucky," I said.

"It was more than luck," she said. "Sometimes I think father may have been right about you."

"How can you say that?" I chuckled. "You're sitting here homeless, sore, and dehydrated."

"But at least I'm sitting here," she said.

At one point, Appia couldn't stop coughing. It was a reaction to her body trying to rid itself of some of the pollution it had inhaled. It wasn't long before I was coughing too. I thought the respirator might ease our discomfort, but the cartridge was too clogged. I pulled it apart to try to clear it, but by the time I was done, our coughing fits had ceased.

I cleared ash away from two more windows to let in more light, while Appia began looking for water. She discovered a door to an adjacent room, but found nothing except clutter. "It looks like a storage room," she said as she felt around inside. "This must be the back of the villa."

"Be careful," I said. I saw another entranceway, so I took a look.

"What is it?" Appia asked.

"I think it's a corridor." It was indeed a corridor; however, it was very difficult to follow in total darkness. We felt our way along a wall until we came to a large, dimly lit open space that had to be an atrium. An eight-foot-high mound of ash directly below the center of a partially collapsed ceiling made identification difficult. A large section of the roof had fallen in from the back wall to the compluvium, and while that didn't bode well for the structural stability of the rest of the roof, it did offer better light.

There was a room to our left as we entered. Inside we found a heavy, rectangular wooden table set against the far wall and several nearly dry oil lamps. There was a counter next to the table and a small brick oven next to it. There was a fine film of volcanic dust on everything.

"It's a kitchen," Appia said. She found several chunks of bread, but our true eureka moment happened right after the discovery of the bread. To the right of the oven stood a pair of large, covered, ceramic crocks, both containing potable water. I could hardly believe our luck. I rocked the containers to assess how much there was. There had to be gallons. Appia found two dusty cups, and we drank. Water is indeed the elixir of life. We could talk clearly again and take pain medication for our dull headaches. We found figs along with the bread, but the figs were bad. We dusted off the bread as best we could, but our need to eat was greater than any concerns about ingesting a little dirt. We also found pieces of sliced chicken in a covered bowl, and whole eggs in another, but we decided it was best to leave them alone.

I hobbled over to a spot where the lower slope of the central ash pile abutted the wall. There was another corridor. It was as dark as night inside and I had to feel my way along a wall. The first thing I came to was a doorway closed off by a heavy drape. The room was small and musty, but seemed relatively free of debris. I felt my way into the room. I was hoping to find fueled oil lamps, but all I found was a single wooden bed and flimsy night table. I returned to the corridor and found a second bedroom next to the first, but still no oil lamps. Farther down the corridor I came to a third room that needed no introduction. A latrine would provide us with an unexpected luxury. The corridor was blocked beyond that by a wall of compacted volcanic debris.

I started back to the atrium but found another entrance. There was just enough light to see it was open ended. I found a small dining room first and then a storage area. There were still no oil lamps, but what I did find was a small bath, but no standing water. The walls and roof appeared to be solid. I picked up a few items I knew Appia would enjoy, such as perfumes, a comb and mirror. We had been concerned about fire, but I found nothing burning or evidence of smoke.

I discovered a stairwell on the way back. It was right off the atrium and led to an upper floor, but I decided to join Appia before doing any more exploring. I found her sitting on the bench draining the residue from a pile of empty oil lamps into a cup. "I think I can make at least two good ones from all of these," she said.

"Can we light them?" I asked.

"Of course," she replied. "Everything we need is here. How was your search?"

"There's a lavatory," I said as I handed her the items I'd collected from the bath. "There is a bath, but no water."

"Smells good," she said as she sniffed one of the vials of perfume.

"I was thinking," I said, "we won't need all that water for drinking. Perhaps one crock could be set aside for washing."

We dragged the lightest crock from its place in the kitchen to the atrium by spinning it on its base. We found the cleanest cloth we could and began washing away the ash that covered our bodies. The process was painful at times because of tenderness due to a variety of burns and abrasions, but that layer of volcanic dust may have kept us from being more severely burned by the extreme heat.

Appia's legs looked irritated and uncomfortable from having trudged through the abrasive grains unprotected. Her feet were even more of a concern because of how the sandal straps had cut into the skin. The wear marks didn't appear to be infected, but they were nonetheless worth watching.

My feet were badly torn up and blistered by my escape from the mountain, but luckily the worst spots had remained protected. There were blistered areas on both of us, probably made by the heat flash, and the metal chain attached to Appius' medallion had left a heat mark around the back of my neck. There were patches of reddened skin on both of us, especially on the backs of our arms and legs where the burning heat from the blast was most direct.

"That looks awful," Appia said when she saw the large bruises and small cuts on my back and thigh that were easily visible even in the bad light.

"I'm sure," I said as I stretched to try to see them, "but I can't complain. It could have been worse." I felt over the small lump at the back of my head. Apparently, I got lucky. The brunt of the stone's impact was against my shoulder and neck, which saved me from a severe concussion or worse. An inch higher and I'd never have gotten off the mountain.

Once our bodies were cleaner, our clothes were next. Appia worked to brush out ash, while I emptied my vest pockets before cleaning the gun. The gun was about all that was left of the items I'd originally brought with me. Thalese had the compass and watch. I'd lost the lighter somewhere in the ash. I had ten codeine tablets left, and happily discovered there were two packets of antiseptic wedged in a side pocket. I still had the epinephrine injectors.

The sky actually brightened. At first, I thought it was my eyes continuing to readjust to the darkness, but soon shadows began to appear. I was pleased by the unexpected light, but paid little attention as I was busy cleaning the gun. I was reluctant to part with it despite how much I'd come to hate it. It might still be useful as a tool. It turned out that some bath oils worked well as lubricants.

Appia had disappeared at one point, and it wasn't until she called that I realized she was gone. "Getha!" she yelled from someplace above, "you've got to see this!"

"I'm coming," I replied. I made my way to the stairwell where she was waiting at the top.

"Come!" she said excitedly. I followed her to a comparatively well-lit room where I was rendered speechless by the view from one of its tall open windows. "Was that Vesuvius?" she asked while pointing at the hazy silhouette of a huge gaping crater in the distance.

"That's it," I said. The volcano continued to belch heavy volumes of ash and stone from its bowels, but the new cloud was much lower to the ground.

For the moment, the winds had shifted the bulk of its mass slightly to the east, bettering our visibility, but the sky was in no way clear overhead.

The newly fallen blanket of ash was venting its heat into the atmosphere in thin wisps of steam across the entire plain. I had understood the history of the event before I came to the era, but like everything else, there was no possible way to be prepared for the living experience. It was an alien world, desolate and colorless, littered with pockets of protruding brickwork and scattered building debris, and completely unnerving to see the city that had become my home so thoroughly blasted into a field of smashed masonry and rubble.

Broken and jagged tops of the western and southern walls were still visible, but the force of the surge had stripped the rooftops of every building completely off, staining the rutted, surrounding grey landscape with darker areas of debris. What had been forest was knocked down in neat little rows of grey, bark-stripped trunks that pointed like a reaper's finger straight at us.

"What do we do now?" she asked.

"Stay the night," I said as the volcanic cloud shifted west again, obscuring our view. "We seem to be safe enough here. And there's really no place to go, at least for the time being."

"We've got bread," she said, "and plenty of water."

"Rest is what we need most," I said. "It will be a fairly long and difficult walk out." Appia was still at the window staring into the darkness.

"It was a pretty powerful scene," I said sadly, "and you've been surprisingly quiet about it. Do you want to talk?"

"No," she replied, "not now."

We returned to the ground floor where I took one more look at Appia's sore feet. She closed her eyes while I applied antibiotics. I suggested we make use of the bed chambers I'd found and she agreed. She found a striker and lit one of the oil lamps. I dragged the bed from one room and placed it next to the bed in the other.

I felt like I was too tired to sleep, but sitting on a mattress was such a wonderful sensation. The last conscious thing I remembered was thinking about how used to the ground vibrations we'd become. It reminded me of sleeping on a train and I drifted off into a real sleep.

We had survived the unsurvivable, but we were still holed up in an unstable structure with little food, no running water, and poor sanitation. The air was polluted with sulfurous gases as Vesuvius continued to belch ground-hugging clouds of foul smoke that blanketed the entire region south of the volcano.

We could barely walk the next day. Thunderstorms and a very heavy acid rain forced us to move upstairs when the first floor flooded. That was followed by a river of mud when a portion of the roof and back wall beyond the bath collapsed.

It rained hard all that day and into the next, but we had nowhere to go anyway. I decided our best bet was to head for the port town of Stabiae. Thanks to our brief view of ruined Pompeii, I had a pretty good fix on our location. Stabiae was also destroyed, but I knew from history that naval vessels landed there two or three days after the eruption.

After three days of being cooped up in an increasingly more inhospitable venue, we decided to leave as soon as the rain let up. Our final evening beneath the volcanic cloud brought fresher air, and for the first time in days the outside world was silent and the ground peaceful at the same time. The sudden calm was the missing piece that allowed us to finally give way to more sensual emotions. It seemed incredible that the physical expression of our feelings for each other had waited so long. What began as gentle caressing became more than just the bonding of two needy people; it was the bonding of kindred souls.

There was a wispy, sulfurous mist drifting through the room at first light. I had hoped for better visibility for our escape, but instead we were thoroughly socked in by fog. I considered staying another day even though the rain had stopped.. I studied the remaining bread that had become both stale and moldy in spots, and then I checked the condition of the potable water to find it had turned milky. There was a rancid smell rising from the flooded floor below. That settled it. It was time to go.

We dressed quickly and moved towards the windows that faced Stabiae. At least we'd begin in the proper direction. I helped Appia down first before climbing out myself.

"Which way?" she asked as we peered into the fog.

"That way," I replied with a wave of my hand. "What's left of Stabiae must be out there somewhere."

"Why Stabiae?" she asked. "Why not Nucerea?"

"I sent the others to Nucerea to get them to safety as quickly as possible," I replied. "Stabiae was not a safe option then, but it is now. It's the closest port, and I know for a fact the navy will have landed there by now."

"Maybe the others are still in Nucerea."

"I thought about that too," I said. "They're not expecting us so most likely they're either in Salernum or already on their way to Rome by now."

The footing wasn't nearly as bad as I expected. We were walking atop ten feet of ash, but with all the rain and ground vibration it had settled into a firmer base that was more easily walkable. It didn't take long before we were beyond view of the building and stepping across an eerie, monotone landscape. All around us were lifeless shapes and long grey shadows. What was once a grove of trees had been transformed into a field of grey, limbless trunks, all leaning hard to the south.

"This is spooky," Appia whispered as she took my arm.

Much of the debris forced us into directional changes, but with all the trees leaning one way, it was a problem easily corrected. The sky brightened as we walked, but it only served to enhance the haunting sensations the scene had already evoked. The horizon remained a blurry haze of random shadows that limited our field of vision to about one hundred feet, and the ground seemed more lunar than earth-like.

Our moods brightened with the brightening sky. The fog thinned over our heads to expose a most welcome color, so we stopped to look up at a brilliant blue that had seemed forever lost. Wisps of fog blew by as if trying desperately to close the gap, but at long last the hideous volcanic soup was starting to lose its grip.

At one point we passed through a valley that sent us right back into complete fog again, and then we crossed a plain where visibility became even worse. When it seemed as if we were socked in for good, a clear, salty breeze appeared, and with it came real change. It was wonderful air, and I closed my eyes to take a breath. The effect was so fantastic that I hardly noticed Appia's grip tightening around my arm. I wanted to enjoy the fresh smell, but with a sudden tug, she brought my attention back to earth.

The fog was gone, and standing before us was a small group of startled soldiers. I immediately went for my gun, but Appia said, "No."

"Where did you come from?" the lead soldier asked.

"Back there," I replied, and I pointed behind us.

"But nothing lives back there," another said.

"We did," Appia announced proudly.

A third soldier, obviously a commander, stepped forward and asked in a far less friendly voice, "Exactly who are you who appears to have stepped out from beneath the veil of the gods?"

His aggressive attitude irritated me, and without thinking I replied in an equally strong tone. "Exactly who are you to ask?"

"Relax," Appia whispered.

"As a representative of Emperor Titus Flavius Vespasianus," the commander said, "it is you who needs to do the explaining."

"This is Appius Marius Valerianus Getha of Pompeii," Appia stated. "And I'm his sister, Maria Secunda. My friends call me Appia."

The soldiers stared for moment in silence, and then backed up slightly. "Appius Marius Getha of Pompeii?" the commander asked in far less challenging tone. "The Appius Getha?"

"Perhaps," I replied. "I'm sure I'm not the only one with that name."

"Then tell me sir," he said, "have you a servant, a former gladiator?"

"Caelus," Appia said.

"It is him!" a voice announced. "The son of Hercules!" Two soldiers knelt and bowed their heads. The others quickly followed, leaving me in a quandary as to what to do next.

"Relax," Appia whispered, "we can use a few friends right now."

"Commander Marcus Nexus Virillius," the commander announced with pride as they all rose to their feet. "We who stand before you had the honor of taking part in the counterattack that put an end to the insurrections against your earthly benefactor and the emperor." I acknowledged them with a nod and a degree of apprehension as they heeled to attention when the emperor was mentioned. "Forgive me for not recognizing you."

"Have we met?" I asked.

"Yes," he replied, "at your villa. The emperor was there and we met briefly."

I tried to recall the encounter, but I was introduced to a great many people during those hectic and difficult days following the assassination. His face wasn't familiar. "I think I recall you now," I said politely. "You held a kind of shiny metal..."

"My helmet," he said with pride. "I was holding it."

"In the red band, the figures..."

"I had those custom made," he said with surprise. "You have a remarkable memory. Again, I apologize for not recognizing you."

"I'm surprised you could at all," I said. "I imagine these past few days have not been kind to my appearance."

"How can we be of service?" Marcus asked.

"We need to get to Rome," Appia stated.

"We were heading to Stabiae to find transport to Rome if possible," I said.

"Stabiae is destroyed," he said sadly. "In all my years of service, I've never seen such devastation. There are no transports out, but if you don't mind putting up with galley-style accommodations, we will ensure your safe passage to Rome."

"That would be most welcome," Appia replied, "thank you."

"We landed late yesterday," he said. "My orders are to assess the situation and gather information."

A young soldier appeared with a message for Marcus. "It's from the emperor," he said excitedly. "He's asking for an update on the situation."

Marcus shook his head and looked towards the bay. "Hustle back," he said, "and have Crassus send this, *Confirmed, entire region from Neapolis to Stabiae destroyed beyond recognition,*" and then he looked at me. "Tell him to add, *Report incomplete. I will update him in person.* Can you remember that?"

"Yes sir," he replied as he too was staring at me. A soldier next to Marcus stepped back and whispered something in the young soldier's ear. "Really?" he replied with a smile.

"Now go!" Marcus commanded, and the boy took off over the ash towards the coast.

"News of the eruption has already reached Rome?" I asked.

"Yes," he said, "but only the early reports. The emperor knows nothing of the level of devastation, which is what makes your appearance most fortuitous. You've given me cause to deliver the news in person."

"To Rome?" Appia asked.

"Yes," he replied. "I will send word to the base. I'm sure there will be no objections. We'll forgo Misenum and go straight to Rome. We'll leave at first light. If the winds are with us, we may arrive there ahead of the message I just sent, so unless you have any objections, let us escort you to the ship. I'm sure you must be hungry." He gave orders for the rest of his group to finish their sweep of the area and then we were on our way.

It wasn't a long walk. The town of Stabiae was in ruins as expected, but perhaps not quite as completely shattered and deeply buried as Pompeii. The naval vessels were moored to the west of the city, just off the newly created shoreline that jutted out up to a mile or so in places beyond where it was prior to the eruption.

"It's a big ship," I said as we approached the bow of Marcus's galley. The word quinquereme came to mind. "I'm surprised you can get it so close without grounding."

Marcus led us to a set of crudely constructed steps that ran up the side and over the railing. I'd seen galleys like it from my perch above the bay, but I never imagined how rugged they were. I knew it was military by the protruding ram device set just below the waterline. The metal trimmed bow was shaped into a reversed goose head at the top. I was impressed by the tight fit of the clapboards and the way the double row of rectangular port holes were carefully cut into them.

We boarded and Marcus led us to a small cabin near the stern. "I offer you my humble quarters," he said.

"That's very kind," I said, "but we don't want to displace you."

"Thank you," Appia said as she stepped by me and entered the cabin.

"I'll find you a divider for privacy," he said. "There is one mattress, but I'll have a second brought in. I'll also send fresh water and food, so relax and enjoy."

I thanked him and entered the room. It was very small, but sturdy like the rest of the ship, and very welcome. There was a wooden bench against the back wall where I sat, while Appia sat on the narrow bed made from a wide plank that was affixed to the wall. It had foldout legs and hinges so it could be folded against the wall when not in use. Marcus was pleased that we accepted his offerings, and after thanking him again, he left us.

"How about a hug," I said. We embraced, but our personal moment didn't last very long. Heavy footsteps outside were followed by a knock. A pair of slaves entered with a second mattress. They were followed by a third with a heavy piece of fabric that he proceeded to affix to the ceiling as a divider. A fourth filled the wash basin with water. We attempted sponge baths after they left, and with that done we sat separated by the divider.

"What are we supposed to do now?" I asked.

"I don't know," she replied with a chuckle.

"Why the divider?"

"Propriety," she said. "We're brother and sister. Unfortunately, it's best we go along with it."

Food was brought. There was a legume broth and cinnamon biscuits. It felt good just to be eating again; after which, we napped.

In a technical sense we slept in our separate sections, but there was a two-foot-high gap between the floor and the bottom of the divider. We placed the mattresses side by side on the floor, but still on opposite sides of the divider.

"There's something you should know," I said as I took her hand. "It's something your father was going to tell you, but he never got the chance."

"What is it, Getha?"

"I don't know exactly how to say this," I said, "so I'll just say it. Your natural mother is really Leita."

She smiled. "I know that."

"Your father told me. He felt badly that…what?"

"I know."

"You do?"

"I've known for years," she said.

"How did you find out?"

"My mother told me," she replied.

"Lucretia?"

"Yes."

"And Leita knows you know?"

"Of course, she does," she said.

"Oh."

"Father and his little intrigues," she said with a chuckle. "Sometimes I think he outsmarts himself."

I awoke the next morning to the sound of a rowing cadence. The sea was calmer, producing only a gentle rocking as we left port and headed into open water. The sun was rising from behind a foggy volcanic haze that had thinned and was beginning to dissipate for the first time since the eruption began. The mountain appeared gutted, hollowed out, leaving a gaping, steaming caldera open to the sea; its battered northern and western slopes were all that remained of its former identity. It had become the shape I knew as Mount Somma in my time, but without Vesuvius.

The landscape was ashen and lifeless, etched with light and dark pyroclastic spillways and desolate, meandering dry gullies. Herculaneum and the coastal towns as far south as Oplontis were entirely gone, without so much as a single rooftop to mark their burial sites. Wherever my time ship was, it was buried along with everything else, leaving me permanently marooned. A wave of sorrow gripped me.

"You're missing your home," Appia said. She couldn't look at the devastation onshore, choosing to watch me instead.

"At least that one issue has been resolved," I said. When I took her hand, she finally looked at the desolate plain that had been her home. Tears welled in her eyes.

"I loved him so much," she said.

"He knew that," I said.

"But I never told him. I never said good-bye."

I drew her close to my side as we watched what had been her world disappearing into the distant haze. As the oars were pulled in and the sail unfurled, we realized nothing could ever be the same, and yet circumstances had created a common ground from which to begin anew, as neither of us could ever go home again.

PART II

Auribus teneo lupum

I hold a wolf by the ears

XXV

∞

Aine's discovery of the photo of two modern shell casings fused amid a time-melded clump of two-thousand-year-old Roman coins at Pompeii was as energizing as it was disturbing, but it still required study and verification. The artifact was housed in the Museo Archeologio Nazionale di Napoli, but after multiple correspondences between Christina and the museum Director's Office, she was denied access to it. Her scholastic achievements, while impressive, as noted in the letter of denial, were not in any of the accepted research disciplines, nor was her stated reason for access to the artifact considered compelling enough.

Her denial was not entirely unexpected. The museum was very protective of its possessions, as it should be, and her stated reason was well worded, in Italian, but amounted to little more than a wish to view the artifact out of curiosity. She certainly couldn't state the true reason. However, she clearly underestimated the degree of scrutiny her request would receive. She was banking on her academic accolades to be the deciding factor, which, of course, they weren't. The director's office receives similar requests from researchers every day, all backed by impressive degrees, but perhaps her biggest mistake was not offering any thoughts on how her viewing might benefit the museum. Lesson learned.

A follow up request for photography was her next course of action, and after adding this new request to a kindly worded reply to the denial letter, Christina received several detailed images of the artifact. The photos arrived in a manila envelope with a disclaimer stamped in red stating that the artifact was a hoax. That determination was based purely on visual examination. Modern day shell casings did not exist when the coins were buried in 79 CE, and therefore, it had to be a hoax despite forensic testing that indicated otherwise.

Of course, the artifact was not a hoax. The fine resolution of each photo was enough to confirm the shell casings were exactly the kind Aaron had taken with him, and after further study they confirmed the casings were spent and not unspent rounds.

The next question was, who fired the gun? Aaron seemed to be the logical answer, but that was by no means a certainty. The working theory was that Aaron had survived after bailing out of the time ship, but there was no evidence to support that. Therefore, anyone finding the weapon, or stealing it, might have been able to figure it out – "might" being the operative word. Modern culture is all too familiar with firearms; however, such an understanding would not necessarily have been intuitive in a culture where no such items existed. First, they would have to know it was a weapon, and secondly, they would have to understand the relationship between the gun and the bullets. Of course, if the gun was discovered already loaded, that understanding would be accelerated.

If nothing else, the artifact meant that Aaron may have survived after he left the ship. For that reason, Aine returned to the library in search of any historical evidence that might be interpreted as the use of a firearm in Pompeii prior to the eruption of Mt. Vesuvius. She was aware of how difficult such a search would be given that Pompeiians didn't have experience with guns. She knew she'd have to rely on ancient descriptions of events that had gun-like elements in them, if such descriptions even existed.

Once again, luck was with her. It wasn't a history book that drew her attention, but a book on ancient myths and legends. The book had been returned to the shelf with the jacket cover askew. When she pulled it from the shelf she saw the cover picture. It depicted a man in a toga with outstretched arms firing lightning bolts from the palm of his hand. There was a Roman temple behind him, and behind the temple was the outline of a mountain. She was shaking as she turned the pages to find the story related to the cover picture.

This legend was born from a purported historical event within the walls of Pompeii, entitled, *An Insurrection Against the Emperor and the Imperial Family*. There were no definitive eyewitness accounts, only fragmentary pieces of later recollections that may have come from survivors of the eruption. Those recollections referred to a man with the power to control thunder and lighting, create violent storms of wind and hail, and toss javelins a mile through the air. The legend described this man as standing a head taller than most, and having a strong, but relaxed physique that belied the power he held within. This man is described as a "neoteric Hercules" with the capacity to single handedly vanquish whole armies, and who, on a hot summer day in Pompeii destroyed an entire mercenary militia created by disgruntled patricians to assassinate the emperor who was in Campania at the time.

Unlike the Julian period, where volumes of writing have survived regarding the Caesars from Julius to Nero, there was frustratingly little historical documentation of the Flavian era. Aine looked for any factual data relating to this so-called *Insurrection*, but no facts were forthcoming. The legend of a new Hercules remained just that, a legend, but Aine wasn't so sure. The description of the man standing a head taller than most might be an exaggeration, but Aaron was a little taller than average in his own era, and the firing of a gun could easily appear as the conjuring of thunder and lightning from his hand. The rest could be understood as embellishment, as the retelling of an event can take on a life of its own.

None of this was the hard evidence that Aine sought, but it was enough for her to believe there was a better than average chance that the "Hercules" in question was indeed Aaron, and that became the theory the team decided to adopt as well. The question then became, why did Aaron decide to use his weapon in such a manner, which was a clear violation of the *Principles of Conduct?* After all, he was the author of those very rules, and swore an oath to uphold them.

XXVI

∞

It was with great relief that we passed through the jetties that protected the entrance to Ostia, the port of Rome. Stiff winds and rolling seas made for a difficult passage with little sleep, but the air was warm and relatively dry, feeling more like summer than fall.

The oarsmen rowed the ship at a relaxed cadence across the calm harbor waters, and then carefully maneuvered it into position alongside a concrete pier. Commander Virillius requested that Appia and I remain on board while he personally arranged for our transportation.

The port was a hub of activity. There were nine other ships being unloaded with another ten anchored outside the harbor awaiting their turn. Crates and barrels of all sizes and shapes were being moved by literally hundreds of dockworkers. Beyond the quays and the semicircular landing platform that defined the shape of the inner harbor were a series of brick, multi-story warehouses that blocked our view of the landscape beyond.

"How do you feel about taking a barge upriver?" Commander Virillius asked upon his return. Appia gave an approving nod and I agreed. "I looked for a carriage," he said, "but the best I could do was a smelly mule cart. The barge will be slow, but a lot more comfortable. I promise."

"I'm sure it will be," I told him.

"I can assign a few of my men as escorts."

"We've been enough of a burden," Appia said with a smile. "I'm certain we can manage from here."

"You're not a burden at all," he said, and then he led us down the wooden ramp to the landing and through the bustling warehouses to a grain barge tied to a wooden dock that paralleled the riverbank.

"Thank you," I said. "I won't forget what you've done for us."

He crossed his chest with both arms in salute. "It has been my honor to serve. Feel free to call on me again."

Appia added her thanks and we boarded the heavily laden barge. We were immediately greeted by the tillerman who pointed to a pile of sacks by the railing. I didn't know what was in them, but after a little shaping they made for comfortable seats.

The crew consisted of six pole handlers, a tillerman, and a collection of about twenty shore workers. The barge had a small mast, but I saw no sails, only long ropes leading from the bow to the group of workers on shore. When the tillerman gave the word, the ropes were pulled taut, slapping the surface of the water as the barge began to move upstream against a slow, yet steady current. I looked back to thank the commander one more time, but he was already gone.

Appia and I were exhausted, and it wasn't long before we dozed off. I awoke just in time to recognize the spot where I got my first look at the ancient world. I was starting to unlock more memories. I remembered sitting at the controls of the time ship when it unexpectedly began to slow down and lose altitude. It appeared to have begun its final descent earlier than planned, but that was less concerning than an apparent warning message in bold red text that popped up on the console. Unfortunately, it was either in a code we hadn't deciphered, or alien language, but in either case it was unreadable.

The warm midday sun and wonderfully fresh air were comforting and Appia slept soundly against my shoulder. Her cuts and bruises were healing with no signs of infection. Both of us had lots of blisters and bruises, along with muscle aches and joint stiffness, but all our aggravations seemed unimportant next to the greater feeling of having survived.

When we reached the first of the city piers, the original shore crew gave way to a fresh crew who jockeyed the barge into position behind several others. I was just about to nod off again when the tillerman tapped me on the shoulder and pointed to a wide plank being lowered between the boat and a stone-paved landing.

"Where are we?" Appia asked groggily.

"I think we're here," I replied.

The tillerman may have been smiling pleasantly, but it was clear he was anxious for us to leave to avoid holding up river craft queuing behind us. Appia rubbed her eyes and stretched while the tillerman graciously assisted us as we were both a little unsteady on our feet. He accepted our thanks with a bow, and then hustled back to the helm to get the barge moving again.

"Can you find the villa from here?" I asked Appia since I had no idea where we were going.

She studied the scene for a moment and said, "No problem." It took some added time to negotiate around the many obstacles and busy shore personnel working the landing, but once across we found a stairway that led to a spot well above the river.

"How are you feeling?" I asked, noticing how gingerly she had taken the stairs.

"Sore," she replied, "especially my knees. But it's nice to be on solid ground again."

"That's a fact!" I heartily agreed.

We passed between a pair of large warehouses and through a tightly packed apartment district. Appia warned me to watch out for debris that might be tossed from windows, something I seemed to have knowledge of. I was also aware of the nervous glances we were getting. We looked a mess in our tattered cloaks and battered bodies. We were still covered in mountain grime despite our feeble attempts to cleanup aboard the naval vessel; however, it made the walking easier in crowded passageways as people stepped away from us to avoid contact.

The city congestion ended abruptly once we were past the apartments. The heart of Rome lay to the northeast as we trekked on a southeasterly course along less congested streets that led to more open countryside. There were impressive villas sandwiched between clusters of umbrella pines and an aqueduct that stretched from Rome to the distant hills on the southern horizon.

We passed a pair of multistory villas on the left and another on the right, and then we came to a great archway where the aqueduct crossed the road. It was most impressive. There was another villa on the right side of the road about a hundred yards beyond the archway. This villa was different. It looked more like a fortress than a country home, surrounded by a solid, seven-foot high, white masonry wall. Only the second story was visible from the street. When Appia stopped before the imposing main gate, constructed out of interconnecting strips of black, iron rod, I knew we were home.

"Is this it?" I asked.

"It is," she replied.

"What's with the iron bars? It looks more like a prison than a villa."

"Otho used to live here," she explained. "It was abandoned when Vitellius came to power. Vespasian gave it to father after Rome's liberation."

"Otho must have known he had enemies," I said as I tugged on one of iron bars. It didn't budge.

"I'm sure," she smiled, "but this is a very old villa, and Rome wasn't always as peaceful as it is today." There was a latch, and once lifted, the heavy gate swung aside with surprising ease. The moment we entered the grounds we heard voices coming from an upstairs window, and then the front door opened and Paris appeared.

"By the Gods above," he cried out, "it is you! Therasia, come quickly! Appia and Getha are here!"

"Paris!" Appia cried out as she hobbled ahead to greet him. Therasia came running out right behind him.

"We just heard the horrifying news," she said with tears in her eyes. "We've been so worried about you."

"Has anyone else made it here yet?" I asked.

"No," she replied, "just you so far. Who else is coming?"

"Everybody's coming here," I said.

"What really happened down there?" she asked. "We've heard stories of earthquakes and fires that consumed whole cities. They say Neapolis is in ruins."

"The stories are true," I replied. "Pompeii is obliterated." I noticed several unfamiliar faces peering intensely at us from just inside the doorway. "All the cities along the bay from Neapolis to Stabiae are completely destroyed." My words were followed by a chorus of groans.

A striking young man of fair complexion stepped out to meet us. "How can that be?" he asked. "What could have made the gods so displeased?"

"The gods had nothing to do with it," I said. "The towns were built too close to an active volcano."

"A volcano? I'm not sure I know what that is."

"And you are?" I asked.

"They call me David, my master," he replied with a half bow.

"David? That's a curious name for this region."

Therasia smiled and said, "David was purchased from eastern traders, but he obviously isn't of eastern birth."

"I don't know where I was born," he said, "but I'm here now."

"And we're glad he is," Therasia said, and she gave him a warm glance.

I followed Therasia and Appia into the house.

"How's the baby?" Appia asked.

"Growing like a little weed," Therasia replied with a proud grin. "He has his daddy's eyes."

The atrium was quite stunning with bright sunlight pouring in through the compluvium. High walls created spaciousness while elaborate frescos added vibrant colors.

“Do you know everyone?” Therasia asked Appia, and she motioned the servants closer.

“I do, but Getha doesn’t,” Appia said.

“But we know of Master Getha,” David said. “We’ve heard the stories.”

“Where’s Paris?” Therasia asked.

“He’s with little Paris,” a woman servant replied. “He sent me out to meet our new master.”

Therasia turned to me. “This is Julia. She’s actually our cook, but today she’s been watching the baby for me.” Julia was a tall, thin woman, nearly Thalese’s height. She had curly black hair and a very childlike face. I mistook her for a boy when I first saw her standing in the doorway.

She stepped forward when introduced and knelt before me with her head bowed as one might do in the presence of royalty. The formality of her greeting may have been to honor my place in the family, but it wasn’t comfortable. I didn’t know how to react, so I simply thanked her and asked her to stand.

“And here’s Fabius,” Therasia said. Fabius was a stocky, older man who stood a little over five feet tall. He had deeply set brown eyes and short, greying hair. “He oversees our work force both here and in Ostia.” Fabius stepped forward and knelt before me as Julia had. “And you’ve already met David,” to which David stepped forward and knelt next to Fabius. “David coordinates shipments. He works closely with Fabius. They spend much of their time in Ostia, so you probably won’t see them during the course of a normal day.”

I motioned them to their feet. “You’re a fine-looking lot,” I said, “however, there’s no need to kneel before me. I know that’s what your trained to do, and perhaps it’s normal, but…” and then I paused to find the right words.

“But Getha isn’t normal,” Appia chuckled, nudging me with her elbow.

“Appia’s right. I’m not like other so-called masters and such formality is not necessary around me. I’d prefer that you don’t bow or kneel.” Therasia started to speak but I cut her off. “Just let me finish. My name is Getha. Not master. Not Master Getha. Just Getha.”

“But decorum dictates otherwise,” Fabius said with a bewildered look on his face.

“I can’t believe Appius required that level of formality from you,” I said.

“But you are new to us,” he replied, “and we wish not to be disrespectful or offensive.”

“You aren’t either of those things,” I said. “Just be yourselves.”

"Moving on," Therasia said, "we have Cornelia. Cornelia is relatively new to the household. She's learning her duties, which are primarily domestic." Cornelia immediately stepped forward and started to kneel but caught herself. She was a pretty woman of about eighteen. She had long, straight, jet black hair, and an overall dark complexion reminiscent of Nubia. She looked confused so I stepped closer and took her hand.

"And lastly," Therasia said, "this is Claudia." I stepped to the right and took her hand. "She's been here the longest. She's our record keeper. She records all income, whatever type, and nothing happens business wise without her input. Even Thalese has learned to rely on her when he's here, and that's quite a compliment."

"Indeed, it is," I said, and I stood back to address the entire group. "Appius has spoken to me on many occasions of how proud he was of all of you, and it's an honor to finally have a chance to meet you." They began to kneel, but then looked at each other as if confused. "Relax," I said, and following an uncomfortable pause, Therasia waved them away.

She ushered us into a large summer dining room. Once situated, Julia appeared with wine and Fabius with cooked chicken breasts. The aromas brought back warm memories of my first meal in Pompeii.

"Have you any news of my mother?" Paris asked as he entered the room.

"Not yet," I replied, "but I have every reason to believe they're safe and on their way here."

Therasia took her place next to Paris. "What about Caestus and Maria Prima?" she asked. "Are they coming here too?"

"I don't know," I replied. "We went to Oplontis to fetch them, but they weren't home."

"No one was home," Appia said sadly, "not even the servants." Cornelia entered the room carrying a pitcher of water, followed by David who stood near the doorway as if awaiting orders.

"Actually," I said in a cheerier voice, "despite the magnitude of the disaster, I believe many people escaped. Maria Prima may be with friends in Neapolis."

"I suppose," Appia sighed.

The chicken was tempting and Appia and I ate even though we weren't terribly hungry. My mind wandered when the conversation turned to domestic issues, and when the meal ended everyone sauntered off in different directions, including Appia. I seized that opportunity to step outside for some private space.

When I looked up at the brilliant, blue sky another bit of lost memory returned. I remembered looking up at a similar sky just before I was struck in the head by a falling object tossed from an upper story window. It was a ceramic bedpan or something similar. It happened in Rome on my way back to the ship prior to my arrival in Pompeii. It explained my head injury, at least in part, although, my injured hands and shoulder were more consistent with a fall. Was it possible I fell out of the ship? At Pompeii, no less? On course, and on schedule? I had to chuckle. Nope, not a chance. Most of my lost memory had returned, but not enough to finally solve that riddle.

"There you are," Appia said as she stepped out from inside the villa grounds. "What are you doing out here?"

"Sitting," I replied. "Getting used to our new home." My sore legs had tightened, and I was still a little unsteady getting to my feet.

"Are you okay?" she asked as she took my arm.

"I think I'm going to be sore for a while longer."

She chuckled. "You sound surprised."

"I'm not."

"I think you're doing well after what happened to you."

"I suppose," I sighed, "but it seems like every time I start to feel good, something happens. I don't think you've ever seen me without bumps and bruises."

"You look good to me," she said with a smile. "Anyway, I thought you might like to see where you'll be sleeping."

We returned to the main house. She led me through the atrium and into the courtyard. It was a smaller open space than the one in Pompeii, but it was comprised of mostly the same elements, including a complete portico supported by columns, well-groomed plants and lots of statues.

"You're in the room on the left," she said. "It's the farthest away from the rest of the household."

The room was a hub of activity. Cornelia was feverishly at work dragging a dusty chair out through the doorway. She had already removed a collection of odd items such as wagon wheels, a bundle of wooden stakes, and a sack of planting soil. Julia was inside lowering a bed frame that had apparently been resting on its side.

"Another storage room?" I asked. The room was dimly lit, having only two small, one-foot-square windows cut into the back wall. The air inside was churning with dust. The musty smell reminded me of our recent days holed up beneath the volcanic cloud.

David entered the room. "Before I take my leave," he said with a subtle look of dismay as he studied my new digs, "I want to personally welcome both of you to the Villa North. I think you will find we have a very good staff here, and I feel certain you will be as pleased with our performance as was our late Master."

"So, David," I asked, "when will you be returning?"

He scratched his head. "In three or four days, depending. I've got to make a short trip up the coast tomorrow. Is there something you require before I leave?"

"No," I replied, but instead of leaving he became fidgety as if there was something else on his mind.

"What is it, David?" Appia asked.

He scratched his head again. "I have a question for you, master. I mean Getha. If you don't mind."

"Of course not," I said, "please…"

"We heard from Paris and Therasia that you freed the entire household staff at Pompeii. Is that your plan for us too?"

It was a good question, and my first thought was how unfair it would be to deny the staff in Rome the same benefits I'd given their peers in Pompeii. "Yes," I replied. "I'll get together with Thalese and we'll figure it out." My second thought was that I shouldn't have spoken so quickly. I needed to be extra careful regarding any future unorthodox decisions since I no longer had an active volcano to negate my mistakes.

He smiled and said, "Thank you," and left us.

I turned to Appia. "Is there a reason why I'm in another storage room?"

"It's the most private room," she replied.

"Okay," I said, still looking a bit puzzled.

"It's the best spot for us," she said, "to share our private time."

"Okay," I said, "but I'll bet all the other bedrooms have drapes or doors for privacy."

"They do," she smiled, "but then people will know we're together."

"You mean like lovers?"

She chuckled. "We're not like lovers. We are lovers. Or do you disagree?"

"Oh no," I said, and I took her hand. "I wholeheartedly agree, but why is that so important? I want the family to know about us. I want to shout it to the world!"

"As do I," she said, "but the timing isn't right. There's been so much change. It might be better to let things settle down first. I would hate for our intimacy to add to all the uncertainty and confusion that these people are already burdened with."

"Call me stupid, but I don't see the point."

"It's a morality issue," she said, "perhaps a legal one too."

I really didn't understand. "Everyone knew about my relationship with Nubia. Nobody told me that was immoral or illegal. In fact, your father encouraged it."

"You're comparing plumbs to pomegranates," she said, "and by the way, he's your father too."

"I know that."

"Yes, you do," she said. "You and I are brother and sister by law. By law, our intimacy is incest."

"It's no such thing!" I said. "We're not blood related. I was adopted!"

"True," she said, "but it doesn't change the facts. We are brother and sister by law, and our current relationship would be considered nefas, or contrary to divine law. We won't be hauled off to prison for it, but it may deeply offend the very people whose aid we will need the most if we hope to keep the family and businesses together. It's a moral issue that can't be ignored."

"Here's a question," I said, "am I still your brother, or as head of the family am I now your father?"

She shook her head again and hugged me. "You're hopeless," she said. "No, you're not my father. But before you try to change the subject again, do you understand what I just said?"

"It means we can never wed," I replied. "It means we'll have to be sneaky, and I'm not very good at sneaking."

"Do you really want me for your wife?" she asked.

"Of course I do," I said. "I know marriage is basically a political tool here, but to me it's about love. That's the ideal from where I come from. And I love you."

"It can also be about love here as well," she said warmly, "and I love you too."

"Do you wish to take me as your husband?"

"I do," she replied with a big smile. "You know that."

"Then we must find a way to make it happen," I said.

"I don't know how."

"We will figure it out," I said. "I'll play the silly game of secrets and sneakiness for a while longer, but not indefinitely. After that, they'll just have to deal with it. Good enough?"

"It's not just the household, but the clients," she said. "We need them now more than ever. We can't afford to lose any one of them over an avoidable morality issue."

"The clients stay out there," I said and I pointed to the main house. "They aren't to come into the courtyard. They most certainly aren't invited into our bedroom whether it's here or over there. And they aren't going to know a damn thing about us!"

"Okay," she said with a chuckle, realizing it was useless to try to have a meaningful discussion when I was that overtired. Instead, she cuddled up with me on the bed, but the sudden appearance of Fabius and Cornelia in the courtyard abruptly cooled the warming trend we were heading toward.

"It's going to be strange sleeping without you at my side tonight," she said sadly.

"It will be."

"You once told me your given name, but I've forgotten."

"It's Aaron," I said.

"Aaron. Correct me if I'm wrong, but isn't that an eastern name like David?"

"I don't know," I said following an extended yawn.

"It's curious that you come from the west and he comes from the east, yet you share eastern praenomen."

"My homeland is a melting pot of people from all lands, and thus a mixture of names."

I was just starting to nod off when she asked, "Did you leave a special woman behind – before you came here?" Her voice quivered as it seemed to be a difficult question for her to ask.

I sighed. "I suppose I could say no, but that wouldn't be the truth," I replied.

"Oh."

"But that relationship was different," I said.

"You must miss her very much," she said sadly. "I can't imagine how I'd feel if you were suddenly gone forever."

"I do miss her," I said. "She was a very good friend, and we cared for each other a great deal."

"Do you love her?"

That was a tough question that didn't have a clear answer. The problem with time travel is that personal feelings regarding people who haven't been born yet are muddled and confusing at best. There's no sense of connection. My memories of Christina had returned, and I knew she was real, but my mind treated her reality as a contradiction, and my feelings for her out-of-place, perhaps even illogical. "I did," I replied, "but in a time that has no more substance than a dream."

"Oh," she uttered.

"I love you," I said, and I hugged her. "Christina is a special friend. I won't deny that. But I also know I've never loved anybody as much as I love you. My heart is yours to keep."

She smiled and drew me back into a warm hug. "To think that just a year ago I didn't even know you existed."

"A year ago, I didn't exist," I reminded her as I could barely keep my eyes open.

"Sleep, my love," she said, and she kissed me on the forehead. I would have kissed her back if I hadn't faded so quickly. Following a second kiss she left and walked back to the house.

XXVII

∞

I awoke to bright sunlight from the small windows over my head. There were voices outside the entrance and a general commotion in the courtyard.

"Do we wake him?" I heard a woman say.

"We must," a male insisted.

"Master Getha," I heard. It was Julia.

"Yes," I replied as I made a feeble attempt to sit up. I was terribly groggy.

"Please master," Julia said nervously. "It's the emperor."

"Okay," I chuckled, "I'll play. The emperor who?"

"The only emperor," she replied excitedly as she stepped into the room, immediately followed by Cornelia carrying an armload of grooming essentials. "He's come to see you. Emperor Titus has come to see you! He's here now, waiting. Right in our home!"

"Emperor Titus?" I said while Cornelia began grooming me, which was more of a bother since I didn't want servants doing those things for me. "I wonder what he wants?"

"I wouldn't know, master," she replied, "but Fabius is finding you a proper toga right now. He'll be here in an instant."

"My name is Getha," I said with a yawn as I stood to get my bearings. "Forget the toga. This will be fine," and I picked up the fresh tunic Cornelia had laid on the end of the bed.

"Just that?" she questioned. "For the emperor?"

"Why not?" I said. "I doubt he's here to discuss fashion." Julia gave me a baffled look and then turned to leave.

"Is Appia up?" I asked before she had reached the doorway.

"Yes," she replied.

Fabius entered. He seemed to be very stressed and anxious. "I must go next door to see about a toga," he announced between breaths. "There is nothing of proper size here. I'll be right back."

"No need," I told him. "Relax."

"But, master?"

"It's Getha," I said, tiring of reminding people.

Cornelia wouldn't let me go without a quick shave. I didn't realize how scruffy I'd become with the better part of a week's growth to remove. The shave completely woke me up, and I was fully alert when I crossed the courtyard to the main house. I could hear a chorus of anxious voices tossing about light banter which came to an abrupt halt the instant I appeared in the room.

My eyes were drawn to a stocky man, dressed in a pure white but otherwise plain toga, standing next to the impluvium at the center of the room. He had wide shoulders and a thick neck along with a slight double chin. His hair was dark brown and curly, but trimmed closely. His gaze was striking as he seemed to be sizing me up. There were four highly polished soldiers standing at attention by the doorway.

"This is both a surprise and an honor," I said nervously, and then I made a half bow for lack of knowing what to do.

"The honor is mine," he replied as he stepped towards me, which struck me as a curious thing for an emperor to say upon meeting a subject for the first time. "I have heard a great deal about you, first from your father, and then mine, and most recently from a Commander Marcus Virillius."

"I know him."

"You seem to have impressed him very much. So much so in fact, he put himself at personal risk by circumventing my guard in order to get an immediate audience with me. It seems that wherever you go you have quite an effect on people."

"I wouldn't know about that."

"Indeed," he said doubtingly. "Anyway, Commander Virillius believes you have a special understanding of the terrible events to the south, and if you do, I should like you to share those insights with me." Despite his confident demeanor, I detected a hint of distress behind the facade. "I've sacrificed in every conceivable way," he added, "but with every report the news gets grimmer."

"May I speak freely?" I said.

"Of course."

"What I tell you may be difficult to understand," I said, "but just hear me out." He nodded. "This tragedy has nothing whatsoever to do with the gods. No amount of sacrificing will work." He stared at me. His look was a little worrisome. "It's true."

"Impossible," he said. "That makes absolutely no sense!"

I was surprised by such a strong rejection of my words, but after a calming breath I said, "Nonetheless, I speak the truth. The event is related to the physical structure of the ground beneath our feet, not the gods." Once again, I was attempting to find a way to explain an event of nature to someone who believed the gods controlled all things natural. "However, there is a great deal you can do to ease the suffering of the people displaced by the event. Unfortunately, sacrificing isn't one of them."

"Physical structure?" he chuckled. "Is this some riddle about the underworld?"

"No," I replied, realizing our conversation was going nowhere. "Just ground, dirt, rocks…all compressed, creating physical stress and pressure," and I squeezed my palms together to support my point.

"Getha knows of what he speaks," Appia said. "You can trust him."

The emperor looked at me, and then he quietly stepped over to the wall where he took a seat. "This is preposterous." He paused for an instant and then added, "Ground, dirt?" He shook his fist in frustration and then looked at us. "But you two survived where others didn't."

"There are other survivors," I said. "I'm sure there are many who left the stricken area in time."

"But you came from the stricken area after the destruction," he said. "You survived the mountain's wrath."

"We were lucky," I said.

"From what I've been told, you have a knack for creating your own luck." It was at that point that Cornelia and Julia appeared with a plate of honey rolls. "This business to the south is very disturbing," he said as he took a roll, "but I was hoping for something more from you. Some way to appease the gods."

"I can't help you with that," I said.

At that moment, a commotion arose outside near the front gate where the emperor's entourage waited. It not only drew the immediate attention of the guards, but the emperor as well. I heard Paris speaking in an unusually high and frantic pitch, and Fabius calling for help.

"Oh no," was all I could say as I hustled outside into the bright sunlight. Paris, Fabius, and Thalese were crowded around someone stretched out on the ground. That someone was Leita. I rushed to her side, literally pushing people out of the way in order to reach her. Appia was right on my heels. "What happened?" I shouted. Leita's breathing was coming in short, stressed, asthma-like wheezes, and she had bright red blotches all around her neck. There were more around her ears and down the front of her chest. Her face was growing ashen.

"Getha," she gasped in difficult breaths, "it hurts," and I could feel her fingernails digging into my skin as she gripped my arm.

"It's a bee sting!" Thalese cried out. "She was stung on the back of her arm a short while ago." I glanced at the wound and found the stinger still imbedded. I pulled it out. Her respiration was growing worse by the second. I grabbed Appia and told her to fetch my vest. Without question she was up and gone.

"Trust me," I told Leita as calmly as I could. "You're going to be all right."

"I always…" and she wheezed in a way that nearly stole all her breath.

"Don't talk," I said. "Just relax. Concentrate on breathing. Think breathing. That's all. Just breathe."

"Hurts," she uttered with painful difficulty.

"I know, my friend," I said with kiss to her sweaty forehead. "Just breathe. Keep breathing."

More blotches were showing up on her shoulders and I could feel her body tensing as she progressively became more oxygen starved.

"Here!" Appia said as she tossed the vest to me. I took out one of my two EpiPens.

"This may sting a little," I told Leita, "but this sting is a good one." I removed the cap and pushed the auto-injector against her upper thigh. It clicked, and after counting slowly to three, I removed it and quickly tucked it back into my vest.

"Relax," I whispered to Leita as Appia placed a pillow beneath her head. "Just relax." All we could do was wait, and fortunately the epinephrine worked its magic quickly. In about a minute her eyes were more alert and her breathing less labored.

"Amazing," Thalese uttered, while all around us watched in silence.

"How do you feel?" I asked Leita as I wiped away errant strands of hair that had blown across her face.

"I can breathe," she said in a wheezing but clearer voice. "My chest still feels tight."

"Is she going to be all right?" Paris asked while pacing nervously about.

"I think so," I replied. "Put something under her feet to keep them elevated for a little while longer." Leita was looking up at me with affection in her eyes.

"I always trust you, Getha," she said.

"I'm glad to have you home," I said.

I leaned back and got up so Appia and Paris could greet the person who was in fact their mother.

"It's great to see you again, my friend," I said to Thalese, and I greeted him with a hearty handshake. "I was getting concerned."

"You needn't be," he replied. "Everything was as you predicted."

"Where's Nubia and Caelus?"

"Not far behind," he replied. "They're still in Ostia, but both are fine," and then he saw the emperor. "By the gods above, I had no idea!"

"It's not a problem," I said.

"That was his litter we just passed. I wasn't thinking!"

The emperor was standing right behind us, carefully studying the scene. He glanced at me briefly, and then at Leita. She had been helped to her feet and was gingerly walking about with Appia and Paris at her side. "Keep a close eye on her," I told them. "The fix is temporary. I may need to treat her again." In fact, I was expecting to, but several minutes had passed and she was still breathing acceptably well.

"We're just taking her inside," Appia said.

"She needs to lie down a little longer," I said. "Elevate her feet."

The emperor stepped over to Leita. "How do you feel?" he asked.

"Better," she replied in a stronger voice, but seeing who he was, she became excited and tried to kneel.

"No," he said, and he caught her before she went to the ground. "Please, there's a time for that, but this isn't it." I walked over to help her. "Was it a bee sting?" he asked.

"Yes," she replied. "We were riding in a hay wagon and it must have been in the grass."

He smiled and rubbed her head affectionately before turning to me. "I see you wear the pendant of my father."

The medallion Appius had given me was hanging outside my tunic. It must have popped out during the excitement. "Yes," I replied, and he took a closer look. "It was a gift from my father. I wear it to honor his name as I do to honor your family through him."

"I am honored that you hold my family in such good favor." He looked at Leita. "I think I should be concerned were it otherwise." I didn't see the same confidence in his eyes that I'd seen earlier. "Let's step back inside. I'd very much like to understand your way of looking at things."

"May I speak?" Thalese asked politely.

"Of course you may," he replied. "Your advice has always been welcome."

"Listen to Getha," he said emphatically. "He may express thoughts that don't seem to make sense, but he has special insights. He tried to warn us about the mountain months ago, but nobody listened."

"I just heard you say how everything went as predicted," he said. "May I ask what you meant?"

"Master Getha not only knew the best escape route," he said, "but what to expect from the mountain, and when. We owe our lives to him."

The emperor looked at me. "Come, Appius Getha, let's talk."

XXVIII

∞

When the emperor left, it was midday and time to eat. Rather than crowd everyone into the dining room, I suggested we dine al fresco in the courtyard. Leita, Appia, and Thalese were relaxed, but the rest of the household seemed strangely tense compared with the day before. I noticed conversations were hushed and happening around me rather than with me. Julia and Fabius were sitting the farthest from me, and never seemed to look in my direction unless I appeared to be looking away. Cornelia would smile nervously and stop talking when I'd glance at her, while Claudia was the only one other than myself not conversing. Even Paris and Therasia appeared to be uncomfortable.

I looked at Leita, who was smiling and conversing with Appia. She was alive because of me, which constituted a conscious violation of *The Principles of Conduct*. This time I had no comforting rationale to fall back on. She was stung by a bee during an escape plan of my design from a place that may well have been where she was supposed to die. I may have altered history twice on her behalf.

It appeared the hard decisions I had once declared I could make were tougher than I could possibly have realized. Leita was not the only beneficiary, and yet despite my guilt for having broken the rules, I couldn't look any of them in the eye and feel like I'd done anything wrong.

The *Principles of Conduct* were well-meaning guidelines, but not worth the paper they were printed on. Their efficacy required ideal conditions in a world where ideals are never fully realized. One little breach, intentional or not, nullifies the whole thing, as actions designed to correct breaches are inherently contrary to those very guidelines. However, understanding this didn't liberate me from the need to restrict my influence, but perhaps it did offer a little localized wiggle room.

"What's got you so preoccupied?" Appia asked while slicing off a piece of cooked chicken from the plate in front of her.

"Just thinking," I replied. "I've got to be careful. I'm starting to have dangerous thoughts."

"How dangerous?" she asked in a seductive whisper that Thalese noted.

"Whoops," she giggled after catching his glance. "I don't think I can be very serious right now, Getha."

Her light-hearted banter was infectious, and soon everyone had relaxed a little. People began to release some of the stress that had been building over the past several days.

The subject soon turned to the eruption and how the family made their escape. Thalese and Leita spoke of the heat and burning cinders. Both displayed marks where the hot ash had stuck to their skin. Their descriptions of the poisonous air, and how the earth shook while they trudged through deepening ash in near total darkness were so graphic as to cause me to recall more than I wanted to.

They spoke of Nubia's strength and Caelus' bravery, and about how they had to leave the wagon behind when it became stuck in ash. It saddened them to have lost the wagon with its valuables, but that was a small price to pay for their survival. They traded the mule to a farmer just outside Nucerea in exchange for food and shelter.

For the next half hour Appia held them spellbound with her rendition of our escape. Her understanding of the event sequence was truly remarkable, and frighteningly graphic when she explained her impressions of Herculaneum's final seconds.

Caelus and Nubia arrived that evening along with a frisky Democritus, who headed directly for Appia the instant he saw her. It was comical to watch Caelus, who'd managed to control him through all that Vesuvius could throw at them, suddenly unable to hold him once he'd caught sight of his good buddy.

"We're a family again," Nubia said with a smile as Thalese and Leita joined us. There were hugs all around, including a horse that wouldn't be left out. I stepped into the kitchen to see if there was any wine available for a little impromptu celebrating.

"May I ask you something?" Claudia asked as she followed me.

"Of course," I replied.

"We need to know what's going on," she said nervously. "Pardon my frankness, but your words have done little to allay our fears. Frankly, I've found them a bit ambiguous. You're supposed to be head of the family, yet you shun tradition in a way that gives the impression of weakness. But by the gods above, Getha, we all know you're not weak."

"Curious," I said. "As a slave, this must be a very difficult moment for you."

"Leita told us we could be candid with you," she said. "She said you will listen even when the questions involve your actions."

"That's true. I understand there are things that need to be said, but I need time to learn and assess, and let you all do your jobs as you have since Appius' passing. I trust you. In time I hope you will learn to trust me."

She glanced away when I finished, appearing flustered and even more confused. "We've heard you don't want to be head of the family despite our former master's wishes," she said. "Is that true?"

"I'm here," I replied. "I am the head of this family and I'm not going anywhere."

"You have made a great start with the emperor," she said. "We couldn't have asked for better. We need to appear strong regardless of our current weaknesses. A strong family leader does more for family wellbeing than anything else."

"I understand," I said. "There's nothing to worry about."

I found a pitcher of wine and brought it out to the atrium. I asked that everyone join me in a brief celebration of our survival, and then I assured them that I was not going anywhere. I made it clear that my primary function was the health and welfare of the family and all those whose wellbeing is dependent on the estate. My point was to include everybody, including those in service in Ostia and any of the workforce who survived Pompeii and chose to rejoin us in Rome.

The next two days were used to reorganize and get everybody situated comfortably within the villa. Despite the crowded situation, everyone managed to find a spot that could be considered their own space.

When David and Fabius returned from their travels we could finally meet as a group to discuss organization and how best to combine the two households. We had redundancy regarding duties, but I made it clear that a reduction in staff was not an option. I also stated that I would rather have tasks shared in a way that offered individuals more leisure time. That's how I began the discussion, and then I turned my chairperson duties over to Thalese; after which, Appia and I left. She returned to the main house while I went to my room to get some sleep.

Appia joining me around midnight and left at first light. The next thing I heard was, "Time for morning meal." It was Thalese. I opened my eyes to see him standing in the doorway.

"Already?" I said groggily.

"Yes," he replied, and then he asked if he could step inside for a moment.

I told him he didn't have to ask, to which he replied, "It's only proper." He stepped closer, but seemed to be having difficulty expressing himself.

"Is something wrong?" I asked.

"No," he replied with a nervous grin. "But I do have something to say."

"Please do."

"You and Appia don't have to sneak around."

"Sneak around?"

"Please," he said, "don't play dumb. It's fine. We're good. We're all good."

"You know about Appia and me?"

"Yes, we do," he said warmly. "Leita and I have always thought you two belonged together. She even predicted this would happen."

"How did you know?"

"How could we not?" he replied with a comical grin. "It doesn't take a Plato to see changes in close friends who've grown closer, especially Appia. Her words. The look in her eyes when she looks at you. I might add that you share that look when you're with her."

"Has she spoken of our relationship?"

"Not knowingly," he said, "but it's obvious. We also hear her at night. There's no possible way to come down those creaky old stairs silently."

"You've made your point."

"I might add that our early risers listen for her return so they won't embarrass her with an accidental meeting."

"So," I said, "everybody knows."

"Yes," he replied. "It's okay."

"With everybody?"

"Yes."

"But she's my sister, albeit by adoption," I said, "and the laws are clear. I don't believe the law makes a distinction."

He shook his head. "You are the master of this household. This is your domain. What you do here is whatever you want. Yes, there are laws, but there is also a larger truth – the reality – and that is the true way of things."

"Are you talking in a public sense or just within the household?"

"Within the household," he replied. "Nobody here will think any less of you or Appia."

"Have you told Appia yet?"

"No," he said. "I thought I'd leave that to you."

I had to laugh. I was quite relieved. "How did the meeting go?" I asked.

"I hope everybody came away less confused."

"I think we cleared up a lot of issues," he replied.

I sighed. "I do have a quandary. I'd planned to enfranchise everyone here just like I did in Pompeii. I told David I'd do that."

"So, what's your quandary?"

"You know my situation," I replied. "I can't keep making changes that aren't common to this era."

"We're just one small villa," he said. "Do you think what happens here matters to anybody beyond our gate?"

"I don't know," I said with a shrug. "I'm just trying not to screw up history any more than I already have."

"Then why did you give the emperor an entirely new way to understand the natural world? Isn't that far riskier to your history?"

"I had my reasons," I replied. "Apparently, the myths about me weren't contained by the volcano. I'm hoping I avoided a future problem."

He smiled. "I don't think the future will be harmed by anything you do in this household."

Leita appeared at the doorway. "There is a smartly-dressed, snobbish fellow here insisting he speak with you. He would not state his purpose."

"Really?" I said as I finished dressing.

"He could be an imperial messenger," Thalese said. "They are quite well trained and strict about formality."

Thalese was correct. He was an imperial messenger sent by the emperor, although, he looked like a hotel doorman to me, and a rather snooty one at that.

"Are you Citizen Appius Getha of Pompeii?" the messenger asked.

"I'm from Rome now," I replied while trying to find a Latin equivalent for the term *lighten up*. "But yes, I am Getha."

"I have a message for you sir," he said, but then he said no more.

"Well?" I asked.

At first he appeared puzzled, and then he gave Leita and Thalese a stern look.

"What's the message?" I asked, as he was starting to try my patience.

"Sir," he said in a hushed voice, "this message is directed at you. Just you."

I looked at Thalese and Leita, and then at Julia and Paris who were drawn to the atrium by curiosity. "This is my family," I said. "We have no secrets."

"Be that as it may," he stated flatly, "my orders are to deliver this message to Appius Getha, and no one else. What you do with it afterwards is your business."

"Come everyone," Thalese chuckled while beckoning for the others to join him in the courtyard.

"Okay," I said to the messenger, "everyone has left. The message please."

"Yes," he said as he brought his body to attention. "His highness, Emperor Titus Flavious Vespasianus, cordially invites you, Appius Marius Valerianus Getha, and your sister Maria Secunda to his Palace on Palatine Hill."

"When?"

"Tomorrow," he replied. "There will be an imperial escort here in the morning and you may bring along any personal servants and belongings you wish. My emperor asked me to add that the palace is fully equipped and staffed."

"Belongings?" I said. "That sounds like more than just a short visit."

"My emperor is hoping you will choose to stay for a few days," he explained. "My emperor has instructed me to add that there is no obligation. I will wait here for your reply."

"He needs an answer this instant?"

"No sir," he replied. "Take your time. I'll stand over here by the doorway until you've decided."

"You can sit if you wish," I said. "There's a bench right there."

"Thank you, sir," and he sat.

"That's why you had me clear the room?"

"Sir," he replied, "the contents of a message have no bearing on the instructions regarding its delivery. Emperor Titus instructed that this message be delivered to you. He did not specifically exclude others from being present during its delivery; however, he did not affirm it either. Therefore, proper conduct dictates this message be delivered in your presence only."

"Okay then," I said with a smile. "You will have your answer shortly," and I hustled to the courtyard to consult with Thalese. He and Leita were conversing by my room.

"Appia and I have just been invited to the imperial palace," I said. "Titus intends for us to stay for several days. What do you make of it?"

"I'm not surprised by the invitation," Thalese replied, "but I am surprised by the suddenness. I'm sure he's looking for advice. After all, you gave him a lot of information..."

"I know," I said.

"You aren't thinking of turning him down?" he asked with concern.

"I don't know."

"You need to go," he stated firmly. "This is a tremendous stroke of luck. Nobody touches imperial favorites, which will buy us time to recover our assets and shore up our weaknesses."

"Unless Appia has any objections," I said, "we'll go. She was invited too, and I can bring whomever I want, as well."

"Good, perfect," he said. "Leita should go. It will be good for her."

"And you."

He smiled. "Yes. I am a bit of a redundancy myself. Claudia has better knowledge of this city and its workings. I trust her. I expect it won't be a short visit."

"Are imperial visits usually days or more?" I asked.

"Yes, they are," he replied. "Most visitors come from long distances. When it takes a guest several days or longer to travel, you don't send them right back home."

"I understand that, but I'm not coming from far away."

He shrugged. "That's just how it is. We should be thankful for it."

"What's all the commotion?" Appia asked as she joined us from the main house. "And who's the marblepuss inside?"

"A messenger," I replied, "from the emperor. You and I have been invited to the palace."

"When?"

"Tomorrow," I replied. "Apparently we're expected to stay for a few days."

"Of course," she said excitedly, and then she turned to Leita. "Would you do me a very big favor?"

"Of course," Leita replied.

"Would you pick up my blue wrap from the fullers? They said it would be done today, and if we're going to the palace…"

"Whoa," I said as I raised my hands. "We haven't decided if we're going yet."

"Of course, we're going," Appia said. "Unless you don't want to go. You do want to go? Don't you?"

"Alright," I said with a sigh. "We'll go. There seems to be no good reason not to, and Leita, I'd like you to join us, and you, Thalese. I'm not letting you off the hook either."

"You should be happy," Thalese said. "Think about it. You chose this time in history. You yearned to visit our world. And now you're here, and not just as a visitor, but as an official guest of the emperor himself. Can it get any better than that?"

XXIX

∞

"We're not quitting," Christina stated, but even she wasn't feeling very hopeful. It wasn't the first time she'd made that statement during a time of gloominess when each new discovery made the goal seem more unreachable. However, this time, Kamden surprised her with a proactive response.

"I'm not quitting," Kamden replied, "and in fact I believe it's time for action."

"What do you propose?" Liam asked.

"Well," he said as he rocked back in his chair, "we need to accept certain assumptions. I believe the legend of the *Insurrection Against the Emperor and the Imperial Family* is based on a real event, and I believe Aaron was the central character of the legend. In order to use that event as a target point for a rescue mission, I need an exact date."

"Fine," Liam said, "but what about temporal backwash? I assume backwash is still an issue."

"It is," he replied, "but there are indications that backwash isn't a constant. It may well be that the ship's very brief, millisecond stop at Pompeii minimized that affect."

"But you don't know," Christina said.

"Not with certainty," he replied. "It's hypothetical. But your future humans had the same idea."

"Any estimate on how this will help?" she asked. "Best case."

"Best case?" he said with a shrug. "A May 79 rescue might be possible."

"Didn't Emperor Vespasian die in Pompeii in June of 79?" Liam asked.

"He died on the 23rd of June," Aine said after doing a quick search on her phone, "but he died in Reate, not Pompeii. In fact, there's no reference to Pompeii, only that he left for Rome after having taken ill in Campania."

"Okay," Kamden said, "so we know the *Insurrection* took place before June 23."

"Then let's aim for the 21st as a ballpark target date," Liam said.

"Ballpark isn't good enough," Kamden replied. "I want the day."

"Ballpark may be the best we can do," Christina said sadly.

"Then, so be it," he said, "but let's be sure we've turned over every possible stone before we make that call. If the *Insurrection* happened in January or February it won't do us any good, but at least we'll know and move on."

"If May is the best case," Christina said, "what's the worst?"

"Well," Kamden said thoughtfully, "if my hunch is wrong, we could end up arriving anywhere between June and December."

Christina sighed. "If we arrive in December there will be no Pompeii."

"I know," Kamden agreed. "There may be no Pompeii in August either. But if backwash does force our arrival past August, I'm banking on recent archaeological support for a fall eruption. October would be great, but November even better."

"It's all just so much supposition," she said.

"Granted," he said, "our window of opportunity is tiny and uncertain. Our earliest arrival date is somewhere between May and December and the eruption of Vesuvius is somewhere between late August and November. All of this effort, all of this work," and he picked up a handful of datasheets and slapped them back down on the table, "may well be for nothing anyway."

"That's hardly positive," Aine noted.

"Look," he said sounding exasperated, "we're going to make the trip, regardless. The place may be destroyed by the time we land, or we land and can't find him, but we won't know any of that until we're there."

"And the date of the *Insurrection* will help somehow?" Christina asked.

"Yes!" he replied. "It's the one and only day in history we know precisely where Aaron is. If it's in May or June I can program it. If backwash is as I suspect, I can nail it. As you've so often stated, Chris, we'll have just the one shot at this.

"He's got a good point," Aine said. "We haven't even discussed how we go about canvasing a completely foreign region noninvasively on best guesses. And we won't have unlimited time either. I think it's worth the effort to try to find that date."

"Agreed," Liam nodded.

"Good," Kamden said and he looked at Christina. "I made a promise to you and I'm going to keep it. So, humor me and get that date."

"How do you propose we get this mythical date?" Christina asked. "I'm not being sarcastic, but the legend is vague. I've spoken with Roman historians from UNH and Harvard. Nobody knows. Nobody takes it seriously. Most believe the legend was invented after the eruption, perhaps by survivors seeking a redeemer or something like that."

"Yes," Kamden said, "but they don't know what we know, so they have no incentive to dig deeper. The answer may still be there for us to find."

"So," Christina said, "where do you suggest we look? Aine has covered just about all the libraries from here to New York City."

"How about Naples?" he replied. "How about that archaeological museum? I'm sure their archives are full of historical documents that are not available anywhere else in the world. Hire a translator. Even better, hire somebody from their staff!"

"They've turned me down once already," she replied. "I don't even have an artifact to focus my request on this time."

"Then tell them the truth," he said. "Tell them you're researching the legend. Ask them for permission to view any related materials. Tell them that all your research will be handed over to them for their suggestions and approval before you publish it, and allow them the right to publish it in their vernacular. But you already know all of this."

"What if they don't like my writing or conclusions?" she asked.

"Christina," he said with soft tap on the side of her head, "hello! What difference does it make? You won't be writing anything anyway. Just get me that date and come home. Okay?"

"I'm sorry," she said with a warm smile. "You're right. I can do that. I'll prepare a formal request in the morning. Are we all agreed?" All nodded their approval.

XXX

∞

A small but impressive caravan of regal guard and two fancy carriages arrived outside the Villa North at approximately noon. It was our official transport to the imperial residence on Palatine Hill, otherwise known as *The Hill* to locals. The carriages were for Appia and me and our belongings, but not Thalese and Leita. I wanted to walk, but Thalese thought it best to follow protocol, at least until people got to know me a little better.

We passed a series of large structures on the left that may have been granaries; after which, we came to an arched passageway that appeared to be a main gateway into the city. It was the Servian Wall. This wall system began as a defensive line made up of fences, earthen piles, and ditches. It was originally known as the Romulus Wall until it was expanded by Servius Tullius, the sixth king of Rome, with large blocks of tufa stone.

Not much of the Servian Wall survived to my era, but there was enough for me to recognize this section as being part of that structure. The central arch was braced by a pair of tall, round, defensive towers that gave the entrance a medieval look. The entire wall system was about seven miles long and ringed the entire city at the time of its construction. If my calculations were correct, we were in the area of the Aventine. There was signage in bold letters stating that wagons were not permitted inside the city proper between sunrise and sunset. After having just passed through some very congested streets I could see why. Apparently, carriages weren't considered wagons.

We continued through the archway and entered the city, which was a hub of activity, but not all of it easy to witness. Class distinctions were obvious, and behind all the pristine togas and fancy wraps were the drab figures of slaves and the landless poor. They were everywhere and unavoidable. Their plight was clearly worse than what I'd seen in Pompeii. It was difficult to look upon them and simply pass their lives off as just being a piece of history.

The Rome of 79 CE was a big city, even by modern standards, but the sounds around me belied that fact. There were no mopeds or busses, only a steady, low-level background hum of conversations and the clatter of human activity that seemed to be coming from all directions. There were the occasional banging and thumping sounds of construction, along with the echoes of pottery crashing against paving stones, which was a little disquieting. Those sounds came mostly from narrow side streets, of which many were dirty, cluttered and occasionally vile smelling, but also familiar.

The main palace was clearly visible as we reached the peak of Palatine Hill. It looked like a conglomeration of separate but connected buildings. What appeared to be the main section, built on the northwest end of the hill, was connected via a passageway to a newer section that was constructed out and over the cliffside overlooking the Forum. Our caravan stopped in front of a colonnaded entranceway to that main section.

I recalled my history, and that the main section of this palace was known as the Domus Tiberius. Yet, I couldn't readily see any logic to its design. It appeared as a compartmentalized multiplex, its central sections very different architecturally than the sections to the right and towards the Forum. Once inside, we entered the grandest atrium I'd ever seen. There was a large impluvium at its center with an accompanying compluvium above it, but the compluvium was closed off by what looked like a roll away wooden cover.

"This is the emperor's audience chamber," Appia said as we made our way across the highly polished, multi-colored marble floor. "The building originally belonged to Emperor Tiberius, but it's been rebuilt a couple times, so it doesn't look like it used to."

"Why all the rebuilds?" I asked.

"It burned once," she replied, "and later Emperor Vespasian just wanted to make changes. Of course, this rebuild was supposed to be temporary while he built a new palace on the southwest corner of the hill, but that never happened."

Several impeccably dressed slaves appeared from a doorway at the far end of the room, and behind them, came the emperor. "Greetings!" he said while displaying a wide smile. To that, we all offered the obligatory bow.

With a snap of his fingers, his servants picked up our belongings and disappeared with them into a corridor on the right.

"Appia," he said as he gave her a warm hug, "why don't you and your servants follow mine and see to it that your things are stored properly while I have a few words with Appius Getha."

It was then that another caravan pulled up in front of the palace and more people entered the audience hall. They were mostly slaves and soldiers who were differently dressed than the ones who'd escorted us. Titus seemed unconcerned until the appearance of a lavishly dressed man with a clear family resemblance.

"Good," Titus said happily as he stepped towards him. Upon greeting his guest, he added, "You are just in time to meet my newest friend." The look I received from this visitor felt cold enough to freeze the sweat on my brow. "This is the Appius Getha of Pompeii," Titus said. "I'm sure you must have heard of him by now."

"I have," the man said coolly. "I was told he was coming."

I was nervous but smiling as the emperor motioned for me to join them. "This is my brother, Domitian," he said.

"How long do you intend to stay here?" Domitian asked gruffly as he stepped closer. He seemed to be trying to match my height with a momentary lift of his heels.

"I don't know," I replied. "Not long."

"He's my guest," Titus said, noting the enmity in his brother's voice. "I asked him to come."

"I'm sure," he replied. I could sense a tension between them, and I was glad when Titus asked if I'd like to see my quarters, but when he started for the door, Domitian stepped between us.

"I'm not so easily fooled as my dear brother," he stated in a harsh whisper. "I'm going to find out who you really are."

"You can do what you want," I replied, and I purposely used my height advantage to hide my nervousness. "I promise I'm no threat to you."

"Then I suggest you disappear," he said as he poked a blunt finger into the center of my chest. "I don't need you here."

"Are you coming, Getha?" Titus asked. He was already at the entrance.

"Yes," I said following a brief stare down with his brother.

"Stay out of my way," Domitian said, and rather than reply in kind I stepped around him and rejoined Titus who was heading for the main entrance.

"Nice to meet you," I said. "Perhaps we might do lunch sometime."

"What?" he uttered.

Titus noticed my discomfort, and he had a good idea as to why. "What did my brother say to you?"

"Nothing much."

"I know better than that," he said.

"For some reason he isn't happy I'm here," I said. "I don't want to create problems for you. Maybe I should go home, and you can visit us there."

"Don't pay any attention to him," Titus chuckled. "He always tries to assert himself with new people. It's just a bluff."

"It didn't sound like he was bluffing."

"Regardless," he said, "I'm the emperor, and whomever I choose to have as my guest is none of his business. Once you and he get better acquainted, I think there's a good chance you will become friends."

"Perhaps," I said, although I had strong reservations.

Titus had led me outside while the others had used the corridor. "Am I not sharing quarters with my family?" I asked.

"Of course," he replied as we approached the large hardwood door of the newer section of the palace. This part of the complex was a multistory addition that was built right out over the cliff face. Its foundation was on the Forum floor.

"Unless I'm mistaken," I said, "didn't the Emperor Gaius have something to do with this part of the building?"

"It was his residence at one time," Titus replied, "but it's been greatly renovated since." Rather than stepping inside, we walked over to the where the cliff dropped off sharply to the Forum level below. "We call this part of the building the palace annex," he explained. "It's like an extension of the hill itself. I put you on the far side, so you'll have a great view of the Forum."

"It's quite a building," I said. I noticed an adjacent exterior service stairway that zigzagged down to the Forum. Some of the steps were cut from the stone face and others were constructed of wood.

"It will be," he said as we approached the entrance to the annex. "We're still renovating. There is stairwell down to the Forum from inside too, but we keep that door locked for obvious reasons."

We entered the annex and into a lamplit, but darkened corridor. Titus pointed to an adjacent door, explaining that it was an enclosed walkway back to the palace. He said the buildings were not originally joined, so there were lots of oddities in the design.

We headed down the corridor, practically to the end, where we came to a door on the left which Titus pushed open. Suddenly we were bathed in daylight. The room we entered was large and rectangular, with a high coffered ceiling and four tall, rectangular windows. One was located at the opposite end of the room and the other three were along the wall to the right.

"What do you think?" he asked.

"It may well be the most beautiful room I've ever seen," I replied as I stood in awe of its splendor. The frescoed artwork on the walls, especially to my left, was vibrant and alive with color. A pair of carefully rendered figures in a lover's embrace were painted over a background of intricately detailed temples and villas, while images of birds were used to frame the scenes.

The floor was elegantly tiled with white marble, and on the immediate left, by the doorway, was a bronze basin, and above that, a highly polished metal mirror. There was an embroidered couch and two posh chairs, and at the far end, over in the left-hand corner, was a bed, its carved wooden headboard was set back against the wall. The bedspread and pillow coverings matched the reds of the walls. Flanking it on both sides were hand carved nightstands, the legs of which looked very catlike.

There was even a full-size, standup closet near the bed. It wasn't just a piece of standing furniture, but the real thing, set into the wall. I didn't see it at first because its flush, wooden doors were painted over as part of the wall art. The only giveaway was the latch.

"I take it that it meets with your approval?" Titus said with a pleased smile.

"Very much so," I said as I stepped across the room to the far window to take in the view. "This is really incredible."

There was some weathered and rickety looking scaffolding on top of a lower level buildout attached to the annex, but it in no way hindered a view that was like something out of a dream. From where I stood, I could see over the terra-cotta tiled roof of the Basilica Julia to Capitoline Hill and the splendid Temple of Jupiter. Its golden highlights were shimmering in the midday sun.

I moved to a front window where I could see over the rooftops of the Temples of Dioscuri and Julius Caesar, giving a fine view of the Via Sacra and the upper Forum. Across the way were the sunlit columns of the Basilica Amelia and nearby, the Curia.

The Forum was a busy place. There were women in attractive pastels, and men clad in tunics and white togas. There were the scarlet women as well, doing a little strutting of their own. Nobody seemed the least bit bothered by their presence.

"I tried to find you another musty storage room," Appia said as she entered the room, "but I guess you're stuck with this."

"Isn't this something!" I said enthusiastically.

"It is," she agreed, and she joined me at the window.

"Well," Titus said with a clap of his hands, "I think I'd best be running along. I'd better see what my brother's up to."

"I'll be here," I said. "This is amazing."

"I'm glad you like it," he said, "and before I forget, I'm having an informal gathering tonight. Just a few friends, lots of food, not to mention a touch of the grape. It'll be fun." With that he was gone.

"Curious fellow," I said to Appia. "I still don't know why we're here."

"He likes you," she replied as she wrapped her arms around me. "I like you too."

"He's got something more on his mind."

"So do I," she said playfully as she took my hand. I didn't argue as I seemed to be sharing similar desires, which unfortunately had a timing issue. The moment we started to get comfortable we heard footsteps coming down the corridor.

"Hello!" Thalese said before entering the room. "Are you decent?"

"Decent enough," I said as I straightened out my tunic. When I told him to come in, I got a lighthearted jab in the ribs from Appia who was still fumbling to get her wrap configured. Thalese entered the room carrying an armful of my clothing, most of which I hadn't packed, but others believed I would need. "You didn't have to do that."

He was smiling as he rubbed his hands together. "I'm going down to help Leita with a few things," he said, "and then I'll be back up."

"No need to rush," Appia said.

"That's right," I added. "You and Leita relax, take some time for yourselves."

"There are some things we need to talk about."

"But they can wait," I said.

"They can't wait for long," he said. "There's a few things you need to know for later."

"I'm sure," I said, "but they can wait for an hour or so."

"A summer hour," Appia said with one of her more spirited grins.

Thalese smiled and nodded. "Of course," and he backed towards the exit.

"And close the door," Appia added.

There was enough time to get comfortable together, but we were exhausted too, and we were asleep when Thalese, accompanied by Leita, returned about a summer hour and a half later. The knock on the door startled us, but after a moment of fumbling around, we made ourselves acceptably presentable.

"Sorry to disturb you," Thalese said as the pair entered the room, "but it's getting towards evening and the emperor will be expecting you soon. I just saw him in the courtyard in conference with his brother."

"In conference?" Leita chuckled. "They were in the midst of a spat."

A pair of palace servants entered with more of my belongings that I hadn't packed, much of it I didn't even know I owned. Apparently, the Villa North staff had been busy acquiring everything they felt I would need since my unexpected arrival, from toiletries and clothing to writing tablets and associated materials, and it appeared to be purchased in bulk.

"Titus and Domitian were arguing?" I asked, to which Thalese quietly signaled for me to hold my thoughts until the servants had left.

Leita and Appia were enjoying the view of the Forum from one of the front windows. One might not guess they were related at first glance, especially because of their hair. Leita's hair was curlier and dark brown, featuring a few steaks of grey, while Appia's was a lighter chestnut color, and straighter; however, it was easy to see the subtle hereditary similarities between them when they stood together. They were similarly proportioned, virtually the same height, and they shared hazel eyes. They even had the same laugh, and on that note, it was heartwarming to see Leita smiling and laughing again.

"The brothers are known to go at it from time to time," Appia said once the servants were gone. She and Leita remained at the window.

"What are they fighting over?" I asked.

"Hard to tell," Thalese replied. "I think Domitian arrived in a foul mood to begin with. He's like that sometimes."

"He's not so bad," Appia said. "I've always found him most charming."

"And you would," Thalese chuckled. "It's obvious he's had his eye on you, especially since your visit to Emperor Vespasian's winter home on Capri."

"That was years ago," Appia said, while still in conversation with Leita. "He liked me because I was a cute kid."

Once we were ready, the four of us walked to the palace together. I led the way with Appia at my side as my sister, with Leita and Thalese following closely behind as our servants. I might add freed servants. They may not have been allowed the same accoutrements of the higher classes, but I made it clear to everyone they were not slaves.

The palace atrium, or audience room, had been transformed into a great feast hall featuring low-rise, highly polished wooded tables set rectangularly around the central fountain. There were at least 50 guests present already, lying or sitting on portable wooden furniture and cushy mats set out around each table. The large, square compluvium was now open to the sky, its covering removed, while below it, a spit sat in the impluvium. There were huge chunks of beef, or buffalo, or something of the sort, being turned over a fire by servants. I would have expected the room to be smokier than it was, but with the large front doors open, most of the smoke drifted up and out though the compluvium. Thalese led us to our places; Appia and I sat.

Domitian and his entourage arrived, and as Appia had predicted, his attitude towards me had changed. "I hope my harsh words this afternoon didn't cause you any undo discomfort," he said to me. "I was upset about other matters and I took that out on you." He sounded sincere, but he was also looking at his brother when he spoke.

"No need to apologize," I replied. "I'm sorry that my presence seemed threatening to you."

"You don't threaten me," he said with the kind of smile that would make even the most successful automobile salesperson envious.

"Be that as it may," I said. "I'm simply here at the invitation of your brother. I can't exactly turn down a request from an emperor, now can I?"

Domitian studied me closely for a moment, and then he broke into a foolish grin and said, "Of course you can't. You're my brother's friend and thus my friend as well." He offered his hand in friendship. Once we'd shaken hands, he moved on to his place opposite us.

"What did I tell you," Appia said. "He's not so bad."

The food was excellent and the wine quite appropriate. There were at least seventy guests in total, all dressed elegantly. If this was indeed an informal gathering, I had to wonder what a formal one was like.

Leita sat quietly, enjoying the conversation, while Thalese was watching the guests. "Did you know the emperor's brother keeps staring over here?" he asked me.

"Yes," I replied. "He's not the only one."

"But he's not just any guest," he said.

"He does worry me," I said. "He threatened me today. Do you think he could know something?"

"He actually threatened you?"

"He most certainly did," I replied. "He said he was going to find out who I really am."

"We can't allow that to happen," he said.

"No kidding."

"I'm surprised," he said. "I don't see how he could know anything. Any records found in the ruins of Pompeii would only add support to your name."

"What about Ephesus?"

He nodded. "I think you're overly concerned, but perhaps it's time for me to look into it. I can certainly find out if anyone's snooping around. I may even need to take a trip to Ephesus."

I took a swig of wine and looked up and saw Titus walking towards me. I was hoping he was headed someplace else, but he wasn't.

"Friends," he said in a voice loud enough for all to hear. All talking abruptly stopped. "Many of you have heard the stories of a powerful stranger from the south who's bravery and deeds rival those of the mighty Hercules himself."

"Oh no," I said. Appia squeezed my hand to remind me to relax.

"I proclaim here and now," Titus said in dramatic fashion, "for all the world to know, that the stories are true. That the powerful stranger from the south is real, except he's no longer a stranger. This is The Appius Getha of Pompeii." The room went silent, that was, until Domitian decided to speak.

"Far be it for me to question you brother," he said, "but how can you be so certain?"

"My dear brother," Titus replied with a tight-lipped smile, "as Caesar I need offer no proof but that of my word. That's a privilege of the position."

"Are you then proclaiming this Appius Getha to be the son of Hercules?" Domitian said.

Titus was clearly caught off guard by his brother's inappropriate outburst, and after a momentary pause he said, "I know you mean no disrespect brother, but I think you should go a little more slowly with that wine."

"You have a point brother," Domitian chuckled, allowing all the other guests to do the same, "and I make my apologies to both you and your special guest."

"Actually," Titus said, "that is a valid question. And one I'm pleased to answer. Not only do I have sworn statements from firsthand witnesses to his deeds, I too have witnessed such an event." He was beginning to get very theatrical, in a way that would have made Appius proud. "I witnessed Appius Getha, the very Appius Getha you see here now, give life back to a dying servant with just the touch of his hand!"

He motioned for Leita to stand up, which she did reluctantly.

"What are you doing?" I whispered to Titus but he ignored me.

"I swear before the College of Pontiffs and the Altar of Jupiter," Titus proclaimed, "that this event was so." Following a weird moment of solemnity and contemplation, Titus changed the subject and invited everyone to feast, and the party began.

I was relieved when the evening was finally over. On our way out, Titus returned to our table. "Thank you, my friend," he said to me. "I know I put you on the spot. I promise not to do that again."

"I would appreciate that," I replied. He slapped me on the back and returned to his place at the head table.

"If you'll excuse us," I said to Thalese, "I believe Appia and I have a little unfinished business to attend to."

"At this time of night?" Thalese asked. Leita gave him a friendly nudge. "Oh."

"How about if I awaken you a little later in the morning?" Leita said. "An hour?"

"Make it a summer hour," Appia replied.

Appia and I were the only occupants on the entire floor because most of the structure was still being restored; although, it looked like that work had been suspended. I wasn't sure why, but it probably had something to do with the transition of emperors and funding priorities.

XXXI

∞

Dawn arrived far too quickly. It seemed like I'd just dozed off when I heard a light tapping on the door. Appia was sleeping soundly by my side. I pretended I hadn't heard it, but the tapping returned.

"Getha?" Leita said as she opened our door about an inch.

"It must be morning already," I replied, which caused Appia to stir.

"I'm sorry to have to call you this early," she said, "but the emperor awaits you and Appia in his chamber. I have Appia's clothes right here."

Appia sat up. She was groggy, and once on her feet, she slowly hobbled over to one of the windows. When Leita entered the room, I saw her looking at Appia with concern. Appia was without clothing and leaning against a waist high windowsill. The windows were large, and practically panoramic, perhaps a little dangerous as they were not finished. There were posts and markers for wooden framing and possibly a grill. There were large wooden shutters on the inside to seal the openings, but since there were no mosquitos to harass us, we left them open for the breeze. They were designed to bathe the room in light at both ends of the day, and also great for viewing, whether looking out, or in this case looking in, perhaps at anyone who might be hanging out the window, literally.

"See anyone out there?" I asked Appia.

"Lots of people," she said with a yawn, and she leaned out a little farther. "I think everyone is up but us." I looked at Leita who was shaking her head.

"Do any of them see you?" I asked.

"Um, well, yes," she replied. "As a matter of fact, lots of eyes are...oh dear!" She literally hopped backwards folding her arms across her chest.

"A bit of an exhibitionist, are we?" I chuckled. "I didn't know that about you," to which she heaved a pillow at me, but with a silly grin.

There were cool and warm water spigots above the basin. Another nicety was having a latrine in the next room. A valve regulated flow, providing a continual flush to a system that drained directly into the ground beneath the Forum. It was all really quite ingenious. There was water pressure as we were still below the height of the aqueduct. The Claudian Aqueduct was a very large and tall, multistory structure that ran directly into Palatine Hill.

Thalese joined us shortly after we'd bathed, sponge style, while Leita was helping me shave. He'd awakened well before us and had begun his inquiries into Domitian's activities regarding me.

"Domitian is investigating you," he said. He handed me a piece of soap similar to what Appius had in Pompeii. "I believe you wanted more of these."

"I did," I said. "Thank you. What's he up to?"

"He's testing the validity of the myths about you," he replied, "but his inquiry may be of no use to him if he's trying to discredit you."

"He may just be trying to seek the truth," I said. "I know I would in his place."

"In any event, he's not learning much. I know he found one of the few mercenary soldiers who survived. This fellow claimed to have been witness to your lightning bolts. He said you put slivers in the back of his head, but struck his friend directly in the face. That bolt took most of his friend's head off."

"Slivers?" I said.

"Yes."

"Maybe at the gate?" Appia said.

"Oh," I said. "That was bad. The slug must have shattered and ricocheted off the stone."

"It was awful," Appia said sadly. "We were trapped." She came over and took my hand. "I don't think you expected it to be that bad. You looked shocked."

"I don't know what I expected," I said. "There was no time, and we had to move."

"I'm sorry," Thalese said, noting how sullen Appia and I had become. "The real news is that Domitian hasn't been looking into your legitimacy at all. I don't see a need to visit Ephesus at this time. In fact, I think it would be prudent to avoid drawing any attention to that area, which my leaving could cause."

"I agree," I said. "How long has Domitian been investing the myths? We only met yesterday."

"I don't know," he replied, "but probably since his father, or better yet, since his brother has taken such a keen interest in you. He's quite the pragmatist. I'm sure he's envisioned you as a likely swindler looking for a way into his family's wealth and power."

"Which makes a lot of sense from his perspective," I said. "I'd feel the same way. I can't fault him for that."

"Anyway," Thalese said, "I think this is good news, but I will keep my ear to the ground, so to speak."

"Will you give us a little time?" Appia said to Thalese and Leita. "Tell the emperor we will be there shortly."

They nodded and left. Appia and I looked at each other. "I can still see that soldier's face," I said. "It doesn't go away. I killed people. I killed that man. I never thought for a second I could ever do something that heinous. If I did, I would not have brought that weapon with me."

"They murdered my father," she said with unusual anger in her voice. "They tried to murder us. They planned to murder Caelus and Nubia with her unborn child. They beat and raped my mother. I'm sorry that you had to do what you did, but I'm glad they're all dead."

Once we finally made it to the courtyard, Titus was there waiting, having already eaten and dressed. There were several litters and bearers, with a full complement of servants along with twenty members of the Praetorian Guard all holding at attention before us. Thankfully, Leita saw what was happening and had prepared a satchel full of food and drink for us to take. She was way ahead of us because we didn't even know we were going anywhere until that moment.

"I'd like to show you around my town," Titus said, and he looked at me. "I'm told you haven't been here for quite a while. Am I right?"

"Yes," I replied.

"It's time to fix that," he said. "This is your city now!"

When he called for the litters and bearers to take their places, I stopped him. "Do we need to ride in those things?"

"I could arrange for a carriage."

"I was thinking of walking," I said. "I think we'll see a lot more that way."

"Okay. Walking it is."

It was a beautiful day with a brilliant blue sky, lots of greenery and bird-song, and a few noisy cicadas that made me smile. On the walk from *The Hill*, down to the Forum, Titus spoke of Appius and his heartfelt admiration for his courage and the strength of his family. He spoke of the long-lasting friendship between our two families. He thanked me for my encouragement and suggestions. He had already taken action by ordering the construction of three large military style camps in the Neapolis area for refugees from the disaster. He believed that these temporary camp facilities would also relieve the stress of overcrowding in cities near the disaster zone. He had just gotten word that refugees were already moving into those sites with construction going on around them.

The first stop we made was at the unfinished Flavian Amphitheater, known in my time as the Colosseum. Titus took us around to all the completed areas, including a stroll beneath the stadium floor. Workers demonstrated the various mechanisms that operated hidden doors and raised platforms for us. As expected, there was scaffolding everywhere, so we needed to keep a careful eye out for dangers above as well as where we stepped.

It was indeed a magnificent structure, but I couldn't escape thoughts of its eventual purpose while watching cages being built and tested. I realized the day would come when I'd be asked to view one of those horrific spectacles. I decided to compile a list of excuses that would keep me from ever having to do that.

We left the Flavian Amphitheater and strolled along the Via Sacra to the famous Roman Forum. Wherever we went we drew crowds, and I found that uncomfortable. There was someone actually speaking from the rostrum. He was an older man dressed rather plainly in a basic tunic, but he stopped midsentence at the sudden appearance of the emperor. It was comical in a way, because he had no throng of eager listeners hanging on his every word. Instead, his crowd consisted of maybe ten youths who appeared to be more interested in mocking him than listening. I felt sorry for the guy, but not sorry enough to find out what he was talking about.

The Curia was a much more impressive building than the brick substructure that survived to my time. This version had a columned portico at the entrance. What I didn't see was the Arch of Septimius Severus, which I realized couldn't possibly have been built yet. Stepping inside the Curia brought welcome relief from the crowd of people we were attracting. When I nixed the litter idea, I didn't realize their function helped keep people at a distance as well. Fortunately, we had the Praetorians to provide that service, because people were getting a little too close for comfort.

Titus spent about an hour discussing a military conflict in Britannia with a few of the legislators inside. From what I heard, the army had pushed into Caledonia and set up forts. It was apparently a triumph for Titus, but he was more concerned with manpower shortages. He needed a strong presence in Britannia to maintain Roman gains there, while having to organize an effort in Asia Minor.

We left the Curia and made our way up the winding steps to the Temple of Jupiter high atop Capitoline Hill, its gold trim glittered in the bright sunlight. From the Temple steps we had a wonderful panoramic view of the city and river. The breeze had picked up, making the surface of the Tiber sparkle, while adding a slightly unpleasant reminder that the fish market was not far away.

We completed our tour with a stroll through the Forum Boarium to the Circus Maximus where we were led to a steep path that returned us to the top of Palatine Hill. There were several buildings that hung right out over the edge, facing the Circus Maximus. Once we reached the top of Palatine Hill, Titus sent our entourage back to the palace, leaving just Appia and me with him. He took us to a spot a little farther down but still on the same side facing the Circus.

"I now own all the buildings along this frontage," he said. "I'm going to do away with them and build my new home right on this spot. I'm going to leave that side alone," and he pointed northwest to a complex of buildings that included a small temple, "but the Circus side is mine."

"They look like nice places," Appia said, but then she looked more closely. "Is that fire damage?"

"That's correct," he said.

"Is that from the fire during Emperor Nero's time?" I asked.

Titus smiled. "Hardly. They're part of the citywide rebuilding program Emperor Nero initiated after that fire. Nobody has ever really lived in them. Hooligans set these homes alight. We were lucky it rained. I keep a posting here at all times now. We haven't had any issues since."

We walked to an open area at the southeast corner of Palatine Hill where I knew Domitian would one day construct the grandest residential palace ever to grace the hill. There was a beautiful grassy spot to sit. It was warm and wonderful with a soft breeze carrying the light scent of spices.

"What do you think of this spot?" Titus asked as we scanned the city below. The Circus Maximus was right there running parallel to the slope, and beyond lay the river and much of the city to the south and west.

"It's very nice," I replied.

"I'm glad it meets with your approval," he said with a smile, "because this can be your new home."

"What?" I said. Appia looked as dumbfounded as I was.

"Well," he said, "what do you think?"

"I don't know what to say," I said. "Why me?"

"Why not?" he replied. "You're a hero to many people, especially to the south where your name is spoken in the same breath with the mighty Hercules. You need a residence befitting of your status."

"I don't know," I said. I knew I could never accept his offer, but I couldn't flat-out turn him down either. "I need time to consult the omens." Appia looked surprised by my comment, but I knew it would make sense to Titus.

"Of course," he said.

"You know Getha," Appia said, "it would really help out our family."

"I know."

We resumed our tour of *The Hill*, passing a pair of large open pits where buildings once stood. We continued on to a point overlooking his big, new amphitheater.

"It still impresses me," Titus said as we stopped to look for a moment.

"What's its capacity?" I asked.

"About 35,000," he replied, "give or take. Another tier might bring that number to 50,000."

"That's a lot of people," Appia said.

"I suppose it is," the emperor agreed. "Of course, the Circus holds over two hundred thousand."

"I noticed lots of tents around the Circus," I said

"We've got an event coming up," he said. "Those are fans. Some come from great distances to enjoy a few days of racing."

On the way back to the palace we stopped at the place where it was believed Romulus lived. There was a hut with an altar that was supposedly his. I had my doubts as to how such a primitive structure could have lasted for so long in such a well-preserved state, but Titus explained that it had been restored a multitude of times.

We finished our walk just in time for an afternoon meal in the courtyard, followed by a relaxing hour at the private palace bath, after which, Titus left us and Appia and I returned to my room in the annex where Thalese caught up with us again. "How was your day?" I asked.

"Fine," he replied. "How about yours?"

"Titus wants us to live here," I said. "He has a site all picked out that overlooks the Circus Maximus."

"Really?"

"It's true," Appia said. "He's planning a new palace for himself in the same area. I'm sure it will be a part of that."

"That's a good thing," Thalese said. "News from home isn't great."

"What's wrong?" I asked.

"We're losing cargos," he replied. "The goods originally slated for Rome are fine, but the ones on their way to Pompeii are being raided."

"By pirates?"

"No! By other shippers, some of the very people Master Appius had agreements with. They think we're too weak to defend them and they're acting like vultures on a carcass. They're telling the captains that we have no funding left to compensate them."

"If my name is so well known," I said, "why would they dare do that? I bet Hercules never had that problem."

He shook his head. "These raiders aren't from Pompeii or that area. They're from here. They're taking advantage of the confusion with those cargos. I expected outside interference, but I was hoping those skippers would continue onto Rome. It appears that's not the case. This represents a huge loss that we can ill afford. The emperor's offer is perfect."

"For what?"

"If you choose to live on *The Hill,*" he said, "that's a message for all to see. That would all but solidify our place in Rome, and then we'll be untouchable."

"That will stop them from raiding us?"

"Eventually," he said. "It may take time for word to spread, but that's not a problem because we'll get it all back, or the equivalent."

"No pressure here," I said sarcastically, "but I can't do it."

"Why not?" Appia asked. "You told the emperor you were consulting the omens. Since when?"

"I know what I said. That was to buy time to come up with an acceptable way to say no."

"History?" Thalese said.

"Yes. Domitian is to build a massive palace complex there. It will take up that whole end of *The Hill.*"

"That's tough," he said, "but what if history wasn't an issue?"

"What do you mean?" I asked.

"You could simply say no to that spot," he replied. "Tell him it's too close to the Circus. The noise and all that. Then suggest that you'd prefer being where you are right now. I know for a fact he has no set plans for the annex yet."

Appia's eyes lit up as she looked at me. "What's wrong with that idea?"

"I can't emphasize enough how important this stroke of luck is," Thalese added, “to our family and our future. We are doing our best to recover what’s been lost, but there are no guarantees. All you have to do is humor the emperor for a while and everything will work out.”

“You both think I should do it?” I asked.

“Yes!” was the response from both in unison.

I got up and looked out the window at the Forum and buildings beyond. There was no mistaking where I was. The late evening sun painted the scene with the same warm pastel yellows and oranges as it did in the Rome I knew two thousand years in the future.

“Alright,” I said.

“Good,” Thalese said with a sigh of relief. Appia gave me a hug.

“For our family,” I said, “but you should know, I’m not comfortable with it.”

“Getha,” Appia said, “relax for once. Look at where we are. No one will bother us here. What could possibly go wrong?”

XXXII

∞

Christina gripped Kamden's arm as the big jet trundled down the runway, quickly decelerating before making the turn towards the main terminal at Capodichino, Naples International Airport. Christina's request to the Director's Office of the Museo Archeologio Nazionale di Napoli received a quick and positive reply. She was given permission to view the museum's materials related to the so-called *Insurrection Against the Emperor and the Imperial Family*, along with documents related to the myth of the neoteric Hercules, provided she agreed to a museum selected staff assistant, who would oversee her work, assist with materials procurement, and act as a translator. That was perfectly fine with Christina. She knew the museum was just trying to protect their works and reputation. Once she agreed, she was sent a letter from the director that allowed her entrance to the museum one hour prior to the daily public opening times.

Christina had a chronic fear of flying, but when flying was the only option, she was always able to summon the inner courage necessary to get on a plane. She briefly considered boarding a cruise ship for the ocean crossing portion of the trip, but time and logistics made that idea impractical. Kamden saw this as an opportunity to share some personal time with her away from the lab, and she was not opposed to the idea of a travel partner, but he was just as fearful of flying as she was. His desire for her was just a bit more powerful than his fears, so together they figured they could find comfort through their shared phobia.

The flights from Boston to Rome and Rome to Naples were smooth and event-free and twelve hours after their departure from Logan International Airport they were checking into their hotel in Naples. Jetlag took a backseat to the joy of being on solid ground again.

They arrived at the museum at 8 AM the very next morning. Following a brief wait to get added permission to allow Kamden admittance with her, they were let in by the guards. They were greeted by an assistant director who introduced them to the staff assistant, a young woman named Giulia who had recently completed her doctorate in Roman studies. Christina couldn't have been more pleased. There was a discussion in the Director's office and paperwork to sign followed by a break for espresso.

All in all, it took two hours to complete the process and another hour to be granted provisional permission for Christina to enter the records room. It was just a formality, but one dictated by protocol. Christina and Kamden were taken to the records room, but only Christina was allowed entrance. There hadn't been enough time to add him to her request, but they were assured he would be granted access in another day or two. Once inside the records room she was assigned a desk and shown the procedure for handling ancient documents. Special gloves were provided, along with acid-free implements designed for turning fragile pages.

The preliminaries were completed at around 12:45 PM, making it a perfect time for lunch; after which, Christina could finally begin her research. Giulia recommended a trattoria not too far away. Christina was fine with it as long as they served pizza. She'd heard so much from Aaron about how good the pizza was in Naples that she had to have one. In fact, Aaron had told her only marinara and margarita pizzas counted as real pizza, so margarita it would be.

On their way out they passed through a long corridor lined with lots of ancient Roman sculpture. There were artifacts in cases as well, including the keel of an ancient boat, but that wasn't what caught Christina's eye.

"Hold up," she said, and everyone stopped in their tracks. She must have looked like a deer caught in the headlights as she needed a moment to process and accept what she was seeing. But then she smiled. "Oh my god, Kam! Look, just look!"

"I am looking," he said, but he saw nothing that seemed out of the ordinary.

"Do you see it?" she asked, her voice trembling.

"No," he replied.

"You're looking right at it!" she said. "Think, Kam! You've seen enough photos. Am I right, or am I crazy?"

His jaw dropped. "You're not crazy," he said. "Unbelievable. Unfreakinbelievable..."

"We'll have to eat a little later," she told Giulia as her hands were shaking. "I've got to call home."

"Why?" Giulia asked as she tried to understand what all the excitement was about. Christina and Kamden could barely contain their obvious joy.

"I'm so sorry to have made you go to all this trouble," she told her, "but I found it. I found what I'm looking for."

"You have?" Giulia said with a questioning look of utter surprise.

"I have. But we have to go. Thank you."

"But…"

Before she could finish her sentence, Christina and Kamden were off and practically running for the exit. They left the museum and hustled around a corner so as not to be overheard by the museum staff. Christina almost dropped her phone from excitement as she dialed.

"Hello?" It was Liam. "Is that you, Chris?"

"I found it, Liam," she said, her lips trembling. "I found it!"

"The sign?"

"Yes!" she cried out.

"He actually made a sign!" Liam said.

"He most surely did," she replied with tears welling in her eyes, "many times over. It's been in front of us all the time. You're not going to believe it, Liam. You and Aine are just not going to believe it!"

XXXIII

∞

It was near the Calends of December when a messenger came with the news that Nubia had given birth to a healthy baby girl, and that both mother and daughter were doing well. Leita could add another successful birth to her midwife resume. I don't know why I found the news so upsetting. I'd accepted the situation and the child was getting a good home. I was greatly relieved there were no complications, but in a personal sense I struggled. I felt like crying and didn't even know why.

Appia found me shortly after the messenger left. "Have you heard?" she asked, full of energy and excitement.

I was at the window staring out over the Forum. "Yes," I replied as I continued to stare off into the distance.

"When can we visit?"

"Any time you want," I said.

"Me? Aren't you coming?"

"No," I said. "I'm not ready."

"Getha?" she said. "They'll be terribly disappointed. You know this child will bear your name."

"I know. I'm not crazy about that either."

"I don't understand you sometimes," she said. "You do know that Caelus and Nubia are a couple?"

"Yes," I replied. "They asked for my permission through Thalese. They don't have to do that. They're free too…"

"Be that as it may," she said. "They want to honor you, and they want this child to know her father. This should be a happy day for all of us, including you."

"It is a happy day," I said in a saddened voice.

"Getha," she said as she put her arms around me, "this despairing over things beyond your control has to end. I know you hurt. You try to hide it, but I still feel it. I fear it will tear you apart. You are one of us now and you know it. It's time to believe it."

"I'm sorry," I said.

"Don't be sorry. There's nothing to be sorry for. Just hold me and let our feelings be the foundation we build on."

I agreed with her sentiment, but not to visiting Nubia and her baby just yet. Appia was disappointed but understanding. She and Thalese left for the Villa North that evening while I remained at the palace. It was strange sleeping alone for the first time in months, and even stranger waking up that way. The first thing I did once up was warm up with a little jogging followed by a cooldown and a midmorning meal. Despite everything, I managed to keep up with my exercising.

That afternoon I cleaned and assembled the gun. My thought was to fire off what rounds I had left, thus ending the risk to history the weapon might still pose. I suppose I could have disposed of all of it by tossing everything into the Tiber, but I saw no harm in enjoying a little target shooting for the last time. There was a large, rectangular depression in the ground over by the Circus Maximus side of *The Hill*. A building stood there at one time, but aside from a few clumps of cement-bound bricks, there was nothing left of it. Just the same, it looked like a safe place to set up a target range. It was a good distance away from the palace and other occupied buildings, and the depression was deep enough to partially deaden the sound. It was a race day at the Circus and the roar of the crowd would muffle the rest.

I placed the gun in a satchel and headed across to the site. I had just seven bullets left, so I picked up seven small clay pots along the way to use as targets and set them up on sticks at the far end of the depression. I was pleased to find the level of noise coming from the Circus to be very high, and that it remained high for several minutes at a time depending on the length of the race. I loaded the barrel with six rounds, which left just one. I stood about ten yards away from the targets. I positioned myself back to them, and then I cocked the hammer, waiting for the moment when the crowd would erupt at the start of a race. I planned to destroy six of the targets in rapid succession, reload, and destroy the seventh.

The moment the crowd erupted, I spun around with arms outstretched, drawing a bead on the first terra-cotta pot, but I didn't fire. My finger never left the frame. Instead, I was shaking so hard I nearly fired by accident as I lowered my arms. I couldn't shoot. What had once been a game to me was a game no more. The screams of the crowd had produced a sudden flow of mental images, of blasted flesh and bodies falling in the forum at Pompeii. I backed up and sat in a corner of the pit. I dumped the unspent shells and gun back into the satchel. I left the pots and walked back to my room. It didn't take long to disassemble the gun and return it to its hiding place in the closet.

It was midafternoon by then, so I decided to head over to the palace kitchen for a snack. The kitchen was well stocked with just about anything anyone could want, so I got excited by the idea of creating the first Italian sandwich, but that excitement was short lived when I saw a few of Domitian's servants hanging around by the palace atrium. I was too hungry to turn back, and since the kitchen seemed like the last place would I run into Domitian, I kept going.

"Getha," Domitian said with a start when I entered the room. Apparently, he wasn't expecting to run into me either.

"Hello," I said politely. "Good to see you."

He gave me one of his disbelieving glares. "Here to hunt up a snack?"

"Well," I replied with a smile, "I was thinking I might try to make something called a sandwich."

"A what?"

"A sandwich," I said. "Can I interest you in one?" It was at that moment a pair of kitchen staffers appeared. They were laughing as they entered, but our presence brought their cheerfulness to a sudden halt.

"We were just about to start preparing evening meal," one said apologetically, "but we can come back."

"You can stay," I said, and then I turned to Domitian. "Do you want to take a chance? I haven't made one of these things for a long time." The two staff members offered bows and left.

"Okay," he replied, "I'll try one."

I had no difficulty locating leafy salad material, lots of vegetables and various edible oils. Breads came in all shapes and sizes, which I opted for a whitish kind that just happened to be much longer than it was wide. The meats were a bit of a problem. Meat was fresh daily, but I didn't always trust it. Refrigeration was nonexistent, leaving salt and the cool of cellar lockers to retain freshness. I cut off a few thin slices from a cooked block of pork that smelled fresh and was still warm. By the time I was done, my creation was more like a warm pork sub than an Italian sandwich.

Domitian had been quietly watching me create it, and when it was done, he couldn't help smiling. The thing was huge.

"I guess I won't need to make two," I said, and so I cut it in half to share.

It was actually quite good, and by the look on Domitian's face he liked it too. "You call it a what?" he asked.

"A sandwich," I replied.

"Never heard of it."

"That's because I just made it up," I said with a smile. I had a pretty good idea that putting meat between two slices of bread wasn't a new concept, but the unusual combination of what I'd put between the slices made it different.

"It's an odd name," he said. "I wish you'd show my cook how to do this. It really is delightful."

"I'd be glad to," I said. "But there are no set rules. I look at what's available and make it work."

"I understand you're quite good at that," he said as he poured wine into cups for us. Wine wouldn't have been my first choice, but accepting it was more important.

"Like I said, this is the first time I've made one of these things in a long time."

"No," he said, "I mean everything. Wherever you go you seem to make it work, so to speak. Your name was unknown to anybody a year ago, and yet here you are today, living in the imperial palace as a mentor to the most powerful personage in this or any other territory."

I shook my head. "You've got me all wrong. I'm here as a guest only. It was not by design."

"I'm not afraid of you," he said.

I looked at him. It took me a moment to reply. "You have no reason to be."

"A lot of people believe you to be a god," he said. "Some very important and influential people. A lot of military men, and not just the common soldiery but commanders too. To be honest, I don't see it."

"Nor do I," I replied. "I'm not a god nor have I ever claimed to be."

"I'm pleased to hear that, but then how do you explain why so many people, respected people, like my father and my brother, find divine qualities in you?"

"I can't," I said, "not in a way that makes sense."

"Then explain it in a nonsensical way."

I didn't know what to say. "I've been lucky. I think in times of desperation people look for somebody or something to cling to, to give them hope. Events get exaggerated. I didn't ask for that, nor do I want it, and it exasperates me. I'm human. I'm just a plain, garden variety human, no different from anybody else. I keep telling people that." He looked up from his sandwich and gave me a doubting look. "You don't believe me?"

"Well, no, not really," he replied.

"Why not?"

He chuckled, "You're still here for one thing. You can go back to your villa anytime you please. And tell me this, who strives to be something less than his potential? You've got followers for crying out loud, many in the upper levels of the military no less! You've got the makings of a strong powerbase. And I'm supposed to believe this is all some haphazard accidental happenstance! I don't think so."

"Look," I said. "I know what you're saying, but the reason I'm living here is in support of my family. After the disaster people were stealing our cargo ships and undermining our strength as a family. That stopped the instant I moved in here. If I hadn't accepted your brother's offer, we might have lost everything."

"Granted," he said, "that's a valid answer. But why are you still here? That issue was resolved."

"I'm helping your brother now," I said. "He has challenges ahead, especially down south where I have knowledge of things others perhaps don't."

"Like what?"

"It's hard to explain."

"I'm sure it is," he chuckled. "Try me."

"No," I replied, to which he recoiled a bit. "I would rather you ask him. I'm tired of that conversation. He can better tell you why he wants me here anyway. Okay?"

He stared at me for a moment. "Okay," he said. "Here's what concerns me. I see my brother in a politically weakened state while your powerbase is getting stronger. It's not unknown for one in a position such as yours to try to take advantage for personal, self-serving political ambitions."

"What self-serving ambitions might they be?"

"Well," he smiled, "you tell me."

"I can't," I said. "I already told you my reasons."

"You have no interest in being the next emperor?" he said with a straight face.

"Emperor?" I said. "Are you kidding? No! No way! I hope that was a joke."

"No," he said, "it's not a joke."

I was shaking. "Believe me. I have no ambitions like that. In fact," and I caught myself midsentence because I almost said, "when your brother dies." Fortunately, I didn't. "If something dreadful were to happen to your brother, it's imperative that you succeed him. Should that day come, I will support you as I have him."

"Oh," he said sarcastically, "I have no doubt of that."

"I do support him," I said. "I mean that. And I would support you too."

He stared at me again. "Okay. Then prove it."

"How?"

"Appia," he replied.

"What?"

"Let's call this a hypothetical, but if I were to wed your sister, our powerbases would be linked. That would satisfy both our ambitions, don't you think?"

"You have a wife."

He shrugged. "She'll be well taken care of."

"The answer is no, and no, and let me see, how about no."

"I thought you'd say that," he said. "She's your lover, isn't she?"

"She's my sister," I replied.

"Interesting conundrum, sister and lover. One I'm sure the gossip mongers might enjoy. Of course, such a familial corruption can take on a life of its own whether true or false."

"Are you threatening me?"

"Hardly," he smiled. "It's more like friendly advice."

I sighed. "I was actually hoping you and I could be friends."

"We still can," he said with a smile. "I quite like you, all else aside. You have a quick wit and you're not stupid. Perhaps you're too much like me, but you hide your ambitions remarkably well. Perhaps you're even more dangerous than I realize."

"I think we're done here."

I returned to my room shaken and shaking, wondering what had just happened. I'd played hardball with the second most powerful man in the Empire. It was a bluff, but that didn't matter. He considered me a rival, perhaps even more so now, and as such, I was clearly causing a problem between brothers who didn't seem to need much provocation to take issue with each other.

XXXIV

∞

The unusually warm winter morphed into an unseasonable cold spell that felt even colder because the clothing wasn't adequate. After a week of near freezing temperatures, a warming trend arrived that brought several days of steady rain. The Tiber ran fast and high, flooding its banks in the low areas, making river travel difficult. Titus stayed at his private villa north of Rome during the heaviest of the rain and remained there until the weather cleared. When he returned, he called Appia and me to his study.

"I had a very interesting chat this morning with your most loyal servants, Thalese and Leita," the emperor said. "They sought my help to legitimize a marriage between you two."

"What?" I uttered. Appia looked stunned.

"I don't know if the romance came before the adoption or vice versa," he said, "but that is of no consequence. You and Appia are legally brother and sister. Adoption is a serious business, and yours needed help. The kind only an emperor can give."

"What help?" I asked as a chill ran down my spine. I had to wonder if the cat was out of the bag, so to speak.

He was smiling. "I don't know all the details, Getha, nor do I want to, but you apparently lacked the usual prerequisites of rank necessary to satisfy the scope of acceptability for this adoption."

"I'm freeborn," I quipped.

"Birth status wasn't in question," he replied, "but your life prior to your adoption was. Your military service was void of distinction. You had no property, no political…anything. Nothing on parchment. And I don't mean to offend you."

"You haven't."

"Of course, we all know you're powerful and divinely gifted, but until recently nobody knew that except Appius."

"I did," Appia said.

Titus smiled. "I'm sure you did. But my point is this, a man of wealth and political acumen doesn't adopt an adult male heir of lesser prominence. It's just not done. And you're from Ephesus. That's the same as being a foreigner to an old Pompeiian patrician. Yes, you qualified for adoption, but that's of little practical use without local acceptance."

"I wasn't aware that my adoption was so problematic," I said.

"Happens all the time," he said. "There will always be questions regarding any adoption, especially where large estates are involved. It's not uncommon for such questions to be settled by a council, or even by an emperor, but your father was smart. He knew how to avoid such entanglements. He made his case, and my father literally gave his imperial seal of approval."

"I appreciate that," I said, "but what's your point? We already know we can't wed."

He smiled in a very warm and kindly way. "My point is," he replied, "I can make it happen."

"Wonderful," Appia said.

"How?" I asked.

"There is imperial precedent for this type of union," he said. "Your father is also deceased. It will take some haggling with senators. I may have to call in a marker or two, but I believe I can fix it for you."

"Okay," I said tentatively as Appia took my hand.

"But I ask something in return," he said, while I thought to myself, here it comes. "I need you, both of you, to sail with me to Neapolis. I would like to publicly formalize your marriage in Neapolis, near your home, before the people who adore both of you. They need heroes. They need a reason to celebrate. Your union can be the spark that unites a region still reeling in the wake of disaster."

"That's a stretch," I chuckled. "Isn't incest still an issue?"

"Not for you," he replied. "Not down there. You're Hercules to them. Your divine heritage is through Hercules, whose father is Jupiter. Jupiter is married to Juno, and they're brother and sister no less! What could be more perfect? I've also put together a fleet of cargo ships full of food and clothing to follow us in. We'll come bearing gifts. What do you say?"

I looked at Appia who was beaming. He had his answer.

Emperor Titus gave us only two days to prepare for travel and we were going by ship. I'd read that all sea travel was curtailed during the winter months due to the difficulties related to navigating in seasonally rougher waters and bad weather. That turned out to be partially true. Long distance shipping from places like Alexandria and Ephesus was halted except in times of desperate need such as a severe grain shortage in Rome. Desperation didn't change the risks involved, as losses due to weather minimized the benefits, often making the entire effort wasted. However, coastal travel for short distances continued to and from Rome. The seas were generally rougher, but to many travelers, the time saved was worth the discomfort, and if a storm did pop up, there was always a port to provide shelter.

Emperor Titus had another surprise for me. He had arranged for Caelus to accompany us to Neapolis.

We met Caelus in Ostia at about 3 AM (a guesstimate) on the day of our departure. He had received a formal invitation to embark with Appia and me for the trip, but no duties were specified, so he expected to be assigned to some form of seaboard labor, but he wasn't. The emperor had specifically invited him as an honored member of his entourage.

Caelus' heroics were becoming legendary in the south, first as a gladiator, but more recently, and importantly as a hero from what was locally termed the *Insurrection Against the Emperor and the Imperial Family.* It referred to the day Appius was assassinated in the Forum at Pompeii, but a desperate longing for heroes among survivors in the wake of the Vesuvius disaster had blown the events of that day out of all proportion. Caelus' strict dedication to the ideal of duty and honor, and an unflinching fervor to go headlong into battle regardless of the odds, made him a role model, unheard of for a former slave and gladiator. The emperor needed a lift in public opinion. By employing Caelus, Appia and me, he wasn't leaving anything to chance.

It's easy to dismiss ancient sea travel as being backwards for lack of modern equipment, but sailors of that era learned and internalized a lot more from observational experience than modern sailors have had to in modern day. That wasn't to say modern sailors were lacking in anything, but different ages required different levels of specialized and localized knowledge which became superfluous over time with improvements in technology. That was what allowed ancient sea captains to navigate with confidence in the dark of night, under partly cloudy skies, using tiny pin pricks of flickering light along a meandering coastline that was often obscured by the way ships dip, roll, and rise through troughs and waves.

The sea became progressively calmer as we approached the bay of Neapolis. The first light of dawn had broken, making the coastline visible again. Appia and I got up early and sat bundled up in a blanket by the railing as we sailed around the naval base at Misenum to enter the bay beyond. What began as a flotilla of six vessels, arrived as a group of three. The heavily laden cargo ships wouldn't arrive for another eight to twelve hours.

"Look," Appia said as she tugged on my arm.

Vesuvius was still center stage. Its central core was completely blown away from its midpoint to the sea, leaving only the 3800-foot high crescent shaped remnants of the northern slope. Steam continued to rise from the gutted caldera like some great open sore in the Earth. Neapolis was visible to the left on the inner bay. From a distance the city didn't look badly damaged, but as we slowly sailed closer the damage became more apparent. There were collapsed buildings and others without roofs. The port was functioning. It looked like all the concrete piers were intact.

As for the rest of the villas and towns along the inner bay between Neapolis and Stabia, there were none, literally none. The shoreline sprawl of coastal structures ended at the southern suburbs of Neapolis, melding into a grayish/tan, moonlike desert wasteland, void of all life, and yet, overhead there were birds. The gulls were back, if they ever left, the first signs of recovery. We tried to find Pompeii, but we couldn't. It was too far away to make out any of the surface rubble that marked its gravesite.

Word of the emperor's arrival was spreading through the city rapidly. The sight of crowds lining up along the quay to see us gave me a moment of pause. It reminded me of the crowd in the forum at Pompeii on the day Appius was killed, but this time the gun was back in our room in Rome.

Our first planned stop was a large refugee camp south of the city, deeper into the disaster zone. It was a giant square, with paths between blocks of tents organized along a grid. This one had military-style barracks as well, which were aligned on the southern and western walls just outside the camp. The walls were no more than staked outlines. There was no war so there was no need to waste building materials on fortifications.

A makeshift rostrum was constructed and setup on the open ground between the quay and the camp. It was an ideal location, offering room for hundreds of spectators without encroaching on the camp. Just how hundreds of spectators would be able to hear the speeches without the aid of microphones and amplifiers was a mystery, but it was a perfect day, with a bright blue sky and almost no breeze, so acoustically it was as good as it was going to get.

When we arrived, there were at least a couple hundred soldiers and civilian volunteers waiting anxiously for us. Cheers went up as the four of us made our way to the rostrum. Our guards took their places around the rostrum when we climbed the stairs to face the gathering masses. The moment the emperor stepped forward to speak, the entire camp erupted with a series of hails. Titus raised his arms in the air, and when he lowered them the crowd went silent.

"Friends," he said a loud, booming voice, "what I have witnessed today is nothing short of a miracle. What you have done has not only saved countless lives, but may well have saved the Empire itself!" He read the names of officers and soldiers who risked their lives in acts of unselfish heroism. He made extra special mention of those who entered damaged or burning buildings to rescue trapped survivors during the first days following the eruption. His words were met with enthusiastic cheers, followed by complete silence. I realized the silence was a way large crowds had collectively learned to better hear what a speaker was saying at a distance.

"I have with me today," he said slowly and deliberately, "a person of whom all of you have heard, but few have ever met. His name is legend, and I proclaim before all of you now that I have witnessed the power that he so humbly harbors within." As he spoke the crowd began dropping to their knees in silent reverence.

"Step forward, Appius Getha of Pompeii," Titus said with arms outstretched. "These are your people. They are our friends."

I stepped forward and acknowledged the crowd. Titus lifted my arm with his to even greater applause. He encouraged me to say a few words, which I did. I can't recall what I said, but people cheered. I doubt anyone could hear me anyway. I stepped back.

The emperor introduced Caelus and encouraged him to speak. He looked terrified. This is the same man who could perform in the arena before hundreds of fans, but he was never asked to speak before. However, like the dutiful person he was, he stepped up and spoke. "Hi," he said, and he stepped back. The crowd loved it.

The emperor then introduced Appia. She stepped forward, waved and tried to step back, but Titus took her hand. "I have a favor to ask," he said to the crowd. Everyone went silent. "I have a Writ of Appropriateness signed by the Senate in Rome. This document allows me the honor of granting marriage to you," and he looked at Appia and me, "Appius Getha and your lovely bride Maria Secunda." He turned back to the audience and raised his arms. "Yes or no. How say you to this marriage? A marriage between Getha, the ultimate strength of Hercules, and Appia, the essence of female purity and divinity. HOW SAY YOU ALL?"

There was a deafening roar that suddenly rose up from a very excited audience. I couldn't tell if it was a yes or a no, but by all the smiles I had to assume it was positive. Titus certainly did. He asked me to join hands with Appia to which he said in a loud and booming voice, “I proclaim this marriage valid! You are officially wed!”

XXXV

∞

After the emperor's final words, we were taken back to Neapolis and to a cleared area near the shore not far from the ship. There were tables covered with a gaudy abundance of food and wine for our pleasure. I questioned the wisdom of that given the conditions of a region barely able to feed itself. Titus said it wasn't his doing or part of his itinerary. He said that sometimes we must allow for situations that may seem wrong to us but might offend our hosts if we turn it down.

We returned to the ship to find city dignitaries waiting for us. Prior to our visit to the refugee camp, the emperor had instructed local officials to do a search for Appia's sister Maria Prima and her family. They began by checking the most recent lists of registered refugees in all the camps, but they were not on that list. A search was done of the most likely public places refugees might have gone in the city, but that turned up nothing. Appia was told it was too early to give up hope. They were planning a more in depth canvasing of the city that should discover any friends who might have seen them or taken them in.

Appia thanked them for their efforts. She was saddened but also comforted by the knowledge that everything that could be done was being done. I don't think either of us held out much hope. It made sense that they would have come to Rome if they'd made it out of Oplontis safely.

We left the next morning at first light.

The mountain was as quiet as the seas had become. Steam rose in puffs and stringers from the inner most depths of its new crater.

"You handled yourself well," Titus said as he joined me at the railing. I saw what looked like small fires on the barren land south of the mountain.

"Are soldiers camped out there?" I asked.

"Not to my knowledge," he replied. "There are a few people looking for their homes. I was told of looters and fortune hunters too."

"Good luck with that," I said.

Leaving was bittersweet for Appia and me. We were married. That was the best part, but the region held a lot of difficult memories that remained unspoken.

Appia was pleased that I'd become more liberal with the scientific information I shared, but liberal wasn't quite right. I was being more calculated. When Emperor Titus first approached me for an understanding of the disaster, he seemed to be vacillating, perhaps awaiting answers from me. I couldn't let that happen. History recorded him as the author of the relief efforts, and that's why I motivated him with out-of-era knowledge to ensure history stayed on course.

The concept of military style refugee camps was also on me. It began as an off-the-cuff suggestion to a contingent of young officers onboard the warship that transported us to Rome, and unbeknownst to me, the idea was passed on to the emperor by Commander Virillius, resulting in the massive refugee shelter and reintegration system we'd just witnessed.

It took three full, wind-hampered days to reach Ostia, but aside from an issue with fog on the second day, the trip was relatively uneventful. David was in Ostia when we arrived at first light, and Caelus chose to remain with him. The rest of us rode in a caravan of mule drawn coaches, headed by the imperial standard and protected by Praetorians. Appia and I rode with the emperor.

The road had its share of paving issues, but our coach actually had a suspension. I could feel it. There were certainly bumps and jerks, but the sharpness was tempered, and I fell asleep. When I awoke, we were passing the Flavian Amphitheater on course for Palatine Hill. At the base of the hill were more Praetorian Guard set to relieve those who'd made the trip from Ostia with us. The stop afforded me the opportunity to witness a changing of the guard protocol that wasn't often seen. The emperor was disinterested, except for the short delay it had caused.

The delay was no longer than five minutes, if that, and we were once again on our way. It seemed silly to be riding at that point, but I was feeling lazy and we were in no real rush. We slowly climbed the hill and made the turn to the right and onto the path that took us to the main entrance of the palace. There were more Praetorians awaiting our arrival there, which was strange since the duty of guarding the main entrance had been cancelled by Emperor Vespasian some years earlier.

When our coach came to a stop before the palace, it was a guardsman who opened the door for the emperor rather than a servant. The guardsman saluted and then said, "Prefect Cassius Civitus makes his apologies. He was taken ill this morning and has returned to the barracks."

"Thank you, centurion," Titus replied, clearly bothered by the news. He turned to me and added, "I had specifically asked him to be here. Granted, he's ill, but he could have at least sent someone I know who knows something, and not some kid." Titus headed directly for the palace.

"Something's not right," I said as I helped Appia from the coach. "I don't recognize any of these guardsmen."

"Where's Thalese and Leita?" Appia asked.

"I don't know," I replied. "Travel schedules are not very precise. They may not know we're here."

Appia and I didn't have much in the way luggage, and both small trunks were delivered to our room in the annex while we were still in conversation by the coach. It was a sunny day with a gentle breeze, and even in winter the air carried whiffs of herbal scents that brighten moods, but my mood wasn't brightening. There were guardsmen all over the place.

"You're being paranoid," Appia said.

"I suppose I am," I said.

"I don't think they're even posted," she said. "They're just hanging around. They're probably an escort for some noble who's waiting inside to see the emperor."

"Since when do Praetorians escort nobles?"

"You know this history," she said. "Is there a problem with the Guard? Is there an attack on the emperor on this date? That seems to be what you're hinting at."

"No," I replied. "History records no such event."

"There you go," she said with a smile and a hug.

"There I go," I said.

We had just about reached the entrance to the annex when the emperor rushed out of the palace and asked us to wait. He was all smiles as he hustled along the path between the palace and the annex. He gave me a strong pat on the back. "Don't you need a witness?" he asked. Appia and I looked at each other. We didn't have a clue. "I got you two married, but until you," and he looked at Appia, "are safely across the threshold I can't promise the omens will be favorable."

"Are you talking about lifting her across the threshold?" I asked. I had no idea that tradition went so far back in history.

"Not me," he chuckled, "you!"

"Okay," I said with a smile. Appia was beaming.

"After you," Titus said, and I opened the heavy wooden door and stepped into the candle lit corridor. I closed the door behind us, but we hadn't gotten more than ten feet down the corridor when I heard the door open, but when I turned it slammed shut.

"That's odd," I said.

"What is?" Appia asked.

The emperor stood there with a puzzled look. "Maybe it was the wind."

"Maybe if we were in the middle of a thunderstorm," I said. "That's a heavy door."

I grabbed the door handle and pushed. The door didn't budge. "What the…" I fiddled with the handle. It was releasing, but the door was so solidly jammed it was like pushing against a wall.

"Hmm," Titus muttered with his hands on his hips. "I'll see that gets repaired first thing."

If I wasn't paranoid before, I was then. I stepped over to the adjacent door that led to the palace atrium. I needed to see what was keeping the outside door from opening, but when I pulled on that door it wouldn't budge. It made no sense that a door opening inward would be jammed, and especially no sense that both doors were jammed at the same time."

"Oh shit," I said in English as my blood pressure rose.

XXXVI

∞

"What?" Titus said. He may not have known the swear word, but he felt the sentiment.

"Getha," Appia said, "you're frightening me."

"We have a problem," I said as I looked around the corridor.

"Let's not lose our heads," Titus said, and then came the sound of heavy boots charging up the stairwell opposite our room. "People love us."

"Apparently not everyone," I said as I grabbed Appia's hand and turned to run towards our room.

"By the gods above," Titus called out as he followed us, "why are we running?"

"I hope I'm wrong," I said. All I knew was that we had to reach our room before those on the stairwell did. I pushed the door open and sent Appia and the emperor ahead of me. When I slammed the door shut, I slipped just as an arrow whistled by my shoulder, impaling itself in the door. Another smashed into the bronze mirror showering us with splinters.

"Sheesh!" I cried out as I lowered my shoulder against the door just in time to engage the heavy iron bolt. Titus and Appia were both on the floor. "Anyone hit?"

That's when the battering began. There had to be several attackers out there banging against the door trying to break it. It was a solid door, but it was made of wood and I could tell by the flexing that it wasn't going to hold.

"Give me just one sword," Titus said, seething with anger.

"I've got something better than that," I said. I turned and looked at Appia and the pained expression on her face. "I'm sorry, I have no choice." My course of action was clear. Titus had to live. I'd have to deal with any repercussions after the fact.

There were several repetitive hard blows against the door as the wood began to give way with a series of frightening cracks. "That's an axe!" Titus said.

I slid across the floor to the closet where I'd hidden the gun. I was upset and panicking, and when I grabbed the cloth holding the pieces of the gun it unrolled and everything fell out.

"I don't believe this is happening," I muttered as I fumbled with the parts, but luckily, it was a simple assembly.

It took two tries to snap the chamber into place. Seconds felt like hours. The bullets had rolled away in various directions, but I scooped up four of the seven and quickly loaded them into the barrel.

"Titus!" I yelled. "Tell them who you are. Tell them to stop or they die!"

"How will that stop them?" he asked. "They're after me!"

"Just do it!" I ordered. The center of the door began to break from consecutive hits with an axe. I saw the blade briefly as it split the wood apart.

"I am your emperor!" Titus screamed. "I AM YOUR EMPEROR! Stop now or the Gods will strike you dead!"

Silence. It lasted for maybe ten or fifteen seconds. We heard voices followed by footsteps going down the stairwell, but then the banging began again. The door was done.

"I am so sorry," I said, and I stood and fired two waist high rounds at the door. I figured that offered the greatest chance of hitting something. At just about the same instant a pair of arrows zipped by my head, crashing into the wall and door.

"I've had just about enough of this crap!" I stated, and I turned and stepped towards the back window. There were a pair of archers not more than thirty yards away standing on the weathered, wooden scaffolding that I'd noticed the day we arrived. They were ready to fire again, so I quickly took aim and fired at the one on the left, hitting him in the midsection. He dropped immediately. The other slipped and fell, probably four stories.

The corridor was silent and there were no more arrows.

"What did you do?" Titus asked as I dumped the empty casings onto the floor. I picked up the other three and reloaded. "My ears are ringing."

"I hurt them," I said sadly. "I didn't want to do that, but I had no choice…no choice." I wanted to cry.

"What now?"

"Okay," I replied as I regrouped. "You can open what's left of that door. But stand back so I can cover you."

Titus crept up to the door and drew back the bolt. The door had buckled in the center, and by pulling on the handle, the whole thing came apart and fell to the floor. I stepped ahead him with the gun out in front of me. There were two bodies on the ground. One was dead. The other was still alive, but gravely wounded in the chest. I felt sick.

I'd forgotten about Appia. I looked back and found her rocking in a fetal position in the far corner of the room. She pulled back the instant I touched her, but when she realized it was me, she grabbed onto my arm as tightly as she could.

"I'm not going to ask you if you're okay," I said. "Neither of us are, but are you hurt anywhere? I don't see any bleeding."

"Getha," she whispered, "it's not your fault."

"We need to get out of here," I said. "We can go through the temple."

"Agreed," Titus said.

Appia was on her feet. I took her hand and stepped by Titus. Titus dragged the live assassin into the room and tied him to a bedpost. I don't know what he was thinking. The man was unconscious and still losing blood. It was a horrible sight. The idea that he might somehow wake up and run away was ludicrous, but the whole scene was. No one knew that better than me.

"I should have listened to you, Getha," Titus lamented as we made our way down the stairwell to the temple. "There's never a good time to be complacent, especially an emperor."

"Yes," I said, "but we can't be so fixated on security that we wall ourselves in either." I had the gun in one hand and Appia's hand in the other. I may have appeared to have calmed down, but I was like a tightly wound spring inside, compressed and set to go off at the slightest movement. My purpose was clear. Titus had to live.

When we reached the old atrium, we headed straight across to the set of heavy metal doors to the temple. Those doors were locked on our side but not blocked. The temple was empty so we entered.

"Now what?" Appia asked. "Where do we go from here? Who can we trust?"

"Does it really matter?" Titus replied. He looked at me. "You've got the power of thunder and lightning in your hand. Use it," and he started for the big doors that opened onto the Forum.

"Wait!" I said. "This power is limited. I can't take on an army, and for all we know that's what's waiting for us out there."

"We can't stay in here," he said, and he turned for the door.

"Please, just wait!" I said. "We need a plan. Who can you trust out there?"

"My Prefect, Cassius Civitus," he replied.

"But we were attacked by Praetorians," I reminded him.

He shook his head in frustration. "Not Cassius! I can't imagine him doing this to me. He's not just Prefect, but he's a longtime personal friend. If he wanted to kill me, he could have done it a hundred times over, and a lot better than these clumsy fools." He sighed. "And Cassius has nothing to gain by my death, and everything to lose. He's not the culprit. I'll stake my life on that."

"Yeah, well," I said, "you are staking your life on it."

"What if Cassius has been attacked too?" Appia asked.

"We'll know soon enough," Titus replied and he shook his head. "Of all times for my brother to be away. He hung around the palace all fall, but he's nowhere to be found when I need him!"

"Could it be a senatorial plot?" I asked. "I don't know any senators well enough to make even a best guess."

"I don't know," he replied in frustration. "The sessions have been productive and focused on the issues down south. There is concern about the borders, especially in the north. I've had to do a balancing act with manpower. Not everyone agrees with me, but it hasn't been contentious at all. None of this makes any sense."

Appia tightened her grip on me and looked at Titus. "Is it possible the attack was not meant for you?"

"Who else could it be?" he asked, and then he looked at me. "Why would anyone want to kill your husband…or even you?"

"I don't know," she said, "but think about it. Our bedroom was clearly the target."

"And I was with you," he noted. "And somebody actively blocked the annex door as soon as we were inside. They had to know I was with you."

"Not the assassins," Appia said. "They were on the stairwell when you joined us. They couldn't know."

"It doesn't matter," Titus replied. "My father proclaimed that any attack on your family is an attack on mine. We can't stay here, so I'm going."

"Then let me assess the scene first," I said.

"No," he said. "I'm not going to hide in here like a jellyfish while I allow somebody else to fight my battle. Where's the honor in that? We're leaving together and we're leaving right now. Just use what powers you have."

"I told you," I said, "my power is limited."

"Limited?" he said. "What does that mean? I saw what you did. I've never seen anything like it. You're punches went clean through a door!"

"I know," I said, "but I can't stop an army!"

"Then we die," he barked. "Problem solved."

"Problem begun," I muttered to myself.

"I have a plan," he said, "so let's go," and, unfortunately, I couldn't hold him back.

"Then let me go first," I said, and with a pull, the giant doors of the temple swung open.

"They're gone, Getha," he said as he stepped past me and out into the bright sunshine.

He was right. There were no soldiers waiting to ambush us and no arrows to duck; just startled citizens who were clearly not expecting the sudden appearance of the emperor.

Appia and I followed him in a forced march directly to the rostrum. I remained alert for any sign of trouble, while Titus seemed to be growing visibly angrier with every step. There was a man speaking from the rostrum, but after one look at the emperor he scrambled out of the way.

"Where's your standard?" A voice called out from a gathering crowd. "Where's your guard?" He looked like a senator by his attire.

"Getha is the only guard I need!" Titus replied sternly as he turned to face a quickly growing audience. He clenched his fists in anger. "I'm not happy!" he yelled. "I've just returned from an exhausting trip to the disaster zone around Neapolis, and how am I greeted? I'm greeted by a cowardly attack on my person and on the person of Appius Getha and his," and he smiled at Appia, "his lovely wife Appia!" He raised his fist high in the air adding, "If any of you gutless bastards are within earshot of my words, run, and run, and keep on running, because when I catch you that hour will be your last!"

"You wish to add anything?" he asked as he looked at me.

I was scanning the scene for threats, so I wasn't expecting to speak. "Um, no," I said. "You've covered it all."

"There will be handsome rewards," he announced, "for any information that leads to the capture of these spineless assassins."

That's when Cassius Civitus appeared running towards us with about twenty other veteran members of the guard. I didn't know what to think, so I watched intensely for any threatening movement towards Titus, but none were forthcoming. They quickly set up a protective ring around the rostrum, which offered the chance to finally relax. If they wanted to kill us, they could have.

"Cassius!" Titus yelled. "Where have you been? You were supposed to meet us at the palace!"

"We were ordered to the south crossroads," he replied. "We were told to meet you there."

"I never gave that order!" he said.

"The order was imparted by Quintus Acillius Serranus," he replied.

"Serranus?" he said with disbelief.

"The order stated that you were arriving by carriage rather than ship due to heavy seas," he said.

"What?" Titus said. "Think man! If we'd come by carriage we'd still be on the road. Probably another three days. Things are starting to become clearer. That order was a trick."

"Who is Serranus?" I asked.

"A nobody," he replied sarcastically.

"Why did your prefect take orders from a nobody?" I asked, but Titus was still addressing Cassius.

"Where is my brother?" Titus asked him.

"He received word that his wife took ill," he replied. "He left the palace this morning."

"They tricked him too," Titus said.

"Who is exactly is Serranus?" I asked.

"He's a snake in the grass," he replied. "This proves the attack was meant for me!" He turned back to address Cassius. "I need a rider to notify my brother immediately of this treachery. He may also be a target."

"Tell me more about Serranus," I said to the emperor as we made our way back to the palace.

"Quintus Acillius Serranus is a former senator and an elder who now serves my brother as an aide and liaison between him and the senate," he replied. "There's no doubt in my mind now. This plot originated in the senate."

"To what end?" I asked.

He looked at me and shook his head. "Somebody believes that killing my brother and me will create an opening from which to take power. Killing both of us might just do that, and I'm sure they meant to kill you too. Naturally, that requires lots of planning and manpower. The only men with the resources capable of pulling it off are senators."

Wine was poured upon our arrival at the palace, but I was thirsty so I turned it down in favor of water. A moment later, Cassius Civitus appeared.

"My emperor," Cassius said, "we have begun interrogating the assassin in the annex but he's gravely wounded and keeps passing out."

"Did you learn anything at all?" Titus asked.

"The only word he uttered was a name," Cassius said to Titus. "I asked him just four words: Who ordered this attack? I repeated them over and over until I got an answer. His answer was Domitian."

XXXVII

∞

Titus looked stunned.

"When you asked him those four words," I said, "were you torturing him too?"

"Maybe," he smiled. "Sometimes a little arm twisting gets results. It can sometimes make the unconscious, conscious."

"It also makes people agree to a lie just to make the pain stop," I said.

"Yes," he agreed, "if such was the case, but it wasn't. And who in their right mind would accuse the emperor's brother if it didn't happen?"

Titus shook his head. He turned to a female servant who was passing by. "When did my brother leave?"

She bowed. "He left this morning my emperor."

"When this morning?" he asked.

"Midmorning," she replied.

"I arrived at midmorning!" he said.

"Yes," she said, "that's right. Your brother was in the peristyle when you arrived."

"What?" he said disbelievingly. "That's impossible! Where was his carriage…his servants?"

"They left yesterday my emperor," she replied. She was getting visibly upset.

"I can have you flogged for making false and egregious statements!"

"Wait!" I said and I grabbed his hand as it appeared as if he might strike her. "Don't you lay a hand on her!"

"I wasn't going to," he said gruffly.

"Good," I said. "I don't think she's lying."

Titus glared at me. "But that places my brother here with the assassins."

"Yes, it does," I said, but I wasn't sure what to say next. History was once again at a dangerous crossroads. If this attack was ordered by Domitian, then it wasn't a part of the history I knew. Domitian was supposed to become the next emperor, but a conviction of such an egregious offence would derail the succession of emperors. I couldn't let that happen regardless of what he may have done. "Just because he was here doesn't really mean anything," I said.

"But it does," Titus said. He sat down. He looked hurt. "I'd like to place blame elsewhere, but those were Praetorians that attacked us."

"Are you sure they actually were Praetorians?" I asked. "Or were they hired assassins dressed like them?"

He was shaking his head again. "They weren't guardsmen I'm personally familiar with. What about it, Cassius?"

"I can't answer that," he replied. "I wasn't here this morning. Serranus met us in the forum before I had a chance to review the palace guard."

"This plot took a great deal into account," Titus said thoughtfully, "including postings and staff. I will review your conduct, as well as that of all on duty officers and staff at a later date. Right now, I need you to get me information. Did you send out a contingent to find my brother?"

"I did sir," he replied. "Two on horseback as you directed."

"Thank you," Titus said, and he motioned for Cassius to take his leave.

Titus sat again. "What a nightmare," he said. "Whether innocent or not we'll know where he is when our riders catch up with him."

"I'm sorry," Appia said as she took a seat next to Titus.

"My brother hasn't always had kind words for me," he said, "and I know he has political aspirations, but I didn't expect he would go this far."

"We can assume Serranus is involved," I said. "That may still mean the senate or a senator is involved."

"Serranus is my brother's man," he said. "Yes, he has close ties in the Senate, but there's no way a senator could manipulate the guard and staff to this degree. This had to have come from my inner circle."

"My emperor," Appia said, "the most important detail we need to determine is who was the actual target of this attack. That makes a difference as to how you proceed with your investigation."

"I think we must assume the attack was against me," he said. "What would anyone have to gain by eliminating the two of you? And with such a show of force."

"I understand," she said, "so please don't be angry with me for disagreeing with you."

"All ideas are welcome," he said with a warm smile.

"I believe the target could only be my husband," she said.

"What makes you so sure?" he asked.

"We know the attack targeted our bedroom," she replied. "How often have you visited us there in all this time? Once? Twice? An assassin would have to wait indefinitely for an opportunity against you. That makes no sense."

Just then a Praetorian Guardsman arrived with the news Titus had hoped not to hear. His brother was witnessed leaving the city on horseback, without his usual entourage, and in the company of a few soldiers. That all but confirmed Domitian's guilt, which became official hours later following the capture of Quintus Serranus.

In the coming days we learned that Domitian had fled north with a small army of supporters and conspirators. He was last seen on the move between Mutina and Parma. It was a difficult time of year to be headed in that direction. There were many people, including senators who felt he had trapped himself. They believed it would take no more than a thousand men to push him to the Alps where he'd find all routes north impassable until spring. They would take custody of him there.

That's where they lost him, and I wasn't so sure he took an alpine route either. He could have taken a coastal route and circumvented the high Alps altogether. The remarkable part of his escape was how little his small army left behind for chasers to follow. Ancient armies plundered the countryside for food and other necessities, but his group was just small enough and smart enough to avoid angering locals and leaving obvious trails. Snowstorms may make ancient travel and camp life miserable, but for an escaping army, they have the benefit of hiding tracks. Having safely escaped the Italian peninsula also meant a campaign to capture him had to wait until spring.

Rome was on edge. Emperor Vespasian had given Rome ten years of stability, which led to confidence and prosperity, but with the specter of civil war once again rearing its ugly head, fear ran rampant among the upper classes and the Senate who expected severe reprisals should Domitian win such a war. They demanded physical and legal protection, and the walls of the city reinforced and manned with troops again. The Senate enacted legislation naming Domitian an enemy of the state, subject to immediate execution when captured. It was a kneejerk reaction to a situation that was unclear at best. Unfortunately, Titus was losing what popularity he had, which had been trending upward since the eruption of Vesuvius. What was worse, he no longer had a successor or heir in the event of his passing. It was assumed Domitian would succeed him, but with that option now in the gutter, the Roman Senate, in the name of the People of Rome, demanded the emperor choose an heir.

Thalese was the first one to break the news that I was on the top of a list of one name selected by the emperor to present to the Senate to fill that role. It would mean my adoption into his family, which in turn meant all that I own would become Flavian assets as well. Thalese found it extraordinarily good fortune. I found something much less.

"No, Thalese," I said. "I cannot do that." He had found Appia and me lounging in our room in the annex. Appia had no immediate reply.

"Do you have any idea what this will do for our family?" he said.

"That argument worked when we had lost just about everything," I said, "but we're doing quite well just the way we are. I'm not even supposed to be here, and a thing like that puts me dangerously close to being documented in history. No, absolutely not. That's final."

"Is a civil war between these two brothers documented history?" he asked. "If so, who won?"

I glared at him. "No, it's not."

"Fine," he said. "Then how do you plan to stop it from happening? I'm sure you're blaming yourself for this historical anomaly, so knowing you, you must have a plan."

"Aren't you the one who keeps telling me to give it a rest; it's beyond my control?"

"And you're the one who keeps ignoring it," he replied.

I chuckled, but I was being sarcastic. "Okay, so there's a civil war and Domitian wins. He's the next emperor. He's supposed to be the next emperor anyway, so I'm good."

"Getha," Appia said, "you're not good. This is eating you up inside. If Domitian wins, he will seek revenge and restitution. You know that. He will certainly come after you, which means all of us and all you own too. If you really had the power of your legend, we'd be fine, but you don't. We'll be hunted and there won't be a safe place for any of us."

"And," Thalese said, "if Titus wins, which is more likely, Domitian will not survive. Kiss your history goodbye."

"It just gets worse and worse," I said. "I've tried to fix my mistakes. I've tried repeatedly, and what's my success rate? ZERO! No successes. If anything, I've made things worse."

"All that means is you're overdue for success," he said. "The one certainty is that you lose regardless of who wins if you're on the outside looking in. You're going to have to be a player to have any chance to manipulate a better outcome. Maybe that's impossible, but you won't know if you don't try. You have the advantage of knowledge, and you have us."

"I can still work with Titus whether I'm an heir or not," I said. "He listens."

Thalese shook his head. "You're not hearing me. Titus could find himself on the outside looking in too. The Senate is scared. They're losing faith in the emperor. They can't depose an emperor by themselves, but they can approach someone else who has the resources and potential military support to unseat him, which might also mean war. The name I've heard lately is Imperial Legate Justinian Florus."

"A military commander?" I said.

"That's just a rumor," he said, "but you can put all that to bed with just one word – yes."

"That's wrong on so many ethical levels," I said. "Most of my mistakes have been accidents, amnesia, stupidity, whatever. But this would be a conscious choice."

"You're going to hate me for saying this," he said, "but if you turn Titus down, his image will suffer grievously. Nobody will understand your reasoning. The senate might see it as a rejection of Titus and his policies. The perception being that the great Getha of Pompeii has abandoned him. That's the same as saying the gods have dumped him too. On the other hand, if you accept the offer, the senate will relax."

"They don't even know me," I said. "They think I actually have some bizarre link to the gods."

"Perception Getha," he said.

"Yes," I said sadly. "Let's consider the goal. The goal is for a peaceful change in leadership between Titus and Domitian in a little over a year from now. The Senate, along with all those who fear him and hate him will have to miraculously accept him. There can't be any purges or retributions or proscriptions or any of that, and I don't even have a plan. I don't know that any kind of a plan is possible."

"Then do what you do best," he said, "figure it out as you go."

"You're sure Titus is going to propose this adoption?" I asked Thalese.

"I am," he replied. "He needs an adult heir and he asked for my opinion. I suggested you."

"Why am I not surprised," I said.

"He was merely asking me to confirm a decision he's already made. It will be announced in the Senate tomorrow."

"He won't discuss it with me first?" I said.

"It's his prerogative," he said, "but if you truly feel you must turn him down, do it now, before he brings it to the Senate. However, if you do that, you won't get a second chance." He paused for a moment and then added, "Should I find him for you?"

I hung my head. I couldn't think anymore. "No," I replied.

"I'll be right here with you," Appia said as she took my hand.

"As will I," Thalese added.

"We'll take it a day at a time," she said, "and see what happens."

I sighed. "Yeah, okay."

On the Kalends of March, 80 CE, I became Titus Flavius Getha. Within a little over a year, I'd gone from a banged-up stranger lying unconscious on the side of the road to the second most powerful person in the most powerful empire in the world. And my mom was concerned I'd never make anything of myself.

Part III

XXXVIII

∞

It was a sunny and unseasonably warm late March morning, but that did little to erode my feelings of gloom and foreboding following the failed assassination attempt. The history I knew had been severely altered, and my attempts at damage control had failed spectacularly. However, it was heartening to see Thalese and Leita chatting and smiling as they left the palace annex together. They had each other, and that was a good thing.

"I don't want to speak too soon," Thalese said to Leita as they stepped outside, "but I think things are finally beginning to look up."

They were smiling as they left the annex because they were on a mission. They were tired of the depressed emotions of those they cared for, and of their own volition, were striking out to buy surprise gifts for Appia, Getha and the emperor. They were hoping the combination of presents and good weather would bring back some of the smiles that had so recently been lost.

"Getha is the one I'm worry about," Leita said. "I've never seen him so withdrawn."

Thalese agreed. They took the exterior service stairway to reach the Forum at a point near the Temple of the Vestals. "He's got a great deal on his mind," he said. "It worries me that he doesn't talk about his dilemmas anymore, at least not since the adoption. Everything he says lately is superficial. It's not like him."

"Appia's worried too," Leita said. "He doesn't talk to her anymore either. Not seriously anyway."

"We've got to watch him."

"Watch him how?" she asked as they stopped just before entering the Forum. "You make it sound like he's in some sort of danger."

"I think he is."

"What danger can threaten him?" she asked. "He has the power of thunder and lightning at his command. No enemy can hurt him."

"Leita, my good friend," he replied, "his deadliest enemy comes from within. We must do our best to see him though his crisis as he has seen us through ours."

"He wouldn't do harm to himself?" she said in a wavering voice. It was a question she didn't really want to have answered.

"I don't know," he said. "He's admitted such thoughts in the past. I think it would be prudent for us to keep an eye on him. His demon is unique, and I think we need to make every effort to show him what he means to us. That's what'll save him."

"You're a wise man," she said. "So, what shall we get him?"

"I'm not sure exactly," he replied while rubbing his chin. "He likes Egyptian antiques. Not the garbage stuff, but the real thing."

"We can do that," she said, "but I think I know something else that might go further towards brightening his mood."

"What?" he asked.

"A visit from his daughter."

"I don't know," he said. "That's a little risky if he's not ready."

"He'll never be ready if he isn't pushed a little," she added. "But my heart tells me that will change once he actually sees his child. That will be one less emotional burden for him to carry. I think it's worth the risk."

"Perhaps you're right," he said, "but let's get him something today anyway."

"Of course," she smiled. "So, where to first? The market?"

"Perhaps," he said as they trekked across the forum in the direction of Mamertine Prison, but halfway across Leita stopped.

"There's a clothing shop near the Forum Boarium," she said. "I wanted to pick up a spring wrap for Appia. I saw one the other day I liked. We can do that first."

"We can," Thalese agreed, but his focus was moving elsewhere. Across the forum were two conspicuous strangers standing in front of the steps of the Basilica Julia.

"What do you see?" she asked.

"Look at those two over there," he replied, "the tall man and the woman."

"Where?" she asked while squinting to focus. Her vision was considered generally good for her age by Roman standards, but she was a little near-sighted.

"They're on the steps now," he said.

"I see them," she said with a smile. "Foreigners for sure."

"They are indeed," he said.

"They're obviously from someplace where clothing doesn't count for much," she chuckled. "Get a load of those wraps!"

"I see them," he said, but he wasn't smiling. "Think back, Leita. Look at the man's clothes. Where have you seen a wrap with the same flaws?"

She squinted again to sharpen her vision. She immediately knew what he meant. "Oh my," she said, "Getha."

"I concur."

They watched as the strangers continued in the direction of the Temple of Julius Caesar. The pair looked tentative and perhaps lost.

"It might be prudent to get a closer look at them," he said. Leita agreed.

XXXIX

∞

The coming of spring brought the warmth and sunshine that would ordinarily stimulate joy and optimism, but in the spring of 80, Rome was living under the specter of civil war. Domitian's exact whereabouts were uncertain, but his trail led to the northern frontiers where he was mustering support from legions along the Germanic border. His message was simple, but effective. The office of the imperial seat had been corrupted by a foreign usurper seeking the ruination of Rome and the reestablishment of Carthaginian hegemony of the Mediterranean. He claimed Rome was to become a vassal state serving Carthaginian interests.

To anyone living in Rome, or Carthage for that matter, that message would be laughably ridiculous. There was no Carthage in an autonomous sense. Carthage had been thoroughly defeated and Romanized decades earlier, but conspiracy theories have always been around, using fear and ignorance to find believers. Postings on the fringes of the Empire at this time were particularly vulnerable given the mix of older career soldiers who had settled in the north, with an influx of young, impressionable green troops with no experience. This was in part a result of the earlier transfers of veteran officers and soldiers south to Rome and Neapolis, creating the need for replacements along all northern frontiers.

Domitian saw the opportunity and used it. He was smart by not verbally attacking his brother, attacking me instead. He made his brother out to be a good man duped into being a puppet for a foreign puppet master who was really running the Empire. His was a call to arms in the name of duty and honor, reminding his listeners that Julius Caesar had once crossed the Rubicon under arms for a greater cause, and just saying the word Carthage created fear.

Thalese caught up with me on the hill overlooking the Circus Maximus. It was a lovely spring day, but my mind was focused elsewhere.

"You want to talk?" he asked.

"About what?" I replied.

"Anything," he said.

I could see honest concern on his face. "I have no answers," I said. "We keep hearing rumors about masses of troops flocking to Domitian, but we can't even find him. If this alleged army has gotten so big, where's the trail? Armies don't tiptoe well."

"Rumors are just that," he said. "The talk I've heard from Praetorians may be more substantial. Most of our Germanic outposts have remained loyal, and even those that have lost numbers to desertion are still capable defensively. I find it significant that not a single outpost has officially declared for Domitian."

"We talked about that this morning," I said referring to the emperor. "We do have word that he's been recognized as Caesar by the deserters who've joined him. His message must be effective. We don't know how he delivers it, but his influence is moving west along the frontier."

"How do you know that?" Thalese asked.

"The reports of outpost desertions," I replied. "Of course, those reports are old by the time we get them, so nothing is certain. Titus has sent a contingent of elite Praetorians to the northern frontier to assure those still loyal that we've amassed an army to win. They hope to locate Domitian too."

"Good," Thalese said. "Perhaps this will root him out quickly."

"I'm not so sure," I said. "If he's over the border we won't find him."

"If he's over the border, the Germans will," he chuckled. "I don't see that going well."

History recorded three disasters during the first year of Emperor Titus's reign, beginning with the eruption of Vesuvius, followed by a devastating fire in Rome, and lastly, a plague. The attack in the annex added a fourth to that list, nudging the fire into third place in the timeline.

Fire was a big problem in ancient Rome. Many grand public structures, and the outer walls of many buildings, featured brick and stone, but interior framing, roofing, stairwells and floors, in fact most of the city, was made of wood, a dangerous mix where open flame provided both heat and lighting.

History had also recorded that Emperor Titus was in Neapolis when fire broke out in Rome in 80 CE. The attack in the annex changed that, as well. He was in Rome when the fire began, and he took an active role in dealing with it and its aftermath. He'd become a more hands-on leader than he was in the original timeline, and after turning his great amphitheater into a refugee center, he visited the stricken areas to personally oversee relief efforts. He brought food and took time to share meals with many of those left homeless by the fire.

His level of personal involvement was unprecedented, a product of his desperate need for a break from all the other stresses in his life, especially the specter of war with his brother. It gave him a singular purpose, and the people in the streets loved him for it. It didn't do his shaken ego any harm either, and it was nice to see him smiling again. The attack in the annex had weakened his public image at a time when his popularity was supposed to be on the rise, so I encouraged him to keep doing what he was doing.

Appia and I needed a break from Rome. The fire was out, and Domitian was rooting around somewhere north of the Alps. His threat to Rome was real, but not immediate, so the emperor granted us the equivalent of two weeks' vacation. Appia and I would spend a couple days at the Villa North and then travel to a resort in the hills outside of Rome not far from the future town of Tivoli.

I hadn't been back to the Villa North since we moved into the annex, but now I was finally ready. Appia was thrilled as was Leita. The emperor wouldn't let us leave *The Hill* without a Praetorian escort as a perk of my position. I told him if the choice was between having a guard or riding in a carriage with a sprung suspension, I'd choose the suspension. He gave us both.

The reception we received when we arrived at the Villa North was both unexpected and overwhelming. The entire family was there to greet us before we'd even stepped from our carriage. All were dressed in their finest clothing.

"What is all this?" I asked Appia as it seemed like we'd walked into the middle of some gala event.

"It's for you, Getha," she said. "They know of your reluctance to take on the responsibilities you have, and they want to show their respect. You're a hero to them, but not in a mythical way. You saved them, and me, and we know it."

"I wish people would stop saying those things," I said. "I've done nothing. They've done all the hard work. They've run the businesses. Our success is because of them, not me."

"Then tell them that," she said, "but not in a way that belittles your part. Never, for an instant, underestimate what you've done. Had you not cultivated a bonding relationship with the emperor, none of this could have happened. They know it, and I know it. And you compromised your *Principles* for us. You recognized that our lives are important too. For that, we will be forever grateful."

All I could do was shake my head. Her words of praise would have been welcome if they were deserved, but I was no hero. I was incapable of making the hard choices, and yet looking at all the happy faces greeting us, it was hard to believe I'd done anything wrong. Leita was the first out of the carriage, followed by Thalese, and since this was the first time Appia and I were coming home as husband and wife, I wanted them to see us hand in hand together.

When we stepped onto the grounds we were greeted with cheers. Nubia looked gorgeous in a lovely maroon wrap with Caelus at her side. In her arms was a child.

I started towards them, but before I got there David stepped up to me. "I guess this is a sort of a local boy makes good thing," he chuckled, "but then again, you're not exactly a local boy."

"That's true," I said, but my eyes were on Nubia.

"I'd like to know exactly what boiling water has to do with fighting illness?" he asked. "I've done as you suggested, but I don't know why."

"David," I said, "it's good to see you, but there's someone I need to meet before I get into any meaty discussions." He smiled and stepped back. I walked up to Caelus and Nubia.

Caelus greeted me with a warrior handshake. "This is indeed an honor," he said. "Son of Caesar! Son of Hercules!"

"Relax," I said with a smile. "It's just me, Getha, friend of Caelus." My attention was drawn to Nubia and the child she held in her arms.

"Hello Getha," she said softly. Her warm smile was most welcoming. "Would you like to meet your daughter?" She loosened the light material wrapped around the sleepy child in her arms, who then yawned, and I could see the perfectly formed little hands and feet. Her face was that of her mother.

"She's beautiful," I said. "She looks like you, Nubia."

Nubia smiled. "She has your eyes, Getha."

"She's just napping," Caelus chuckled like a proud parent. "You should see her go when she's awake. She'll be walking soon, that's for certain."

"I'm happy for both of you," I told them. "This child obviously has a good home and the right parents."

"She's your child too," Caelus said.

"I know that makes you uncomfortable," Nubia said, "but she is a part of you, and I know you feel it."

"She is beautiful, isn't she?" Appia said as she hugged me closer.

"We have a favor to ask," Caelus said, and he looked at Nubia. "Maybe now isn't the right time."

"Please," I said, "ask."

Nubia smiled. "We want Appia Getha to have a good home should something of ill will befall us. We'd like you and Appia to consider raising her should we become unable."

I looked at Appia. Her feelings were clear. She was practically hopping up and down to answer, but waiting for my reaction. "Caelus, Nubia," I said, "no need to consider. We're honored, and of course we accept. Absolutely." It was handshakes, big smiles, and hugs all around.

"Perhaps she could know me as an uncle," I said.

"An uncle?" Nubia chuckled. "I don't think so. She will know exactly who you are."

"She will know the pride of her heritage through you, Getha," Caelus added.

"And through you," I said as I looked at the child asleep in Nubia's arms. "Both of you." Nubia was right, I did feel a connection.

"It takes an entire family to raise a child, Getha," Nubia said warmly, "and that's what this is all about. You taught me that."

Appia took a turn holding her namesake as did I. I'd never held such a young child in my arms before, but it wasn't as frightening as I thought it might be. I had Appia Getha to thank for that as she wriggled and turned around in my arms until she made a comfortable spot, and then she went right back to sleep.

When we gathered for evening meal, everyone had a chance to question, discuss and talk about anything. I fielded several questions about the emperor and what he's like, and more questions about Domitian and the threat he posed to the Empire.

I thanked them all for their hard work and the success of our businesses. I announced that my personal profit was to be used to renovate the villa, and that each one of them would have his/her own room. No more sharing.

That brought Caelus to his feet. "To Getha!" he called out.

"To Getha!" was the response as they all stood.

"And to you," I said as I lifted my cup.

That night Appia and I stayed in the converted storage room given to me when I first arrived at the Villa North, except it had been completely refurbished. No longer was it dark and dank, but bright, with a skylight, and a huge double bed. It was a wedding gift.

Our welcome couldn't have been warmer or friendlier and relaxing. During the next two days I forgot about concerns on *The Hill*, figuring no news was good news. I played with little Appia Getha, who had completely stolen my heart with a smile. Nubia announced that she was pregnant again. It was indeed a happy time.

The villa was a little crowded with all of us there, so Appia and I decided it was time to get away to the resort we'd talked about. We told Thalese we were going, but we couldn't give him an exact location because we didn't know. I didn't even know the name of the resort area; other than one day it would be called Tivoli. I think it was called Tibur. However, Thalese was uncharacteristically concerned about where we'd be and how long we'd be away. He even went so far as to suggest we wait for a better time, but the weather was superb. I told him we were thinking of only four or five days, which seemed to satisfy him for the moment.

The idea of escaping for a few days of blissful frolicking away from the ills of the world didn't include an escort of Praetorians. I suppose we could have snuck away unseen by walking out the back and hitching rides on various wagons, but I really liked that carriage with the suspension. I could nap in that thing without loosening teeth every time we hit a bump. As a plain, garden variety citizen of Rome, I could dispense with the guard, but not as the son of the emperor. The guard came with the title. I suppose it didn't really matter. It wasn't like they were with us every place we went. They just had to be in the area. I gave them spending money and told them to have a little fun. Supposedly, they weren't allowed to accept gratuities, but I said unless the emperor had specifically stated that as an order, my word as his son superseded all other ranks.

We chose a hillside inn that overlooked the city from across the plain. Hadrian would one day build a villa the size of a small city below us. Our arrival was a complete surprise to the locals, but I did my best to assure the innkeeper that we required very little attention. In fact, we wanted to be left alone. The view was wonderful, as was the food.

We were hardly the first to discover the spot, as it was full of wealthy Roman tourists seeking a hideaway from their daily pressures and routines. Some of them recognized us, and I recognized a few of them as well, but everybody was there for the same purpose, and nobody bothered anybody. It became our honeymoon, and we stayed a couple days longer than planned, a full ten days basking in an escapist reality. We didn't want it to end, but we'd told Thalese we'd only be away for four or five days, so we decided it best to return to the villa before the emperor sent out a search party. I was glad to see the Praetorians used the time for their own enjoyment, but they were quick to return to form when I announced it was time to leave.

It was a beautiful day, which made the ride back easier, but once on the road I had a feeling of foreboding. It's easy to associate such negative feelings with some supernatural connection, but I think it's also a natural, emotional response when returning to the real world after having been liberated from responsibility for several days.

Unfortunately, my feeling of foreboding had validity. We walked into chaos when we arrived at the Villa North. There were search parties looking for us, and Praetorians everywhere on the grounds. All I could think was Domitian must have attacked. That would explain all the craziness we walked into. It also meant I was wrong about his ability to raise a whole army and sneak it through the Alps to Rome unseen.

Thalese came rushing out of the villa the moment we stepped from the carriage. Behind him was the shadowy figure of an imperial messenger.

"What is all this craziness?" I asked Thalese as he approached. "Domitian attack?"

"Oh, Getha," he said, with uncharacteristic stress in his voice, "worse."

"Worse than that?"

"Yes," he said solemnly. "The emperor is dying."

XL

∞

It took me a moment to process his words. "That's not possible," I said.

"Apparently, it is," he said.

"How?"

"Illness."

"It's not his time," I said in a hushed voice. "That's not for another year at least."

"I'm sorry, Getha," he said. "He's very ill. He asked to see you yesterday. Word is he lost consciousness overnight."

"Damn!" I blurted out as Appia took my arm. "Thalese, this can't be happening. It's all wrong."

"Maybe you made an error with the date," he said. "Remember at Pompeii? You were a day off with the date of the eruption."

"A day is not a whole year," I said. "No mistake. The mountain erupted in 79 CE by my calendar, which makes this 80 CE. Titus won't die until 81, and in September no less!"

He shook his head. "I don't know what to say."

"Is he sick or possibly poisoned?" I asked. The fact that the situation with Domitian was not following history made anything possible.

"I don't know," he replied, "but you'd better get to *The Hill* right now."

I agreed. The carriage was right there. Tears were welling in Appia's eyes as she took my arm, but I asked her to stay. I asked that nobody join me. If the illness was plague, I didn't want anyone else exposed. Thalese insisted he needed to be with me. He knew protocol and could act as my liaison with regard to priests, senators, and city officials if the emperor remained incapacitated for any length of time.

I relented and took him with the stipulation that he use the soap I made and keep his distance from anyone exhibiting signs of illness; although, the idea that I'd need such expert assistance while the emperor recovered seemed extreme. The imperial messenger accompanied us as well, and it was a very solemn ride to the palace. He said the emperor took ill only two days ago and the illness had progressed rapidly. The more he described it the more it sounded like cholera. His symptoms began with intense abdominal pain accompanied by severe diarrhea and vomiting. History had recorded a plague in the city after the fire, but the emperor was not supposed to be a victim of it.

The palace was near pandemonium. There was a crowd at the main entrance being held back by Praetorians. I refused to speak to anyone as I made a beeline straight for the emperor's quarters. My hope was to find the severity of his condition exaggerated, but that would not be the case.

In a haze of incense, and surrounded by physicians, Titus laid on his bed face up and comatose, his ashen cheeks tinted with a ghastly blue.

"Have you the power to resurrect the dead?" one of the physicians asked.

"No," I replied. I was momentarily stunned. "But it's not his time."

"People die," the physician said. "Caesars die. It is the way of things."

"But not Emperor Titus," I said, and I looked at Thalese. "This isn't right. This isn't what's supposed to happen." I was in a state of shock and disbelief. "I never should have left."

"Could you have prevented this?" Thalese asked.

"I don't know," I replied. "I don't know anything right now."

"I didn't think so."

"I have no more special medicine either," I said, and then I looked at the physicians. "What was the emperor doing before he became ill?"

"He's been busy," one of them answered. "He spent much of his time visiting burned out districts, offering aid to the homeless."

"Is plague also in those districts?" I asked.

"Yes sir," was the general reply, "especially near the river."

I shook my head and looked away. "That's it," I told Thalese. "Titus wasn't supposed to be this personally involved."

Titus changed after our visit to the disaster zone. He saw firsthand how successful the refugee camp idea worked, which, as I learned later, couldn't have happened in the original timeline. In fact, prior to my first discussions with him about the disaster, his plan was to hold off relief efforts until he had a clearer understanding of the disaster. He wanted statistics first, including a refugee head count, before determining an appropriate response. I gave him information, both directly and indirectly, way too soon, and when he spoke of a desire to get more personally involved, I encouraged him. I didn't see the harm. I didn't expect him to be breaking bread with refugees in the fire gutted, plague districts of Rome either. The conditions were ideal for cholera, and his new hands-on approach to leadership did the rest.

I stepped back to try to organize my thoughts. I was an emotional wreck and had to get a grip. I couldn't allow my grief, or my culpability, to hinder my capacity to act. History was beyond fixing, so my focus had to be damage control, and soon, because the consequences of change cascade quickly. I asked Thalese to join me in the corridor where we could talk freely.

"What next?" I asked him.

"I think you know," he replied. "Word will spread quickly and military leaders will be hailing your name before the day is done."

"I can't do that," I said. "I know I've said that about so many things and relented, but this time I have to make a stand. I just plain can't do it."

He smiled. "Oh, but you will my friend, you will. It is your destiny."

"You're no help," I muttered and I left for the atrium and the exit. I figured the best place for me to think was in my room, but getting there wasn't easy. I was immediately confronted by a room full of senators and clients looking for answers. Cassius Civitus, and several veteran guardsmen stepped in front of me as a kind of shield that offered welcomed space. If I thought I could sneak away without having to address anybody, I was wrong.

"At this point in time," I said, "it appears our emperor has passed on. He has been proclaimed so by his physicians. That's all I know. This is a terrible event that I have no words for. I'm as shocked as all of you are."

Yes, I was shocked, but the shock didn't stop there. I was asked when I would be addressing the people of Rome. Thalese whispered that I needed to do that right away in the Forum. I told them I needed a little time to prepare my words, but when I stepped forward to pass through the gathering, Cassius turned to face me. He crossed his chest with his right arm and raised it in the air and called out, "Hail Getha! Hail Caesar!" to which the rest of his guardsmen followed suit.

I couldn't deal with that. I remained polite, but then I bullied my way through everyone and hustled with Thalese across to the annex where I locked the door behind us. We continued to my room where I locked that door too.

"Listen to me, Thalese," I said. "I CAN NOT become the next emperor."

He looked me in the eye and said calmly, "You not only can, but you must. And you will. It IS your destiny."

"Destiny?" I chuckled. "You've never spoken to me this way before. What's going on?"

"I can't say," he replied. "All I know is that the only way you can achieve your goal is to become the next emperor."

"What do you mean, you can't say? That implies knowledge of something I'm not aware of."

He smiled. "I misspoke. I meant, I don't have an answer, but when you are emperor you will have total control over whatever you need to achieve your goals."

"You never misspeak," I said. "You know language and protocol better than anyone I know."

"No one is perfect."

"Which goals are you referring to?"

"You have but one goal," he replied, "and that is to fix history to what you remember. You can do that as emperor."

I sighed. "That ship has already sailed. Once news of this reaches Domitian, he's sure to attack us. That means civil war. If I win, Domitian loses all political options and possibly dies. If he wins, Rome's senate and elite will be decapitated through revenge and proscriptions. He'll be emperor, but such retribution will end the historical line of imperial successors entirely. A protracted war? That may well cause an early end to the Empire."

"That's a lot of negativity," he said. "You've got to trust in yourself. Do what you do best. Take action when opportunities appear, and the only way to do that is by becoming emperor. And don't let protocol or even honor stand in the way of any undertaking that will satisfy your goal."

"The only possible way I might diffuse this problem without war is if I surrender to Domitian. He will see I'm not after the Imperial Seat. In fact, I'll offer to accompany him back to Rome where I'll use my influence to make him emperor."

Thalese grinned. "That's a bad idea on so many levels, not to mention delusional. He'll kill you for one thing. He won't listen and he'll never believe you. If the senate finds out you're thinking of doing that, they will quickly turn to somebody else to lead your army into battle. They aren't about to rest on Domitian's sense of fair play and forgiveness for their survival."

"I get it," I said.

"No," he said, "you don't or you'd be taking my advice."

"You do know," I said, "that by becoming emperor, I will be further damaging the history I'm trying to fix? There was no Emperor Getha."

"It's called a compromise," he replied. "You're adding an emperor to history to have the control necessary to safeguard the line of succession that will follow you. If this civil war results in the death or permanent political downfall of Domitian, you must serve in his place because only you know what he did from your history. You won't have that option if you turn down this request."

He was right. I knew quite a bit about Domitian's reign as it came down to us. There were a lot of gaps too, but it did seem possible I might be able restore the subsequent succession of emperors, as emperor, even if Domitian was no longer a part of that historical record. It certainly wasn't ideal. I didn't have his temperament, which played a role in his rein and eventual demise. He was assassinated too. Regardless, my first priority had to be the restoration of Domitian's rightful place in history.

"Why do you have to be so damn smart?" I sighed.

"It is your fate," he said.

"Did you ever think the Senate might not even ask me?" I said.

He shook his head and said, "You're already emperor. The Senate is a formality. You will be called to the Curia, perhaps as soon as this evening or tomorrow. You will be told you're their choice, as if they actually have a choice, and if you don't object, you'll be unanimously ratified on the spot. The point of a public ratification is not to pick a new leader. It's to show the world that Rome remains strong and unified."

"What happens if I fail to fix this mess I've made? There are no more options."

"You will not fail," he replied confidently.

I just looked at him. He seemed so calm and sure of himself. "Okay," I said. "I believe I must give a speech in the Forum. I'll think of something on the way."

"Like you always do," Thalese chuckled.

"Let's just clean up and get ready. There's not even enough time to mourn. He was my friend too you know."

"He certainly was that," he agreed.

XLI

∞

I washed and dressed. Thalese thought a toga would be more appropriate than a tunic, even my best tunic, but I declined and he didn't argue. The day was hard enough without adding physical discomfort to it too. The people and Senate would simply have to understand.

Cassius Civitus and eleven other veteran members of the guard were awaiting us when we emerged from the annex. "Hail Getha!" they called out in unison.

"The Senate is calling an emergency session," Cassius announced while at full attention. "Your attendance is requested, my emperor."

"Thank you, Cassius," I said, "but Emperor Titus remains emperor until another is selected. Until that time, as his son, I will act in his name."

"If that is your wish," he replied, "but you have been declared Caesar by our contingent, as all legions are now hailing you thus."

"Be that as it may," I said cordially, "I plan to speak at the rostrum prior to convening with the Senate. Please send someone to apprise them of that. I won't speak for long. I feel I must address the people of Rome first so that they know what has transpired. Rumors have a way of turning ugly if left uncorrected for too long."

"Understood," Cassius said.

"I can do that," Thalese said.

"No, you can't," I said. "You got me into this, so you're not going anywhere."

"It will be done," Cassius said, and he turned to one of his guards and sent him to deliver the message.

"Thank you," I said.

Cassius and the remainder of the guard formed a circle around Thalese and me. The standard of the emperor was brought to Cassius from inside the palace. I asked that it be left with Emperor Titus for the time being.

When Cassius began leading us down the roadway towards the opposite end of the Palatine, I stopped him. That may have been the traditional route used by emperors to enter the Forum, but I wasn't ready to consider myself an emperor yet. I told him to take the stairway because it was closer.

It took us perhaps ten minutes to reach the forum, and because we took a rarely used route without a standard, we reached the rostrum without being held up by the gathering crowd. Before I spoke, I asked Cassius to send a Praetorian to the Villa North to apprise the family of what's transpired, and escort Appia to *The Hill* if she wished to join me since it was unlikely I'd be back anytime soon.

When I stood atop the rostrum and looked over the crowd, I was astonished by the number of people who had gathered. I mentioned that to Thalese, but he wasn't surprised. He said that when news of any event reaches the ears of the citizenry, they always come to the Forum for answers, which made sense.

I took a deep breath and began my very impromptu speech. I didn't know what I was going to say until I said it. "Fellow Romans," I said, "fellow citizens, friends…I am Getha of Pompeii, the son of our emperor, the great Emperor Titus. Hail Titus!" I lifted my arm as others were doing, and after a moment I let my arm drop. "Today our emperor joined the pantheon gods. A great leader to all of us, and a great friend and companion to me. I grieve his loss, as I know all of you before me feel the same. These are troubled times. These are times of need. I come to you now as the son of our great emperor to assure each and every one of you that we will remain strong. Rome will remain strong. The policies and special initiatives our emperor so successfully began will continue unchanged. His rebuilding program will be initiated. And the threat to the north will be crushed." There was a sudden roar as everyone seemed to be cheering at once. I raised my hands to speak. "Thank you for your patience. We will stay strong! And in the name of Emperor Titus Flavius Vespasianus we will become stronger!"

The whole place erupted with shouts of "Hail Getha." I turned and looked at Thalese. I expected a response, but nothing that enthusiastic.

He smiled. "What did you expect? You didn't speak like a son. You spoke like an emperor."

"I wanted them to feel secure," I said. "I wanted them to know nothing was going to change."

He was shaking his head. "Only the emperor can make that promise. Only the emperor can back up those words. You are the emperor. I know it and they know it. The army knows it. The Senate knows it." He paused for a moment. "And Getha, you know it too."

"I suppose I do," I sighed. "Alright, let's get this over with." It was a short walk to the Curia. I stopped to study it for a moment. "A funny thing,"

I said to Thalese. "Domitian is supposed to rebuild this building. He's supposed to expand the amphitheater and build massive new structures on *The Hill* too. If we can't fix this situation, I'm going to have to build all that for him."

"That should keep you out of mischief," he chuckled in a nervous attempt at humor.

"The problem is," I said, "I have only a vague idea of what all those buildings are supposed to look like."

"I think that's the least of your concerns right now."

"I guess I've procrastinated long enough," I said. "How about you?" He nodded. I think he was more nervous than I was. Actually, I wasn't very nervous at all. I felt numb more than anything else. I knew what was going to happen. I knew I had to go through the motions. I didn't care how I looked. I didn't care what people thought of me. None of that mattered. I just wanted to go back to my room and crash.

There were a lot of Roman senators, about six hundred total, but only one hundred were active at this time. There were many more than a hundred at the Curia which made for a very tightly packed session. I was given a seat next to the Consul who opened the meeting. All the benches were filled to standing room only at the sides. Everyone was impeccably dressed, while I remained tunic clad, but it was my best tunic. Thalese stood at my side, which was against the rules, but nobody spoke up against it.

The motion was put forth that I be the Senate's choice to replace Emperor Titus as holder of the Imperial Seat. The motion was quickly seconded, followed by a vote; in this case a simple show of hands. I was surprised by that, because important decisions were usually determined by a quorum, but then I realized the vote was more for show. The backing of the Guard and local legions gave me enough authority to proclaim myself emperor at the moment of the emperor's passing, a claim that would be valid indefinitely barring assassination or until somebody with a bigger army took me to task. I was also Titus's heir, but in point of fact, the Senate had no legal power to install or depose an emperor. However, their support was most certainly needed if not indispensable. To accept their ratification before accepting the Imperial Seat was a gesture of good faith that showed my willingness to work with them. Thalese was correct. The ratification was unanimous. I did as expected and accepted the honor.

XLII

∞

That evening I returned to the palace and wrote a letter to Domitian. I wrote of his brother and my feelings regarding his family. I wrote of how I understood his motivation for the attack on me, and that I held no grudges towards him. I called him my brother, and offered safe passage to Rome so we could talk and bury our differences. Thalese helped me make sure of my wording because I wanted to be exact, and making mistakes on parchment results in a redo. I sealed it with his brother's seal. Sending it would have to wait until I knew where he was.

It took two months to finally find Domitian, and when we did, he was already south of the Alps. He had come down from around Mediolanium and was camped along the Po river just east of Cremona with a military force. The fact that he was on the move didn't surprise me, but that he was so close did. That placed him only about two hundred and fifty miles north of Rome. I immediately initiated the defensive plan Titus and I had worked out months before.

Initial reports from unofficial sources estimated his force to be in the neighborhood of eighty thousand men, which was enough to start a minor panic in Rome. I almost bought into it, but eighty thousand seemed way too high, and after talking with Cassius we came up with different figures. The desertion rate along the northern frontier was still running higher than everywhere else, but it was not nearly enough to populate such a large military force. Our best guess based on statistics was five to eight thousand. There were desertions in the east as well. There was ample reason to believe they went to Domitian too. They amounted to possibly another six hundred men. The only other source of military manpower would have had to come from tribes across the frontier, but that was extremely unlikely.

We were relatively confident with our assessment, but to be certain we sent our own scouts, with my letter, to Domitian's camp. They were dressed as couriers rather than praetorians, and while their official duty was to deliver my letter, they had the experience and expertise to assess the strength of his forces. I asked them to take their time and be thorough because I'd rather wait a few days longer for accurate information than receive a flawed report that was rushed.

I had capped my forces at fifty thousand. Most were older and veterans who had served under Titus in the East. This force was mobile, tactically experienced, professional, and capable of defeating larger armies of lesser experience. There was no way that Domitian could possibly match us in quality and speed. If winning the war was my main goal, I'd have felt pretty confident, but my goal was to avoid war.

The one headscratcher was why Domitian was forcing a civil war with no obvious chance of winning. He wasn't a stupid person or suicidal, leaving me to wonder what we might have overlooked with regard to his options. Was he delusional enough to believe our soldiers wouldn't draw arms against him? His claim to be the legitimate heir to the Imperial Seat hadn't gained any traction south of the Alps.

Gathering intel took a lot of time in the first century and communicating that intel could be a slow process. The local rumor mill was ramping up the public's fears and anxieties to new levels. One rumor put Domitian's manpower at one hundred and fifty thousand, based on a mythical pact he'd signed with eastern hordes. Supposedly, he had promised them a free reign in Rome to rape and pillage. That was to be payback against Romans who had turned against him. It was easy to get drawn in, but I stuck with our more factually based figures.

On July 17, I received answers from our scouts, who, after finding a way to deliver my letter, infiltrated Domitian's army by posing as soldiers from an eastern province. My patience had paid off. Domitian's numbers were fewer than ten thousand troops, of which none were from Germanic tribes or Asian hordes. There were some veteran soldiers elevated to leadership roles, but for the most part they were inexperienced troops.

A week later, Domitian moved his army to a plain north of the town of Sutrium, probably hoping to use the lakes and hilly terrain to his advantage. He was only about thirty miles from Rome too, which rattled the Senate and pubic, but not my commanders. However, it did mean we were on the eve of battle.

I knew Domitian had scouts studying our position, which was no secret. I wanted him to know what he was up against, and to make sure of it, I sent him another letter. I made it clear that I was numerically stronger, with better equipment and more experienced leadership. I said I did not want a civil war, but if he brought it to me, I would be obligated to crush him. I repeated much of what I'd written in the previous letter. I said I wasn't asking him to surrender, but rather to meet to negotiate a truce with honor. I promised him safe conduct to and from the selected meeting site, and if negotiations failed, he would be free to return to his troops.

I apprised the Senate of my attempts to reason with Domitian so my letters could not be used as propaganda against me. I also told them civil war was imminent, and should that happen, I ordered my commanders to seize Domitian and not kill him. I needed him alive, but then I had another thought.

"Can we abduct him?" I asked my closest commanders. Nobody seemed to want to answer the question. "What if we send our scouts back to infiltrate his ranks again, but this time to abduct him? No leader, no battle, and I can finally meet with him. I'd call that a win, win."

"What about honor?" I was asked. "There's no honor in that kind of victory."

I shrugged and smiled. "There's no honor in any of this. We are two Roman armies fighting each other. That's a statement of weakness and failure of our way of life no matter who wins. I think the only way to avoid that is to nullify this threat before it becomes a battle, and that includes abduction if necessary. Time is rapidly running out. I think it's necessary."

"That's a good deal easier said than done," Cassius pointed out. "He undoubtedly has close associates and perhaps bodyguards."

"That means he's less wary too," I said. "He won't be expecting it."

"He'll be wary of assassination," he replied thoughtfully, "but maybe not abduction. He might even ignore anyone around him who appears to be unarmed."

"I think we should try," I said. I asked that I be present when our scouts were apprised of the plan, and I wanted volunteers. I also wanted to personally swear all involved to secrecy.

It didn't take much of a sales job to get our scouts to return to Domitian's camp. They had observed him quite often during their factfinding efforts, and he seemed pretty sure of himself. He didn't have tight security around his tent, and he strayed away from it quite often to talk with his men. They thought he came across as a decent leader who was unfortunately on the wrong side of the issue. I told them, and I was very specific, that honor wasn't a concern. They were to grab him at the first opportunity, bind him, gag him, sneak him out through a sewer if they had to, but not to torture him or abuse him.

They wanted to know their limitations if he yells or becomes too hard to hold. I said, if they have to knock him out, okay, but only as a last resort, and do not kill him. They suggested one other man be added to their abduction team. He was apparently highly skilled at quelling unruly captives without deadly violence, and I was assured of his loyalty to me. It sounded like he did it with pressure to the carotid artery. That would be preferable to a head injury. I agreed.

The plan succeeded. My scouts abducted Domitian without a fight. They had been studying his habits, and noticed his trips to the latrine behind his quarters were unescorted. The man who would be emperor was unceremoniously grabbed while seated on a throne of sorts, knocked out with a carotid sleeper hold, bound and gagged and stuffed in a laundry hamper used for storing armor. They simply walked away with the hamper without anyone questioning them.

I was elated by the news, but when I heard the details of his latrine capture, I immediately ordered that particular bit of information remain secret. My hope was to salvage his honor; therefore, it was imperative to protect him from ridicule as well. Having Domitian in custody presented its own set of difficulties. The first issue was to find him a secluded sanctuary that would protect him from his enemies and himself. Suicide was not out of the question. I asked Cassius to select people he trusted to guard Domitian while I located a sanctuary.

Half of Domitian's army had surrendered by midday. Most of the rest quickly dropped arms as an order I drew up offering full amnesty for the soldiery was being spread. By midafternoon I was able to send in troops to capture the last of the holdouts and assess damage.

XLIII

∞

This isn't so bad, I thought, as I released the buckle of my safety belt and eased back into the seat. It seemed like I could finally relax. The air was dry, but relatively clean, and the only sound was the comforting drone of powerful jet engines.

I knew I should sleep to avoid jet lag, so I tried to stretch out, but I wrenched my foot when the person seated in front of me tilted his seat back. To relieve the pressure, I pivoted to the side, but ended up scraping my shins against the lower edge of his seat. When I lurched forward to ease the pain, my food tray dropped and bounced off my nose, and with a start, I woke up.

Apparently, I couldn't get upgraded to first class even in my dreams, but rather than flying, I was laying comfortably on my back in my own bed at the Villa North. The calming chirps of birds in the nearby courtyard quickly replaced the drone of engines. Once again, I was looking up at the imperfections in a white, stucco ceiling, recalling the moment when an attractive young woman dressed in a green, flowing wrap first touched me with her kindness.

More than six years had passed since the morning Appia entered my life, and the warmth of her presence was my greatest comfort. She stirred briefly when I pressed a kiss to her cheek, but then she fell back to sleep.

No matter how enjoyable the moment, I couldn't completely clear my mind of the matters of state. I had been emperor for nearly five years, but change was in the air. The time to step aside was at hand, and I could only hope that my efforts to pave the way for Domitian had paid off. I'd methodically sabotaged myself with decisions and inactions that annoyed the Senate and senatorial class because they benefited the lesser classes. That needed to happen so they'd look elsewhere for leadership, but at the same time I had to keep the military happy so they couldn't be used against me while I was restoring Domitian's public image. There were no guarantees, but with Thalese's guidance I had some success.

It wasn't easy. Domitian's public image was so badly damaged after his defeat at the popularly named "Battle of Sutrium" that there were public outcries for his execution. I pointed out that Sutrium wasn't a battle at all, sarcastically adding that neither the Roman army nor the City of Rome were attacked, and for all we knew, Domitian was simply out camping with a few thousand of his good buddies.

There were no honors, titles, celebrations, or even bragging rights for breaking up a camping jamboree, therefore, the people and Senate of Rome preferred to call it a battle. As such, the Senate bestowed upon me all the lofty official titles commensurate with battle-worthy feats, my first as emperor. That put me on a higher pedestal, into rarified air with the likes of Julius and Augustus Caesar, not to mention Vespasian and Titus, and thus making it that much more difficult to hide my name from history. That meant I had to keep Domitian in exile on the island of Ischia longer than I had hoped in order to protect him from those who felt I hadn't dealt harshly enough with him. It was an issue of honor, which meant his life was at risk.

His unceremonious capture left him a broken and humiliated man. He would have welcomed the cold blade of an assassin. He even tried to bribe prison guards into doing the deed, but with the help of Cassius Civitas, I selected my people well, and his life continued. He mellowed once I'd assured him that the finer details of his capture would remain secret. However, rumors abounded, but rumors were just that – rumors – and thus readily discounted without proof.

I waited several months for the public and political backlash against him to cool down before quietly recalling him to Rome. I spoke to him of reconciliation, and how I planned to offer him a full pardon as the first step to restore his honor before making him my successor. I couldn't risk confiding the true nature of my reasoning, so I spoke to him as a fellow Flavian. I spoke of family pride and the need for unity to ensure the future glory of Rome, and to that end I was willing to step down.

I believed he would understand, but like so many other assumed beliefs, he had a different take. He knew public opinion was against him. He knew he had to accept my pardon, but he didn't for a moment buy my reasoning. Life had taught him that power wasn't something a rational person gives up except out of weakness, and since he didn't doubt my sanity, he believed I was hiding a serious weakness.

How the hatred must have seethed in him when he was led to the Forum to humble himself before me by reciting an oath of loyalty. It disturbed me to have to do it, but as Thalese predicted, it neutralized much of the anger against him. That allowed me to publicly forgive him for his attacks against me, citing his actions as being the result of a feud between brothers, and not against Rome.

Such an unorthodox and benevolent resolution to a situation involving high treason came as a surprise to most Romans, and no one seemed to know quite what to make of it, especially since there wasn't even a trial. Pardons that seemed unworthy often pointed to graft, but this situation defied common reasoning because I was generally believed to be above reproach. Not even the rumor mill could dig up anything substantial to explain my inexplicable action, despite several creative tries. My personal favorite was that Appia had visited Domitian on Ischia and was carrying his child. I had no idea why that would make him pardon-worthy, but it was worthy of a good laugh.

The pardon may have spared his life, but a lot more needed to be done to ensure his political future. To start with, I offered him the chance to take residence with us on Palatine Hill. That way I could assign him to a deputy position, which would be a first step in rebuilding his power base. However, such a power base would have to begin as an extension of mine, and while that sort of thing was common in politics, it would not suit Domitian's strong ego. He didn't just turn down my offer, but appeared insulted by it, and that very afternoon he quietly exercised his option to leave Rome.

The pardon was a gamble, and it appeared I'd lost. My sources told me that Domitian went north to Volaterrae where he still had friends, but there was no local confirmation of that. He held me personally accountable for his dishonor, and not because of his exile, or the humbling experience of a public oath of loyalty, but because I was the one who ordered his abduction before battle. By doing that I had robbed him of the chance to die with honor.

His terse rejection of my offer was a smart political tactic, and one I hadn't foreseen. By questioning my honor for having approved such a dishonorable, "un-Roman" plan of capture, he had an argument worthy of debate among the citizenry. It had little impact at first, but as my popularity slowly waned, his was showing signs of being on the rise. Memories were short, and by my fourth imperial year, many of those in the Senate who once feared him were quietly offering him support.

That wasn't how I planned it, but the result was the same, so once I realized what was happening, I played along by ignoring his attacks on my honor, which left many Roman's shaking their heads. There would be more head shaking to come, especially when I initiated a grandiose building program to match my understanding of what Domitian had done in the original timeline. I began by expanding the Flavian Amphitheater, and then I cleared space for a new palace complex on Palatine Hill. I even tried to find the architects Domitian was supposed to have employed.

My strategy was a balancing act that involved a lot of guesswork and a lot of stress, but I stuck with it, and after four long years, it appeared that for once one of my plans was finally going to work.

XLIV

∞

"Hey you," Appia said groggily as she snuggled more tightly against me. "I hope you're not thinking of getting up just yet?" She was barely awake, yet she had a playful twinkle in her eyes that meant I wasn't going anywhere. It was a warm, lazy morning at the Villa North, tailormade for the sharing of passion, followed by a nap. For once there was no place we needed to be until the hunger for food replaced our hunger for each other.

"I think I smell fresh honey rolls," I said as we awoke to start the day for the second time. It was already late morning and the comfortable warmth we enjoyed earlier was giving way to the heat of midday.

"I suppose we must eat," she agreed. There was the familiar sound of busy birds in the courtyard, along with hushed voices.

"Don't you need to be up for something this morning?" Appia asked.

"Not really," I replied.

"Are you sure? I thought Thalese said…"

"Nothing that can't wait," I told her. "Antoninus may be sending clients by to try to sell me on that thing…"

"Intersection dedication stones," she said.

"They're not stones," I said. "They're really statues…"

"More like friezes carved from stone…"

"Whatever," I said. "It's more like shameless self-promotion."

She smiled. "It's still part of the job."

"I know," I said with a kiss, "but that isn't until midday."

"I think it is midday," she chuckled.

I studied the bright patches of sunlight crisscrossing the room. "I guess you're right."

The voices in the courtyard grew louder, and then came a knock. "Emperor Getha?" It was Claudia. "I hate to bother you..."

"But?" I said.

"You have guests."

"I know," I said calmly. "I'm coming. Tell whomever it is to relax and have a honey roll."

Appia was still chuckling as she stepped over to the wash basin. "You really don't care who it is, do you?"

"When I take a break from *The Hill*, I'd like it to actually be a break."

"I know," she said.

"I just want out. No more imperial shit, and finally I think we're close." I dipped my fingers into the basin and playfully flicked water at her. She replied with a few flicks of her own that led to a brief water fight followed by hugs.

"It will be nice when every morning can be like this," she said lovingly.

"Soon," I told her. "I can feel it. Domitian's been more active lately. Support for him in the Senate has grown. He knows it. He wants to be emperor. All I need is an hour of his time, and I know we can work out a quick and honorable transition."

"But Getha, he still hasn't responded to any of your messages. That worries me."

"I know, my love," I said. "It concerns me too, but I still have support of the military. To act against me would be suicide. He needs me, especially since many of his newly found patrician buddies have not entirely forgotten the past."

"All I want is for it to be over," she said. "You've sacrificed your political strength for him, and he doesn't understand why. He doesn't understand you! All he can see is that you're vulnerable."

"He doesn't have to understand me. What he understands is he needs the military and therefore he needs me. That's why he's in the city. Honor must be served in a way that satisfies his followers. Given our history, he can't just suddenly befriend me, but he wants the imperial seat pretty badly, so I expect to hear from him in a day or two at the most."

"I don't know," Appia said as she helped me straighten out my tunic. "I hope you're right."

"How do I look?" I asked as I spun around.

She chuckled, "As if you really care."

"I care," I said as I helped her with her wrap, "sort of."

"Sort of?" she smiled. "Go see what they want," and she gave me a playful push out the door. "Save a honey roll for me. I'll be right there."

The sun was hot and bright on my face. It felt good. Halfway across the courtyard I saw Leita hustling towards me. "Come," she said excitedly. "Your friends are here."

"My friends?" I chuckled sarcastically. "You mean Antoninus? I would hardly call him..."

"No," she said, and she grabbed my arm. "Real friends, Getha. Your friends. From home...your home!"

"My home? This is my home."

"Yes," she replied, "Ceristina."

"Ceristina? You mean…Christina?"

"Yes, Ceristina. Come…hurry!"

"But it can't be," I said as I followed her into atrium.

"See," Leita said with pride, "real friends." My heels ground to an immediate halt. Christina and Liam were standing directly opposite me on the other side of the impluvium.

"How are you, Aaron?" Christina said with a nervous smile. Her words were spoken in a tongue that I knew well even though I hadn't spoken it in years.

From behind me came the familiar clatter of sandals as Appia burst into the room, only to stop dead in her tracks at the sight of the two strangers.

"Tell me this isn't a dream," I said in English as I inched my way towards them.

"It's not a dream," Liam replied. Christina was suddenly too choked up for words, so I stepped forward to give her a hug.

"You actually came," I uttered in a quivering voice.

"Of course we did," she said, her body trembling as was mine.

"But how?" I asked. "The ship was buried in the eruption."

"It wasn't buried, Aaron. You sent it home."

"I sent it home?" I had no memory of doing that.

"You did," she said, "but that's not how we knew where to find you."

"Some historians call you the *Vain Emperor*," Liam said with a chuckle. "How many busts of yourself did you commission anyway?"

"I can't remember," I replied. "I was mostly concerned with likeness. They'd be useless otherwise. You have no idea how many I rejected."

"It was a brilliant idea, Aaron," Christina said, "brilliant, and we found you."

"I thought the ship was lost. I just wanted you to know what happened to me. Plus, it was a way to possibly satisfy our project goal. It was all I could think to do. I can't believe it. I can't believe you're really here."

"Believe it," Liam said as he joined us in a group hug. Thalese and Leita were standing by the kitchen entrance smiling like a pair of proud parents. They didn't seem in the least bit surprised by the appearance of such distant strangers.

"You probably haven't met everyone yet," I said as I wiped the moisture from my cheeks, and then I turned around to find Appia standing in the doorway looking forlorn, very lost and alone.

"We've met Thalese and Leita," Liam said.

"It's all right," I told Appia in Latin. "These are my friends. They're our friends," and I stepped back and took her hand. She was understandably tense as I coaxed her forward.

"Christina and Liam," I said in English, "I'd like you to meet…"

"Appia," Christina said. "I knew it the moment she entered the room. She's adorable, Aaron."

"Do you also know that she's my wife?"

"Yes," Christina said warmly, "I know that too," but when she offered her hand to Appia, Appia drew back. "It's an honor to meet you," Christina said, and she bowed her head.

"You've come to take my husband from me," Appia replied as she pulled herself tightly against me. I saw fear in her eyes. I looked at Christina who knew exactly what Appia had said.

"I didn't expect to ever see you again," I said.

"I know, Aaron." Christina said, but with a warm smile. "And now it's time to make things right. It's time to bring you home."

"You have no idea how long I've yearned to hear those very words," I said as I held Appia close, "but my life is here now. Changes are coming. I have a plan. I won't have to be emperor much longer. Appia and I are going to escape from all of this, to our own little exile, to where I won't be able to screw things up anymore."

"Changes are coming," Christina said, "but not in the way you think," and she turned her attention back to Appia. Speaking slowly and clearly in Latin, she said, "You are correct. We have come for Aaron, your husband, but we have also come for you, Appia, his wife."

"What?" I said.

As if on cue, Thalese stepped into the center of the room. "This is a day of great cheer!" he announced, but my eyes were fixed on Christina.

"That's right, Aaron," she said. "Both of you will return with us."

I swallowed hard and looked around the room. People were quietly filtering in from other parts of the villa. "But this is Appia's home," I reminded her in English. "She may not wish to go, and I won't leave her."

Appia took my hand. She didn't have to understand English to know what I'd said. "I will go wherever you must go, my love. My home is with you."

"It's not a matter of choice," Thalese said. "We made this decision for you because it's the only decision possible. You will not survive if you stay."

"Will not survive?" I said. "You mean I'll die if I stay?"

"No," he replied. "I'm saying you and Appia both will die if you stay."

XLV

∞

"When? How?" I asked.

"That's not important," Thalese replied. "What's important is that Domitian succeeds as history requires. That is what you've wanted for so long, and now it's going to happen."

I looked at Christina. "I guess I didn't totally wreck history after all?" and then I looked at Liam. "Or were you right; history can't be changed?"

"Actually," Liam replied, "the jury is still out. There were changes, obviously, but in the overall? I'd have to say no, history wasn't changed."

"That's right," Christina said. "We now know history can be altered on a localized level, but what that really means is anyone's guess."

"Is there a way to go back and fix those localized changes?" I asked. "One of them would be the death of Appia's father."

"What are you asking?" Appia said with a tug on my arm.

Christina shook her head. "No. We discussed the idea of trying to meet up with you at a point before you first left the ship. We sought other ways we might extract you earlier than this, but all options were prohibitively complex, impossible, or ultimately too risky."

"That means you've put history at risk again by coming here."

"Yes," Liam replied, "and we've had some lively debates on the subject."

"You, Aine, and Kam, perhaps," Christina said, "but Aaron, there was no debate. I was coming even if I had to do it alone."

I took a deep breath as it was all starting to sink in. Appia stepped up to Christina and took her hand. "I'm sorry for the way I spoke."

Christina responded with a kindly smile. "No need to apologize. I could never leave the man I love either."

"I know that," Appia said warmly, "or you wouldn't be here now."

Her comment left Christina momentarily speechless, but then she smiled and looked at me, "I wondered what she'd be like, Aaron. She is indeed someone special."

"We've been to hell and back together," I said. "She was the first person I saw when I awoke in this world, and I'd have died long ago without her.

She's been by my side through everything," and I was starting to get emotional. "Thalese, Leita, Caelus, Nubia, everybody…they saved me in every way possible. Believe me, I didn't want this. I didn't want to be emperor. It's just that every damn time I tried to fix things, I made things worse! You'd think I'd have learned, but no…"

Christina grabbed my arm to calm me down. "You can relax now, Aaron. You succeeded. Domitian will become emperor, and localized historical anomalies caused by OUR presence here, not just your presence, because we all had a hand in this, will be contained."

"Well done," Liam added.

"It's our turn to do the thinking," Christina said. "We have a plan in place and it's time to go home."

"Alright," I said. I was impressed by both Christina and Liam's working knowledge of Latin, and that both she and Liam were properly attired.

Thalese suggested we move to a more comfortable venue in the courtyard, which was also away from the main entrance and the risk of exposing them to visitors who might ask questions. We were led to a lovely spot by the fountain where Cornelia and Julia had already set out pillows for us. Therasia appeared with honey rolls, which Appia and I particularly enjoyed since we hadn't eaten.

"How soon do we leave?" I asked.

"Soon," Christina replied. She and Liam were now speaking exclusively in Latin. "Before the Ides of August."

"Okay," I said. "That gives us most of two days."

"Not exactly," she corrected. "We go tomorrow, the day before the Ides. Tomorrow morning to be exact."

"Morning?" I sighed.

"I'm sorry."

"Why so soon?" I asked.

"Because it's necessary," she replied, seemingly reluctant to give a better reason.

"Because you will be assassinated if you stay," Thalese said to demonstrate the gravity of the situation.

"We need at least a twenty-four-hour window," Christina said.

"Assassinated?"

"Both you and Appia," Thalese replied. "Both of you die!"

"Who would do such a thing?" I asked. "Especially to Appia."

"Domitian," he replied.

"That doesn't make sense," I said with surprise. "He's the first person my commanders would hunt down if he kills us."

"It doesn't matter," Thalese said, "because now it won't happen, and time is short."

"Where will we be attacked?" I asked.

"In the annex," he replied. "Ambushed in the corridor. Of course, it has to be the corridor," he chuckled. "You'd need a twenty-foot battering ram to get through that bedroom door of yours. That thing is better fortified than a city gate."

"I'm scheduled to return to *The Hill* this afternoon," I said solemnly. "I'm usually in town for the Ides, but I was thinking of staying here tonight."

"According to our research," Christina said, "you spent tonight at your residence on Palatine Hill. That's according to multiple sources, so we're quite confident with that data."

"But why Appia?" I asked. "Domitian actually likes her. The earlier attack was not meant to do her harm."

"It's not important," Thalese insisted.

"It is to me," Appia said somberly. "We were friends at one time."

"Is she killed because she can identify those who will attack me?" I asked.

"No," he said. "His plan is to kill both of you. With you, it's personal and political. With Appia, it's just politics. It's about garnering senatorial support."

"I know I haven't many friends there," I said.

He chuckled. "And you deliberately did that to yourself. You wanted them to seek out Domitian and they have."

I shook my head. "I may have alienated the Senate, but I don't see how killing us garners their support. Does their support even matter? It's the military that really counts. Unless I'm totally out of the loop, they still support me, which means I must be alive to pick Domitian as my successor. I don't see how he benefits otherwise."

"He's not going to kill you himself," Thalese said. "He has arranged for your assassination in a way that places blame elsewhere. In that way he can appear to be the hero who avenges your deaths."

"Where might that blame be placed?"

"I believe he has a pair of senators in mind," Thalese replied. "Of course, the rest of the Senate will be quick to speak in his favor to avoid becoming suspects themselves. The military will line up behind him when he publicly feigns frenetic anger in his quest to seek revenge, and then there's the public. Appia's death will add to a welling public outrage."

"I see," Appia said somberly as she took my hand. "He must kill both of us. That will ensure loyalty from your supporters. I may only be a woman, but I'm your woman."

"You're not 'only' a woman," I said.

"You know what I mean."

"That is what happens," Christina said. "Hypothetically there was more damage done to history from your death than anything else our project caused. It appears Domitian may have used the event to settle old scores to eliminate a rival or two."

"May have?" I asked.

"We don't know for sure," she replied. "The twenty years following your assassination are the most skewed between the original and new timelines. All that extra historical data you carried on board was invaluable in making that determination."

"Yes," I said, "but now you propose to change history again by extracting us prior to a major historical event. Our assassination was not in the original timeline, but it's there now, and history seems to have corrected for that."

"History didn't correct for anything," Christina said. "What appears to have happened is that history outside the altered zone diluted the changes over time until the two histories became virtually indistinguishable. We expect; however, that there is a point at which a large enough historical change would indeed create the cascading effect we all fear."

"And that doesn't worry you now?" I asked.

"Not really," she replied. "All we're doing is removing you and Appia at the point of your historical demise. The other lives that are spared in the process will be those that survived the original timeline. This will be a third variation, but there is no reason to suggest it might cascade."

"I have to ask," I said, "who does Domitian find to assassinate us? I've had the Praetorians on special alert ever since he came into the city."

"Yes," Thalese said, "and you keep sending your most trustworthy guardsmen to places like Neapolis."

"Where they'll do the most good," I said.

"That's right," he said, "and didn't Emperor Titus do the exact same thing?"

"Yes, I guess he did."

"And what happened then?" he said. "Men like Domitian are creatures of habit. If something fails the first time, they'd rather perfect it than start from scratch. Your own actions have played right into his thinking."

"Are you telling me it's the Praetorians again?"

"You've trusted the hiring to others," he said. "Sound familiar? Domitian's used your benevolence towards him against you."

"I guess that makes sense," I said sadly. "But you're right, it's not important now because we're leaving. At least we'll have one more night with the family."

"Well," Christina said sadly, "not exactly. You must spend tonight at your official residence."

"Tonight?"

"Yes."

"That's tough," I said sadly. "I suppose once we leave, we won't ever be able to come back. Am I right?"

"I'm sorry," she said, and she looked away.

"Ever?" Appia asked.

"I'm afraid so," I said.

"What about my mom? Can we take her with us?"

I glanced at Christina, but her expression wasn't hopeful, and then she looked at Appia. "We chose this time because we can save your lives without damaging our world. You and Getha are the only known causalities of the attack. That's why we can't take anyone else. I hope you understand."

"Do you really think adding Leita would cause history to cascade?" I asked. "She's older. She's probably past childbearing age…"

Christina sighed. "That's perhaps true, but we don't know with certainty, and there are other considerations, including the dynamics within your family once you're gone, which is why she and Thalese will remain here together. I am very sorry, Appia." Appia hung her head as a tear fell quietly to the ground.

"Perhaps there's still a way Appia can remain here," I said. "Maybe she can hide…"

"No," Appia said firmly. "My life is with you," and she gave me a hug.

"Are you absolutely certain?" I asked.

"Yes," she replied.

I turned my attention back to Christina and Liam. "We will need time to say our good-byes."

"Of course," Christina said, "so let's go over the plan, and then you'll have the afternoon."

"We had to cut it as close as possible," Liam explained. "The less time we spend here, the less chance of screw ups."

"Your Latin is pretty good too," I said with a smile.

"I try," he replied. "Chris and I have worked very hard on our language skills for this day."

"I can tell. You've even picked up on much of the local dialect. I'm amazed."

"We can discuss all that later," Christina said. "There is one more thing. You must restrict your goodbyes to those within this household. Thalese has assured me of their trustworthiness. Your escape must remain a secret outside these walls. The transition of power must happen quickly with no opposition, and that won't happen if your supporters have reason to think you might still be alive."

"That must mean the plan is to make it look like we we're killed?"

"That's correct," she replied.

"That'll be a neat trick," I chuckled. "How can we be rescued and assassinated at the same time?"

"You're not going to be assassinated," Christina said. "You're going to stage your own deaths. We've tried to think of every conceivable scenario, but it was the input from Thalese and Leita that's been most valuable. They've added a cultural element that allowed us to choose the direction we've taken."

"They helped you plan?" I asked.

"Yes," Christina smiled.

"How long have you and Liam been in this era?"

"Since daybreak," she replied.

I shook my head. "You've worked all this out since daybreak? That makes no sense." There were knowing glances and smiles between Christina, Liam, Leita, and Thalese. I looked at Thalese. "You knew they were coming today?"

"We have been here before," Christina confirmed with a warm smile, and she looked at Liam.

"Our first trip was a recon mission," Liam explained. "The only one possible. The next trip had to be the rescue. That was four years ago in your time. That's when we found Thalese and Leita."

"Actually, they found us," Christina corrected. "It seems our misaligned attire reminded them of when you first arrived. Thankfully, you trusted them with your secrets."

"I trust them completely," I said.

"They made it possible to develop a better strategy than what we originally had in mind," she added, "and we didn't have to involve you, which might have affected your actions."

"We were here for three days living out of the ship," Liam added, "but we had to leave with a plan in place," and he looked at Thalese and Leita, "because they needed to know how to prepare for your rescue."

"Maybe there was a better option," Christina said, "but this was the best we could come up with within that limited timeframe. Once we left here, we were committed."

"We knew there were still major obstacles to overcome," Liam said, "but we managed it and here we are."

"You've known about this for four years?" I asked Thalese.

"About that," he replied, and he looked at Leita.

Leita nodded. "Yes."

"I can't believe you two kept this secret for so long," I said.

"It was important," Thalese said.

I looked at him. "That's why you used the word destiny so often. You knew the future."

"I know what will happen if you stay," he said, "but that has also given me insight into how it will playout in this new version."

"We'll miss you, Getha," Leita said, "but we're happy for you too."

"I'll miss you too. More than you ever know," and then I turned to Christina. "Will they be all right?"

"We'll be just fine," Thalese assured me. "Domitian will protect us. The only way he can win the loyalty of your supporters is by honoring your name and protecting your property. I'd say official deification and a couple nice arches are in the offing for you as well."

"Right," I chuckled.

"You laugh," Christina added, "but he's right. You were deified after the assassination, and Domitian commissioned two arches in your name."

"That's funny," I said, "because there are people who think I'm already some sort of god."

"We know," she said. "Pliny the Younger wrote of a cult that likened you to Hercules. He apparently met you and found you big in stature, but surprisingly human."

"A wise man," I explained.

"But you do have a strong cult following," she said. "We're counting on it. You'd better fill him in, Liam. It's getting late."

"Alright," Liam said. "This evening you and Appia are to return to your home on Palatine Hill," and then he handed me one of two fabric satchels he was carrying. "You're going to need this."

I peeked inside. "What is it? It looks like one of those hokey bombs you see in movies. But of course, it can't be."

"Be careful, Aaron," Christina warned. "It's C4."

"What?" I uttered.

"Well," Liam said, "it's not exactly C4. It's a specialized variation of military plastic explosive. It works basically the same way. But it's stable, so you don't have to be super careful. You can probably hit it with a hammer and it won't go off without a detonator."

"The detonators are wrapped separately," Christina added, "but they're with it."

"A bomb? Are you kidding me?"

"People must believe your dead with no lingering questions," Liam replied. "And they have to believe it without having your bodies for positive identification."

"That goes for everyone," Christina said, "the Senate, the public, the military – especially the military. Everybody must believe you died in the explosion; otherwise, Domitian may not receive enough support to secure his elevation to power."

"If there's any doubt, any doubt at all," Liam added, "others may use that time to find another leader. The military might even pick somebody from within its ranks to challenge Domitian if given too much time to think about it."

"I understand that," I said, and I looked in the bag again, "but a bomb?"

"We know you live in an unoccupied section of the palace," he said.

"Yes," I said.

"Good. You will assemble the explosive tonight in your bedroom and then set the timer and place it under your bed in the morning."

"Remember, Aaron," Christina said, "you are being watched by your enemies. They must believe that you and Appia are in your bedroom when the bomb goes off."

"This is the best plan you could come up with?" I asked.

"It will be fine," Liam said. "Thalese has already smuggled a ceramic crock full of entrails from the amphitheater into your bedroom. That will add realism to the explosion."

"Animal or human?"

"You don't want to know," Thalese said, "but this mixture will lead the priests to identify it as you."

"The priests are pretty good at identifying that stuff," I reminded him.

"Yes," he said, "but I know what they look for."

"The explosion will pulverize everything," Liam said, "and splatter enough visible forensic material to allow investigators to conclude it's you and that you're dead. Remember, they can't do blood typing or DNA testing, or even fingerprinting."

"I'll admit it's pretty gruesome," Christina added. "Thalese knows better than any of us what the priest will believe."

"All you have to do," Liam said, "is place the pot in the center of the bed. Drape night clothing over it if you wish. Set the timer for ten to fifteen minutes. I'll leave that up to you. Push the bomb under the bed and get the heck out of Dodge. I believe you have a private escape route that exits onto the Forum."

"That's correct," I said.

"What the heck is Dodge?" Appia asked.

I laughed. "It's just an expression. It means we need to get away from there in a hurry."

"Oh," she said. "From your native language."

"How big of an explosion will this be?" I asked.

"The bomb is not designed to destroy the building," he replied. "It should make a big hole in the floor and closest wall, maybe the ceiling above your bed. That will leave three walls and lots of wreckage to catch the splatter."

"Also," Christina added, "you need to stay in the general area until you hear it go off. In the unlikelihood of failure, you'll need to reset it with the backup detonator."

"Failure?"

"It won't fail," Liam insisted. "It can't. We have no room for error."

"What about fire?" I asked. "The inside's all wooden."

"Minimal risk," she replied. "It's not an incendiary, but this version is designed to have a powerful shockwave. It will blow things apart."

"It's specifically designed to avoid fire," Liam said. "It's meant to clear rooms without causing secondary effects. If you want to wipe out a few terrorists in an apartment complex without destroying the homes of other tenants, this will do it. That's why it was designed."

"Okay," I said, "but I still don't see how this can work. Explosions just don't happen in this century. People won't know what to think."

"Exactly!" Christina said. "We're counting on that, and you should know better than anybody how this society reacts to the unknown."

"You're thinking they'll assume it's an act of the gods," I replied. "Probably Jupiter since he controls lightning and thunder, but that can still be a pretty hard sell."

"Thalese will help sell it," she said. "He's done all the prep work. He's already created a term to explain the blast – divine lightning."

"Jupiter is correct," Thalese said. "Over the past several months I've taken the liberty of consulting priests regarding the idea that Jupiter has new plans for you. More recently I've arranged evidence that will appear as if you and Appia have been making special offerings to Jupiter."

"And they bought it?" I asked.

"We'll see," he smiled, "but I expect so. I was very thorough."

"I'm sure you were," I said.

"Once the bomb goes off," Liam added, "you are to meet Thalese at the round temple in the Forum Boarium. He will escort you to the ship. He knows where we parked."

"Good," I said.

"Do you have any questions?" Christina asked.

"Nothing at the moment," I replied.

"Then it's time we get back to the ship," she told Liam. "It's getting late."

"Why don't you stay here?" I asked. "Use our room."

"It's a tempting offer," Christina replied, "but we need to minimize our contact, so all our food and water is in the ship."

"I wish I could show you around," I said as they got up to leave.

"We'd love that," she said warmly, "but it's best we stick to the plan," and she gave me a hug. "We'll see you bright and early in the morning."

I accompanied them to the street, causing the guards to abruptly snap to attention the instant I appeared.

"This is really spooky, Aaron," Christina said under her breath. "Do you ever think about the fact that you're the most powerful person on Earth?"

"I try not to," I replied, "and I certainly don't feel like it."

"You're not just the emperor," Liam chuckled. "You're an emperor with a bag full of C4."

"That's just makes me more dangerous," I said, "not powerful."

"Don't be so hard on yourself," Christina said.

"Anyway," I said, once we were past the guard, "they'll start following us if I walk any farther."

"All right," she said with a hug.

"Will you be okay getting back from here?" I asked.

"We'll be fine," Liam replied. "It'll be great having you back. We'll all be able to breathe again."

I nodded. I couldn't think that far ahead. "I'll see you in the morning, and thanks."

"Good luck, Aaron," they said with fingers crossed.

"Good luck to us all," I replied, and I watched them until they were out of sight.

I returned to the villa and headed directly to my room with the satchel.

Appia had left to spend time with her mother, and when she returned, she was upbeat despite her obvious sadness. "Everybody will be here before we leave," she said. "They've been planning this for four years. It looks like we're the only ones who didn't know."

We took a few minutes to look over our personal items to decide what we could take with us. We couldn't take much because personal items help to add visual support to the cover story, so we decided on one item each. Appia had a lovely necklace from Egypt that her father had bought her, and I had my medallion that symbolized my acceptance into the family. I wore it every day even though I generally kept it under my clothes. We also took a robe and nightshirt to place over the explosive for added realism.

I thought it best to bring back the remaining items I'd arrived with, which included my tattered vest and the gun. It was corroded, and nonfunctional, but better disposed of in its own era.

Once we'd finished packing, we took one last look around the room. Appia put her arm around me. She was shaking. "How are you holding up?" I asked.

"I'm scared," she replied.

"Me too," I said.

The happy sound of children playing drew us to the window. People were beginning to arrive. I smiled when I saw little Paris chasing Appia Getha around the statues. Nubia followed right behind with somebody's lost sandal. It was little Appia's, of course.

"She bears your name," Appia said, "and one day she will understand the honor of her heritage."

XLVI

∞

After we said our tearful goodbyes, we returned to *The Hill.* Upon our arrival we walked through the palace to make sure everyone knew we were there. We took evening meal with Darius Lucillius on a terrace facing Capitoline Hill. His kindly manner completely belied the fact that he was a central figure in the plot to kill us. After the meal we retired to the annex, leaving word that we were not be disturbed until midmorning.

It was with some trepidation that we walked past the guards who would soon be tasked with the job of killing us, but it was important that there be no doubt about our location when the bomb went off. I knew we were at risk if Domitian's plan of attack was based on opportunity, but that seemed unlikely. Domitian had been burned badly once before, and I was certain that he'd be far more conservative the second time around. The upcoming Ides was also well suited for his purpose, because he would not only know our location, but the locations of those he intended to blame.

Thalese had left us a pair of plain, brown, hooded cloaks folded next to the large crock of entrails. It would be dark when we awoke so we moved those things to the middle of the room where we could easily find them. There was little else to do after that, so I checked the alarm clock Liam had given me and we went to bed.

Neither of us got much sleep. Appia was concerned that we'd oversleep, and I was continually listening for anyone entering the annex. About the time I nodded off, the alarm sounded.

"Is it time to go?" she asked.

"Yes," I said, and I gave her a hug.

Only the faint light of early dawn gave definition to the room. The air was cool and moist, and the floor cold on our bare feet. We washed quickly and dressed in our makeshift disguises. Appia helped me lift the crock and place it on the mattress. I connected the timer and detonator to the explosive.

I looked outside at our route and set the timer for twelve minutes. That seemed like enough time without a long wait once we were clear. The building was quiet, as was the city below except for the rustling of birds huddling in a niche beneath the sill. I quietly shoed them out of harm's way.

"Are you ready?" I asked.

"Yes," she replied. We hugged, and then I pressed the button initiating the timer and set the bomb under the bed.

We made our way as quickly and quietly as possible through the corridor and down the narrow staircase to Caligula's old atrium.

"Wait," I said, and we stopped.

"What?"

"Listen," I replied. "Did you hear that?"

"Hear what? The building creaks like that every morning."

I shook my head. "It's not that. It's probably nothing."

"Relax, Getha," she said and she took my hand. "I'm sure it's nothing. Let's go."

I unbolted the door to the temple and then stepped across the polished stone flooring to the huge front doors. I opened one side just enough for us to squeeze through.

"This is it," I whispered as we pulled our hoods up over our heads. We peaked outside to make sure we weren't being observed before quietly stepping into the brightening, early morning light. We closed the door behind us. We were nervous, so I reminded Appia that we needed to walk at a normal pace despite the urge to rush.

I glanced up at our room as we made our way across the Forum paving stones. I thought I saw something move in the window. It was like a shadow, or maybe a bird, or maybe my imagination. "Do you remember if I closed the door to our room?"

"I don't know," Appia replied. "Does it matter?"

I grabbed her arm and stopped. "I don't know." I saw it again, but more clearly. There was somebody in our room. "Oh shit!"

Appia saw it too. "Who can that be?"

"I have no idea," I said. "Talk about shitty luck. I've got to go back."

"Is there time?" she asked, and she grabbed my arm when I started to pull away.

"I have to try," I replied as I pulled myself free.

"No!" she cried. "You can't fix everything!"

"I can't have another death on my hands, either," I said, and I hustled back to the temple with Appia in tow. Once inside, we quickly made our way through the old atrium and onto the stairwell. I was practically running at that point, and running out of breath by the time I reached our floor. There was nobody in the corridor, so I took a couple breaths. I asked Appia to stay put, and then I headed straight for our room. I got there just as Domitian, of all people, was coming out. He looked startled.

"Your door was open and I…" was all he could say before I grabbed him and shoved him onto the stairwell landing opposite our room. He tripped and I immediately fell on top of him. It couldn't have been two seconds later when the blast went off. Its earsplitting boom shattered the early morning stillness as a shower of splinters, spikes, and plaster blew over us followed by a frothing cloud of particulate debris. My ears were ringing, as I'm sure his were as well, and when I got off him, he looked stunned. I pulled him up onto his feet. "Getha? What…" he uttered.

"Shut up!" I said and I pushed him against the wall. "Now, you listen to me for a change! I never lied to you. I never wanted to be emperor." I pulled him out of the stairwell to look at the room that was now shattered and smoking with gaping holes in the floor, the ceiling, the walls, both interior and exterior. "Take a good look," I said. "I did that. I summoned that power."

Appia was in the corridor by the central stairwell looking perplexed. I knew we needed to be gone before we were seen, but I also needed to talk to Domitian, so I grabbed him again and pulled him along with us down that central stairwell. He was still stunned and shaking.

"If you're going to kill me," he said in a shaky voice as I was practically dragging him down the steps, "at least give me a sword to preserve my honor."

"I'm not going to kill you," I said angrily as we entered Caligula's old atrium. "I'm here to save your sorry ass so you can be the next emperor. Was there anybody else in the room with you?"

"No," he replied. "I was just…"

"You weren't just anything," I said. "You were making sure we were in our bedroom before ordering your assassins to kill us."

"I don't know what you're talking about!"

"I know all about you're damn plot," I said.

"I thought your friends said we were killed on the Ides?" Appia asked. "That's tomorrow."

I nodded. "True, but we went out of our way to make certain the guards saw *both* of us enter the annex last evening. It was important everyone knew we were in our room when the blast went off."

"Was your friend's information wrong?" Appia asked.

Domitian stood there looking both confused and perhaps a little shell-shocked.

"No," I said, "it wasn't. History recorded *me* staying here last night, not you. You had plans with Leita. You weren't coming until today."

"That's right," she said.

"But that offered you," and I stuck my finger in Domitian's chest, "the chance to move up your timetable. Am I right?"

Domitian was shaking so hard his voice quivered. "I don't know what…"

"But it doesn't matter now," I said as I stepped back. "Appia and I are leaving for good. Do you hear me? We are leaving for good!"

"For good?" he uttered.

"For good and forever," I said. "You won't ever see us again. Nobody will. If you still want to be the next emperor, then listen to me now and follow my instructions to the letter. Do you understand?"

Domitian actually listened to me this time and I lied through my teeth. I told him his senses were correct, that I was as human as he was, but unlike him, I was granted special powers by the gods. I explained the concept of divine lightning, and that through Jupiter I had destroyed the room in a way that made it appear we were killed in order to cover our escape. I stated once again that I never wanted to be emperor, but this time I finally gave him a reason he understood – that Jupiter had other plans for me. He had no issues using the deception of our deaths to achieve power. I strongly suggested he listen to Thalese and use him as a resource. I did not tell him anything about the time ship or time travel, but I made it clear that if he didn't do right by my family, I would come back and deal with him personally.

All that took time we didn't have. Domitian needed to be one of the first people on scene at our room to play his part, and we needed to escape unrecognized though a crowd that was forming outside in the forum. On top of that, I didn't entirely trust Domitian. His Praetorian assassins were undoubtedly prepped and awaiting word to attack. He could still call upon them to track us down to ensure I would be gone forever.

Despite my concerns, we had to risk it and go, although Domitian didn't look like he was ready to go anywhere. All of his usual bluster seemed to have been sapped out of him. He took a seat on a dusty old bench. I had to coax him back to his feet and lead him to the stairwell.

"You do understand what I told you," I said, "right?"

He looked at me. "Yes," he said.

"There should be splattered entrails everywhere," I said. "That will help you to proclaim us dead."

"I know," he said.

"You are the emperor now," I stated emphatically.

"I am the emperor," he uttered.

"And Appia and I are gone," and I turned away, but he grabbed my arm.

"My brother was right about you," he said, "wasn't he?"

I looked him in the eye. "Goodbye," I said, "and don't try to look for us. You won't find us."

Appia and I pulled our hoods up over our heads. She carefully opened the door leading into the temple. "I don't see anyone," she said.

"Then let's get out of here," I said as I doublechecked to make sure Domitian had left.

Appia took a moment to dust me off so I didn't look like I'd just come from a blast zone, after which, we made our way to the huge front doors of the temple again. I peeked outside to where a crowd of about fifty people had gathered, but their attention was on the gaping hole that wasn't relegated to just one wall, but also the corner of our room, exposing the remains of the interior on two sides. I sent Appia out first, as being seen together near the palace might give us away as well. I told her to head straight to the Forum Boarium and I'd be right behind her.

I left the door ajar and watched her walk along the front of the Basilica Julia. No one gave her a second glance. Once she was out of sight, I followed. I stepped outside and closed the big door behind me. I was aware that some people had noticed me, but by acting in a casual way, I didn't appear to be drawing added attention.

I suppose I should have kept going, but once I was amid the crowd, I couldn't help one last look at our room. It was utterly destroyed. There were chunks of brick and wood all over the ground too. The bomb turned out to be more powerful than planned, but there was no fire. I could only hope there was enough left of the entrails to do their job in the deception, but the deed was done, so there was no point in worrying about that.

"Anyone ever tell you that you look like the emperor?" a rather short, rotund man, in a tan tunic asked as he stood at my side looking up at me. That comment certainly gave me pause, especially when another man turned around to check me out.

"You know," I replied, "I get that all the time, but I hear he's a lot taller."

"Definitely," he said. "You're tall, but not that tall. He's a good foot or more above most men."

"You've seen him before?"

"Only at a distance," he replied, "but you look like his statues."

"Yeah," I chuckled, "they're all over the place. He must have an ego the size of an amphitheater to commission so many."

He laughed and then pointed to the damaged building. "Somebody said he sleeps in that room."

"I wouldn't know," I said, "but if he was in there, I can't imagine it went well for him."

He nodded. "If the gods willed it..."

"I agree," I said. "Anyway, I may have his looks, but I don't have his wealth. I have to work for a living."

"What do you do?" he asked as I turned to leave.

"Vulcanologist," I stated.

"What?"

"Plastering," I replied as I shook off more dust from my cloak. I quickly ducked behind him and made my way past the Basilica Julia. It took me about five or so minutes to reach the Forum Boarium where Thalese and Appia were anxiously waiting.

"Hurry," Thalese called out.

"I thought you were right behind me," Appia said.

"I was," I said, "but somebody recognized me."

"What?" both said in unison.

"Relax," I replied, "I handled it."

"Did you see any Praetorians?" Appia asked as we began our trek out of the city.

"No," I said, and I looked at Thalese. "I couldn't lock the door between the temple and Caligula's old atrium. The door is closed. I hope that won't be a problem."

"Not a problem," Thalese said, and he smiled. "So, you saved Domitian's life."

"I did," I replied.

He was still smiling. "You didn't save him just to preserve history either, did you?"

"You know me all too well," I sighed, and then added, "but it did give me the chance to toss him around a bit."

"Toss him?" Appia chuckled. "You manhandled him."

"I wager that felt good," Thalese said.

"I hate to admit it," I replied with a smug grin, "it did. He bought the whole divine lightning spiel too. That should make it easier for you."

We started seeing more and more people as we left the city, but the sight of us, three plain-clothed figures passing along the river trail was hardly cause for concern. We picked up our pace once we were beyond the wharves. It didn't take as long as I thought to reach the ship. It wasn't far from where I had landed in 69, but I never would have found it without Thalese.

The woods were dark and tangled, but the clearing was right where it was supposed to be, and in the middle sat the time ship. It was practically invisible because of its chameleon-like ability to mimic the colors of its environment.

"That's your special ship?" Appia asked with wonder.

"It is indeed," I replied, and as we stepped closer, the oval hatch opened and Christina stepped out to greet us.

"I was starting to get worried," she said, sounding quite relieved.

"Perfect timing," Liam exclaimed. He was inside the ship. He could see us, but we couldn't see him.

"How did it go?" Christina asked.

"That was some explosion," I replied to avoid a direct answer.

"Okay, Aaron," she said as she looked me over. "Is that sawdust? What happened?"

There was still some grit in my hair. "Just plaster dust and splinters," I replied.

"Do I want to know?" she asked.

I chuckled. "We had a little problem. Improvising under pressure seems to be something I do best. Well, maybe not best, but I've had to do it a lot. And for once I believe we're okay. We'll talk later."

"Will she be all right?" Christina asked, noticing how tightly Appia was clinging onto Thalese as they shared their final moments together.

"She will be," I replied.

"It would be ideal if we could leave now," Liam said.

"Relax," Christina told him. "We've got time."

Appia was in tears as Thalese escorted her to the ship. "Remember what I told you," he said, "and everything will be alright."

"I'll never forget," she replied, "ever," and she hugged him one last time.

Christina offered her hand to Appia. "Let me help you inside."

"I should be getting back," Thalese said as he looked at me while wiping away the moisture from his cheeks. "There's still much to do."

"I feel I've left you with such a burden," I said.

"No," he said. "I'm glad for it. It gives me purpose and keeps me focused."

"Will you be all right?"

"Yes," he replied. "My heart will ache, but it's okay because we know you and Appia are continuing on the path of life."

"Be careful, my friend," I told him.

"Always," he replied, and we embraced.

"Thank you for everything. I couldn't have had a better friend, but you're so much more than that…you're a brother."

"You broke your most cherished rules for us," he said. "I will never forget that. Never!"

"There is one final official duty I must perform as emperor," I said, "or perhaps more as head of the family." I looked at the face of the medallion Appius had given me one more time before taking it off. "As Appius Marius Caupo once gave this symbol of family unity and strength to me, I now present it to you, Thalese."

"What are you doing, Getha?"

"I think you need a title to go with it," I said.

"What do you mean?"

"How about Thalese of Pompeii?" I said. "In honor of our home and our survival."

"I like it, Getha," he said with a smile.

"Thalese of Pompeii, my friend, my brother, I present this medallion to you."

"Getha?" he said as I placed it around his neck. "I can't accept this."

"You most certainly can," I said. "It's your family now."

Christina had gotten Appia seated and was adjusting her safety belt when she happened to glance outside. She saw me giving the medallion to Thalese. "Is that medallion solid gold?" she asked Appia.

Appia looked as she wiped away her tears. "Yes, it is," she replied. "Emperor Vespasian gave it to my father, and he gave it to Getha when he made him part of our family."

"Wow," Christina commented. "A thing like that must be priceless, but of course Aaron must know that."

"He knows," Appia said with a warm smile. "He knows exactly what it's worth."

With a firm handshake I bid Thalese goodbye. "Good luck, my good friend and thank you," and I walked back to the ship. "I wish there was a way I could know how this all turns out for you and our family."

He nodded and smiled. "Perhaps there is. I have an idea, but we'll see. Good luck to you my brother."

I stepped inside the ship and watched Thalese as he positioned himself a safe distance away.

"It's hard to leave with so much left unfinished," I said as I took my seat next to Appia.

"He knows what he's doing," Christina said, "and it's time for you to come home."

"Are we ready?" Liam asked.

"I think so," Christina replied as she waved her hand over the opening, closing the hatch. "Thalese is where he needs to be."

Thalese was quietly standing by the tree line clutching his medallion with both hands.

"Here we go," Liam said, and in the next instant Thalese's image blurred away to nothing. Appia sat in complete silence, her eyes closed, and an arm tightly wrapped around mine.

"Was that smooth or what?" Liam said with pride over his take-off.

"Very nice," Christina replied.

"That's 12 hours," he added. "Probably a little slower than you remember, Aaron, but we've learned the body acclimates to time travel better with controlled acceleration and deceleration."

"We've already gone into the future about half a day," I told Appia. "That means it's night in Rome right now."

"24 hours," Liam said.

"We're up to a full day," I told Appia.

"Now we're starting to really move!" Liam exclaimed, trying to perk us up. "35 years… 50…"

"It will take three hours and forty-two minutes to complete the journey," Christina said. She was studying Appia who was quietly absorbed in thought.

"Would you like anything?" I asked Appia.

"Just hold me," she said.

"We've got sandwiches," Christina said.

"Sandwiches?" Appia said as her face brightened. "Like what Getha makes?"

I smiled. "I was hungry one day, so I invented the sandwich."

"That's not quite how history recorded it," Christina chuckled, "but you both need to eat something with one of these pills." She opened a bin and took out a small, brown container filled with blue and yellow capsules. "It reduces the temporal shock, or what we now call Displacement Disorder associated with time transition. It eliminates memory issues and confusion like you suffered before."

"I know I'm still missing some memories," I said. "Like I told you, I don't remember much about my trip from Rome to Pompeii or even leaving the ship."

"You had a head injury along with time related issues," she said. "It may never come back, but we'll get you the best help we can. Both of you. You both look healthy, but there will be health screens and lots of checks and tests to make sure there are no issues."

"How long have I been gone in your time?" I asked.

"Three years, two months, six days."

"What about my family? I asked. "I said nothing before I left which was pretty stupid given the risks. I could have at least told them I was going to Italy."

"They're fine," she said. "Your mom knows. I probably should have spoken with her sooner, but I didn't know what to say. I feel badly for what your family went through."

"That's not your fault," I said.

"Your mom's a remarkable woman, Aaron. She helped us. She helped me though some tough moments, too."

I glanced at Appia. She looked asleep with her head against my shoulder. "Does she know I'm bringing home a wife?"

Christina smiled. "She does, and she's already bought wedding gifts. She says she wasn't sure if you'd ever get married, but she knew if you did, it wouldn't be to a local. I guess she has you pegged."

"She does indeed," I said.

"Of course," she said, "you will need to get married again in our time to make it official. Your mom has ideas for that, as well."

"I'm sure," I said as another thought crossed my mind "What about Appia's citizenship? She will need to be in the system somewhere."

"All taken care of," she replied.

"Does that mean you've gone public with the project? We weren't going to do that if history can be altered."

"We aren't going public," she said, "and Appia can become a citizen in a couple years after you're officially married."

"Okay," I said, "but won't she need documents to show she's a citizen of another country?"

"Yes. She's from Italy."

I looked at her questioningly. "I suppose technically that's true, but she doesn't speak a word of Italian. Are you telling me she really is an Italian citizen…legally?"

"Yes," she said with a smile. "It wasn't so difficult. She enters our era with no history, no past, no property, nothing. She has a clean slate to start with. That made it relatively it easy."

"That sounds familiar."

Quietude

∞

Appia's arm tightened around mine as the big jet powered into the clear evening sky over Boston. She was understandably anxious. It was, after all, her first conventional flight, and yet I saw a look of resolve in her eyes. Ghostly dreams of the distant past were calling her home, and now she was ready to go.

Christina and Kamden, on the other hand, were having considerably more difficulty acclimating to the flight despite having much more experience in the air. They shared a fear of flying that left them wide-eyed and tense, gripping the armrests hard enough to turn their knuckles white. Neither had to join us on this trip, but Christina had a strong personal need to come, while Kamden had a strong need to be with her.

Business class comes with comfort, decent food and drink, and lots of video entertainment, but Appia and I were more involved with each other, sharing moving excerpts from Thalese's *Letters to Tacitus*. When Thalese said he would try to find a way to update us with family news, he did. I had told him of the kinds of materials historian's in my era used to try to understand his era, including the correspondences between the historian Tacitus and Pliny the Younger. When Tacitus wrote to Thalese for a better understanding of the "enigmatic" Emperor Getha, the clever and ever resourceful Thalese used those letters as a way to write to us. He would reply directly to each question, but end with a paragraph of thoughts he told Tacitus he wished he could share with Appia and me had we survived.

I'd found an unabridged, hard cover edition of Thalese's *Letters* at a weekend flea market in Dover, NH. The fact that it was dog-eared and yellowed only made it look and feel more appropriate.

Tacitus found his musings so insightful he continued the dialog for many years. In this way we learned that our escape plan actually worked to perfection. The family survived intact, and in fact, flourished under the Flavian banner until the assassination of Domitian in 96 CE, precisely when it was supposed to happen. Thalese had already befriended Nerva based on what I'd told him prior to my departure. Nerva shared consulship with Domitian, and became the next emperor. His reign lasted for two years. During that time, he adopted the military commander Trajan to be his successor.

Fabius and Claudia had passed away by 98 CE, but remarkably David, Thalese, Leita, Caelus, Nubia, and Appia Getha were still living. There were gaps in the writings as some of the letters didn't survive. We knew Caelus had passed away around 104 CE, but not how, and nothing of Nubia's death, or anything at all regarding her second child. The most difficult letter told of Leita's passing. She'd been ill, perhaps a cancer, but that she'd lived for nearly sixty-six years was remarkable. She passed with Thalese and Appia Getha at her side.

Appia Getha wrote to me through Thalese in one letter. His wording to Tacitus was this, "Appia Getha is proud of her connection to Emperor Getha. Appia Getha thanks him every day for giving her life. She knows the truth. She prays on the altar of time that one day he will return to find her, and find satisfaction in the workings of her life that he has inspired. Her hope is that he will be as proud of her as she is of him, her father." Tacitus actually questioned that passage, finding it curiously cryptic. Thalese replied with answers to other questions, completely ignoring that one.

It was a difficult passage to read knowing I couldn't respond. I wanted to know what those workings were, and I desperately wanted to know her. To this day I have not entirely ruled out answering her prayer, but with the time ship rendered inert, that opportunity is most likely past.

The ship's ability to return to its Date of Origin lasts only as long as it remains turned on. It may have been in a kind of hibernation mode for millions of years by the time we found it, but it was never turned off. The difficult decision was made to render it inert in order to avoid any future misuse. Liam and Kamden figured out how to do that, and it was deliberately done without knowing how to reanimate it. Whether or not being inert is a complete shutdown is not known, but seems likely, as the portal no longer closes and the hull doesn't change color or repair scratches. If at some time in the future it is reanimated, there's a very good chance its Date of Origin will be updated to the date of its modern restart and not the Jurassic.

Appia Getha would have been about 28 years old when that letter was written, which meant Thalese was well into his seventies. He equated his longevity to my suggestions regarding basic hygiene, which he and Leita subscribed to and she taught to Appia Getha.

There were only two more letters that survived, and the last was only a partial. In it Thalese talked about Trajan, offering a positive outlook for the future of the state. Near the end he said he was very tired, and that he missed his family desperately, but for one who lovingly remains at his side. That "one" he described as having been a joy and an inspiration. We presume he meant Appia Getha. He ended it with "Farewell" instead of his name. There would be no more letters.

We managed to eat in between readings and tried to stay hydrated. We slept for nearly three hours. By the time we awakened we were flying in sunlight over the Alps. Appia knew of the Alps from having traversed them with her family on their way to and from Gaul, but the view from the plane gave her a new perspective on what had to have been difficult traveling.

Our overseas flight landed in Rome on schedule, giving us plenty of time to make the connecting flight to Naples. It was gloomy and wet when we arrived, the mountain shrouded in clouds. The fact it wasn't a sunny day didn't bother me, but having hired a private water taxi service to take us across a stormy bay to Sorrento did. It seemed like a great idea when I booked it. Water taxis are efficient, reliable and fast, covering the sixteen-mile route in about fifty minutes. They avoided the daily traffic jams on the A3, along with the added risks of road construction and tunnel detours; however, heavy rain and rough water threatened to be the equalizer. To my great relief the taxi had a comfortable, dry cabin, and the bay was relatively calm.

From Appia's perspective, and to a lesser degree mine, there was nothing left of 79 CE Neapolis to evoke memories of the distant past. That changed once we were about halfway across the bay. That's when the sun broke through the clouds and the green, fertile slopes of modern Vesuvius came slowly into view – its gritty, tan peak catching sunlight above a thin, land-hugging haze. The mountain's shape may have been different, but its familiar omnipresence was unchanged. Appia was tense as she took hold of my arm. I know how crazy this must sound, but it was as if the mountain was calling to us in some quasi-mystical way. It was just a mountain, a geological construct of earth and rock, and yet we felt something more.

Sorrento was built on a high precipice. Its 300-foot cliff face rose before us as we made our way into the small port below. From there we took a cab to our hotel in the adjacent town of San Agnello. I'd booked two sea view doubles on the top floor to give us truly grand views of the bay. The plan was to spend the afternoon recovering from jetlag and make the trip to Pompeii in the morning after a full night's rest.

The weather had cleared and the sea was sparkling. There were seabirds everywhere catching updrafts, soaring and circling while calling to each other in a birdsong that traversed the ages. I stood on the terrace soaking it all in while Appia's eyes were mostly focused on the mountain and the plain to the right.

"It looks like there are a lot of towns all around Vesuvius," she noted. "There are even buildings on the slopes. Those are all buildings, right?"

"You are correct," I replied. "The whole inner coastline from Naples to Castellamare di Stabia is a continuous series of towns."

"They must know about the mountain," she said, "or is the mountain no longer dangerous?"

"Oh," I said, "it's just as dangerous, and they know it. The mountain has been quiet for a long time."

"It was quiet for a long time in our time too."

"So true," I said, "but today the mountain is continuously monitored with seismic equipment. There are evacuation plans. I suppose they trust in science to provide ample warning. Whether that's enough or not, who knows?"

"It still seems terribly risky," she said. "Even if people survive, they'll lose everything."

"You can almost see Pompeii from here," I said. "It's on the inner bay just beyond that chunk of land that juts out."

"I know this view," she said. "I've been here before. How long will it take us to get there from here? It must be much quicker in machines than it used to be by carriage."

"I'd estimate an hour or so to the site depending on what time we catch the train."

"The site," she said. "That's such a strange term for our home."

"It's an archaeological site now. That's why it still exists for us to see after so many hundreds of years." I saw her wipe a tear from her eye. "There's still time if you want to go."

"I can wait until tomorrow."

"No," I said, "we can't."

She turned and gave me a big hug. "It happened over 2000 years ago, Getha. Why does it feel like only yesterday?"

"Because it was practically yesterday for us," I replied. "In a way I don't think we ever really left."

Christina and Kamden looked exhausted when we stopped by their room to tell them of our change of plan, but Christina was all smiles. She was expecting that would happen and the two of them were ready to join us. Her comment was, "We figured that. We wouldn't miss it for the world."

The towns around the Bay of Naples are served by what travel guide and writer Rick Steves appropriately labeled "a rickety but reliable rail service" called the Circumvesuviana. The trip from the San Agnello Station to the Pompeii Scavi Station, as we know it today, made about twelve stops, depending on the season, and took about forty minutes. It was a pleasant ride when it was not overcrowded, offering some spectacular views of the Bay and Mt. Vesuvius along the way. The four of us had a good, lighthearted conversation lasting right up until the train slowed upon approach to our Pompeii stop. There were tall grasses lining both sides of the tracks, but above them was our first view of the ruined city we once called home.

Despite the destruction, and the city being a mile farther away from the coastline, I didn't have to tell Appia what she was seeing. "We're here," she uttered somberly.

I suffered a momentary bout of confusion when we exited the station, as if caught between eras. Call it temporal or displacement confusion. It's akin to temporal amnesia, but less acute. Both maladies come under the heading of Time Displacement Disorders. I knew that whatever I was feeling was probably worse for Appia. She looked as if in a daze.

It was a very touristy stretch of roadway between the station and the site, and while I usually brushed aside any vendors who approached, I engaged an elderly man selling roses. I bought two long stem red ones for Appia because I knew where we were going first.

We entered the ancient city at what was now called the Porta Marina Gate. We smiled at each other because that was not where the port was. We climbed the steep, stone-paved roadway past the bathhouse and through the double-arched entrance. I ran my hands along the interior wall just before we stepped back into the light. I had to stop for a moment. The sensation of displacement returned but with less confusion, and this time it was accompanied by a strange sensation best described as a feeling of my own presence among the ruins.

"So, this is the Pompeii you knew before you met me," Appia said as we walked past the broken remains of barely recognizable structures.

"It is."

"There's not much left," she said, "just crumbling walls. No color. No life."

"But you can still feel something," I said, "can't you?"

"I don't know what I'm feeling."

Christina and Kamden had gotten ahead of us and were already part way across the Forum by the time we got there. Only marble and brick columns and first level entrances hinted at its former grandeur, but it was enough to complete our connection as we looked beyond the groups of tourists and into the past.

"You must be feeling it," I said. "I know you do. This town's still alive. It's in the air. It's all around us."

She nodded. "I do, and it's scaring me. It's like it's trying to reclaim us."

"You two alright?" Christina asked as she and Kamden joined us.

"We're fine," I replied. "It's just a little overwhelming."

"I'm sure," she said, but it was clear they weren't picking up the same sensations.

We walked with them across the Forum describing as best we could what it really looked like in antiquity. Appia was a veritable encyclopedia on who owned what and lived where, including all the local gossip, some of which I didn't know, but it explained a few things.

Once we left the Forum, we headed in the direction of what was now called the Herculaneum Gate. That gate held a particularly difficult memory for me. It was where I killed a man with a gruesome shot when he tried to stop us from leaving the city after Appius was murdered, but that was not why we were there.

Appia took a deep breath and looked at me. She was anxious. I looked at Christina. "I hope you don't mind, but we need to go this way alone. We'll rejoin you shortly."

"What's down there?" Kamden asked.

Christina understood. "Come on, sweetie," she said as she took his arm and directed him back towards the site cafeteria. "How about some ice cream? My treat?"

The street beyond the gate was lined with tombs. Appia squeezed my hand, took another deep breath, and calmly led me down to what remained of her family tomb which, while long since shorn of its markings, was recognizable. The small door to the burial chamber was gone so I pulled away a clump of grass to expose the interior.

When I stood back, Appia knelt before the chamber, bowed her head and placed her roses inside. "Goodbye, my father. I love you." She stood and we hugged. Tears welled in her eyes. She trembled at first, but then calmness washed over her as if a great weight had been lifted. She looked at her hand. She removed the silver ring from her finger and placed it inside the tomb between the roses. It slipped between the stones as if it was sliding back into the past. "Father," she said. "I want you to know that I'm alright now. I'm safe and I'm happy."

We stood in silence for a moment to gather our thoughts, and then we walked to a spot above the tombs where we could see the entire plain to the sea. A large rock stuck out from a thicket of grasses, and with Appia's hand in mine, we took a seat on its smooth surface. It was nearing sunset and the warm glow of the late afternoon sky was beginning to paint the landscape, with its many towns and wooded spaces, in vibrant colors. The sea sparkled as seabirds passed overhead enlivening the air with their sounds. The feeling of déjà vu was inescapable, as was the timeless vision of a solitary mountain, whose bountiful façade of vineyards and farms once again masked its abiding disquiet from within.

We were home.

CPSIA information can be obtained
at www.ICGtesting.com
Printed in the USA
LVHW090720210521
688043LV00024B/1198/J